Shots Taken

Kate Byrne

*For the ones who are learning to stop painting themselves
with the brushes of others.*

Author's Note

This book is for the hockey romance genre and its readers. It's full of little Easter eggs that nod to the hockey *and* the romance that make up my enduring love for these books. I hope that those who favor one part over the other find things about it they enjoy, connect to, and leave reflecting on.

However, this is a work of fiction more than anything, which means I have taken some necessary liberties to keep the story moving and streamlined. I know there are more than six players on a team, but in this case, we will focus on the starting six of the New Haven Midnight. Throughout the planned series we will likely meet more players, but I do not want to overwhelm readers with too many names too soon in book one.

Additionally, while great thought has been put into staying as accurate as possible, there are embellishments and changes made to procedure, policy, and general structure in the front office support of a professional team, and to an extent, the league. These are not meant to distract from the overall plot, but to help ease its telling and give our characters the "happily ever after" they deserve.

For those that enjoy having reference material in a fictional world with numerous characters and moving parts, there is a Player Roster located at the beginning of the book, and a Hockey Handbook in the back for your use.

STARTING LINEUP

NIKITA BALADIN
GOALIE

AUGUSTUS KELLY
DEFENSEMAN

OBADIAH JAMES
DEFENSEMAN

CHARLIE KANE
RIGHT WING

CROSBY WELLS
CENTER

HENRI TEXIER
LEFT WING, CAPTAIN

Chapter 1

Violet

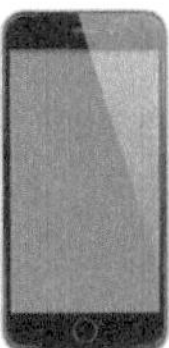

"Don't forget to print your ticket."

"Dad, I have it in the app on my phone. *And* there's a confirmation in my email."

"Which would be fine if you remembered your portable charger," my dad's voice chastises from the speaker on my phone. It's currently sitting on the nightstand as I struggle to shove three more shirts into a suitcase on my bed. The zipper strains against the extra clothing.

"One time. It happened *one time* when I was seventeen, Dad. Guess you're just never going to let me live it down." I grunt one more time, leaning heavily on the top of the luggage. Only once did I *almost* miss a flight because I hadn't charged my phone the night before. Approaching the gate with 3 percent power and a prayer hadn't been one of my finer moments of air travel. "The charger is currently plugged in next to my purse. I'll have it with me. Promise. Ha!" I shout victoriously as a satisfying little jingle sounds, signaling the meeting of the zippers.

"What's going on, Violet? I can't see anything!" Dad calls

through the speaker. He's been staring at the ceiling since I set my phone down. *Oops.*

I pick it up again, tilting to show him the bulging black suitcase.

"I got everything in one!" I raise my arm in a celebratory pose. I can see my dad's face relax, his lips thinning, and I know what he's going to say next.

"And how many boxes are being shipped?"

I turn the phone so he can see my face again and bite on the inside of my cheek.

"A dozen."

"Twelve?!" Dad's voice rises just a pitch, his dark eyebrows climbing up his forehead.

"That makes it sound like so many!" I sigh exasperatedly but give a laugh. "A dozen gives the impression of being manageable. Easy."

"It absolutely does not," Dad answers. "It sounds expensive."

"What's a little transatlantic shipping cost when it means your favorite daughter is finally coming home for good?"

"You're my *only* daughter." Dad tries to sound irritated, but I see the smile creeping at the corner of his lips.

I've lived in London for three years, and Dad has begged me to come home at the end of every single one of them. It's always been just the two of us in the family, but I grew up with plenty of time apart from him. It was a natural byproduct of having a professional hockey player as a father.

I took a chance when I finished my undergrad, applying to a prestigious overseas program solely for the experience. I grew up with travel as part of life, so moving to London to complete my Master's Degree in Statistics seemed like a natural choice. When my schooling was finished, I took on what I thought was my dream job: a sports statistician internship for an international hockey team. The dream lasted six months before I switched to a less glamorous position at the Whitehall Football Club.

Despite the requests to return home, Dad was supportive of my acceptance in London, even if it came at a time when he was starting his first season as the head coach for the New Haven Midnight. He was the youngest head coach in the NHL, an unexpected life change, but a welcome way to keep the game he loved so much in his life.

Nine years ago, Callum Andrews went from the most feared defenseman in the league to retiring in the blink of an eye during a fast and furious playoff series. A brutal entanglement on the ice left him with injuries that would have led to a recovery time eclipsing the entire next season. While he would have been willing to do anything to get back to playing, at thirty-six, he saw the injuries for the sign they were: his career as a player was over. Instead, he rehabbed his body, played stay-at-home Dad while I finished high school, and began working as an assistant coach when I went off to college.

Now forty-five and just about to start his fourth pre-season, Dad is excited to have me around. Despite their record when Dad was a player, The Midnight haven't won a Stanley Cup in nearly forty years. Now, after building a team of strong talent, The Midnight have started making waves in the NHL under his leadership, reaching the playoffs the last two seasons. Dad and I have always had hockey, from watching his career as a child to the Face-Time calls after games he coached. I am excited to return to Connecticut. I can't wait to see how my dad works with the organization he spent his career playing for.

"Who's in charge of shipping the boxes?"

Dad's voice pulls me back to the quiet of my bedroom. I glance around at the empty shelves, blank mattress, and barren walls. My heart gives a little pang at the finality of moving back home.

"Bea will take care of them tomorrow." I flip the camera to show Dad the doorway where my best friend has appeared. Her curly brown hair is tied on top of her head, but stray curls fly away from her face, touching the doorframe where she leans. Her warm brown eyes are watery as she looks around before giving me a soft smile.

Beatrice Farrow barged into my life on the first day of post-graduate university when she snagged the seat I wanted in a lecture. When I took the one next to her, she introduced herself, and we never looked back. Bea and I became inseparable; room-mates and family when Dad's schedule made going home for the holidays hard. I'm going to miss her so much.

"Hi, Cal." Bea waves as she walks in, a dismissive sniffle to keep her tears away. She traces a finger over the top of the boxes stacked nearby before giving a disapproving look at my suitcase. "You have more than one suitcase. You should use it."

"I only get one checked bag for free. I don't want to pay fifty bucks for another!" I reply as Bea tests the zippers. The bag does look like it could burst at any moment. Bea frowns and pins me with a look. It reminds me of the summer we took a trip to Germany, and I complained the whole time about my backpack being heavy. Bea had packed far less and split it between a back-pack and a carry-on tote. I guess I just like keeping things simple, even if they're not easy.

"But she's sending twelve boxes. *Very* frugal, this one," Dad grumbles in my hand. Bea leaves the room and walks back in with a large weekender bag. She drops it on the bed before lifting a finger and pointing. Her silent instructions are clear. I roll my eyes but hand her my phone to begin shifting clothes out of the over-packed suitcase. Now that I'm on camera, I hear my dad pick up the conversation with Bea once more. I'm lucky they get along, but having Dad visit every summer in his off-season has helped them connect. "Thank you for sending over Violet's things. Will you be taking her to the airport?"

"Wouldn't be anywhere else." Bea's voice holds a little tremor. We've tried not to talk about my leaving too much over the last few weeks. Our conversations resulted in nothing but blubbering tears and snot on each other's shoulders when we hugged. Bea is staying in her native city—happily employed at Cunningham & Hartford, a prestigious marketing firm. I helped her with mock interviews and perfecting her resume for the internship they offered during our last year of school. Then, when she got it, Bea worked her butt off and was offered a full-time position after graduation.

Whitehall offered me a full-time position as well, but my heart wasn't in English football. I loved keeping stats and helping teams grow based on the data I could provide, but I only worked for the club because it was the furthest professional sport from hockey I could think of here. I hated leaving Bea, London, and the entire life I built here. But I had spent so much of the past year running away from a lot of things; running a little further seemed necessary to start over. Especially if it promised me a chance to be happy. It was time to go home. Even if it meant missing my best friend more than I was able to think about. *And* having to figure out what to do with my life.

"Good. Just make sure she's there two hours before the flight in case there are any issues," Dad continues from the phone, and Bea rolls her eyes with a smile.

"We've got it," I try to reassure him as I take the phone back. I'm still holding him in one hand as I pick up my suitcases from the bed with the other. Bea steps in and wheels the larger one down the hall to set it next to the front door. I bite my lip as reality crashes into me again. *I've spent my last night in this flat. I'm really leaving.*

I clear my throat to rid myself of the emotion threatening to overwhelm me. I need to stay focused. "Are you still picking me up?"

I glance down at Dad, just in time to see him look away and grimace.

"I take that as a 'no.'" I frown at him.

"I was planning on it," Dad replies as Bea comes back into the room. "But then Todd scheduled a meeting to talk about Bridger's contract."

"I thought The Midnight released Bridger? What is there to talk about?" I sit on the empty bed. Bea settles on the floor next to my legs. She leans against me, listening quietly. Bea doesn't really like hockey, but I don't know if it's because it isn't as popular here or because she knows I'm having a difficult time loving it right now, and she wants to be supportive.

"Remember, you're not supposed to know that information. Anyway, he wants to activate his fucking trade clause, cutting us off at the knees for salary cap this season." Dad's getting fired up. He usually does when talking about the finer inner workings of the hockey team. Especially if it involves decisions the team's owner, Todd Montgomery, has made. The guy has an abrasive ego and a big bank account. He has very little understanding of how to own and operate a hockey team. "I could murder someone for agreeing to that fucking ridiculous stipulation when we signed him two years ago," Dad goes on. "Bridger turned out to be an absolute dipshit, but the team will get punished for getting *rid* of him because we can't go after the talent we want *and* pay out the rest of his contract. It's almost six million dollars! Motherfucker."

"Tell us how you really feel, Cal," Bea calls toward the phone with laughter. I giggle along. For an easygoing, level-headed guy, my dad can get *enthusiastic* at times when it comes to his job.

Which means he starts to cuss.

A lot.

"Sorry." Dad lets out a breath. "All of that means I can't pick you up like I wanted to. But I'm sending someone I think you'll be happy to see."

"I'm going to try and ignore how, coming from anyone else, that would feel vaguely ominous." Bea pinches my leg. I slap her hand away. *I'm going to miss this.* "Who is it?"

"I don't want to tell you." Dad is grumbling but also smiling.

"But if I don't know who to look for, I'll end up taking an Uber," I push back. "And if my phone isn't charged, it could die on the ride. You wouldn't want that, would you?"

I know I'm playing dirty. It's not nice to toy with how protective Dad gets when I travel, but it seems to work.

"Fine. He'll be mad at me for ruining his surprise, but you have a good point," Dad concedes. "It's Obadiah."

"Obie's coming to get me?" I can't keep the surprise from my voice as my eyebrows shoot up my forehead. Bea twists to look up at me, a huge smile on her face.

Obadiah James. My other best friend.

Obie and I grew up together in the way only children who spend too much time together can: as close as actual siblings. Our parents met when they were teenagers—Obie's parents are a few years older—but remained close even when Dad's NHL career started. Our houses were three blocks apart, and I would stay with them when Dad had a road game. Obie's parents also stepped in at other times to help when Dad wasn't available, so I wasn't always with a nanny. Obie became the brother I never had.

Obie went on to follow in my dad's footsteps, playing in the NHL in Los Angeles after a year of college. We've been best friends our whole lives. Being on the same continent again means we don't have to just theorize about all the trouble we can get up to via text messages, we'll be able to do some of it. I'm surprised to learn Obie's in Connecticut. He managed to keep this a secret from me in our near daily conversations.

"Is he home to visit his parents? I bet Temperance and Palmer are thrilled!"

Temperance and Palmer James are my other unofficial set of parents. With my mom out of the picture, I grew up in their house and with their support because of Dad's schedule. Aunt Tempe took care of me, along with Obie, whenever Dad was at practice or an away game. Uncle Palmer took Obie and me to Dad's home games when they fit with our school schedule, enduring the experience with two overly eager kids trading smack talk and falling asleep in equal turn on the drive home. The Jameses embraced hockey life, supporting my dad by loving me.

"Not exactly." Dad grins. The corners of his mouth twist up so I can see the mischief behind it. "We just signed him. Despite Bridger's fuckery, Obie's a Midnight now."

"Wait. Wait. Wait. Obie's going to be on your team?" I look down at Bea, whose surprise mirrors my own. Bea and Obie have never met in person, but since they're my two best friends, they've gotten to know each other in our share of group chats and video calls.

"Yep," Dad responds succinctly. Before I can ask any other questions, Dad clears his throat and fixes his stare at me. "Better get off the phone now, kid. You need to finish up and get to the airport."

"Oh, all right. I have so many questions, though," I protest. Dad gives me a little smile.

"Going to need some patience. Don't go texting Obie about it, either. He'll know I gave away his secret, and I'll lose all professional credibility with him. Can't have that before the season starts." One of Dad's fingers waggles in front of the phone camera, filling the screen.

"But I can text Aunt Tempe!" I tease. Dad lets out a huff, knowing he's been outsmarted for the moment. Bea offers me a high- five for being so clever. I slap at it as Dad's voice pushes me to get moving.

"I want updates. Thanks for everything, Bea!" His voice softens as he gives me a look that has his eyes just a little misty. Or maybe it's my own that makes the picture waver a little on the screen. "I can't wait to see you tomorrow. I love you, kid. Be careful."

"I love you, too," I answer more thickly than I anticipate before tapping the red button to end the call. I slip it into my back pocket. Bea disconnects the portable battery pack to tuck into the side compartment of my purse.

"Right," Bea announces to me after a beat of silence.

It's always made me laugh; that irrepressible British thing that steers a conversation or deflects an emotion in such an easy way. Americans can't begin to mimic it. Linking her arm through mine, she brings us out of my room into the main part of the flat. She heads to the table by the door for her keys, jingling them excitedly. "I'm not letting you leave me without one last attempt to drown you in a proper pint. C'mon then."

I let out a good-natured groan, but I grab my jacket from the hook. Not long after becoming friends, Bea single-handedly made it her mission to find just *one* type of beer I could consume an entire pint of. Three years, two months, and eighteen days later, the score stands at Violet Cameron: 18, British Beer I like: 0.

Chapter 2

Crosby

The ice cuts away perfectly from my skate as I slide toward the center line. It's loud in the arena tonight, the state high school finals enticing a big crowd. This rivalry also brings out the rowdiest supporters for both teams, with the tension thickening in the dry air. As I brace down toward the center face-off circle, I suck in a deep breath, blocking out the increasing noise until there is only a pleasant thrum of anticipation. I can hear my heartbeat pulsing in my ears instead as I pinch my eyes shut, laying my stick across the tops of my knees.

There's a spray of ice against my pads as my opponent settles into place across from me. I open my eyes to calmly look through the plastic of the visor portion of my bubble mask at him. He's shorter than me, more obviously so as he crouches into position, tapping his stick lightly against the circle. As I study his face, there's a drop of sweat working down his temple and a small twitch at the corner of his eye. This kid is nervous.

I set the blade of my stick on the red circle, purposefully not *tapping at his. He flicks his eyes down to the ice, and when he looks back up, I wink.*

As his eyes widen, the ref blows the whistle, and the puck drops to the ice.

Whatever thoughts I've been stuck on all day—Dad not being at this game, the upcoming draft, the familiar doubt of not being good enough—fade away with the singular slice of my stick along the ice.

Game on.

I know how early it is without opening my eyes because the six a.m. alarm is crying out an insipid repeating melody from its perch on my nightstand. I would groan against it, interrupting my sleep during the off-season, but dreaming of that night isn't something I want to return to.

Instead, I roll carefully to the right, press the button to turn it off, and sit up, stretching my arms over my head and move my neck around slowly. After a shit night of sleep, I'm actually looking forward to my morning run, hopeful it will clear my head of bad memories and give me focus before I hop on a call with Coach in a couple of hours.

Without much thought, I fall into my morning routine: a nice long shower, followed by a stretch. I'm pulling on athletic shorts and a shirt, tucking a pair of socks under my arm, and slipping my phone in my pocket while heading downstairs. In the kitchen, I lift the remote and turn the television on, clicking until it lands on the NHL channel.

"The Midnight have confirmed they will not be seeking the option to keep Alex Bridger for the remainder of his contract."

My eyes fly to the screen across the open-concept kitchen/living room where the anchor sits behind a desk delivering the kind of news that will change my life. I awkwardly pull on the sock I'm wrestling with before leaning my elbows against the counter.

"It appears the decision was originally discussed at the conclusion of The Midnight's season, which ended in a disappointing elimination in the second round of playoffs but only confirmed this week. Midnight front office staff, players, and Alex Bridger himself have kept the news quiet as it appears Bridger is now enacting a failsafe clause in his contract. With more details on what this clause is, how it impacts the team, and how The Midnight will be moving forward, we go to Tara Upton. Tara?"

"Thanks, Dave." The blonde woman on the television I vaguely recall talking to once or twice gives a flat smile before speaking again. *"There's been no official statement released from the New Haven Midnight front office, but we do have confirmation owner Todd Montgomery is due to sit down with head coach Callum Andrews later this morning, in what we can only imagine is the first of many strategy sessions."*

My phone buzzes in my pocket. I pull it out and push the side button, declining the call from my best friend. *He'll get over it.*

I set the phone on the counter and lean my elbows across it, paying closer attention to the screen as Tara continues her report.

"The release of starting center Alex Bridger is a surprise move but maybe not a fully unexpected one. In the two seasons Bridger played for New Haven, his numbers faced steady decline while his penalty minutes rose. The frustration between Bridger's performance, the team, and Coach Andrews was palpable at times throughout this postseason. Bridger was even benched halfway through The Midnight's series against Columbus, replaced by Crosby Wells."

My phone buzzes against the top of the granite with another incoming call, and while part of me wants to continue watching the report now that I've been mentioned, I can't decline when Coach Andrews' name flashes across the screen.

I turn off the television and answer before the next ring.

"Hello, Coach."

"Ah shit, you've seen it, huh?" Coach Andrews' voice is strained, and he gives a heavy exhale. "Fuck, Wells. That wasn't how you were supposed to find out."

"Not exactly sure what I'm finding out, Coach, but I'm guessing we're having our meeting now and not later." I lean back against the counter for a moment. "Bridger made it pretty clear to all of us after the last game that it would be unlikely he'd stay in a black jersey for another season. And now that he's gone, I can say freely how much I won't fucking miss him."

Coach gives a halfhearted laugh before he sounds serious. "Yeah, well, maybe it was never his color."

I wait, crossing to the fridge for a bottle of water. It's not until after I open it and take a drink that Coach continues, "There's a lot to work out with how Bridger's departure is going to impact the team. At least on the front office side of things. Thank God we managed to sign Obadiah James before this shit show and have a little cap space to try and make it work. But it is going to take some creative financial strategy to make sure The Midnight will be in a place to keep acquiring the kind of players we need. Fucking hate dealing with salary cap shit." Coach sounds like he always does when it comes to the management side of the organization: annoyed. If Callum Andrews could coach our team without ever having to talk to a single person in the front office, I think he'd be the happiest man on the planet. He lives and breathes for what happens *on* the ice. I respect the hell out of him in more ways than one. "Anyway, Wells, I'm putting you on the first line. Permanently."

The sound drops out from my ears for a moment. *I'm putting you on the first line. Permanently.*

It's everything I've worked for my whole career. I swallow

around the feelings Coach's announcement stirs in me. I'll pick them apart later.

"Yes, sir," I manage.

"Crosby," Coach's voice feels warm through the phone. It's the tone I imagine he uses as a father. It always causes an ache in my chest to ease slightly when he talks to me this way. "I wouldn't have given you the spot if I wasn't one hundred percent confident it's your time. I'd have put you on first line two years ago if I could have. You can do this."

"Thanks, Coach." I sound choked up rather than confident. I grunt to clear the emotion. "I'll make sure to live up to the opportunity."

"I know you will." Coach sighs again. "Gotta run. Time to go deal with the rest of it. See you soon."

Silence sits against my ear. Coach hung up before I could say goodbye, which isn't rude, just his efficient style. I put the phone on the counter where it immediately starts buzzing. THE RUBBER PUCKIES group chat icon—a rubber duck outfitted like a hockey player—fills the screen, individual messages popping up underneath.

TEX

Wellsy. Answer the damn phone.

Henri "Tex" Texier. Left wing. Team Captain. Despite his nickname, Tex is originally from Canada. He's a stoic but fierce leader. Endlessly supportive and the oldest veteran on the team. He's in his mid-thirties but makes rookies look like children learning to skate on the ice. I'm convinced it's some weird French-Canadian magic that lets him play so well at this point. Or maybe it's because he's the only one of us who's married. I don't have any evidence that says marital status impacts player performance, but I think Tex could be the test case.

NICKY

Yes. Answer.

Nikita "Nicky" Baladin. Twenty-three. "The Baladin Wall" as he's called by our fans. One of the best goalies in the league. Nicky was only called up from the Hartford AHL team last season. Why he had been stuck in the minors for so long is beyond me. The six-foot-six Russian beast lives up to his nickname; he nearly blocks out the net when he settles into position. His four-year-old daughter, Natalia, is tougher on us than our coach, but we love her as much as we do her dad.

BONES

Wellsy, we just want to check in after
seeing the news.

Charlie "Bones" Kane. Right wing. Nicknamed for his surgical precision to get the puck past an opponent's goalie. He's twenty-one. Strong and silent. But Bones will give you some of the most profound life advice you've ever heard—once he warms up to you. Despite his age, Bones is easily the most dependable member on our line on the ice. His skills are almost once-in-a-generation.

TEX

And Gus is driving us nuts.

GUS

Pardon the fuck out of me for caring.

Augustus "Gus" Kelly is my best friend. Twenty-six. He reminds me of a golden retriever puppy that seeks out a person when he feels like he isn't being given enough attention. Which might be why he's such a brutal defenseman: he never wants anyone to forget he's there. We're the same age, but The Midnight is Gus' third team in eight seasons. He never fully gelled with the other teams since his draft at eighteen, but we've played together since I came here three years ago.

I quickly check my phone and see two missed calls and eight texts from him. I shake my head before tapping out a response.

ME

I'm alive. Just got off the phone with Coach. Thanks for checking in.

GUS

What did Coach have to say?

TEX

He might not be able to answer that. You know how management is.

GUS

But Coach isn't management. He's COACH.

ME

He's putting me on first line.

BONES

About time. We all know you would have been on it earlier if Bridger hadn't been signed.

ME

Anyone have Obadiah James' number? It's probably about time we add him.

I change topics. If there is any surprise at the news of our new defenseman, it doesn't make it across the screen.

TEX

Taken care of. Say hello to Obadiah. Obadiah, this is everyone.

UNKNOWN NUMBER

Obie is fine. Happy to be here.

I send off a short hello and announce I'm headed to work out. I was originally looking forward to my run this morning, but now I'm eager to hit the pavement and let the monotony of it clear my head. The messages continue to buzz through, but I ignore them as I prepare to leave. I'll catch up later.

The shock of the cold water sucks the breath from me. Cold showers are a brutal necessity of training; they lower inflammation, boost immunity, and help with pain and muscle fatigue. At least that's what the team trainers say, but they don't have to endure the needle-like stings from the showerhead as I stand under the spray. Without the option for an ice bath, this is the best substitute. I grit my teeth and breathe heavily when I hear the timer go off on my counter. Ten minutes never feels as long as it does during this part of my post-workout routine.

Switching the shower off, I grab the towel off the side hook and run it briefly through my brunette hair, the curls springing a little, before running it down my chest for a quick dry. I settle it around my hips as I pick up my phone and shut off the tinny version of a generic ringtone that's acting as the timer.

> **GUS**
>
> **What are you doing right now?**

The text pops up while I'm still holding the phone.

> **ME**
>
> **Just cleaned up after a workout.**

> **GUS**
>
> **You're coming out with us tonight, right?**

I switch back to the message app home screen to review the

collection of missed messages in THE RUBBER PUCKIES. Sounds like the guys decided there is no time like the present to introduce Obie to the rest of the group, setting up drinks at Lowry's, our favorite haunt. The little bar has two pool tables, low lights, and cracked leather booths that surround an open spot that the tipsy use for dancing to the jukebox. Morgan, the owner, pours heavy and is unimpressed when professional hockey players descend on the place. It's become our favorite spot.

I don't really feel like going out. I'm still adjusting to how I feel about this morning's news. It's moments like this that make me wish my dad was still here. I would call him, and I'd hear how proud he is of me. That to be seen as the first choice is everything I've worked hard for. To be trusted to lead the team on the ice even if I don't have a capital C on my chest.

GUS

C'mon, Wellsy. If you don't show up, I'll drag you. You're going to end up in your head about this if you don't just celebrate it.

Gus knows me too well.

ME

Yeah, all right. I'll be there. But the new guy better be buying the first round.

GUS

He's been informed. Especially since he already said he could be late.

Gus' message includes that disapproving face emoji at the end. I set the phone down to finish drying off, chuckling to myself. Gus is a great guy, happy and easygoing, but punctuality is something he takes very seriously. I've never been able to figure out why, but it's part of the reason I don't mind when we have to room together sometimes on road trips. We're never late for meetings or the bus.

ME

Give the guy a break. He just uprooted
his life to come play here.

Gus likes the message, and the conversation ends. I head to my closet to pull out a pair of jeans and a navy blue tee. It's late summer and warm, but it's air-conditioned in Lowry's, so this will be fine. I slip my phone back into my pocket and head back toward my kitchen to put together some food.

I touch my fingers gently along the framed photograph in the entryway, tapping three times on the image of my dad.

Chapter 3

Violet

The airport is painfully busy as I make my way through customs to the baggage claim area. It's mid-morning, and while I managed some sleep on the flight, my internal clock is all messed up. I like taking the early flight because I adjust faster to the time difference, but the first twenty-four hours are always difficult. My body can't decide if it wants sleep or caffeine.

"Letty!"

A loud, booming voice draws the attention of everyone in the surrounding area. I try to cover the smile that wants to bloom on my face by quickly looking away from the source of the noise. This is supposed to be a surprise, but I know exactly who's calling my name, not just because my dad told me. Obie is the only person in my life who calls me "Letty." He's the only one *allowed*.

"Letty!"

At the second call, I lift my head and scan the crowd, looking for black hair. I know I'll find it above the heads of most people.

Obie isn't exactly small, but he's also jumping up and down. I stop walking and laugh.

"There she is! Letty!" Obie is moving through the crowd now, sliding with all the grace he possesses on the ice as he passes people. "Excuse me. Best friend coming through. Look out; she needs a James Juggle."

I freeze when Obie says that, twisting around for a place to hide. The "James Juggle" started when we were teenagers. Obie grew five inches and gained twenty pounds of muscle in one summer as he trained with my dad, making our usual hugs imbalanced. My shorter stature became one of his favorite mechanisms for lifting weights and practicing his control. A James Juggle consists of being upended and hoisted over Obie's shoulder before being spun around, dropped into a bone-crushing hug, and placed back on my feet. It's disorienting.

It's humiliating.

In short, it's awful.

I love it.

Barely managing to drop the weekender bag and my purse at my feet, I cackle loudly when Obie's shoulders press against my thighs, and I'm upended over him. There's a bouncing that drives the curve of his shoulder into my stomach a little, but I keep laughing as I slap playfully against his back as we spin.

"Letty, my girl, you've been indulging!" Obie chides as I flip back into his crushing embrace. My toes skim the tile, but Obie keeps me upright, his teasing smile broad and warm. I press off his chest to level a glare into his green eyes. At least I try. I'm not sure I'm impactful when I'm looking up a solid six inches.

"You did not just comment on my weight. Maybe you're just not benching enough during training." I poke at his pectoral, causing him to squirm a step away. My feet are back on solid ground, so I push harder. "Los Angeles made you soft."

He swats my intrusive finger away, dipping quickly to pick up my bags and sling them over one shoulder before tucking me against his side. With my giant best friend next to me, navigating the terminal becomes a lot easier.

"Guess it's a good thing Cal brought me home to whip me into shape, huh?" Obie looks down at me for a reaction. I aim for surprise, but I think it comes across a little more like a grimace. Obie laughs and squeezes me. "You have always had a shit poker face. Was it the news or your dad that spilled?"

"You know I try not to follow hockey news anymore. Turned my alerts off, deleted the app and everything," I reply. I wind my arm around his waist, steering him slightly under the signs indicating baggage claim. I catch Obie nodding his head. "Dad told me while I was packing. Is it public now?"

"Yeah. The Bridger news broke this morning, too." Obie pauses to look at the video screens that indicate which carousel will have my suitcase.

"That's going to be a mess, isn't it?" I point at the information for number three. We turn together to find the right place, walking casually to wait by the conveyor.

"I'm not really sure. Cal has always kept Midnight things close to the chest, and I've been across the country." Obie places my bags at his feet and crosses his arms thoughtfully. "I played against Bridger a few times. He's not much of a menace on the ice—at least not like he thinks he is. And I haven't had much cause to interact with him outside the schedule." He gives a little shrug. "I have no idea what the team dynamic was like with him here. But I can say the line seems really welcoming in the group chat I was added to this morning."

I see a shy smile cross Obie's face, and I match him. Obadiah James is the best friend anyone would be lucky to have, but despite his outward appearance of being larger than life, he's rather reserved around new people. His old teammates nicknamed him "Monk" for how little he participated in activities with the team off the ice. If he's been added to a team chat already, I'm hopeful it means The Midnight is going to be a better place for him.

"That's great, Obie." The conveyor blares a loud alarm, signaling the arrival of luggage. "They're going to be lucky to have you."

"I'm excited." Obie's eyes roam the bags that begin to circle us. "What color is your bag?"

"Black."

"Ah, so easy to find." His sarcasm makes me glare at him over my shoulder before I go back to scanning the sea of black suitcases.

"Mine has a red phone booth keychain on it." I made the impulsive purchase at a souvenir kiosk inside Heathrow Airport before checking in at the airline desk. One final reminder of the place I had called home.

"There it is!" Obie calls as the claim spits out my bulging suitcase, red keychain swinging playfully as it makes its way to us. With a single lift, Obie adds my wheelie case to my existing luggage, deftly hooking the straps of the weekender over the pull handle and pushing out of the growing group of passengers. I follow in the wake behind him.

"How tired are you?" Obie asks as we break through the sliding doors outside. He pulls a set of dark Ray-Bans from his back pocket before looking over at me. I reach for my purse from where it's stacked atop the weekender, pulling out a pair of sunglasses for myself. It might be mid-morning, but late August on the East Coast is no joke. It's bright as hell.

"I slept a few hours on the flight. Dad upgraded me."

"Fancy." Obie is making steady headway to where he must have parked. I follow along, content to let the day sink in.

"I'll definitely need a nap later to try and get myself right. My brain thinks it's the afternoon right now, but it also thinks it should be the middle of the night because I left the flat in the afternoon. It's all mixed up."

"You think you'd be up for going out later?" Obie guides us into the elevator of the parking structure, pushing the number four until it illuminates. A few other people crowd in, forcing me closer to Obie. I yawn and rest my head against his bicep for a moment.

"Dunno. I think Dad wants to have dinner, but I have a feeling today's news is bound to make things go tits up. Why?"

"God, it's weird when you talk like a Brit," he laughs softly. "The guys in the chat, they're the first line. I'll be playing with them a lot. They want to get together for a drink." I look up, but even hiding behind his sunglasses, I see Obie drop his brows. *He's nervous.*

"I'll see what I can do," I answer. "But I think you should meet them without me."

Obie hums in the back of his throat. He was drafted by Los Angeles right out of high school, and despite playing and living there for the last seven years, he didn't feel comfortable playing for the Tide. Obie never thought he could be himself, so I'm hoping a move back home and playing for Dad's team will give him the confidence to open up to his teammates.

The elevator doors open to the right level, where we walk halfway down an aisle, stopping before a sleek black Land Rover with California plates. It doesn't scream professional hockey player, but it is a considerable step up from the family RAV4 Obie drove in high school.

I run my fingers along the stitching of the onyx interior, sinking into the buttery leather and listening for Obie to secure the tailgate. I inhale the scent that indicates Obie hasn't had the car long, or maybe he had it detailed recently. It's clean and crisp but a little artificial. I close my eyes and lean my head back. *Caffeine.* I've figured out I want caffeine.

"Still drink Americanos, or did you switch over to the leafy stuff in England?" Obie slides into the driver's side and pushes the start button. A pleasant rumble starts thrumming through me as we back out and make for the highway, the hour-and-a-half journey north to Connecticut stretching out in front of us.

"I quite enjoy a cuppa, thank you." I infuse my voice with my poshest accent, exaggerated slightly to enhance the joke. Weekend and holiday travels with Bea from London to the continent were made easier if I pretended to be British. I got really good at mimicking half a dozen dialects, picked up from nights in the pub or around the communal kettle in the office.

"They converted you?" Obie sounds offended, but I detect humor behind his words.

"Not today," I grouse. "To Dunkin'—stat."

I've sent a text to Dad and Bea, letting them know I've arrived safely when Obie cracks, asking the question I've been dreading. We've been in the car for approximately thirty-two minutes.

"Have you heard from him?"

I suck down the last few drops of the life-giving Americano before I exhale and rest my head against the pillowy headrest. I close my eyes against the onslaught of memories trying to break through.

Him. The way Obie spits the word means he's only asking about one person: Olivier Ahlman. Swedish Hockey's elite right winger. League top scorer for the last three years. Sweden's reigning Sexiest Athlete. NHL hopeful.

And my ex-boyfriend.

"Not recently." I open my eyes to glance over at my best friend. He's focused on the road, but he nods approvingly.

Olivier and I met when I started working for Anders Lasch, a sports agent who was building his international office in London. He wanted to have his own set of in-house statisticians to help run numbers to refine contracts and build rosters of clients. The internship would give me the opportunity to work on both sides of the sport: game-play data and client contracts. The international travel associated with working with different clubs and teams was an added bonus. Anders was interested in my resume, knowledge, and enthusiasm.

I was assigned to work with a top hockey team in the Swedish League in Helsinki. Most of my work could be done remotely, but I flew to watch games and practice live as often as I could. On one of my early trips, I met Olivier. He swept me off my feet. I was planning my whole life around him, until it ended.

"Good. What an asshole."

"Yep." I stretch my arms out and turn the radio up. I don't really want to talk about Olivier. I'm leaving that part of my life behind. "No more hockey players."

Obie gives me a wry smile. "Sure."

"Well, if you're going to bring up my love life, we have to talk about yours." We are halfway to the neighborhood where we grew up. Where my dad still has a house and I'll be staying until I fully figure out what my next step is.

Next to me, Obie changes lanes as if it will help him get away from our conversation. He picks up his iced coffee, swirling the cup so the ice crashes in that addictive yet obnoxious sound. He pulls a long sip and presses his lips together.

"That bad, huh?" I turn more fully toward him.

"You know why I don't date." Obie's face drops as he speaks. I reach across the console and thread my fingers through his, giving him a little squeeze in silent support. Obie came out to our families when we were sixteen, but he's lived his entire professional life in the closet. To the best of my knowledge, he's never confided in any of his teammates and deflects most questions about his personal life by saying he likes to focus on the game. It's kept the press out of his business, but I know it hasn't been easy for him.

"Sorry, love. I'm sure that's lonely."

"Can be." Obie lifts our hands and kisses the back of mine. He lets go and replaces his own on the wheel. "I try not to think about it too much. Being home will help. It's a new season, time for lots of things to change, right?"

"Let's hope," I reply before Obie starts humming along to the radio, hoping he's right. We spend the rest of the trip singing throwbacks and catching up on neighborhood gossip. It feels good to be home.

Chapter 4

Crosby

GUS

I'm outside.

ME

On my way. You could always ring the doorbell.

GUS

Absolutely not. That's awkward as fuck.

"What's awkward about ringing the doorbell?" I climb into the passenger side of Gus' Silverado.

"I have to wait for you to answer it. What if you don't hear it? Then I just stand out there even longer? Or worse, ring it again?" Gus pulls smoothly off the curb with the twilight orange of the evening light bleeding briefly through the townhomes of the neighborhood.

I roll my window down a little more; the late August air is more humid than cool, but it feels good blowing through the cab.

"If you would just give me a key, I wouldn't have to feel so awkward about the doorbell, *and* I wouldn't be treated like an Uber when I come to pick you up."

"Gus, you're my best friend. I trust you with my life." He sits a little straighter in his seat, puffing his chest out unnecessarily. I grin broadly. "But I don't want to wake up one night with you standing over me asking where I hid the last slice of pie. Again."

Gus turns with his mouth gaping.

"You wound me. You agreed to never talk about that again. The one—and only—time I sleepwalked, and you hold it against me for the rest of my life." Gus shakes his head before focusing back on the road. "Some best friend."

Two years ago, Gus was run against the boards in a hard game against Cincinnati, resulting in a mild neck injury. The road doc gave him some stronger-than-usual painkillers to help take the edge off and get him to sleep. As it turned out, Gus was one of the few who fell into the rare side effect category of developing lucid dreaming while taking them. We were sharing a room on that stretch of road games, and I woke up two nights later to Gus standing next to my bed, demanding I tell him where the last piece of chocolate peanut butter pie was.

It's still funny as hell, and I love reminding him it happened.

"Lighten up." I laugh. "You drowned your sorrows in the peanut butter cups I had in my bag, and we're the only ones who even know it happened."

"Doesn't mean you need to bring it up," Gus grumps. We pass a few minutes with just the sound of Post Malone filling the truck. "So, uh, how are you doing? You know, with everything?"

I've spent all day thinking about how this season is going to be unlike all of my previous years in the league. I wasn't drafted into the NHL until I was almost twenty. I spent my first two seasons in the minors for Austin, working hard to get called up. When I finally joined the Rampage, I thought I was set. I wasn't on first line, but I was always suited up and saw a fair amount of play. It lasted two years. Then I was traded to New Haven, and I've been waiting for my shot.

Now I have it. According to Coach, I should have had it two years ago, but I'm getting it now, and it feels good. Mostly. It's hard to tell when my success is wrapped up in an emptiness that's never fully gone away. The person who should be sharing this with me, who would be happiest for me, died when I was eighteen.

"I know what I'm supposed to feel, but that's not what I actually feel," I reply, turning my face to the window for a moment.

Gus knows about my dad and the accident that killed him. How I became an adult orphan in the final months of high school. How I was so consumed in my grief that I missed my draft slot that year. How I was forced to accept the full-ride scholarship I had at the University of Michigan just to work my way back to the opportunity.

I trained hard and took my guidance counselor's advice to seek a therapist. With the support of my coaches and teammates, I worked as many hours on my mental health as my physical. I spent hours processing the grief of losing my dad. The anger and guilt I harbored about our final moments and the irrational belief hockey somehow was a part of the blame. The journey hasn't always been linear; there have been emotional highs and lows, but I make sure to have a few standing appointments with my therapist throughout the year to check-in. Sometimes, there is still sadness, but often it's just longing. A desire to share these career milestones with the man who was my biggest supporter.

"It probably won't make it better, and I could be talking out of turn here, but I think your dad would be really happy for you." I cut my eyes to Gus. He's offering me a crooked, hesitant smile. I know he can't fully understand how it feels to lose a parent so suddenly, but he tries, and hearing what I know to be true in my heart is helpful. My dad would be happy for me. Proud. I nod quickly in answer.

"Plus, you're a hell of a lot better than Bridger ever was. Should have been on the line before now. That guy's best days are behind him."

"That's what Coach said. Not the best days part, just that I should have been on the line sooner."

"No shit?" Gus pulls into the cracked asphalt lot next to the nondescript building with a faded sign above it that says *DRINKS.* "Well, Coach knows better than anyone else."

With the truck in park and our conversation wrapped up, I close the passenger door and head to the entrance of Lowry's. Scanning the partially filled lot, I spot Bones' sleek Jaguar parked next to Nicky's practical BMW X7. I don't see Tex's red Mercedes, but he could have ridden with one of the others because I know our captain is here. My eyes also coast over a black Land Rover near the door. Like the rest of our vehicles, it feels a little out of place for Lowry's usual crowd, leading me to think it belongs to our newest defenseman. The California plates are also a dead giveaway.

"Looks like the new guy isn't late." I gesture to the car as Gus and I pass. Gus looks and nods.

"Point in his favor, then." Gus pulls open the door where a single sign displays the hours of operation. There's no open/closed sign. If it's between the hours shown, the door will be unlocked.

Inside, the place is pretty empty. It makes spotting our team easy; they're the only group clustered around a table just off the back of the bar. A few solo evening regulars are settled in their favorite corners, working on whatever their usual drink is. Morgan gives Gus and me a nod as the door closes behind us.

"Hey, Morg," Gus calls as we walk toward our gathering. "Can I get Johnnie Blue, neat? Two fingers pour, yeah?"

"You can have light or dark, pretty boy. You know the rules." Morgan pulls a pint glass from the rack. There's nothing fancy about Lowry's. No liquor that costs more than an average paycheck, and the beer comes in a light color or dark. We are never told what's on tap, just that it's cold, and Morgan knows how to pull his pints full.

"A pitcher of whatever the majority is drinking. And it goes on the new guy's bill." Gus taps a knuckle on the bar top in thanks. I offer a smile at Morgan as I pass.

"Thought you liked people being on time, Gus!" Tex's voice calls from behind Nicky as we step up to the group.

"We are on time," I reply, double-checking my watch. Tex laughs.

"Looks like all these years of being an asshole about the function of a clock has finally sunk in." Gus pops himself atop a stool, glaring at our teammates before he settles on the face of Obadiah James. "And this guy won't be half bad if he's already figured it out, too."

Morgan arrives with the pitcher and two empty pints. The ale is light, as it appears all but Bones have opted for it tonight. I pour our glasses, careful to angle it so there isn't too much head on the beer.

"Obadiah, but everyone can call me 'Obie.'" I lift my eyes to see Gus shaking hands with the black-haired defenseman.

"Crosby." I lift my chin in greeting, then pass Gus his drink.

"Top off, boys," Tex instructs. Nicky takes the pitcher, pouring to ensure everyone has a full pint again. Everyone except Bones, but Morgan shows back up with another glass of the stout, swapping it for his nearly empty glass. "All right," Tex begins again when we all have a drink in hand. "This marks the beginning of the best season we've ever played. Wellsy is on the line where he belongs, and our new guy already knows better than to fuck up, right?"

He cuts his eyes to Obie, who gives a little salute of acknowledgment. Tex nods back. "Drink up, Midnight. Rise!"

We tap the bottoms of our glasses and pull long drinks from them, the familiar chant from our fans drowned by hops and barely distinguishable citrus. It feels good to be with my team, and the unease I've wrestled with all day starts to fade into the background as I fold myself into a seat. Maybe I should have had my chance at the starting six before now, but as I scan the faces of men I've known for years and the relaxed smile of my newest teammate, I'm suddenly happy it's only happening now. There's a little tingle in the air around our group. The stirrings of... something. I think my dad would say it's potential.

"Why do we say 'rise?'" Nicky asks. He stretches his long legs behind my stool. I'm bunched uncomfortably under this high top, knees almost knocking the underside, but Nicky has three inches on me.

"Someone in the front office must have thought it sounded cool," Tex answers, shifting our attention toward the pool table. I happily stand to follow. "Which it fucking does. Especially from a sold-out crowd."

I pull a few cues off the wall, handing them out as Bones collects and racks the balls. We divide ourselves into pairs: Tex and Bones, Gus and Obie, and I stand next to Nicky. We silently step back to let the others play the first round.

"There's actually a local urban legend that inspired the saying," Obie speaks up. Gus and Bones are playing the fastest game of rock paper scissors to see who will break. Gus slams his fist atop Bone's scissor fingers to win. He leans over the table and draws back his cue.

"It's also why the team is named The Midnight," Obie continues. The decisive crack of the pool balls bouncing against each other as they scatter punctuates Obie's words.

"How do you know?" Gus asks. He's giving a smirk to our new teammate. I know he would never intentionally make someone feel unwelcome, but Gus isn't above a little teasing to see if personalities settle well. Bridger couldn't tell the difference, so he quickly stopped hanging out with us. "Googling shit to get in good with the new team, Rook?"

"He's not a rookie, Gus," I correct. I have a good feeling about Obie being on the team. And maybe, now that I finally have my starting spot, I want to do a little more for the camaraderie of the team.

"He's still new *here*," Gus replies, unbothered, slapping Obie on the shoulder before the defenseman leans over the felt top to line up a shot.

"I know because I grew up here," Obie says, knocking a solid into the corner pocket.

"No shit?" Gus leans on his cue.

"No shit."

"So, what's the story, then?" I ask as the game resumes. I think knowing the history behind the team would be good. I'm sure it was probably in my player's handbook and introduction when I signed, but I admit to not reading it. For the most part, every team in the NHL has the same rules: *play well on the ice, contribute to the club, and manage your money and your behavior off the ice.* I've always tried to do those things, but a little extra knowledge won't hurt. I don't make a habit of staying in New Haven for long periods of time during the off-season. I prefer heading to my dad's old cabin in Maine.

"There's a grave in Evergreen Cemetery for Mary Hart. She died in the 1800s—don't really know how, just that it was around noon, but she wasn't pronounced dead until midnight. The family interred her quickly after that." Obie levels us all assessing looks to see if we're paying attention. Tex is taking his shot, but I can tell he's listening from how his head is cocked. "Anyway, the legend part is that Mary's aunt dreamed of Mary calling to her from the grave, asking for help. They say the family became concerned, exhumed the casket, and found the inside torn to shreds. Mary's fingers were bloody from trying to claw out. Now, the ghost of Midnight Mary haunts the cemetery and that area of New Haven."

We all stand there in various states of shock by Obie's story.

"And we're *named* after this ghost story?" Gus looks gobsmacked. Obie shrugs. I stifle a laugh behind my hand and check on Nicky. The Russian's usual stoicism cracks as Gus' voice gets a little squeaky as he pushes on. "It's so dark and twisted. That's—that's fucking *demented*."

Tex and Bones are laughing outright at our teammate's distress. I walk over to my spooked best friend.

"You okay, bud?" I take the cue from his flapping hands, passing it to Bones. "It's just a story. But I think it makes us sound kind of cool."

"Oh yeah, 'cool.'" Gus rolls his eyes. "You know, most teams are named after an animal or something badass."

"The only real animals around here are wild turkeys and deer," Obie supplies. The guys are putting up their cues and walking back to the high top. "I guess being named after *Bambi* wouldn't be so bad, but that story is just sad."

"I think I like being named after the ghost better. Definitely more badass than a turkey." I steer Gus back to the table, passing him his drink. He sips and breaks off to talk to Bones. I laugh at his grumbling, hitching a thumb at him when I speak directly to Obie, "Ignore him. He'll never admit to being scared easily, but he asks me to check his room before bed when we go on road trips and he's alone in his room."

"I heard that, asshole," Gus calls back over his shoulder.

"You were meant to." I laugh even harder. It feels good to be out with my friends tonight. I spent too much of the day wrapped up in my thoughts. The concern that I might not be good enough to have a permanent starting spot loops back through my head. I push the thought away; these guys have my back, and Coach wouldn't have given it to me if he didn't think I could do it.

Obie sits next to me, and his light laughter brings me back to our conversation.

"That story taught in school or something when you were a kid?"

"Nah." Obie pulls a sip from his amber ale. "My dad and uncle loved all sorts of things like that when I was little. They'd tell me and my best friend all kinds of weird and wacky stories when we'd have sleepovers and stuff."

"My dad knew a few of the local urban legends back home. My pee-wee team loved having sleepovers at my house after games to hear them." I press my lips together. I'm not sure why I'm offering up anecdotes about my dad. Probably because he's been on my mind today. To avoid further discussion, I press forward, changing topics. "So, you grew up here. Must be nice to be playing at home."

"It will be," Obie says. I finish off my pint with a large swig. "My best friend also recently moved back."

"That's cool." I watch Obie check his phone and frown for a second. "Everything okay?"

"Yeah." He slides the device back into his pocket. "I was hoping she'd come out tonight, but she can't make it."

"Who can't make it? Your girl?" Tex asks, cluing back in on the conversation. He picks up the half-full pitcher and tops off his pint. I wave him away when he offers it to me.

"Who has a girl?" Gus leans in, eyes wide, curiosity sparkling, and all traces of fear gone. "Rook?"

"I'm not getting away from that nickname, am I?" Obie glances at me. I shake my head.

"Not likely. But it could be worse."

"Definitely could."

"Tell us about your girl." Gus bounces slightly on the balls of his feet.

"She's not my girl. Just my best friend. Since we both just moved back to town, I thought she'd want to come hang out, but she let me know she can't make it."

"All right!" Gus whoops. "Another wingman. Always looking for someone else to pick up girls with. The only one here who has a girl is Tex."

"Speaking of which, I should grab an Uber home." Tex drinks the last of his beer. "Pre-season only lasts so long, then it's back to late nights and FaceTime with the missus."

"I can still drive you home. I'm ready to head out for the night," Bones speaks up, the bass timbre of his voice strong in the quiet space. His second stout pint is only a quarter down, and I know he wouldn't offer if he was drunk. Tex nods before tipping his fingers at his brow in a goodbye salute.

"I should go, too." Nicky is texting furiously on his phone. He looks up, a small scowl on his face. "Babysitter problems."

"Sorry, man." I pat the big guy on the back. "Give Natalia a hug from all of us."

When our goalie has departed, Morgan comes by to clear glassware. None of us order another drink.

"Tell us about this girl best friend of yours," Gus starts. I roll my eyes. "Is she cute? Do I get to meet her?"

Obie takes a moment before he begins to laugh. I cock my head in confusion, and Gus looks a little offended.

"She's my best friend and has spent plenty of time around hockey players. You wouldn't stand a chance with her." Obie wheezes a little as he talks. Gus pouts.

I'm intrigued.

Chapter 5

Violet

The deck at the back of the house has always been one of my favorite spots during the summer. The shade from the large trees that divide us from our neighbors offer the right amount of shade on a hot day, and there is almost always a cool breeze in the afternoon. I stretch my legs out on the sun lounger, the feeling of weekend possibility floating around me.

I close my eyes and turn my face toward the sun, basking in it like a lizard on a rock. Connecticut is so different from London this time of the year, and while my jet lag has eased, my sadness over leaving Bea and the life I had there is only marginally better.

A shadow passes over my eyelids, so I crack them open gingerly before shielding them with my hand. Dad stands with his hands in his pockets, a small frown at the corner of his mouth, and a pinched brow. I don't like that look on my father's face, even if it's something I've seen before.

Growing up, I was afraid it meant I had done something wrong. It's taken a long time to figure out the look on his face is more a worry he's not being a good dad than I'm being a bad daughter, so I brace myself for whatever he has to say.

"Hey, Dad." I smile at him, and the crease between his black eyebrows relaxes. "Everything okay?"

He tips his head in silent question to the open space near my legs on the lounge. I bunch up to make room for him.

"Training camp starts Monday. I won't be home much."

"It won't be the first time we've been through it."

I never knew my mother. It never bothered me much. At least not until I was in school and the other kids started asking questions. That made me start asking questions.

My dad met the woman who became my mother when he was eighteen. As a young kid and a rising star in the NHL, he made some choices that, to this day, he's not proud of. He chased a woman who didn't want him, just what he could give her. It took the better part of a season for Palmer and Tempe to make him see sense, but by then, she had dropped the bomb that I was on the way. Dad told her the relationship was over, but he would support me when I came along. Realizing that even a child wouldn't guarantee her the future she wanted, she signed away her parental rights when I was born and took off after the next best offer. It's been the two of us ever since—with considerable support from Palmer and Tempe. But I wouldn't have it any other way.

Dad hums. I push at his leg with my foot.

"What's wrong?"

Dad and I have always managed to talk about things. Even with his schedule taking him away from home so much growing up, we would spend hours on the phone or video calls. He would listen to me complain about how Madison Lee's comments about not having a mom in fourth grade made me cry. He threatened to have David Horton expelled when he got a little handsy at the Homecoming dance freshman year, even though the kid was just high off painkillers from wisdom tooth surgery and thought I was his girlfriend.

"What are you doing, kid?"

"Enjoying the nice weather? Giving myself ten minutes before I need to put dinner in the oven?" I offer hesitantly. I know he's not asking about *right now*. He knows it, too, if the slight eyebrow raise he gives me is any indication. I shrug my shoulders. "I know what you're really asking, but I haven't gotten that far yet. It feels like my whole life imploded this year."

Dad puts a gentle hand on my knee, giving it a light squeeze in silent support.

The truth is, I don't really know what to do with myself. I know coming home was the right decision, even if I still miss parts of my life in London. But it's been two weeks, and I admit I'm beginning to feel restless. It's an unwelcome feeling. I know I'm lacking direction. I'm just unsure where to start.

"Your boxes will be here in a couple of days," he says. I know the tone of voice he's using. Dad is getting ready to tell me a hard truth. He's always led into these conversations with gentleness before dropping the heavy bomb. It made things easier when I was little, but now I sigh and pinch my lips. Dad scoffs, pulling his hand back to clasp them between his spread knees. "You have until Friday to unpack them or store them. I cleaned out the single garage for your stuff if you need it."

"And?"

"And, if you haven't figured out what your plan is by then, I pulled some strings with a friend, and there's a job in the social media department in the front office waiting for you." Dad stands up, walking toward the house.

I follow.

"You know Bea was the marketing major, right? She has all the public relations expertise. I just took an elective in the metric impact trends have on business to hang out with her." I keep pace with my dad into the kitchen, as he begins pulling out the items I prepared earlier for dinner. "I know statistics, not social media."

Dad begins assembling a salad in a large bowl while I uncover the tray of lasagna that will go in the oven. He leans over to punch a few buttons to preheat as I grate a final layer of parmesan on top, trying not to think about how crazy his idea is.

"You know *analytics*, Vi." Dad leans against the counter. "You know the game. This makes sense, even if you're trying to come up with a dozen reasons right now why it doesn't."

I re-cover the tray with foil, opening the oven door despite it not being preheated yet. It's hot enough, and it gives me a reason to pull a face when my back is turned.

"I talked to Ava about it. You remember Ava? She oversees Communications and Public Relations?" Dad asks but continues before I've fully finished an affirmative grunt. "I don't think you'd be responsible for coming up with the content ideas. I think that's Ethan's job. Anyway, you would just be helping with posting and analyzing the feedback. Plus, you know how to interpret the team data better than anyone else up there. They could use the help understanding the difference between power play goals and shots on goal."

"They really don't know the difference?" I stand up, turning to offer him a smirk. "There are fewer people on the ice. Do they even watch the games?"

"See? They'll be completely helpless without you."

My chest pulls a little tight as I lean on the island separating my dad and me. I can't help the frown I feel turning down the corners of my mouth. I've spent the better part of the year trying to distance myself from hockey.

As a kid, hockey was everything in my house. Dad's job ensured it was an essential part of our lives, but my love for the game grew on its own. I knew I wasn't ever going to join my dad on the ice; I'm the least athletic person I know. But I found another way to spend time with Dad when he was working: numbers. I started keeping track of his stats and slowly added his teammates' information in a little green notebook I decorated with hockey stickers. After road games, Dad would call, and we'd talk about his performance or what the numbers could mean.

When Obie started playing, I expanded my recordkeeping to include him and other members of the pee-wee league. I loved every second of it. When Dad got injured, I had already decided to focus on working my way onto the staff of a professional team in some capacity. Going to London to secure my master's and gain more work experience was supposed to be the beginning of a long career. Then all of that changed.

"Vi?" My dad looks at me with a riot of emotions clouding his face. His eyes—a unique shade of blue, so light they almost appear gray—are wide with concern. His lips are flattened in irritation. "Don't let him take this, too."

My breath catches in my throat, a weird kind of hiccupping sob. Dad rounds the corner of the island quickly, pulling me against him in a tight hug. It's the kind of hug that makes me think he could really put me back together if he just held me long enough. I wrap my arms around his waist, breathing in the familiar scent of family and home, exhaling the remainder of my grief.

"I know that bastard twisted you up." Dad's voice is laced with anger, but he works to hold it steady in my ear. "He made you believe all kinds of promises he never intended to keep. Preyed on your love for others, your passion for the game, your kind and joyful spirit. But he doesn't get to own those things about you, now, kid. He didn't take ownership of them when you decided to share your heart with him. They belong to you."

I'm crying against his chest. It hurts and heals to listen to him.

Dad's fingers hold the back of my head before he kisses the crown. He's right. I feel it deep inside. The fire I thought had died shows signs of glowing embers. Sparks begging for fuel.

My directionless grieving and heartbreak suddenly snap apart, the remains being tossed into the fire I want to see burn bright again.

"This will be your desk."

Ethan Savoy—head of social media—gestures toward his left. He's in his early thirties, with dark brown hair and brown eyes behind thick, square frames. He wears tan chinos and a checkered shirt. He looks like a Pinterest result page for "hipster office attire," but it works for him. He's been nice and welcoming as he shows me around the offices, explaining my role and his expectations. My new coworkers give him obligatory nods, and I receive a few bright smiles before they all return to their tasks. He has clear enthusiasm for what he does, sometimes rambling on about how he's been so close to having content go viral or his interactions with the players.

Three sides of the space are enclosed by the usual wall material cubicles are made of, but the fourth is tinted glass. The modest desk against it overlooks the practice rink inside The Midnight complex. The Midnight logo is featured at center ice: black script with a crescent moon shaping the curve of the "d." There's no official mascot for the team—a strategic decision to keep the bold, mysterious aesthetic intimidating and easy to market.

"Wow," I say, tracing a finger along the edge of the desk.

"It's a cool view, right?" Ethan asks behind me. I agreed with my dad when he said it was time to reclaim what I let Olivier take from me. Hockey was mine long before I shared it with him. But trying to embrace this part of my life again and staring at it every day at work are going to be two different things.

"Can I move the desk?" I turn around, unsurprised to see a confused look on Ethan's face. They probably don't get many people wanting to turn down the opportunity to watch professional athletes practice while they work.

"Well." He rubs at the back of his neck uncertainly. "I'll have to ask maintenance, maybe. I think it's attached to the cubicle structure, and those are bolted to the floor."

I do a quick visual inspection of my square. Ethan's right. The desk isn't going anywhere.

"That's okay." I offer up a half-amused smile. "I just didn't want to put myself in a position to be distracted."

"The team isn't here all the time," Ethan offers before laughing. "But you do know you're working in the social media department for a hockey team, right? You're going to have to interact with them from time to time. Some people think of it as a job perk to get to know the players. Between you and me, they might not come off as the friendliest group, but if you work long enough at this, they'll start to get used to you. I've been here nearly five years, and most of them know my name now."

"I was under the impression I would be doing more behind-the-scenes work, not directly working with the players," I counter.

"Most of the time, yeah." Ethan leans against the entrance to the cubicle. He takes his glasses off and removes a pocket square from his shirt to clean them. "However, we all share the work, Violet: content creation—including the ideas, filming, uploading. Analytics and performance. Follow-ups with focus groups. All of it falls under our department. I give my team a long lead; I like to let you explore and play to find what works for you, but I'm always keeping an eye on things." Putting the glasses back on, his voice pitches a little, a firmer edge creeping in. "I don't usually get too worked up about interoffice politics, but Ava hired you without involving me in the process. I'm not mad about it; I've seen your resume, I know what you bring to the table. But this is my department. My team, if you will. I've worked hard to cultivate the right personalities and skill sets to give The Midnight their social reputation and platform. Part of that is our dynamic with the players. We work to get to know them and strive to have them know us. That trust is built on our relationships with them. *All of us.* Everyone in the department films content and travels with the team from time to time. You included."

"Understood," I reply. I offer a tight smile to my new boss. Ethan seems nice, but I get the sense that success is really important to him.

"You do *like* hockey, right?" Ethan asks.

"For my whole life."

"All right." He smiles, my answer bleeding some of the uncertainty from his face. "I'll leave you to settle in. Security should have your permanent credentials ready by the end of the day, so be sure to check in with them. You won't be able to get into the building tomorrow without them. Otherwise, there's a packet on the desk with everything you should need to get started, and I'm at extension 2012 if you need anything else."

I walk back to the entrance of the space, thanking Ethan once more. As I turn back toward my desk, the shiny black nameplate in the upper left corner of my cubicle catches my eye.

Violet Cameron, Social Media Strategist I

"Violet. What a pleasure to meet you. Your dad talks about you all the time." Ava Michaels rises from her sleek black office chair, hand extended. The bright red fingernail polish catches in the light as she clasps my own offered hand. It's a firm but brief shake before

she steps back, leaning on the edge of the glass desk behind her. "I'm so pleased you agreed to come work with us."

She gestures to a plush dove-gray chair next to me before rounding back around to her chair. Ava is a statuesque beauty. Easily brushing the six-foot mark in her three-inch, red bottom stilettos with voluminous blonde waves and green eyes. She is the most professional and stylish woman I've ever met. With her authoritative aura, she would be intimidating on her worst day and likely terrifying on her best. It makes me like her immediately.

"Thank you for the offer." I smile, settling down into the comfortable cushion. "Before we go much further, though, I do have a request."

"Oh?" Ava leans forward on her elbows, brow arching.

"I would prefer my relationship with Coach Andrews not be public information." Ava pinches off a smile as though she knows exactly what I'm thinking. "The organization has changed a lot since he played here, and I spent a large part of the last decade away from New Haven, so there are even fewer people here I know. I've spent my father's coaching tenure at school, so to the best of my knowledge, no one knows our relationship. I'm sure it will come out eventually, but I'd like to try and let the work I do build my reputation first."

Ava's smile breaks free before she taps her finger twice on the desktop.

"That shouldn't be much of a problem. Cal is a private person. It's common knowledge he has a daughter, but no one bothers to ask questions they know they won't get answers to. He doesn't offer up information easily, especially about people he loves. Cal protected your identity throughout his career as a player. That didn't change once he came off the ice. Your last name is Cameron, right?"

"Yes." I nod, a warmth spreading in my chest at Ava's description of my father. "He used his mother's maiden name for my legal

name. Just another layer of protection he could give me growing up."

"Then it's rather easy: you don't mention Cal's your father. Everyone here will get to know you and your work without the shadow of the boss." Ava bobs her chin definitively.

"Isn't Todd Montgomery the owner?" I ask.

"Owning something doesn't mean you're in charge, Violet." Ava smirks. "The first mistake any man can make when it comes to something he professes to love: thinking they control it."

I blink blindly for a moment at Ava's statement. I know she's talking about sports, business, million-dollar investments, and dealings, but her words hit hard against the protective shell I buried my broken heart in. A tiny fissure ruptures, but instead of the advice stinging, it seeps inside the space. A tiny amount of balm on a wound I let fester for too long. Yep, I think I'm going to like Ava.

"All right, as the Director of Communications and Public Relations, which oversees the Social Media Department, it is my job to go through all of the finer points from HR for new hires," Ava's voice draws me back to the moment. She lifts a piece of paper before placing a delicate pair of tortoiseshell reading glasses on the tip of her nose. She scans while reading. "The NHL has a code of conduct for its players—I'm sure you're familiar with it, so I think we can skip that. Your duties are determined by your direct supervisor— that's Ethan Savoy in this case—but wages are regulated by industry standards and me." She flashes a quick smile and resumes reading. She huffs a breath and grimaces. "All other aspects of conduct, procedure, and policy can be found in your onboarding paperwork, but I'm supposed to say this specifically: conduct between employees is expected to remain professional at all times. HR enforces a no fraternization policy in the front office."

Ava lifts her gaze to me. I feel the expectation of a reaction, but she won't get one from me.

"I'm not looking to date while I'm here," I offer.

"It feels like an archaic stipulation, but there's precedence for needing it, I suppose." Ava rolls her eyes, the expression out of place for such a sophisticated woman. It gives me a clear idea of how she feels about things and makes me laugh. She leans forward a little conspiratorially. "Professionally speaking, I should tell you that's the right attitude to have. As a woman, I would just tell you don't let a good opportunity go to waste. My office is always open if you need to talk it through."

A not-so-small part of me wishes this woman was going to be overseeing my work. She's a straight shooter, and I like that. But my heart has had a strict "closed for repairs" sign on it, and I don't think anyone around here is going to change that.

Chapter 6

Crosby

I hiss as I drop further into the swirling jets of the hot tub, leaning back to close my eyes. Training camp has kicked my ass over the last two weeks. Long days, sore nights, and rarely enough time to keep my focus on anything but my spot on first line.

"Holy shit, this feels good." Obie splashes down next to me, forcing my eyes open as little waves of hot water push against my chest. "Why didn't you tell us you had this earlier, Gus?"

"Because then all of you would be here all the time," Gus calls from the back door of the house. The hot tub is situated in a covered corner of Gus' spacious, enclosed patio. He's currently on the phone with Carver's Pizza, securing an order that will likely equal our body weight in food. I certainly won't complain as long as there's a meat lover's thin-crust pie for me. It's time for this week's cheat meal, and the idea of gooey cheese and flavorful toppings has me practically salivating.

"Don't listen to him." I turn toward Obie. The younger defenseman has been a natural fit on the team, and he's been a great person to get to know. On the ice, he plays viciously, teaming up with Gus to form a tough barrier for any seasoned professional to go against. The pair have an uncanny ability to anticipate the other during practice, and I'm excited to see how it will impact our play during the season. "He wouldn't know what to do without all of us every day, no matter how much he complains about us."

"It's a nice change," Obie comments. "I didn't really fit in with the guys in LA."

"Probably helps to be home?" I ask. While he's been getting along with us, Obie is still a little guarded, but I'm not the kind to push. I don't like it when people do it to me, so I make it a habit not to do it to anyone else. His comment about LA piques my interest but not enough to make him uncomfortable discussing it.

"It does make some of it easier. But I've got to find a place of my own. It made sense to crash with my parents since I practically flew here, filled out paperwork, and then started camp. Hasn't left a lot of time to go looking at places." Obie leans his head back. "But I don't think I want to continue staying in my childhood bedroom. God forbid, I try to have a bigger social life than this."

"What'd I miss?" Gus asks as he approaches the edge of the tub, eyes floating back and forth between me and Obie.

"Obie needs to find a place; he's sick of staying with his parents," I tell him.

"Makes sense." Gus' smile curls across his face. Then he plants one hand on the ledge and launches himself into the open space of the hot tub. The splash sends water at my face, which I swipe away with my hand. The water settles, and Gus is sitting across from me, a relaxed look on his face. "Move in here. I've got an extra room."

I give him a surprised look. Gus doesn't share his space easily, but he just continues talking to Obie. "You pay for half the utilities. You'll also be responsible for any food the nutritionists don't send over, yeah?"

"Are you serious?" Obie checks.

"Wouldn't offer it if I wasn't." Gus laughs. "Bring your stuff by tomorrow after morning skate."

"Okay." Obie smiles.

"Ready for the first game, boys?" Gus asks, the roommate situation easily forgotten.

Our season opener is in three days.

Mixed with a bunch of other emotions is excitement. Camp helped me feel more secure in the changes of the last month. Coach has been resolute in his support, and getting to play with Tex and Bones is always easy. We transition the puck seamlessly while making sure the guy who is best set up for the shot gets it. It's a selfless thing. Exactly how it should be.

The only drawback to being the starting center has been the increase in media attention. It doesn't help that The Midnight have been the second or third story on *Center Ice* and the *NHL Network* every day since Bridger's exit.

Bridger ran his mouth when he settled in with his new team two days after the announcement. The dickhead felt it necessary to slam almost every aspect of The Midnight organization, from the locker rooms to the lack of support on the ice from his former teammates. It's been hard keeping our mouths shut about the negativity Bridger was responsible for during his two-year stint, but Coach asked us to keep quiet. It's been mildly beneficial to the team's morale to know his weak ankles and bad attitude will be Miami's problem. And I'll officially be allowed to drive him into the boards when we play against each other this season. Then maybe he can fade away.

But the media has been persistent in other ways. I've had to sit through my fair share of post-camp interviews in the press room, something that hasn't been normal for my career thus far. Until now, my only real media interactions have been the few times I ended up in a scrap or during last season's playoffs when I started for Bridger.

That's all changed. I've been fielding questions all through camp, and there have been moments I've felt uncomfortable with the direction the reporters have taken. For the most part, I've only had to talk about the game, shutting down anything that didn't involve a puck, but I know that's not always going to be the case. Despite my current single status, I wouldn't be surprised if my dating life finds its way into an article or blog, which will suck. I don't want to get asked about my relationships.

I have meetings scheduled after the first game with the head of social media to discuss my promotion in the lineup. Tex assures me it's all completely normal. As captain, he's been dealing with it for years. Still makes me itchy thinking about the attention.

"I think it's going to be great," I finally respond, setting aside those thoughts and choosing to focus on the game ahead. "New York is always tough, but we're ready. Coach has set good lines. We've got some new blood. Your family coming?"

"Not this year," Gus says. His parents and little sister have been at every season opener since he was old enough to be in a league. They live in Minnesota but have never complained about the travel. "Maeve has her senior banquet; they can't miss it."

"That okay? I know how much you like it when they come out," I check with him. Gus just shrugs his shoulders. Even with the age difference, he's always been close with Maeve, and his parents are great people.

"Yeah," Gus brushes off. "When we play in Minneapolis later this season, they're going to come to the game. Plus, Maeve is looking at applying to schools out here."

I nod at him.

"What about you, Obie?" I ask.

"Absolutely. They haven't missed a Midnight home game since Coach joined the team. They've all been around practically since the franchise started." Obie laughs at the matching looks Gus and I must be giving him.

"No shit?" Gus flattens his lips and nods, and I bob my head in shared surprise. Obie lets out a pained sigh as he shifts, leaning forward.

"Guess now is as good a time as any to let you in on a bit of history." Obie sounds serious. I throw a look at Gus, but he seems as clueless as I am. And just as interested. "I'd say I'm surprised it hasn't been made public knowledge, but Cal has always kept things close to the chest," Gus mouths the name back to me. No one ever calls Coach by his first name. Especially so informally. "My parents and Cal went to high school together. They were best friends. When I came along shortly after, he became my godfather. I grew up a few streets over from his house, and he helped train me when I took an interest in hockey."

"No. Shit," Gus repeats, all traces of curiosity removed from his voice. He can say those two words about a dozen different ways. Silence settles, cut only by the steady bubbling sound of the jets.

"All right. That's wild. Keep that close to the vest if you don't want the media to pick you apart," I say. Family is family, and Coach has never given any preferential treatment to Obie since he joined the team, but it's also information that could cause a lot of interest in a guy I don't think likes being in the spotlight.

"Weird," Gus says, shaking his head at the revelation.

Obie nods absently, but thanks me for the advice.

We sip from our glasses of soda that had been forgotten on the edge of the tub, easing into other topics of conversation. The evening slips away comfortably, my thoughts straying to lacing up my skates in three days.

The club's bass thumps through my chest as I walk through the side door. Ahead of me, Gus' head bobs along to the beat of the tune I don't recognize. Most of the team is inside somewhere. I let the music sink into my blood. It mixes with the endorphins from our win, creating a fuzzy high that will hopefully promise a memorable night.

Our season opener went better than I could have hoped. I scored in the first and third periods, helping propel the team to a 3–1 win. After we finished the post-game press, we decided to celebrate. Usually we'd be at Lowry's, but Tex suggested this place to mark the occasion. It's a lively club a few blocks from the arena, but it isn't too full for a Tuesday night.

There are groups of people huddled around belly-up tables with glasses clinking between them as we make our way to the back. We weave through swaying and writhing bodies on the fringes of the dance floor before finally reaching the bar. I lean over the polished dark oak, lifting my hand to gain the attention of the bartender. With Gus still bouncing obliviously next to me, I order two drafts. As soon as the frosted glasses hit the countertop, I pull down a heavy drink. It's my first beer since before training camp, and the hops settle perfectly among the post-game adrenaline rushing through my system.

"Where are the rest of the boys?" I shout to Gus as we head toward an empty table opposite the dance floor but within sight of the bar. He indicates the end of the bar where Tex is tucked up with Allison, his wife. I catch my captain's eye and lift my glass in salute. Allison waves back with a big smile on her face before Tex wraps her up, laying an almost indecent kiss on her. I shake my head at them. Tex met his wife when they were twelve, and the way they've navigated life and his career has always been something I've envied.

"Nicky wanted to get home to Natalia." Gus leans over to explain where the rest of our teammates are. "Bones said he was coming, but who knows where he's ended up. And our Rook was trying to convince his elusive friend to come out tonight."

"I thought we were his only friends in town," I joke, scanning the crowd and taking another drink. I'm just about to ask Gus for more information when I spot Obie easily gliding through the bodies on the dance floor. His arm is trailing behind him, hand interlocked with that of a woman. Whatever I thought I was going to say dies on my tongue.

The brunette has long hair curled in an effortless way, porcelain skin, and full lips. She's clinging to Obie, letting him make a path. Her gaze is sharp as it takes in the club before she lifts onto her toes to pull Obie's shoulder down so she can whisper in his ear. She's average height, and I'm drawn to the curve of her hips encased in tight jeans as she breaks from my teammate. Her hips perfectly balance the swell of her breasts covered by a black t-shirt and the narrow waist in between. The brunette slips around a couple, obnoxiously grinding against each other, releasing Obie's hand and heading toward the bar. I see Obie nod toward our table before he calls back to the woman.

"Thanks, Letty!"

She shoots a hand in the air as an acknowledgment of some kind.

"Who the hell is that?" I yell at Gus quickly. My gut tells me this isn't a date. Obie said he was bringing a friend, so I don't think I'm crossing any lines if I go talk to her. I'm still tracking her as she approaches the bar. Before I hear Gus' answer, I see a guy box her out as she tries to flag a bartender down. Irritation spikes along my spine, and I'm moving, passing Obie without a word.

I'm a few steps away from grabbing the offender's arm and swinging him around when the woman slides a lean leg in front of his hip and checks him back a step. It's so similar to a drill I learned at seven, and it freezes me on the spot. With her place at the bar secured and the guy grumbling loudly as he walks away, I hear her call out a sharp "oi" to get the bartender's attention.

I spot an opening a little to her right, leaning my hip against the lacquered surface to keep observing her. She places her order, braces her hands on the bartop, and blows out a breath, checking over her shoulder quickly. I can't tell if she's looking for Obie or making sure the asshole doesn't come back, but she turns fully to rest back against the bar.

With the bodies around her cleared, I slide closer.

"It's Letty, right?"

Chapter 7

Violet

"You're coming with me tonight."

"Obie, please. I just want to go home, sit on the porch, and listen to Taylor Swift," I beg my best friend as we walk down the back hallway of the arena. I spent the game walking around the crowd with Ethan. We gathered photos and video clips for content while he explained the history of the team and pointed out players to me. I smiled politely at the information I already knew while fighting off the familiar melancholy that came with being around the game. It was difficult, but the feeling was less than before, and it reminded me that I've made the right decision.

Obie just finished the small amount of post-game press he was required to do, but I waited around to congratulate him on a great game. He scored his first goal in a Midnight jersey and helped block ten shots on Baladin in goal.

"Which album?" he asks, stopping to look down at me. I think he already knows the answer.

I sigh.

"Absolutely not," he replies.

"But—"

"No. I've let you gracefully bow out of every other social gathering." Obie loops his tie around his neck. If I had known my plans for a little self-reflection and pity were about to get hijacked by my well-intentioned best friend, I would have left at the final buzzer. "Violet, it's time to be a little less *Tortured Poets* and a little more *Reputation*."

"Which part?" I counter, knowing I'm not going to win this argument. Obie's right. I've avoided every invitation from him to hang out. I haven't even gone over to his new place.

"The 'fuck the haters, I don't need them' part." Obie cuffs his hand behind my neck before pulling me forward to kiss my forehead. "I'm here for you, but I don't want to have to keep you separate from the team. You haven't even been over to meet my roommate. I finally feel like I can fit in here. And having you as *part* of that is important to me. You're my best friend. So, come out tonight. Pretend if you have to, but be there *with* me, yeah?"

"Ugh." I wrap my arms around his waist, sinking against him. "Fine. That's your freebie on the 'best friend card.'"

"This month," Obie amends, and we walk to the parking lot. He pulls his phone from his pocket, tapping a couple of times, and mine buzzes in my pocket. "I sent you the location we're meeting at. Can I trust you'll show up, or do you need to ride with me?"

"You'll have to take me. I hitched a ride with Dad earlier."

"Really? I didn't think you wanted people to know your connection if you can help it. That's why I haven't told anyone." Obie pulls open my door when we get to his Land Rover. I hop into the seat as he rounds the car to the driver's side.

"I had him drop me down the street. I walked in for my report time." I buckle up and set the nav app to link directions through the car's Bluetooth. "I think it's more important that people in the front office don't realize the connection. Outside of the people who know but legally can't say anything, like HR," I consider. "Anyway, with you playing on the team and *insisting* I hang out with you, it's only a matter of time before the rest of the guys know. But I want to get through a few weeks of work without the whispers. Have my efforts be judged for what they are and not who I am."

"Makes sense." Obie drives, waving at the lot guard. "Do you want to tell any of the guys tonight? They know you're coming."

I think about it. There's a part of me that would love to keep my relationship with the team's coach quiet. I've managed to keep a low profile in the hockey world outside of the immediate members of the team Dad played with and a few others he couldn't avoid introducing me to. Otherwise, I rarely acknowledged the connection. It made me feel like I was treated differently, or I was only interesting to people because of who my dad is. It doesn't help that being Callum Andrews' daughter was the entire reason my last relationship fell apart, a mistake I'm not keen to repeat. But I'm not trying to date any of these guys, and they're already on my dad's team. There would be more harm in keeping it from new people than just being upfront about it. *Then again...*

"Who exactly did you tell them I am?" I'm smirking a little. There's this idea teasing my conscience. Just one night of being unknown to the guys on the team. I haven't even been introduced to them at work yet. Instead, I've been spending my days pulling backlogs of data to see where the department's strengths and weaknesses are in content creation and management. It's not exactly ethical to keep back my identity, but there's something in the anonymity that clings to me like armor. It feels safe, even if I know it's temporary.

"I've mentioned my best friend a few times. They know you're a woman, something Gus finds particularly amusing." Obie chances a look over at me as directions to turn left fill the cab. "Probably won't take them long to put together *something* if they've seen you around the practice facility."

"Let's leave it alone tonight, all right?" I give Obie a real smile. It's harmless fun. Not a real lie, just an omission. "If someone asks outright, I'll answer, but it's unlikely to come up. This isn't an interview; it's a celebration of your opening night win!"

"You sure?" The navigation chirps that we've arrived at our destination, and Obie looks for parking. He guides the car into an opening along the curb. He has a shit-eating grin on his face when he looks at me. "What if you end up liking one of them?"

"Never going to happen." I pop open the door, shucking my leather bomber jacket off and leaving it on my seat. The early October night isn't quite as cold as the arena was, and I'll be inside. Obie comes around with a disbelieving lift to his brow. I link my arm through his as we make our way to the entrance. "I don't date hockey players anymore."

Obie shakes his head next to me and rolls his eyes. I slap a hand against his chest in retaliation to his judgment.

"If *Reputation* Taylor didn't need a man to have a good time, I don't either."

"It's Letty, right?"

I twist at the sound of my nickname coming from an unfamiliar voice. I have to tilt my head back to find the source. The guy is tall. He's at least six inches taller than me, probably more. Over six feet, with a firm chest and broad shoulders. They curve slightly inward toward me, as though he's trying to appear a little more approachable. Dark brown hair curls a little at the ends, not because it needs a trim but because it might actually have a curl pattern he knows how to control. His upturned eyes, the color indistinguishable in the club's lighting, have a little glimmer in the corner, hinting at trouble. It matches the flirty yet kind smile he's giving me.

I draw upon an attitude I don't really have, cocking my head and lifting my chin at him. If he were anywhere close to my height, I'd level him with eye contact, but as he practically towers over me, it loses a little of its impact. His eyebrows wrinkle just a moment before he speaks, as if his confidence might be faltering before he gets it together.

"I'm Crosby." He offers his hand. "You know my teammate, Obadiah, right?"

Crosby Wells doesn't look anything like his brooding and serious roster photo. It's surprising and welcoming, and it makes me want to play a little as he waits patiently for my response.

"My name is Violet. Obie calls me 'Letty,' and my other friends call me 'Vi.'" I place a hand on my hip and pick up the beer Obie asked for with my other hand. I use it to point back and forth between us. "*We're* not friends."

Crosby pulls his hand back, hooking it behind his neck for a moment before letting out a laugh. His high cheekbones darken a shade in the mixed lighting, and suddenly I'm glad I'm busting his balls a little more than necessary for an introduction. I need to make sure Crosby stays far away from me, and being prickly is a good way to do that.

He surprises me when he draws a breath and sets his half-finished beer behind me on the bar. It brings him a lot closer, even if he doesn't lean over to face me directly. He smells like vanilla, sandalwood, and a hint of citrus. It's unexpected, stealing away my thoughts of keeping space from him when I let the scent wash over me. His voice drops a little, low enough so I'm the only one who can hear.

"Maybe I don't want to be your friend."

There's something sinfully inviting in the way he says it. The offer is clear but not rude. I like it. Probably more than I should.

A body bumps me from my opposite side, jarring me out of the moment with the splash of beer on the back of my hand. It helps bring back my resolve. I shake my hand, wiping it against the leg of my jeans.

"That really work for you?" I can't quite keep the barest touch of venom out of my voice as I search Crosby's kind but bewildered face. He seems surprised with himself. Or maybe by me. If I were a little more confident, a little less bruised, I would have found the line clever. Instead, it stings with memories of a different man, whispering promises to me he never really meant to keep. My defenses insist I shut him down as fast as I can. "I don't date hockey players."

Without a backward glance, I push off the bar and make for the table Obie's at. It doesn't take me more than a few steps to realize Crosby will be following me, as I spy the other players gathered with my best friend. Flutters still skitter up and down my spine at Crosby's nearness and husky voice, and I push down the blush threatening to rise. Obie will take one look at me and know something is going on. *I can find Crosby attractive without it meaning anything, right?* I school my features as I slide up next to him.

"One draft." I plunk the pint glass on the table in front of him. He smiles down at me before hooking his arm around my shoulders and pulling me against him in a brotherly manner. Crosby travels around to my other side, next to a guy with long, dark blonde hair. It grazes the tops of his shoulders, layered and shaggy, an intentional bedhead look. He knocks shoulders with Crosby before looking at me, smiling widely. It's cocky and sexy, even with the right lateral incisor tooth missing.

Augustus Kelly. Defensemen. Obie's other half on the ice and new roommate. His prolific love life tends to be the topic my coworkers focus on most days, but I'm more interested in his time on ice average in his career—it's increased in his tenure with The Midnight—and how many sticking penalties he received last season—too many. Dad really needs to help him get that under control; it makes Kelly look incompetent, which he isn't.

The only other occupant is a redhead on Obie's other side. He's a little shorter than the others, but with hockey players, it still makes him taller than me, and he's built like a Viking: bulky in the shoulders and thick through his thighs. He has intense amber eyes and a somberness that's equally mysterious and terrifying. Charlie Kane is the youngest player on the team, but there's something about him that makes him look like the oldest. He gives an almost imperceptible nod at me.

"Everyone, this is Violet Cameron, my best friend," Obie introduces me. He points around the table, starting with Charlie. "This is Bones, Gus, and Wellsy. Nicky had to get home, and Tex is around here somewhere."

"Nice to meet all of you. Congratulations on the win tonight," I offer. I make note of the nicknames assigned, committing them to memory. Crosby has moved a step toward me, a hand still in his pocket and a lazy smile on his face. I can see his mind turning over my declaration from the bar. It should have been a deterrent. I should be happy I put up the roadblock. *So why do I feel my pulse flutter at his clear curiosity before he speaks?*

"Obie mentioned you two grew up together and just moved back. Where were you before here?"

"I've been in London for the better part of three years. Before that, I was an undergraduate at Brown." I untangle from Obie, who's smiling proudly at me. I bump my shoulder against him while he lifts his pint glass.

"Do you like hockey?" Gus asks.

Obie sputters around his beer, doing a terrible job at stifling his laugh and launching into a coughing fit. If Crosby looked curious before, he looks downright invested now. He leans forward on his elbows. The table is a high top, hitting me just below my ribs. When Crosby settles, his face is almost level with mine. This close, I can finally make out the color of his eyes: they're leaf green, bisected with sections of golden hazel. *Heterochromia*, my brain helpfully supplies as I struggle not to lose myself in them. I swallow thickly before cutting my eyes toward Gus. His mouth is curved up a little in the corner, playfully, as if he caught me.

"You could say that," I offer. Obie finally wheezes a little as his coughing subsides. "I couldn't really escape it in my house." I see Crosby cock his head. I backtrack before I give too much away. "Being friends with this guy and all."

"Then you know we're a real superstitious bunch." Gus looks over to Crosby, who gives a small shake of his head. Then, out of the corner of my eye, I see Bones offer me an apologetic shrug. A sinking feeling appears in my stomach. "Once something good happens, we take it as an omen. A requirement to uphold."

"Yep. I think I read once that a player kept his daughter's stuffed unicorn in his locker after she gave it to him during a playoff run," I try to deflect, pulling up a memory of me and my dad. I'm not sure where Gus is taking this conversation.

"Right." Gus slaps a hand on Crosby's shoulder. "So you'll understand why we like to make sure for a win, our lead scorer is treated well that night."

I recoil. Obie draws himself to his full height, even against his teammate. Crosby looks like he's going to level his friend with the fire blazing in his stare.

"Shit." Gus sighs, swiping his hand across his face. "Just realized how that came out. Not at all what I meant. I was just kind of hoping you'd dance with my boy here, I swear."

"That was painful," Charlie says. My eyes widen. His voice is *deep* deep. Unexpected. It makes his chastisement of his teammate all the better and loosens me up a little. Obie even deflates from the protective stance he was in.

Silence descends over the group. I pick up Obie's drink, taking a sip and scrunching my nose at the taste. Even on American soil, beer just isn't my drink. I see Charlie turn Gus away from the table, their heads bowed together for a conversation. Obie leans over to join in, leaving me to awkwardly look around the club.

"You don't have to." It's Crosby who breaks the last threads of lingering tension. He sounds sincere and is leaning a little further into my space. The hints of vanilla tingle in my nose. "I'd love it, but it's your choice."

I shouldn't. I'm learning from my past mistakes, starting over. Moving on.

"I'd really like to dance with you, Violet," Crosby whispers into my ear, his breath ghosting across my skin. I chance a look at Obie. He's still talking to Gus and Charlie but gives me a little wink of reassurance. Or maybe he's gloating already.

I turn back to Crosby. He's got a sweet, boyish charm with his hands in his pockets and a free curl sitting off-center on his forehead.

He's not Olivier, I remind myself. *Not all hockey players are the same.*

"Just one dance, Wells," I announce. A blinding smile splits Crosby's face.

Shit.

I forgot *Reputation* Taylor fell in love while making that album.

What an unhelpful bitch.

Chapter 8

Crosby

"**G**od damn it, Obadiah! You've got to know the fucking deke is coming on the *left* in this formation! Get to the fucking puck!" Coach yells from the bench in the arena. There's a whistle from one of our assistant coaches, and we all stop skating, listening as Coach continues his tirade. I lean against my stick, angling my eyes down and trying in vain to keep my thoughts from wandering to last night.

Violet Cameron.

With one dance, she turned my whole world upside down. The way she moved. The way she smelled. The way her lips would lift in the corners only to flatten like her brain was actively reminding her body she wasn't supposed to be smiling.

Violet gave me one dance and left like a thief in the night with all my attention. And, if I were being honest, maybe a little piece of my heart.

I stared at the exit of the club long after she told the group she would be calling it a night and grabbing an Uber shortly after we left the dance floor. Obie walked her out, shooting the group a text, saying he was going to save her the cost and take her home.

When I got home a little while later, it felt too late to text Obie for more details about her. I didn't see him until today at practice, and there hasn't been much chance to ask questions.

"Did you hear me, Wells?"

I snap my head toward Coach Andrews. He looks thunderous. I quickly scan for the information floating between my ears, trying to latch onto the instructions he just finished shouting at me. *Run it again.*

"Yes, sir." I nod. "We're running it again." I push down on my right blade, skating to the other side of the midline and cutting a half circle to settle in. Next to me, Bones taps the ice twice with his stick, calling for the puck from Tex on my other side, and we're off.

Twenty minutes later, I'm sucking down water from a Gatorade bottle on the bench, elbows on my knees as I watch the other lines run the same drill when Coach blows the final whistle. With just a few reminders of when to report back for the short trip in the morning for the DC game tomorrow night, we're filing out of the rink.

"Wells," Coach calls from where he stands at the boards. "Your meeting with social is in twenty. Don't be late."

"Got it." *I don't—I almost forgot.* I hustle up the tunnel, stripping off my gear and skates before diving for a lightning-fast shower. I give a quick wave to the boys as I run out of the locker room.

I pull on my Midnight hoodie in the elevator, shaking my hair a little to work the last of the water from it, wishing I had dressed a little more professionally. This season feels like my first in the league, only more important. I've always wanted to do well, be successful on the ice. But with a bigger spotlight and years of experience behind me, I know I can do *more* now. Showing leadership in all my relationships in the organization is a big part of that, and I'm about to meet the head of social media in black joggers and a pair of Nikes. I know I've been too distracted the last couple of days. This is just the proof staring back at me in the reflective metal of the elevator doors. It doesn't matter that I'm meeting Ethan, someone I know and have worked with a few times before. He's never been my favorite staffer to interact with; something about his working style always rubs me a little wrong.

The doors open, cutting off all thoughts about Ethan and social media, revealing the last person I expect to see.

"Hello, Crosby." Violet stands stiffly in a perfectly distressed vintage Midnight T-shirt tucked into black wide-leg trousers, one hand tucked into a pocket. Her brown curls have flattened into waves as they fall from the high ponytail she sports, showing off her high cheekbones and gunmetal blue eyes. She gives me a little smile before I notice the doors starting to close. I lunge to keep them open and step out onto the floor next to her.

"What are you doing here?" I scan her head to toe, disbelieving that she's here. My eyes snag on the credentials hanging on a clip at her hip. The identification card is similar to the one on my lanyard in the locker room. "You work here?"

"Yep. Come on, it's this way," she clips, taking a purposeful step through the glass doors at our left. My body responds as my brain catches up, walking in stride with her as she weaves us toward a cubicle along the glass windows overlooking the ice I was just on. The space is a little tight with both of us in it, especially since I'm not a small person.

Violet spins an office chair away from the desk pressed against the windows, dropping into it gracefully while gesturing to a similar chair to the right of the cubicle opening. I eye it a little dubiously, then settle into it by tucking my elbows against my sides and drawing my legs up to fit.

"I'm sorry. Ethan is stuck on a call in the conference room, so he asked me to take the meeting with you. I know my 'office' is a little small for this." Violet cringes around the word "office" and frowns as she looks at the space. I follow her eyes, trying to see it the way she does, but I like her cubicle.

There's a little red statue of a British phone booth near a pen cup on her desk. A picture frame with a younger Violet and who, I assume, is a younger Obie sitting on a shelf near perfectly organized black binders. Their faces are covered in chocolate and marshmallow as they hold up matching gooey s'mores. Next to it, is a photograph of Violet and a woman with wildly curly hair along a beautiful coastline. I think I see Cinque Terre in the background.

"So, this meeting is to determine what your requests and refusals are for working with the social media department throughout the season." She pulls a legal pad off the desk, balancing it on her crossed knee to take notes. She's sitting perfectly straight in her chair, body and voice a perfect reflection of the professionalism she's projecting. Compared to the woman I met last night, it feels as if Violet is putting on a persona.

I don't like it.

I want the sass. The shyness. The dichotomy of her personality.

I thought about it last night, lying in bed hoping for sleep but thinking of her instead. I don't think Violet trusted herself very much in the club once she met all of us. The confident woman I watched hip-check a guy to get to the bar vanished as introductions started. I know now she came because Obie asked. She stayed long enough to meet everyone, tantalizing me in the process, but left before anyone could press with the "getting to know you" questions.

Now, sitting in her cubicle at work—*my work*—she's practically robotic.

"Violet—" I start.

"Yes, I should have said last night that I worked here. But I genuinely didn't think I'd come in today and be told I was going to be working with you directly. I thought I'd be able to ease my connection to the team into a conversation further down the road. Or at least not feel so awkward about it when the time came. It was wrong. I'm sorry."

I blink a few times. Violet's drawing in little circles at the top corner of the legal pad. She's not looking me in the eye, and I find I dislike that even more than the efficient delivery of her apology. An apology, I don't think, is necessary.

"Violet," I start again, reaching out to stop her doodling. There's a pleasant little thrum in my blood when I finally come into contact with her skin. She's warm and soft under my bigger and rougher palm. I run my thumb along the inside of her wrist just once before pulling back. "I appreciate the professionalism, but you didn't owe anyone your life story last night." Her blue eyes hold mine as she nods once. It makes the waves in her ponytail bounce a little. "Am I surprised to see you here? Absolutely. Is that a bad thing? No. I could say more, but then *I'd* be the unprofessional one."

The most beautiful shade of pink splashes across her cheeks, and her lips form a little "o" as she lets out a gasping exhale. I like the shape of her mouth that way. A dark corner of my brain sparks to life, trying to figure out how I can make it look like that again for a reason other than shock.

"Well, um, let's just maybe focus on why we're here?" Violet transitions us away from the moment. She's cute when feeling a little flustered or awkward, but I'm happy to switch back to business. For now.

"Sure." I lean back into my chair, letting Violet adjust herself and lock her focus on me. "This is the first year I've had one of these meetings. I'm used to the social team being around a few times a week to film content or whatever, but I've always just been in the background."

"That's because you've been stuck on a line you really shouldn't have been. Management focused on the wrong player," Violet says, making a quick note on the legal pad.

"How would you know I wasn't exactly where I should have been? It takes time to build up the skill and respect to end up a starter." I fold my fingers across my lap, tilting my head slightly at her.

"Crosby, even on the third line, you managed eighteen goals in a season, and last year when you were on the second line, you had a career-high of twenty-nine. That's insane, considering how ice time is split between lines statistically. That record alone should have guaranteed you a spot on the first line whether Bridger was here or not." Violet's voice is finally full of life. Her eyes spark with passion, and she's leveling me with a look that speaks to how little she'll accept an argument back. I shrug. "Not to mention, you had a hat trick in the playoff game you started last season!"

"Still got eliminated." I can't help pushing her just a little. She huffs at me. She's irresistible like this: all fire and brimstone, like a preacher at the pulpit, but instead of heaven and hell, she's worshipping at the altar of what I've built my life around. And, maybe, if my ego ruled my brain, me.

"Yeah, well, that series would have gone differently if you had started all the games. I bet even Andrews thinks so."

"Really?" I'm surprised to hear that. During that round against

Milwaukee, Coach told me he had faith in me when Bridger was benched, but maybe it was more than that. Maybe he had wanted to start me for the entire series. It's a nice idea.

"Who wouldn't?" Violet queries. "Anyway, the point is, you are where your talent can really shine now. And according to my research, you're also a successful draw on the team's social media accounts. Posts featuring you in the past have a 5 percent higher engagement than ones that don't. Since it was announced The Midnight wouldn't be seeking another center, all content tagged with your name is currently increasing traffic to the account as well. It makes sense the organization wants to capitalize on it."

"Wow." I hook a hand behind my neck. First, it was getting a position on the starting line. Then, it was the press. Now, it's social media. I press my fingertips into the base of my skull, trying not to get overwhelmed. I love to play hockey, but I regularly remind myself I don't think I'm built for the attention it brings me.

"Hey." Violet's voice softens into a warm, sweet tone. "This meeting is for *you* to tell *me* what you do or don't want to do. There are some minimal interaction requirements we have to meet because of your contract, but if you don't want to do anything more than that, I'll make sure you're left alone."

"Personally?" I ask. I can't help but hope Violet will be my contact for this department. I'll take any excuse to spend more time with her, to get to know her. She rolls her lips before flattening them against each other. I watch as their plumpness returns when she speaks.

"I don't know. This is my first year working in the department, and while I've been told I might have to work directly with the players from time to time, I was also brought in more to analyze how the accounts perform."

"So, that's not a no."

"It's not a no," she replies, giving me the tiniest hint of a smile —her first since we sat down.

"I'll take what I can get for now, Violet." For the first time in my career, I'm figuring out if I have enough professional gravity to ensure I can pull Violet Cameron into my orbit because I don't think I want to go into this with anyone else by my side.

Chapter 9

Violet

"I can't believe this is your idea of fun. Isn't there some rule in your contract about playing sports outside of hockey?" I secure my seatbelt in the backseat, glaring at Obie in the driver's seat.

"I'd hardly consider *bowling* a sport. More like a hobby." Obie turns and frowns. It's a week and a half into the season. The team has gone on their first road game stretch, with tonight free before a game tomorrow. When Obie texted earlier saying I should come by his place to "hang out," I didn't realize it would consist of the most embarrassing activity known to man.

"Careful now," Gus interjects from the passenger seat. As Obie gave me a tour of their place, Gus invited himself along to play a few games. Once word traveled that I worked upstairs in the team's facility, Gus showed up in the entry of my cubicle, hands in his pockets and head low. He apologized again for how our first interaction hadn't been the smoothest start. He explained he can get a little excited sometimes, running with a thought or idea before really thinking it through. I told him there were no hard feelings. "There are plenty of people who would disagree about that."

"I don't see how there would be an argument," Obie faces off against his roommate and teammate as we drive toward the highway. "Rolling a ball down a lane at a target isn't exactly athletic. Most five-year-olds manage it just fine."

"The definition of the word sport: an activity involving physical exertion and skill in which an individual or team competes against another or others for entertainment," I recite from the Google results. Obie lobbies a dirty look over his shoulder at me. I stick my tongue out in return. "According to that, bowling counts."

"So does my sex life," Gus cracks.

"Who exactly are you competing with?" Obie asks. "When we go out, you're with a married guy, a single dad, a twenty-one-year-old who doesn't like to talk to people, me, and Crosby. I've told you I don't date or sleep with anyone during the season, and I think Crosby might be interested in someone."

I don't miss the way Obie's eyes cut to me in the rearview mirror. My best friend is about as subtle as a check into the glass during a game. Before the blush paints my cheeks or I try to refute him, Gus carries the conversation forward.

"You're right. There is no competition, and there have never been any complaints. Crosby's going to meet up with us. Maybe we can get him to spill who he has a crush on." He half-turns in his seat to look at me.

I'm fighting to show no emotion, aiming for impassive and nonchalant. But if Gus' eyebrow waggle and soft smirk are any indication, I'm not doing a good enough job. Saving me from any further discussion, he reaches over to turn up the music, arguing with Obie about what to listen to.

I sink back into the leather seat, turning over the idea that Crosby might be interested in me. It's not my ego talking when I think it isn't a surprising development. He and I connected the night we met, even if I kept it brief. There was no shortage of attraction. Crosby has a congenial, sincere charm that puts people at ease. Coupled with his tousled, curly hair, beautiful eyes, and strong jaw it would be difficult for any woman to resist feeling drawn to him.

But I've been through this before. I met the charming hockey player who made me feel like the only person in the room. Who had me so blinded by his attention I let my guard down almost immediately, and I paid the price.

I really want to believe I wasn't left so jaded by the experience that I can't find the good in the men that I work with. In fact, as I sit listening to Gus give a TEDTalk on why the *Star Wars* prequels might actually be better than the sequels, it's hard not to want to give them a chance. I don't have to close myself off from spending time with them. Getting to know them. Even becoming friends with them. Including Crosby.

The bowling alley is oddly busy for a Tuesday night, but one glance down the rows of lanes explains it's league night for the over sixty-five crowd. At the counter, Crosby leans casually, a row of two-toned red-and-blue bowling shoes lined up next to him. He shakes hands and hugs Obie and Gus before smiling in welcome to me.

"I have a good idea what size to get these guys, but I wasn't sure about you. It's all paid up, you just have to ask for a pair," Crosby tells me before turning around to wave down the teenager currently spraying a returned pair of shoes. I try not to think about how many pairs of feet have been in the footwear I'm about to acquire.

"Size seven, please," I tell the employee. Lazily, he reaches behind him for a neon-green-and-pink pair with yellow laces. I lift them up and look back at the kid.

"Only pair I have left. Cosmic bowling style," he offers the explanation with a shrug.

"Great." I smile, hooking my fingers into the shoes and laughing under my breath as he returns to the far end, continuing to sanitize shoes.

"At least you'll stand out in the crowd?" Crosby teases from beside me. His smile is lopsided but kind as he takes in the obnoxiously bright shoes.

"Just what I always wanted: all eyes on me as I roll gutterball after gutterball."

"It couldn't possibly be that bad," Gus says, looping an arm around my shoulders, steering me toward our designated lane.

"Oh, it really *can* be that bad." Obie chuckles. Our group sits in the uncomfortable plastic seats to change our footwear. I glare at my best friend because I know he's about to recount something from our childhood that's going to leave me embarrassed. "She once managed to land a gutterball two lanes down." Obie's laughing full out now at the memory. "Just don't stand too close to Letty when it's her turn. Especially if you value your toes."

Gus gives me an uneasy smile before looking down at his feet and back to me. Crosby looks thoughtful but offers a shrug.

"It's just for fun. I'm not worried," he says kindly. He ties off his shoes and stands up. "Be right back. Gus, can you get everyone typed into the machine?"

Gus nods. Obie comes over to sit next to me as I finish changing shoes. He bumps my shoulder. I lean back. There's never any hard feelings between us, and this little silent communication reminds us of that.

A few minutes later, Crosby returns just as Gus finishes setting up the scoring system.

"Vi, I put you first, that okay?" Gus spins around, indicating the lineup. I'm first, Obie's second, then Crosby, and Gus put himself last.

"Want to get the wrecking ball out of the way?" I laugh as I search for a bowling ball I can hold comfortably in one hand. The sparkly orange one has swirls of white, making it look like a creamsicle. I wiggle my fingers into the holes and grip. As I step up to the top of the lane, I exhale, focusing on the white pins at the end. Suddenly, there's a clanging noise, and the metal bumpers pop out of the sides of the gutters. I spin around to the group of guys.

Gus and Obie are smiling, but Crosby is looking anywhere but at me, busy sifting through bowling balls. I wait a beat to see if he'll look up. When he does, he gives me a wink.

"Show us what you can do, Violet," Crosby says.

The other guys cheer me on as I spin back to the lane and hurl the ball. It bounces against the bumpers before gliding smoothly into the far corner, knocking a single pin down.

The next night, I'm waiting in the arrivals tunnel for the team to show up. It's my turn to get some walk-in content to go with the still photos. But waiting for the team to trickle in has sent me scrolling, and I latched onto a trend we haven't filmed yet. It settles in my brain, and I immediately know who I want to pull aside for it. As soon as I see Charlie and Gus walk in together, I flag them down. I explain my idea, with Gus agreeing gleefully before Charlie frowns.

"I understand if you'd rather get on with whatever pre-game you need to do, Charlie," I say patiently. He takes a moment, running his hand through the shock of red hair on his head before he slowly nods.

"I'm doing this once, Vi," he tells me, the frown softening

slightly when he says my name. I smile and nod. "And only because *you* asked."

"Thank you," I say, reaching out to touch his arm. He tenses a little but gives me a hesitant smile that flickers and fades from his face. I take a step back and pull out my phone, swiping open the camera and adjusting the settings quickly. With one shot at this, I want to make sure I don't waste it. Gus and Charlie arrange themselves in front of The Midnight's logo. I line up Gus in the frame, press record, and point at him.

"Do you think they're going to play 'HOT TO GO?'" Gus asks excitedly. I hit pause and turn to Charlie. He sucks in a deep breath, and I hit the bright red button.

"This is a Midnight hockey game."

Charlie's delivery is so deadpan, so unflinching in its severity, I barely stop filming before Gus and I collapse against each other in a fit of giggles.

"This is perfect. Thank you, Charlie," I say sincerely. The video is going to look so great when I cut in footage of the team skating out to their unofficial anthem of "Back in Black" by AC/DC later. Charlie gives me a sharp nod and moves down the hall on the way to the locker rooms. Gus gives me a little salute as he spins on his heels, heading directly toward one of our team photographers.

I'm not looking where I'm going as I make my way back up to the arena to scope out the perfect spot to film the ice introduction. I slam into a body, an apology falling from my lips as I try to hold onto my phone and not end up on my ass. A steadying hand squeezes my bicep.

"All right there, Violet?" It's Ethan. He pulls his hand away and offers a concerned frown.

"Great!" I chirp, even as I take a few extra steps to balance. "Hey, it's okay if I made a different video for the walk-in tonight, right? Charlie and Gus were really funny doing that Chappell Roan trend. Charlie is so serious people are going to die of laughter."

I'm flicking open the screen on my phone to show him when Ethan speaks.

"You mean you didn't film the answers for 'What's your favorite pre-game snack?'" In our weekly department meetings, Ethan has only ever presented himself as someone who appreciates creativity and trying new things. He encourages us to be adaptable, make adjustments in the moment and for the current trends. But as he looks at me, I can't tell if he's upset I changed the plan. I scramble to make things right.

"I can do that. There's still time to grab some of the guys." I shove my phone in my back pocket, intent to turn around and make things right. "I'm sorry, I should have asked."

Ethan waves a hand in between us, literally clearing the air as he gives me a tight smile.

"No, no, it's all right," he begins, shoving his hands in his pockets. His voice sounds calm, but there is a tightness around the corners of his mouth and eyes that makes me think maybe everything isn't all right. "I think the 'HOT TO GO' trend is a good change. Just wish I had thought of it myself."

I press my lips together in a forced smile. It still doesn't feel like all is well, but maybe Ethan *is* just upset he didn't think of the idea. I still feel too new, too unsure in this job, to let it go, so I push a little harder to make sure I haven't messed up.

"So you're not mad I changed direction and filmed something else?"

"I'd be kind of a terrible boss if I spent every week telling my team to go with their guts, only to turn around and get mad when someone actually does, wouldn't I?" Ethan pushes his glasses further up his nose, and I see the way he shakes off the tension of the last moment. "I think it will be a great video, Vi. I'm excited to see how it performs."

"Okay." I breathe a sigh of relief. I start to move past him when he nods.

I wasn't sure how I felt joining the social media department and working on anything other than analytics, but making this choice tonight felt empowering. It made me feel connected to the work and the team in an unexpected way. Having Gus and Charlie's help—even if Charlie looked like a root canal would have been more fun—felt good. I felt supported, like maybe the guys on this team could be my friends.

Chapter 10

Violet

"I can't wait to get my own place. I love my dad, but I'm not used to living with him like this." I'm sitting on my bed in my childhood bedroom, complaining to Bea over Face-Time, the iPad propped against the lamp on the nightstand. It's a Saturday in late October, the midday sunlight doing little to warm my room as I catch up with my favorite girl.

"When do you move out?" she asks while twirling noodles around her fork. I'm joining her for a remote dinner; it's the best we can do with the time difference. I look at my forgotten Pad Thai next to the lamp. It doesn't quite taste the same at two o'clock in the afternoon, especially without Bea adding her unwanted bean sprouts to my bowl and stealing my extra lime wedge.

"Next week on the team's off day. Dad insists on helping, so it has to wait until then. I'm glad I can make the new place work without a roommate, but I'm afraid I'll feel lonely. Obie's already living with Gus, so I can't ask him to move in with me. And my best roommate is still busy living her dream across an ocean." I pick up my fork, shoving a mouthful of noodles and peanut sauce into my mouth. I get a little hum of acknowledgement from the tablet.

"Tell me about the hockey player." Bea gives a wicked smile, abruptly shifting topics.

"They're all hockey players, babe," I deadpan. I know exactly whom she's referring to, but I'm not ready to talk about the man currently testing my willpower.

Crosby has officially become my work project. The day after our meeting, Ethan darkened the opening of my cubicle, announcing I was to run point on any and all content involving the new star center, and I needed to adhere to the specifications we laid out together. I wasn't sure from the look on his face if he was happy about the arrangement Crosby clearly engineered, but I acquiesced. Crosby is willing to film one piece of home content and one away every two weeks, meaning I have to start traveling with the team at least twice a month.

"And you know exactly who I'm talking about, so don't hide behind semantics." Bea points her fork at the screen. "It's been almost two weeks. How is it going with him?"

I flop against my pillows.

Crosby is a consummate professional in the emails we exchange to decide what he's willing to film or when sending a quick approval on a photo. When we meet up in person in the facility—somewhere far away from my dad's offices and the locker room—he remembers everyone's name. From the temps that scurry from the mailroom and the equipment managers to our day security team and receptionists in the building. His personal acknowledgments of them show how much respect he has for his team and the people who work for it. People light up when they see him walking the halls. On top of that, Crosby does his homework, studying the previous videos filmed utilizing the trend we choose, and he's always prepared. It's an absolute dream.

"He's really good at what he does," I hedge. There's a thumping noise from the screen. I look over and see Bea slapping at the camera. "What are you doing?"

"I can't actually smack you in the head for the absolute bullshit you just spouted." She stares intensely at me. I heave out a sigh. Even if I wanted to, I couldn't lie to her; she knows me too well. "I don't want to hear about whether he's good at his job. Thanks to you, I'm well aware the team is already blazing in the standings, and the ESPN notifications I get lead to articles praising the new lines Cal set."

"Wow, Bea, did I rub off on you that much?" I blink innocently at her. When we lived together, she used to grumble at my hockey talk and immediately started outright hating it when Olivier broke my heart. Hearing she's following the team I work for makes me want to cry. *God, I miss her.*

"Not the bloody point! You're torn up about him, I can tell." The curve of a glass comes into the picture. Bea takes a drink before softening her voice. "Come on, Petal. Talk to me."

"Playing dirty, I see." I glare at her use of the nickname she gave me. Bea looks completely unrepentant. "All right. Just—well—we're just talking."

"God, you can talk yourself in circles, woman. Get onto the goods," Bea pushes. Now her expressive eyebrows are waggling.

"He's gorgeous," I finally blurt. Everything slips from me like sand in an hourglass. I can't stop now that I've started. "He has curly hair that doesn't need to be tamed; it always looks perfectly mussed. His eyes are the most beautiful things I've ever seen; the two colors are so unique but fit him so well. He doesn't smile a lot, but not because he's grumpy. He's genuinely funny and positive, but it's almost as if he enjoys spending more time listening to everything before he allows himself to react."

I sigh internally at how considerate and attentive Crosby is when we talk. Eyes always on mine, questions coming at the right time and in a thoughtful way. No distractions like his phone or other people taking up his attention.

"Crosby is patient. He hit on me when we first met, but since then, he's been completely respectful of our work dynamic." I shift in my seat on the bed, grabbing a pillow to do something with my hands, fluffing it absently. "I've seen him twice outside of work since that first night. Once, when he showed up at an impromptu 'Best Friend's Bowling Night,' as Gus called it, and then after the San Diego game at the group's favorite dive bar. There were a bunch of us again, but he did little things to show he was paying attention to just me." I glance up at Bea's face on the screen. Her eyebrows are lifted in silent question, and I fight off the blush that wants to creep up my neck. "Just things like refilling my water first. Saving me the end seat of the booth so I could slide out to go to the bathroom, even if it meant his knees hit the underside of the table. Even with that, there's no pressure. I know he's interested. It's like he's just waiting until I say the word."

I'm practically panting by the end of my explanation because I didn't stop to draw breath. I've held onto these thoughts for too long to have taken the time to linger on any one particular aspect of the man who is currently occupying more of my thoughts than I'd like to admit and working unconsciously to break down my defenses.

"Wow. Not a single word of what you just said was problematic," Bea replies. "So why haven't you given him the go-ahead?"

"Aside from my positively disastrous history with dating the hockey players I work with?"

"One man does not a history make," Bea counters, sounding

like some New Age wise woman. "The occupation of a man who treats you like an *opportunity* and not a privilege to delight in makes no difference. The only job that man is succeeding at is being a world-class asshole."

"I know. It isn't fair to compare Crosby to Olivier. They aren't even remotely similar."

I play with a loose string on my comforter. I twirl it around my finger, parceling out my thoughts. Thinking about Olivier doesn't bring the same pain as it did before. My heart doesn't feel like an exposed bruise. In fact, it strongly beats a rebellious rhythm when I try to consider Olivier and Crosby in the same thought. It pulses at me to leave the past firmly buried there, the tempo increasing when a memory of Crosby surfaces.

"He left breakfast for me the other morning." I look up from under my lashes at Bea. She shovels another bite of Pad Thai and leans forward. It's impossible to hold back my smile. "Just sitting on my desk: a chocolate croissant pinwheel inside this beautiful periwinkle box. There wasn't a note, but the outside had a heart and 'CW' written on it."

"Why is it always so hot when men do that?" Bea sighs.

"It's the attention to detail," I reply and grimace a little. "If he's that observant about my breakfast pastries, how long do you think I have before he figures out his coach is my dad?"

The thumping sound emanates from the screen again. Bea looks furious.

"Violet Mae Cameron."

I hold my hands up in surrender before covering my face with them and groaning.

"I *know*," I push the words out between my fingers. "I think I have PTSD when confessing who my father is."

"I mean, I get it, but Crosby already plays for him! He's not going to use that piece of information to try and better his career."

Bea still looks a little thunderous at my deception, but there's a softness around her eyes that tells me she's trying to be supportive.

"It's just," I start quietly. Admitting this is hard. It draws up issues I spent years working through in therapy as a kid whose mom left. Old, dark feelings creep out of the bowels of my nightmares, and I hate that traces of them were almost allowed to be reignited by one worthless man. Olivier damaged me in ways that went beyond a broken heart. "What if I'm not enough for him, Bea?"

"Petal. If you decide you're willing to try with him, he's going to be the luckiest person in the world. But it won't matter if you're not honest with him. You have to tell him."

I've barely set my blue-light glasses next to my computer when the phone beside it chirps. Rubbing at the corner of one tired eye, I pick up the receiver with the other.

"Violet Cameron," I say by way of a greeting.

"So she does answer the phone," Obie says from the other end. I sigh loudly while twisting down to my purse and extracting my cell phone. Two missed calls and eight text messages.

"I'm sorry, Obadiah. I was busy, you know, *working*," I grouse back at him. "You don't exactly see me banging on the glass when you're running a four-corner D sequence during practice just because I need to tell you something."

"Guess that's fair," he answers. I hear the smile in his voice. I listen closely to the noise behind him. Morning skate wrapped about twenty minutes ago. It sounds like Obie might still be in the locker rooms or training offices. "Anyway, I was just trying to let you know some of the guys are coming with me tomorrow to help you move."

"What?!" I stand up so fast my rolling chair flies backward into the exterior wall of my cubicle.

"You okay, Violet?" I hear my coworker ask from down the hall, concerned at the shriek I let out.

"Yeah. Fine! Thank you!" I answer and grip the back of the chair to steady myself. Obie is laughing in my ear. "Shut up. What do you mean some of the guys are coming with you tomorrow? What guys? *My dad is going to be there.*"

Obie shuffles and the background noise fades a little.

"How many of you will be there?" Sweat breaks out along my forehead. "How did they find out about this?"

"The usual." Obie's voice loses a little of its jovial tone. "Gus asked me what my plans are for our day off, and—well—I live with the guy. I couldn't exactly lie to him. So he volunteered to come with me. And then Bones said he'd come, and it went from there," he takes a breath. "Wellsy's coming, Letty. I've stayed out of your business with him, but he's going to ask questions when you start calling Cal 'Dad' tomorrow."

I press my fingertips against the inner corner of my eyes.

"Shit," I curse under my breath. "I'll take care of it."

"Okay." Obie shuffles again, and I hear Gus and Tex's voices clearly come closer. Obie says something back to them before speaking into the receiver, "Talk to you later."

"Yeah, thanks."

The dial tone drones so long in my ear that it begins to make a buzzer sound before going dead. I replace the receiver on the cradle, picking up my cell phone, and finding my text thread with Crosby. It only contains work specifics, but I know it is time to cross that professional line.

ME

> I know skate just ended, and you're probably on your way to enjoy your day, but any chance you can swing by me upstairs?

It takes less than a second for the reply to come through.

CROSBY

> Sure. I was going to stop at the coffee cart, want anything?

I push back at the way my stomach is trying to launch its butterflies into orbit at Crosby's sweet offer.

ME

> I don't think so. See you soon.

I listen to my email ping on my computer as I wait, spinning in half-circles in my chair, going over and over what it is I'm going to say when Crosby shows up. Despite my growing attraction to him, our relationship hasn't been such that I need to divulge my family history to him. He even told me after we met that I didn't owe anyone my life story. We work together. Talk hockey. I ignore the way my pulse races when he's near me and how I have to stop myself from falling over to try and catch the delicious smell of his cologne.

So why did I feel so awful?

"I was afraid you were just trying to be nice, so I grabbed you a London Fog." Crosby's voice carries through the opening of my cubicle before he does.

Wearing dark wash denim and a black long-sleeve Henley thermal, Crosby is decidedly more put-together than the first time I brought him up here. He clutches two takeaway cups in one hand. The other holds a white wax wrapper disguising some kind of baked good. I trail my eyes up from his impressive hands to his multicolor eyes, soft and warm, and the shy upturn of a smile on his lips. His curls are still a little damp, peeking out from under a crooked black beanie. He extends his hand, rotating his fingers so the cup containing the tea latte is closest to me. I take it automatically and set it on my desk.

"Thank you," I say, gesturing to the chair I know is too small to be comfortable for him but is all that fits in my space. Aside from Crosby, I don't have much cause to have the players in my cubicle. "How did you know I like London Fogs?"

"Last week, in the afternoon, when I asked if you wanted anything, you said you don't drink coffee after 10:00 a.m., but London Fogs work in a pinch. They just make you miss bees." Crosby is smiling, balancing his to-go cup on his knee. He holds out the wrapped pastry to me. "You also said something about how bees make good biscuits, but they didn't have any, so I got a short-bread cookie."

"Bea," I correct, cradling the treat in my hand. Crosby tilts his head in question. "I didn't say 'bees' like the insect. I said 'Bea,' B-E-A, my best friend who's still in London. She introduced me to the drink, and 'biscuits' really are shortbread cookies. I sometimes forget to switch over the colloquial phrases." My nose burns, and my eyes sting a little. I suck my teeth and spin away for a moment looking at the picture of Bea and me on the shelf. Crosby has no idea how deeply his gesture hits.

"Oh, that makes more sense." I nod while he speaks, breathing through the threat of tears. Crosby's warm hand splays across my shoulder blade. "You okay, Violet?"

I bite the inside of my cheek. *I will not cry.* Not at the reminder of Bea. Her words of honesty echoing in my mind. I will rip the Band-Aid off the reason I asked Crosby here and deal with the fallout like an adult. Clearing the emotion out of my throat,

I'm very aware Crosby's hand has not left my back. Instead, his thumb moves in little sweeps against me. I focus on that, letting his ministrations steady me before spinning around and breaking the contact.

"Thank you for this." I gesture at the drink and cookie. "It will be helpful in getting me through the afternoon."

"Sure." Crosby readjusts, his elbows pulling in against his sides. *It looks like he's sitting in a child's chair.* "What did you need to see me about?"

"My dad is Coach Andrews."

Chapter 11

Crosby

"Your dad is Coach Andrews?" I hear the words pass through my lips, but my brain is still catching up to the surprising information Violet just blurted out. She looks as shocked as I feel. Her eyes wide but searching, her hands gripping the armrests of her office chair. She gives me a very slow nod yes.

"Huh," I offer. *The girl I like is my coach's daughter.*

More alarm bells should be ringing in my head, but they aren't. A lot about Violet from the last few weeks is starting to make sense. Her cagey behavior. Her knowledge of hockey. How she and Obadiah have been best friends their whole lives.

"Wait. He obviously knows you work here. It's not like I'm going to be skating suicides until I puke for talking to you, right?" I ask. "There shouldn't be a reason for him to care, is there? We just work together, and we're adults."

I'm not sure if I'm saying it to let her off the hook in case she isn't interested in me or to remind her it's okay if she is.

Violet shakes her head and crosses one leg over the other.

The polka dot skirt of her outfit flutters against her calf. It's almost distracting enough for me to miss the quick flush of pink in her cheeks. But I don't miss it. After three weeks of being professional and proper every time we interact, is it possible Violet has been struggling as much as I have been when we're together?

I've hoped for as much when we're together. When I feel her eyes linger on me or hear her breath hitch every time our fingers brush as we walk the halls. I still see how she fights the smile threatening to break out and the polite laugh she gives when I make a joke.

Every night since we met, I've fallen asleep to visions of the silky brown hair that tumbles down her back and across her shoulders. I wonder if it's as soft as I think it is. *Does it smell like her?* That euphoric mixture of apple blossoms and crisp green leaves I can't ever get out of my memory. It's the smell of summertime and possibilities, a hopeful mixture I lean into and steal lungfuls of when we're in the elevator.

I dream of her eyes, a color so unique it's a mixture of a cloudless sky and molten metal. There are flickers of bright silver in the irises that spark the more animatedly she talks. Those little sparks are mesmerizing.

I've made it my job to know as much as she's willing to share with me in our limited time together. It was a little underhanded of me to insist I only work with her for these social media things, but I didn't know what else to do. She told me she doesn't date hockey players. *But if that were true, why would she think it would be a big deal if I know who her dad is?*

"Violet, is there a reason your dad would care that we work together?" I ask again. "He had to remind me about my first meeting with this department, so I would think he already knows we've met."

"No, he doesn't care about that," she answers. "But he might care if..."

"If what?" The paper of my coffee cup is starting to slip against my palm. I watch her carefully, trying in vain to catch which direction her thoughts are going. I've taken every chance I can get to learn her, but dancing to the newest pop song or answering fan questions hasn't left me nearly as much time with her like this—unguarded. Raw. Alone. I don't know what the little pinch of her brows or the twitch in her jaw mean. It makes me nervous as hell.

"I just don't want you to be surprised tomorrow when my dad is there to help me move, and it's the first time you're learning he's also your coach." Her voice grows in confidence as she speaks, but the way she purses her lips at the end means it isn't what she's actually thinking. I think Violet is relieved this secret isn't between us anymore, but there are more truths she's keeping close. I want her to give them to me when she's ready. I won't take them from her.

"Thanks for letting me know." I try for casual as I drink a sip of coffee. I don't really want it, but I couldn't just show up with something for Violet. I was afraid it was weird enough when I left her breakfast once before. Swallowing thickly, the acidic taste burns a little as it goes down. *This stuff tastes like shit. How does anyone drink it?*

"You're not mad at me?" Violet reaches for her own cup, rolling it between her hands tentatively. The movement matches the tone of her voice.

"Not at all." I smile when she finally takes a drink, smacking her lips just a little before trying to hide a grimace. She sets the cup back on her desk, pushing the drink farther away from where she put it originally.

I laugh, and her eyes fly to mine searchingly.

"I had no idea the coffee cart was so horrible," I huff out after a moment. Violet looks back at her cup and then at the one in my hand. She folds her hands together in her lap and lets out her own laugh.

It's light and full, tickling up from her throat to join my own that's beginning to ebb away. She spins back to her desk to pick up the shortbread, offering it up in between us.

"Do I dare?" she asks, pulling the wax paper away.

"Absolutely not." I wrap my hand around hers and the cookie. I don't miss the way she sucks in a breath at my touch. Taking a chance, I run my thumb along the inside of her wrist, just like the last time I sat here with her. "I wouldn't want to risk you cracking a tooth and damaging that beautiful smile—even if you do hide it from me."

"No, I don't," Violet protests. She hasn't pulled away, and I indulge in the softness of her skin under my rougher thumb.

"You do. But I'll get it out of you sometime. I don't mind working for it." I let go of her hand, plucking the dubious baked good from her fingers before hefting it into the trash. The resounding thunk at the bottom of the basket echoes ominously.

"About tomorrow, I can't be there until the afternoon because I have a standing appointment with our physio in the morning. I think the rest of the guys will be there, so you should have plenty of help." I carefully set my still-full coffee cup into the trash next to the discarded cookie, reaching back blindly for Violet's drink. *No way will she be drinking this if it's anywhere half as bad as her face indicated it was.*

I straighten, arching my back a little to stretch. Sitting hunched over like I'm in a kindergartener's chair hurts. I stand up while I wait for Violet's answer. She stands, too, the lift of her black heels puts her at my shoulder. *Speaking of kindergarten,* my brain unhelpfully supplies as the whole of her polka dot dress is revealed. She looks like a sexy primary school teacher in the black and white patterned ensemble, fitted and flared in just the right places. It makes a certain part of me sit up attentively. *Damn.*

"Is it all right if I text you?"

"Sure," I reply before gesturing to the trash. "Sorry about that. Guess I'll have to make it up somehow."

"Well, I wouldn't say no to finding out where that chocolate croissant came from." Violet smirks.

"If I told you, I wouldn't get to take you there one day. Can't have that." Her lips pop open a little, the light catching on those irresistible flecks of silver in her blue eyes. I'm being more forward with her, pushing again because I like to see how far she'll let me go. I hook a finger under her jaw to close her mouth. "See you tomorrow, Sparks."

ME

I'm heading to your house.

GUS

Okay. Bring pizza. I'm hungry.

ME

Fine. Your usual?

GUS

Yeah. And a large BBQ chicken with extra sauce. Obie and I are watching film.

I park my SUV in the driveway behind Gus' truck, hefting the three pizza boxes from the passenger seat to balance on one hand before I close my door. As I climb the three steps to the front door, it swings wide open to show Gus leaning against the frame. He reaches grabby hands at me, relieving me of the boxes.

"About time. I'm fucking starving." He carries the pizzas through the entry into the living room on the left, depositing them on the large coffee table. There are a few notebooks I recognize from the arena scattered and pens next to them. He lifts each lid until he finds his Hawaiian-style pie, scooping up a slice and eating half in a single bite.

"You're welcome," I say, looping around the back of the couch toward the chair in the corner of the room. I slap Obie's shoulder in greeting as I pass him in his spot on the couch before he leans forward and pulls his box toward himself.

"Thanks, man. I'll send you my share. Just let me know what I owe you." Obie nods in appreciation before taking a deep inhale of the smoky flavor wafting from the open cardboard.

"Don't worry about it." I sit on the plush leather of the club chair, reaching a hand toward Gus, who is currently engrossed in swallowing his second slice. He doesn't see it, so I lean forward and swipe my unopened box from in front of him. I flick my eyes to the screen before digging into my own meal. "That the Portland footage?"

"Yeah, just started watching," Gus says, never taking his eyes off the game while he reaches for his next piece. "Their third line is going to be a nightmare. There's some new guy on the team—absolute goon shit, but he's fast."

"That's Olivier Ahlman. Swedish right winger," Obie supplies. He wears the darkest look I've ever seen on his face. Obie might be quiet sometimes, but he's a generally positive person, even when he's cross-checking our opponents. "I fucking hate that guy. I had no idea he was in the league."

"This is last night's footage. They must have just signed him,"

Gus answers. I watch the player, marked by a number seven on his back fly down his shooting lane before slamming my old Austin teammate into the boards. I grimace a little. The puck wasn't even in play near them, which doesn't make the play illegal—just rough. I've spent my whole life playing this sport, I understand playing hard is part of it. I've had my fair share of contusions and aches to show that it gets brutal. I still hate watching guys play like assholes.

"God damn it," Obie practically snarls as he watches the TV with narrowed eyes. Then, he's dropping his pizza, pushing up from his seat, and heading to the hallway. "I need to make a phone call."

In the silence that follows, Gus and I eat and watch. We don't play Portland until after our road game, but with a new player in the mix, it doesn't hurt to get a head start on understanding what we're up against. The first period comes to an end. I finish my slice of meat lover's while Gus makes some last notes, his empty pizza box on the floor next to the coffee table.

Obie comes back into the living room, a less thunderous look on his face, but there's still a troubled annoyance rolling off him. I'd like to ask him about it, but I don't feel as if I know him well enough to intrude on whatever is going on. Instead, I set my pizza box on the floor, brushing my hands together, hoping I'm not about to make things worse.

"Violet is Coach's daughter," I say.

Gus drops his pen, whipping his head back and forth between us. His eyes are wide, and there's a mischievous grin on his face. He looks like Christmas just came early.

"What?" he draws out the question in a little singsong voice as he looks at Obie. It's like he's doing a terrible impression of Deadpool.

"Wasn't my information to tell." Obie holds his hands up with innocence but offers me an apologetic look. "Just happy you know. Everyone's going to find out tomorrow, anyway."

"Which makes me wonder," Gus turns back to me, "why did you get early access?"

I hear the curiosity in his tone. It's not just because I know before he does. Gus has suspected I like Violet since Obie introduced her to the group. He's spent more time away from work with her than I have due to Obie living here—which he has enjoyed telling me about. Gus has been obnoxious in bringing her up in seemingly innocent ways in conversation, but my best friend can't bullshit me. I see the little smirk he gives me, hear the leading questions he drops, waiting for me to rise to the occasion. I haven't. But it's time to come clean to my best friend. And Violet's.

"She asked me to come see her before I left the facility today. She seemed concerned I would be worried about it." My words are for Gus, but I keep my eyes on Obie. He doesn't give much away, just a little nod.

"Are you worried about it?" he asks. I hear the protectiveness there. Violet has only ever talked about Obie with familial affection. The pair of them behave like siblings when they're together, so Obie sounding like a big brother now doesn't surprise me.

"Not at all." I lean forward on my knees. "I like Violet. A lot." Out of the corner of my eye, I see Gus give a little fist pump. Obie lifts his chin expectantly. "I can tell she has her reasons to be wary, but I don't plan on giving her any reason not to trust me. Not because I'm afraid of what it will do to my life on the team but because she deserves it."

"All right," Obie replies. I nod back to him. I've never been one to think approval is necessary to go after a girl I like, but having support is important. Making the people in Violet's life matter to me as much as they do to her is a good step in giving her the confidence to let down her guard. To let me in.

"I can't be there tomorrow for most of the moving. What can I do to help, Obie? What would she like?" Now that I feel like I have an ally, I'm not above asking for a little insider information.

Chapter 12

Violet

I keep staring at the message. *You told him to come over. You want him to come over. This will be okay.* I've repeated those three sentences for the last twenty-five minutes, pacing around my new townhome, trying in vain to mitigate the sheer chaos moving brings. I shove my phone into my side pocket.

I'm pulling a throw blanket out of a box marked "living room" to put across the new couch when the doorbell rings. I straighten, brushing non-existent dust from the Whitehall FC sweatshirt I'm wearing over a trusted pair of black leggings as I cross to the front door. I managed a quick shower once Dad and the rest of the guys left this afternoon, but I've been unpacking boxes since then. When I finally worked up the nerve to text Crosby, with Gus' enthusiastic encouragement, I belatedly had an existential crisis over what to wear. I settled on the most accessible and comfortable elements of my wardrobe, telling myself this isn't a date, so it doesn't matter.

I'm working on believing that as I grasp the doorknob.

I pull open the door to see Crosby standing on my front stoop in an equally comfortable Midnight hoodie and black joggers. He's looking around at my new house before landing that multicolored gaze on me. It makes my mouth go a little dry when I feel the full weight of his attention.

"Hey." He smiles brightly at me.

"Hi," I answer, fighting the smile I want to give him in return. The one he knows I resist giving. My heart lurched painfully yesterday when he pointed it out; a necessary chastisement that I'm not being myself around him. I'm still hiding away because I'm scared. He was right. Messaging him this afternoon was my first step in trying to change that. He lifts a few plastic bags in his hand between us.

"Thought you might be hungry."

It's then the scent of takeout hits my nostrils. It's full of spices and warmth, immediately causing a reactionary growl from my stomach. I don't even have time to process how that might be embarrassing because the bright red logo of my favorite Chinese place catches my eye. I look up at Crosby and don't fight the grin that breaks out.

"There it is," Crosby says, reaching up his other hand to brush at the crinkle in my cheek. He's caressing my smile, a simple thing, but he's looking at me like I just handed over the Stanley Cup. "I'm not even mad that it's for the food and not me."

I laugh, turning just slightly as he drops his hand, gesturing into the entryway. He steps inside, toeing off his sneakers to line them up next to my own near the door.

"That's my absolute favorite restaurant in town." I point back to the takeout. "I celebrated my birthday there four years in a row as a kid. The owners used to bring me extra almond cookies."

I turn to close and lock the door, hearing Crosby rustle in the bags.

"These cookies?" He's holding up three almond cookies in their signature plastic wrappers with green writing. I feel like I'm eight again, unsuccessfully shoving the extra treat under my napkin while my dad smiles. An unexpected perk of having a July birthday meant Dad was always home. No training. No practices. No games. Just the two of us for a whole month.

"The very ones," I say, reaching a hand out to take the offering. Clutching them close, I lead the way to the eat-in kitchen. There are large IKEA boxes leaning against the wall of the dining space, my new table not put together yet. Uncle Palmer promised to do it tomorrow while I pack for my first away game. I won't be flying with the team, as the private plane is reserved for players and essential personnel only. My commercial flight is only behind them by about an hour, and I have my own room in the same hotel for the night.

Crosby navigates to a free spot on the island to drop the bags and unpacks the containers. Something about the relaxed way he's adopted the space makes me sigh contentedly. Our conversation yesterday changed things between us. I don't know how yet, but I'm finally excited to figure it out.

"I have absolutely no idea which of these contains plates." I point to the stacks of boxes labeled "kitchen" but little other indicators of the contents. I stash the almond cookies next to my unplugged electric kettle. "I hadn't fully thought out dinner plans tonight."

"We have chopsticks." Crosby holds up the paper-wrapped utensil. "I know how to share if you do."

"I'm an only child, of course I know how to share," I say, taking the offered chopsticks and opening containers. There's kung pao chicken, dumplings, Yangzhou fried rice, sweet and sour shrimp, vegetable lo mein, egg rolls, wantons, and two fortune cookies. I'm smiling again, shaking my head a little in wonder. "You have all my favorites."

Crosby clears his throat and looks a little abashed, hooking his hand behind his neck in the way he did the first time we met. It's charming in an innocent way. Honest and sweet. Exactly how I think of Crosby.

"I may have had a little help," he confesses, pulling his chopsticks out and breaking them apart. He rubs them together to rid them of loose slivers, avoiding looking at me as he continues. "I had already decided I'd bring food with me if you texted today because moving means you never remember to eat. At least, I never do. But I asked Obie to help me with what to bring. Hope that's all right."

"It's really thoughtful, Crosby. Thank you." I break my chopsticks and consider pinching a dumpling before spinning around for a moment, looking for the best place to sit. Before I find a solution, Crosby's stacking a few boxes and shifting them to the floor, effectively clearing the island off. He lifts an eyebrow and cocks his head at the empty countertop. I shrug before climbing up. We settle with the food between us.

It's hilarious watching Crosby fold his long legs underneath himself into a crisscross style, but he manages to do so without falling off backward, then picks up an eggroll, demolishing it in two bites. I finally pick up a dumpling, close my eyes, and chew happily around the familiar flavor.

"God, that's so good," I groan. I open my eyes to see Crosby frozen with a steaming orangey shrimp halfway to his open mouth. "What?"

"Nothing." He shovels the shrimp in, blinking a few times as he chews. I reach for the lo mein, twirling the saucy noodles around for the perfect bite. "So, the move go okay today? I'm sorry I couldn't be here to help."

"Things went fine; don't worry about it," I say, angling the straggling noodles into my mouth. When I've swallowed another perfect bite, I ask, "You said you had physio today. Is everything all right? You're not injured, are you?"

"No. No, I'm good." Crosby's looking at the containers, clearly deciding which one to attack next. I pick up the fried rice and hand it to him. He nods in thanks. "When your dad moved me to the first line this season, I reached out to our physio department and set up a regular schedule of stretching sessions and evaluations. We do a lot of them throughout the season and always have someone with us at games, but I wanted to make sure that even on the off days I had someone looking out for me. The more I know about how my body is performing, the better I can use it."

I grip my chopsticks a little harder, twirling them around the pea pods and sprouts. Crosby is talking about his job, and I'm trying really hard to be respectful of that. But the man's body—and talking about how to use it—is doing things to me. The feeling slinks through my blood, rippling and pulsing in a way talking about hockey has never done for me before. *It's been way too long since I've gotten laid.*

I chance a look up. If Crosby knows he just lit a fire in my belly, his face doesn't show it. He's gone after the kung pao chicken, lifting the container to make sure the sauce doesn't drip. But it coats his lips as he takes a bite, and I can't help but follow the path his tongue takes as he licks them clean.

Shit.

"That's—" I start, hoping I've kept the flush off my cheeks, coughing a little to cover any pinkness that may have developed there. If I blame it on the spicy food, maybe Crosby won't notice. "That's smart. It shows a lot of dedication and game intelligence.

It's probably part of why you already have four goals this season. I remember Dad used to have a massage therapist on call."

"Can I ask you a personal question?" Crosby sets his chopsticks across the top of a container. "You don't have to answer. It's just something I've always been curious about and never thought I'd have an answer to."

The way Crosby is asking feels like he isn't pressuring me, but I still take a full five seconds before I nod.

"Like most of us on the team, I knew of Callum Andrews before I came to New Haven. I grew up watching him play. But when your dad brought me on, I wanted to know as much as I could about him. Your name was never released to the media, and Coach hasn't publicly dated anyone that I know of." He's choosing his words carefully, but I have an idea of where he's heading.

"It's just me and Dad," I interject the first time he pauses. "He ended up a single father when he and my mom split before I was born. She made her choice to have me but not raise me. Dad was still pretty new in the league, but he was getting a fair amount of attention, so he put measures in place to try and protect me. I have a different last name. He avoided bringing me around to events with media coverage and tried really hard to give me as normal of a life as possible."

"Do you ever miss your mom? Wonder where she is?"

"No," I say. I give a little shrug of my shoulders. I covered this topic on multiple occasions with the family therapist my dad and I saw throughout my school years. "I've never wanted to look any further than the man who raised me. Sure, it was hard. My childhood was lonely at times: a professional hockey player for a father? He was gone a lot. But his best friends from high school took care of me when he couldn't be there."

"Obie's mom and dad, right?"

"That's right. He became the brother I never knew I wanted."

I pinch another dumpling, taking a bite, gesturing for Crosby to do the same. He doesn't pinch one between his chopsticks, opting for skewering the food on the end of one. He swallows it in one bite. "What about you? Where are your parents? I know from your team bio you're from Maine."

Crosby's hand stills as he attempts to spear another dumpling. The lightness I've felt from him since he arrived bleeds from him, deflating like a balloon. His broad shoulders curl a little, caving protectively around him.

"Hey." I take the forgotten chopstick from him, standing it upright in the box. Instinctually, I lace my fingers through his and squeeze.

"It's all right. I was raised by a single father, too," he lets out, rubbing his thumb across the back of our clasped hands. I love how it feels. There's a roughness to the pad, worn and calloused from playing, but the motion is soothing. Suddenly, I'm not sure if I'm comforting him or he's comforting me. Before I can think too much longer on it, he lifts our hands and presses the briefest of kisses to the spot his thumb touched. "Sorry. I've been thinking about him a lot lately."

"It's okay. If it isn't something you want to talk about, we don't have to," I offer him the out. I can tell he doesn't really want to get into this tonight.

"Thanks." He gives me a shy smile of gratitude. "It's not the happiest of stories, and I'm having a good time with you."

"Sure," I whisper as he pulls back. "Not everyone likes to bond over past parent trauma." Crosby lets out a laugh.

"My therapist would argue finding commonality with someone who understands is a sign of good communication." He stabs another dumpling, lifting it to me. The jovial, upbeat energy returns to him, happiness spreading across his face when I take a bite of the offering. He tucks the rest away with a few quick chews, swallowing with a satisfied sigh.

"Here's to single parents, good therapists, and being well-adjusted adults." I salute, which Crosby returns before we both continue hunting for our next bite.

We spend the rest of the meal comfortably discussing the team, their game tomorrow night in Columbus, and my brief explanation of living in London. I fill that topic with a lot of superficial things: Bea, our quest for the perfect pint, the seasons and sights, what I miss the most. I appreciate Crosby's curiosity. I feel his sincerity; he's genuinely trying to get to know *me*. It makes it easy to open up to him, especially when he is an attentive listener: he's silent or chewing thoughtfully and looks me in the eyes when I speak.

When we finish the containers down to the dregs of delicious sauce or singular grains of rice, Crosby packages everything back into the plastic bags. He deposits the waste in the trash can before opening the closest box and asking where I want the mugs he finds inside. We spend the next hour unpacking and setting up my kitchen before I'm yawning more than talking.

"I should probably head out." We've just stacked the last of the empty boxes, my plates taunting us from the bottom of it. I'm about to tell him he's welcome to stay longer, but another unexpected yawn answers for me. We both laugh, rounding the far end of the island to head to the front door.

"Wait!" I cry, swiping the forgotten fortune cookies and passing one to Crosby. "We didn't open these. I can't imagine worse luck."

Crosby cracks his open, his large fingers deftly pulling the slip of paper from the cookie crumbles.

"If we wait until we are ready, we'll be waiting the rest of our

lives." He pops the pieces into his mouth, turning his expectant gaze toward me.

I split my cookie into two equal halves, extracting the stiff paper from one side, reading clearly: *"Vulnerability sounds like faith and looks like courage."*

I nibble a corner of the slightly sweet and cardboard-textured dessert, staring at my fortune with equal parts disdain and wonder. A tidal wave of emotion threatens to swell within me. The doubts and fears of being with Crosby tonight mix with the hurt and anger of my past with Olivier. I push the feelings of guilt and frustration away as I continue looking at a takeout fortune threatening to upend me after a nearly perfect evening.

Then Crosby is there, pulling the offending paper with his large hand. He takes it from me, affixing it with his own by a small magnet to the outside of my fridge. It's enough distance to bring me back to the present. I look at the fortunes intertwined, the messages so similar, and realize I'm not the only one who is represented there. The man walking back to me has nothing but openness in his eyes. He takes a deep breath as he steps into my space. With the island counter at my back, I have nowhere to go, but at this moment, I wouldn't want to move even if I could. He looks down at me as heat radiates off his chest.

"You want to go out with me sometime?" Crosby's voice is inviting and kind. He reaches out to hook my hand with his. I stare up at him, a battle waging inside. He pulls me slightly closer, playfully, teasingly. There's barely a space between us now, and the resistance I've fought to keep up for the last month crumbles. I let out an unsteady exhale when he leans down repeating himself with a huskier tone in my ear, "Go out with me, Violet."

"All right."

Chapter 13

Crosby

"Obie, do you think you can tone it down a little? You're blocking Henri."

"Left foot first, Charlie. And maybe smile? Or at least look up?"

"Great job, Nicky. Yeah, just... feel the music."

Violet gives direction and encouragement to my teammates as we sway along to Celine Dion for the tenth time. I made sure everyone watched the inspiration video at least three times on the plane, and I've listened to the song so many times I know all the words now. All we have to do is "vibe" as Violet's email instructed with a link to the original video: two guys in a garage being unfalteringly committed to the feeling of the music, stepping side to side before throwing their arms out as the song crescendos. It *should* be easy.

"No, Gus, it's the beat *before* 'baby, baby,'" Violet explains, setting her phone on the ballroom chair. The hotel was nice enough to give us an empty room to film in before we have to get upstairs for a pre-game nap and dinner. She sings the line, nodding along to the beat and exaggeratedly showing when to put her arms out. Gus tries once more, but it's half a second late. "It's like doing a shuffle at practice. Step, step, step, slide. Listen to the beats like that. You've got the right enthusiasm."

Her eyes lock with mine when she hits play on the music and lifts her phone to film. She smiles shyly and counts us in. I dance my heart out, hoping we get it right because this is important to her, but also hoping we have to try it again. This is the only time I'll see her until we're back in Connecticut after the game. Coach likes to keep a tight schedule on the road, and I realize now the only reason we've been allowed to do this is probably because it was his *daughter* who requested the thirty minutes.

"Got it!" Violet cheers, the music abruptly cutting off.

"Thank God," Bones says from behind me. He's already heading for the exit. "Nice to see you, Violet."

"That was fun, Vi!" Tex gives her a side hug. "My mom used to love that song. I bet she can't wait to show everyone at her ceramics class."

He and Nicky leave without much comment. Tex is likely texting his wife about the whole thing, and Nicky is off in his own thoughts. He gets really serious before a game; it's a goalie thing. I hope he agreed to this because we're friends and not because Tex pulled rank. He's had a rough season already, and his moods can be hard to read.

"Thanks for your help." Gus hovers over Violet's shoulder as she presses the button for the playback. She's smiling at him, pointing out the moment he got the move right. "You're coming to the game, right?"

"Nope." Violet packs away her phone into her purse, handing the one that played Celine on it back to Obie. "I'm not responsible for game footage, so I'm going to order a ridiculous amount of room service and stay in."

"Watch us on TV?" Obie asks. Violet rolls her eyes, giving a little sound of annoyance. "Please, Letty? I could use your post-game report."

Obie is giving her the biggest, most ridiculous puppy dog eyes I've ever seen as he puts his hands together in a silent request. I don't think Violet will break. Her eyes are narrowed, her arms crossed. I'm trying not to lose myself in the distraction of the swells of her breasts sitting atop her folded arms when she agrees.

"C'mon, Rook." Gus slaps Obie on the back, steering them out of the room. I give my best friend a slight chin raise in gratitude. I've been dying for more alone time with Violet since she agreed to go out with me last night. We've texted a few times in the fourteen hours since I last saw her. The messages are no longer strictly professional—we're flirting, testing the waters to see how deep we want to go, and I know my teammates have noticed my newfound obsession with my phone.

There's a clatter from the closing of the ballroom door. It means we're alone, and I wait for the moment it registers with Violet. She flicks her eyes past my shoulder just once in confirmation before they settle on me. I don't wait for any of her usual unease to sink in; there will be no uncertainty anymore about who we are when we're alone.

"Are we finished with work?" I ask. Violet's eyebrows pinch for a moment in confusion before she nods to me. "Good. That means I can do this."

I scoop her into a hug. Banding my arms around her waist, I wrap them so thoroughly I can rest my hands on her opposite hips. I haul her close, dipping my nose into the brunette strands she's styled in easy waves, inhaling the summer and promises I feel from her signature scent.

It takes her half a second to respond, but then she glides her hands up my chest until they loop behind my neck. It's a stretch for her, so I sink down a little. Now, her face is snuggled just under my chin, tucked against the base of my throat. Her breath is warm as it tickles against the sensitive skin there.

I wanted to wrap her up like this last night. I almost did after she agreed to go out with me, but my instincts told me I had pushed her limits enough for the night. Instead, with her agreement making my feet practically float off the floor, I let her guide me to the door for a quick goodnight. Even now, with Violet sinking just a brief second into me, I know she's about to pull away. I do it first, untangling our limbs and letting her out of my embrace. I don't, however, let go of my grip on her hips.

"I wish you were coming to the game."

"Maybe the next home game." She gives me a sweet smile. I know I'm getting ahead of myself, and I love that she's willing to call me out on it. "But this is nice."

She lifts onto her toes, initiating another hug. Her fingers toy with the hair at the back of my head. It takes a considerable amount of energy to suppress the shiver trying to slide down my spine. Instead, I hold her a little tighter, humming in appreciation, letting my hands ghost along her waist, her hips, and the very top of the swell of her ass. I haven't kissed her yet, haven't managed to take her on a date, but the feeling of Violet in my arms is right. It settles something that has roiled and rioted with unease in me for years. Like a distant stereo finally being turned down, the silence that follows is peaceful.

"For the first time in years, you're making me want to miss a game," I whisper against her cheek, barely feeling the softness of her skin against my lips. It's a tempting thought to turn just a little and have the feeling imprint itself there. "I could take you to dinner instead, and I could catch up on the highlights later."

Violet pulls back this time, trailing a hand down my arm

before giving it a squeeze. She pushes her hair back behind her shoulder and steps far enough away to pick up her purse.

"Can't have that, Wellsy." She uses my nickname from the ice—switching us back effortlessly to our previous professional dynamic—except it now has a playful edge it didn't before. "Columbus' defense is starting their backup goalie. He's weak on the glove side, perfect for a wrap-around if you can get it behind the net."

"Damn, Cameron. You sure know all the sexy things to say." I bite my knuckles exaggeratedly before smiling. Violet blushes, and her shoulders sink a little. *I know insecurity when I see it.* I wrap a finger up in the ends of her hair, pulling at it a little. She looks up, the silver in her eyes dulled. "Hey, I wasn't dismissing you. I love that you probably know more about my job than I do."

"Okay." Violet nods. My fingers still play with her hair. It is as silky as I dreamed about for a month. I tuck the strands behind her ear, letting my thumb rest on her cheekbone. She leans into my touch for a beat, then flashes a big smile. "C'mon, time for your nap."

She turns toward the doors, and despite knowing we will hide away the flirty words and touches as soon as we cross through them, I can't resist one more volley.

"Will you tuck me in?"

VIOLET

Another win!

ME

Someone gave me a really great scouting report. Bones destroyed the glove side.

VIOLET

All of you played great. Congratulations!

ME

That means you watched right? You had your room service and took notes for Obie? (He's currently reading this over my shoulder.)

VIOLET

I have your notes, you nosy pain in my ass. Go away. (Is he gone?)

ME

He's back in his seat with Gus. We're heading back to the hotel. Too bad you ate dinner already, we could have ordered in together.

VIOLET

I haven't had dessert yet.

ME

Not exactly what I had in mind when I asked you to go on a date with me.

VIOLET

Save that for a second date? I'm in room 1303.

Thirty minutes later, I tuck my phone into the pocket of my joggers, illuminating the button for the thirteenth floor in the elevator. I lean back against the wall, trying to steady the pounding of my heart, waiting for the elevator to carry me the four floors below to where Violet is waiting. Once we disembarked the bus, I made my excuses to the team to get out of a round of drinks at the hotel bar. I came up to my room, deposited my kit bag, took my second shower since the end of the game, and threw on my black joggers and a hoodie.

As the doors close, I study my reflection in the chrome. Just like the day in the Midnight main office, I'm wondering if I should have dressed up, especially now that I *know* Violet is waiting for me. But I wasn't expecting to have any real time with her here, so I didn't pack more than my standard away game suitcase: suit and tie for arrival and departure, sweats for downtime, and multiple sets of socks and underwear. It would be weird to show up near midnight in either of my suits, and I'm betting that Violet will be just as relaxed tonight as she was last night at her house.

Every time I see her at work, I'm reminded of how striking she is: the kaleidoscopic shades of blue in her eyes, the wavy, full brunette tresses she styles to fit her fearless and flirty wardrobe. Violet Cameron is easily the most beautiful woman I have seen since moving to Connecticut. It's hard to take your eyes off her, and having walked around the facility a handful of times now, I know I'm not the only one looking. But Violet doesn't seem to notice. If she does, I'm not surprised she knows how to ignore it for the sake of her job.

But last night, in the soft light of her new home, boxes stacked in half-furnished rooms, she was resplendent. The tight curve of her leggings that showed off her fit thighs, coupled with the artfully draped sweater that offered outlines of her perfect breasts, had me wishing I could peel them away layer by layer to feel her warm skin underneath. Her hair was tied high atop her head, giving me full access to the slope of her neck, teasing me to press soft, sucking kisses to every inch.

It was the perfect kind of torture to have those desires and be so close to the source of them, only to be reminded that despite the very long, self-inflicted dry spell I have been in, I am not ruled by my dick. *I am not ruled by my dick.* I repeat it as the chime announces I'm on Violet's floor.

Violet opens her door after the first knock. She's in gray sweatpants and a simple pink long-sleeved shirt. Her face is makeup-free and glowy despite the standard bland hotel light, and her hair hangs in a loose braid down her back.

I barely make it inside before I wrap an arm around her, pulling her close again. The door closes behind me, and Violet melts against my chest. She stays, not pulling away, and my brain isn't the only part of my body that registers it.

I am not ruled by my dick. The twitch it gives in reply clearly states he's willing to challenge my resolve on that principle tonight. I push a chaste kiss onto the crown of Violet's head and turn us into the room.

It's an identical match to my own, except it's flipped to have the king bed on the left wall instead of the right. Violet slips her hand into mine, leading us to the little table and chairs against the window. The city lights are distorted through the sheer curtain she has pulled closed, and a few silver room service trays sit on the table.

"I wasn't sure what you'd want, so I ordered cookies, a crème brûlée, and a small charcuterie tray. I don't know what the nutritionist has you on or how strict you need to be. Dad liked to joke desserts never counted, but just in case, there's another option. Or, if you're a salty person? Maybe you don't like sweets." I squeeze her hand. She's rambling adorably, the nerves coming through clearly in the way she speaks and how her hand is beginning to slip in my grasp.

"After a game, I'll eat just about anything, but cookies are my biggest vice." I encourage Violet to sit down, dropping myself into the chair across from her. I help her lift the covers on the platters, sighing in satisfaction as huge chocolate chip cookies are revealed. Violet lets out a little groan when she uncovers the crème brûlée. Her happiness at the sight of the decadent treat makes the silver flecks in her eyes light up. "Thanks for inviting me and doing this, Sparks."

"That's the second time you've called me that." She taps a spoon to crack the caramelized sugar while I swipe the first of the cookies, taking a large bite. She waits for my answer, scooping a bite of the custard, passing it delicately through her lips before dragging them along the spoon and swirling her tongue just a bit at the end to ensure she's collected every bit.

I am not ruled by my dick.

"It's—well," I clear my throat, inspecting the chocolate chunks to avoid how embarrassed I feel under Violet's gaze. "You have these silver streaks in your eyes. They remind me of the sparklers I'd get on the Fourth of July as a kid. They light you up, and I can't keep my eyes off you when they do."

Violet's face softens, and she sets down her spoon. She's quiet for longer than I expect, making me shift uneasily in my chair.

"I won't say it again if you don't want me to," I offer. I put the cookie back on the plate, my own hands now starting to sweat with nerves.

"I like it," she finally says, looking at me. There's a sweet smile painting her lips, curling up in the corners. I exhale my relief. "I like *you*, Crosby."

"I like you, too," I reply immediately. Because I do. I haven't been this interested in a woman, ever. With my dad's death and my brief time in college, I barely entertained the idea of relationships. It didn't make me a saint, and I always tried to be upfront with any woman I shared my bed with, but I never bothered to look for something more. Once I made it to the NHL, hockey became my focus. Sure, there have been the occasional hookups. I even dated a really nice woman I met in the grocery store for a month one off-season, but she wasn't interested in dealing with my work schedule once training camp started.

Since then, it's been a steady stream of me, myself, and I. Subconsciously, I think I just haven't wanted to try with anyone who couldn't understand how important my job is to me. But Violet, she gets it. In ways no one else could possibly wrap their minds around. She grew up seeing the good and the bad parts of what an NHL player endures. I've not had to finesse my way through that with her. Telling me she doesn't date hockey players the night we met felt like an extra challenge I couldn't bring myself to walk away from.

I reach for her hand across the table, the need to touch her growing exponentially at her confession. Violet surprises me, standing from her chair and rounding the small table to end up next to me. I turn myself so she's now directly in front of me, opening my legs to give her space to come closer if she wants.

She takes the invitation, stepping into my space, a determined look on her face as her eyes fall to my lips.

I am not ruled by my dick.

Chapter 14

Violet

My body has been in a state of heightened awareness all day. Ever since Crosby wrapped his arms around me in the ballroom, there's been this low-frequency humming just below my skin that I can't shut off. It hummed louder when I invited him to my room. A moment that feels like a fever dream because I panicked immediately after doing so.

I tried to call Bea before remembering it was close to five in the morning in London and that she was likely still sleeping. I gripped my phone before letting a text to Obie fly, begging him to talk me out of the emotional pretzel I was tying myself into.

OBIE

Stop overthinking it, Letty. Just "fuck it,"
right? Oh, but you know, be responsible,
and use protection if it actually becomes
a situation in which you fuck. 🙃

An entirely unhelpful response. The harder I tried to stop thinking of the limitless implications and possibilities of tonight, the more I thought about them.

My pulse picked up even more at that while I dialed room service and placed an order. As I waited for the food—and the hockey player I had reluctantly admitted my interest in—to arrive, I paced around the room. I checked my reflection three times and brushed my teeth twice. I checked my suitcase to make sure all my underwear was tucked into the furthest corner, insanity temporarily making me believe Crosby would go looking.

But it was ridiculous to be nervous. I hadn't invited Crosby over to have sex with him. At least my mind hadn't.

He filled the doorway in his relaxed state: damp curls, bright eyes, flirtatious smile, and the energy of a big road win radiating off him. My traitorous vagina began trying to convince me sleeping with him wouldn't be a bad way to end the night. She hasn't seen any action from something other than my own fingers in nearly a year, and the beautiful man who has disarmed me in almost every way over the last few weeks looks like the perfect way to get back in shape.

Now, as I stand between Crosby's thighs, my heart is pumping so hard I feel it in my toes, and I'm having a hard time figuring out why I *didn't* think about having sex with him tonight. But it's not a good decision. I meant what I said moments ago. *I like Crosby.* And I've learned from my mistakes. I won't blindly tumble into something again. I'll be smart, even if just being in the same space with him feels better than anything I've experienced.

He's breathing hard. It's an almost imperceptible change, but I can see the rapid rise and fall of his chest, his multicolored eyes searching mine. There's a question in them, the reassuring check-in he so often gives me. It's sexy as hell that Crosby has moved slowly since we met. He takes his cues from me, watches and learns before acting. He makes me feel safe and secure in the choices I make. That gives me all the confidence I need to lean forward and touch the corner of his mouth.

I swipe my thumb along the curve of his full bottom lip, dragging at the smudge of chocolate left behind by the cookie. Crosby's pupils dilate, something I can see from being close enough to share a breath. Holding his stare, I bring my thumb to my lips, parting them to suck in the sweet residue.

"Violet." My name is a broken sound from him. It's part warning, part plea.

In my peripheral vision, I see Crosby's fingers curl into fists atop his thighs, holding himself back from touching me.

I don't overthink it anymore.

Fuck it.

I surge forward, pressing my lips to his, spending the last of my courage. As though he knows what I need, Crosby's hands race up the back of my thighs, rising as he stands from the chair. His lips move hungrily against my own, their softness a welcome surprise and the sinful taste addictive. It distracts me as he wraps his arms around me, one hand coming up to cradle the back of my head.

The direction he gives our kiss intensifies with a small brush of his tongue along the seam of my mouth, a request. I open for him, letting him explore with gentle strokes, teasing and pulling my tongue to reciprocate. A small sound resembling a groan or a growl escapes him when I press my hands against his chest, twisting my fingers into the well-worn hoodie, pulling him impossibly closer to me.

With our bodies flush against each other, I feel his hardness through our sweatpants against my hip bone. The low-frequency hum from the day has disappeared. Replaced by a raging fire burning through my veins, fueled by every taste of Crosby's lips and the way he's swallowing the moans I don't bother trying to contain. I rock against him once before tipping my head back, gasping for breath.

Crosby follows me, chasing for a moment before he rests his

forehead against my own. The hand in my hair relaxes, threading through the strands I didn't even notice he had gathered there. But he doesn't release me. He keeps me cocooned with him, a little bubble full of the high of a first kiss.

A kiss that has left me speechless.

"I was not expecting *that* when I showed up tonight." Crosby's voice is hoarse. Endorphins are pumping through my system, heightened by the way he sounds upended from our kiss. I feel floaty and just a little out of control. I try holding onto it, banishing the worry and doubt that threaten like a riptide, a malicious intent to pull me under and away from this moment of happiness. But when Crosby cups my face in the calloused touch of his hands, I realize there's nothing to be afraid of. He's the lighthouse. He's been steadily calling me to shore, lighting my way, and quietly giving me the hope I've needed to battle through the waves of old habits and heartbreak.

"It wasn't what I was expecting when I invited you," I confess. I lean in as his thumb traces along the curve of my cheek, turning to press a kiss against his palm. I like the hum of response he gives me. "But it doesn't make me mad it happened."

"Agreed." Crosby dips and kisses me again. It isn't the heated intensity of the first, but it lingers too long to be chaste. I sigh happily when he pulls back, his eyes sweeping over my face as though he's cataloging everything about this moment. With the smallest nudge, he guides me to lean into his broad chest. The vanilla, citrus, and sandalwood of his cologne swirls around me, sinking in like the warmth of his lips. I love how he smells, how strong he is, but there is a distinct softness about him that's different from his teammates.

On the table, my phone screen flashes with my dad's name. It's a reminder this isn't a conclusion to a date night. We're in a hotel room on a work trip.

"I should probably go."

"Okay," I agree. Cockblocked by a text from my dad is the worst. He turns me out of his embrace but weaves his fingers through mine as he walks across the room to the door.

"When we get back, we have a few days of training, a home game, and then we have two days off," Crosby says once I open the door. He's leaning against the frame, fingers still entwined with mine. He swings them gently between us. There's a distinctly boyish charm to the way he plays with them before pulling his hand away to cup the back of my neck and hold me. "Please come to the game?"

"I'd like that." I mean it.

As the daughter of the head coach, I've always had the option to attend home games in the suite reserved for families of the staff. My school schedule and internship commitments in London have kept me away from seeing The Midnight on the ice under my dad's leadership. Since returning this summer and starting in the front office, I still haven't gone to a game except for work obligations. It hasn't become a sore spot between Dad and me yet, but I know I can't keep putting it off. Especially with Obie not-so-subtly making sure I know my continued absence isn't winning me "best friend of the year" points. Now, with Crosby? I don't have any more excuses to stay home.

"Yeah? That's great." Crosby's smile lights up the dull hallway. It's infectious, and I find myself grinning back at him. He kisses my smile with short, silly pecks. My laughter breaks out in between before he silences me with a long pull from my lips. It's softer, slower than our heated exchange, but the promises in his languid movements have me wrapping my arms around his waist. With a final groan, he pulls away, taking two steps back from the entrance to my room. "Goodnight, Sparks. This might officially be my new favorite way to celebrate a win."

Then he turns down the hall toward the elevator. I keep the door propped open with my foot to lean out and watch him go. He swipes his thumb across his bottom lip before he looks over his shoulder at me and winks. Thank God the doorframe is at my back because I could melt from another look like that from him. Luckily, he rounds the corner, out of sight, and I'm saved from turning into a literal puddle that maintenance would be called to mop up.

I lock the door behind me, wandering back across the room to pick up the crème brûlée and my phone, opening it to see what was urgent enough for Dad to text in the middle of the night.

DAD

We need to talk when we get home.

"Dad?" I call as soon as I come through the front door. After a restless night's sleep, a flight filled with messages from Crosby setting up an official date for after the Portland game, and a day at work listening to Ethan push for more content with the starting six, I'm back at my childhood home to address the text that has darkened my good mood.

"In the office!" Dad answers back. I ditch my shoes, detour to the kitchen for a bottle of water, and head down the hall. Despite the butterflies that have been beating relentlessly in my stomach following Crosby's kisses, Dad's summons without context has made me uneasy.

While waiting for takeoff this morning, I scoured my contract double-checking that Crosby and I won't be breaking any rules by dating. The verbiage stipulates I can't date anyone I work with directly in my department. I replay my conversation with Ava from my first day of work. She emphasized coworkers could not fraternize with each other, and the players were bound by the

NHL Code of Conduct. Neither explicitly says a player and front office employee are not allowed to date, but I'm sure there is a responsible way of dealing with this. Then I felt silly, like I was getting ahead of myself.

As far as Dad's opinion, I'm sure this won't sit well with him. He might even have something to say about it, but ultimately, it's my choice, and Dad won't get to tell me who I can or can't date. If that was the case, I wouldn't have been allowed to go to any high school dances. Still, I've never dated someone Dad has coached. It's an entirely new dynamic we'll—hopefully—learn to navigate together.

I get to the door of Dad's office, watching quietly as he looks back and forth between a legal pad in his hands and the screen of his laptop on the desk. Halfway down the bridge of his nose sits a pair of horn-rimmed glasses. When he first started wearing them, they looked a little old-fashioned, but now they are perfectly in style in the post-hipster era, even if Dad hasn't changed more than the prescription inside them.

His shaggy black hair has some streaks of silver rising from his temples, playing peek-a-boo through the layers he keeps brushed back from his face. It isn't too long, but definitely a hangover from his playing days. In any other industry, someone his age would probably feel out of place with the haircut. But Dad makes it work. I've joked with him for years about how it gives him a roguish quality women would find impossible to resist, a gentle prodding to get any insight into my father's severely lacking dating life. Like most daughters, I don't want details, but I hate the idea of hockey being the only thing in his life he loves more than me.

I've missed him for the last few years. Being so far from home was difficult. I know how much it hurt for him to leave the game as a member of the team. His injuries forced something he wasn't ready to give up. He struggled with the shift his life took, even if he relished being at home with me more. I was in high school, a peak time of naturally limiting parental involvement, but that awkwardness was soothed by our shared love of hockey. Watching NHL games and highlights with Dad in this room, just the two of us, went a long way to bridge the usual teenage angst.

I think sometimes it should bother me more that he traveled so much when I was growing up. But it really doesn't. I had the best secondary set of adults to help me and care for me, and Dad was around for almost every important moment. As a divorced father, his coach was understanding of the milestones my dad couldn't get back if he didn't take me to my first day of kindergarten or take a few personal days when I had chickenpox. He couldn't be there for every bump or bruise, but Dad was never more than a phone call away, and he would stop everything to pick up when my name was on the caller ID.

There were the occasional nannies for school breaks, and they would travel on a road game stretch with me so I could stay close to Dad, but they're all blurred together in childhood memories. When I got older, Dad respected my wishes to stay with the James family instead. The biggest benefit of having a professional hockey player for a father was our summers together. Even when the team made it to the Stanley Cup Finals, Dad was home for my summer break, something most kids didn't get.

Callum Andrews ended up being everything I could have possibly dreamed of when it came to a father. He was patient and kind. A disciplinarian and a doofus in equal measure. He loved me unfailingly. There was never anyone else who mattered to him the way I did.

"Hey, old man," I greet, coming in and sitting on the loveseat he has under the windows.

His head whips to me, the familiar smile I've seen my whole life on his face, making the corners of his blue-gray eyes crinkle and the glasses lift a little. The same warmth that always comes from being with Dad fills me, and despite all the horrible reasons that played a part in returning home, I'm so glad I'm here.

"Thanks for coming, kid." Dad takes his glasses off, depositing them atop his pine desk before circling around to me. He sits down, a small grunt escaping as he settles. He turns enough to prop his elbow on the back of the sofa, leaning his head on his hand. "How was the road game? Did you have fun?"

"It was fine." I shrug nonchalantly. It dawns on me, despite my pep talk in the hallway, I don't really know how I'm going to tell my father I'm going on a date with his new starting center. That I like his new starting center. That I've *kissed* his new starting center. *Okay, maybe I don't need to share that last one.* My heart rate kicks up a little at the innocent questions my dad's asking.

"You didn't want to come to the arena?" Dad asks.

"No. That's not what I was there for. I had a job to do, but I watched from my room," I tell him. I try not to stare too hard at the little stain on the edge of the cushion. The one I accidentally put there when I was twenty by dropping a spoonful of chocolate ice cream one summer. I'm trying not to come across as nervous, even if I feel a little unsettled. "I'm coming to the Portland game, though. Obie's been on me since the season started, and I'm not sure I can put it off much longer. Being there for work isn't the same thing."

If I thought the news of my attendance at a home game would get my dad to lighten up and ease off the concerned vibes he's been throwing out since he texted me, it doesn't. In fact, it seems to have the opposite reaction.

Dad drops his arm from the back of the couch and leans forward a little. His face is serious, as serious as it was when he informed me my county fair goldfish had died a week after I won it. We hadn't ever had a pet, and I think he believed my world was going to end. But at six, I remember saying, "Okay" and asking when we could get a new one.

"About Portland," Dad begins slowly. With unflinching certainty, I know whatever comes out of his mouth next is going to hurt. *This* is the feeling he was trying to protect me from with the goldfish. I was just too young to recognize it. "They've signed Olivier Ahlman."

Chapter 15

Crosby

I'm loading the last dirty plate into the dishwasher when my doorbell rings. I glance at the clock on the microwave, noting it's too early for Gus to be here recounting his exploits from the night. Plus, he'd never ring the bell, and I don't have any texts announcing his arrival.

I dry my hands on a towel, push the start button, and head down the hall. As I pass Dad's picture, I tap three times without thought. The habit is so ingrained I would feel more weird if I *didn't* do it. He's been on my mind a lot the past few days. Ever since Violet asked me about my family. I don't know why I faltered when she asked about them. My dad isn't a topic I seek out to discuss, but years of therapy have helped me be okay with talking about him when asked.

After she divulged she was also raised by a single father, a commonality I wasn't expecting, I still clammed up. My story doesn't end as happily as hers. It ends with the night of my senior year championship game in high school and my father dying in a car accident on the way there. But something in Violet's quiet understanding, her permission to move on from a topic I was struggling with, makes me feel like I can tell her.

The doorbell sounds once more just as I look through the peephole. Violet is standing on my porch, bundled into a peacoat and scarf. November nights have officially started ushering in winter, with the temperatures sinking low after dark.

I've barely opened the door before she barrels into me, cold arms wrapping around me and holding firm. I shut the door behind her and cuddle her close. The chill from outside threatens to send a shiver down my spine, but I just hold Violet tighter.

"Hey, hey, you okay?" I ask, rubbing my hands along her back and up and down her arms.

I want to chase the cold away, but I'm also happy for the excuse to touch her. Every thought since leaving her room has been how to hold her again. It took all my strength to avoid riding the elevator to her office after our skate today. But it didn't keep me from looking up to the glass windows I'd never paid attention to before, searching the panels until I found the one with the brunette and a little red phone booth statue next to her.

She looked so beautiful from where I stood, leaning against the boards. She was focused, staring at her computer while she worked, then smiling when she turned to talk to Leah from accounting at the opening of her cubicle. Violet had a happiness and lightness unlike what I had seen from her during her time with the team. As I lapped Tex in warm-ups, I hoped I may have had a part in bringing it to her.

Now, Violet is huddled against me, holding on tightly like I'm an anchor designed to keep her from floating away from whatever worry radiates off her. Carefully, I lead her back a few steps away from me and further into the warmth of the house. She finally lets me go, looking up at me with a little smile that won't reach her eyes. She begins to unbutton her coat, a silent question to stay, answered when I hang it in the entryway closet.

She still hasn't responded to my question, but she doesn't need to. I can tell from the way she holds my hand as I lead us to the living room that it's more than worry she's grappling with. There's sadness and regret mixed into the emotions flickering in her eyes when we sit on the couch.

"Talk to me," I begin, reaching for her. She came to me for a reason tonight, and I'm feeling driven to make sure I'm exactly what she is looking for. I settle into the corner of my plush couch, guiding her to sit on my lap. She comes willingly, nothing sexual in the way she sits astride my hips, her warm center on my lap. There's just a sad, sweet smile on her lips when I cradle her face to look at me.

"Sparks, please." I run my thumb along the rise of her cheek-bone. I make sure to put enough of a plea in my voice that she will answer. Her eyes glass over, the tears threatening to spill, and I'm willing my blood pressure to hold steady. Something has her rattled. It's setting my teeth on edge but coiling like a snake about to strike won't help her right now. Catching the first tear that falls will.

I do just that, sweeping it away and leaning forward to give her a soft kiss. She allows it; a gentle reminder that even if we haven't started anything conventional between us, I'm here for her. Her lips tremble slightly under my own, the saltiness of past tears staining my tongue before I pull away. She snuggles down into the crook of my neck, hand drawing lazy shapes on my chest while I hold her.

"I studied statistics. Both at Brown and in London. When I finished my master's, I signed on for a one-year internship in my field to give me more real-world experience. The school worked with a set rotation of companies, but my adviser notified me I was being matched with a new firm. They had, of course, donated a lot of money to establish more scholarships for women in STEM, and I fit the requirements they were looking for." Her voice is quiet but steady. I start a pathway with my fingers along the outside of her thigh. Light and reassuring, I let my touch tell her I'm listening. "I was flattered. The position was everything I could have dreamed of. I would be keeping stats on a hockey team from Sweden while helping the firm's owner set up the London office. When I wasn't traveling to watch games, I was helping use the data to build contracts or analyze potential new players from scouting reports."

Violet pauses. Her fingers stop moving along the top of my pectoral, and she drops her hand to wrap as far around me as she can. She still hasn't lifted her head. As much as I'm desperate to see her face, watch her as she speaks to catch a better hint of what she's feeling. I think this is the only way she can get through it. I pause my own movements, curling my hand around the back of her leg, giving an encouraging squeeze. The span of my palm takes up almost half of her thigh. The visual, coupled with the vulnerability in the secret she shares with me, makes Violet feel so much smaller than she is.

"There was a player on the team. Right winger. My boss was his agent." She exhales against my throat. Her breath is hot, but from the way Violet tenses on my lap, her emotions are getting hotter. "He was good. Probably the best in Sweden. And off the ice? He was dazzling."

I stretch out my hand. I didn't realize I had started gripping her so hard. I swallow slowly, having an idea of where her story goes.

"It didn't take very long before we were involved." There's a touch of shame in the way she says it, disappointment lacing through the memory. "Our relationship lasted for months. He promised me... everything I could have wanted. I was getting ready to tell my dad on his next visit that I wasn't planning on coming home. I was going to live in London permanently, and I had found the love of my life."

She sits up, searching my face for a moment. Her eyes have cleared, and there is a determined look on her face. Whatever melancholy her story brought on has cleared. I hold her hips to keep her steady, my fingertips sneaking a little under the hem of her sweater and pressing against her soft, warm flesh.

"He was the *lie* of my life, Crosby." Violet holds my face now, keeping me still while she finishes her story. "He never wanted *me*. His agent—my boss—knew who I was as soon as he hired me and my paperwork cleared HR. They manipulated me. It nearly broke me when I caught him talking to my boss about how I had finally agreed to let him meet my dad. He was finally going to 'have his in' with the NHL, and all it took was 'fucking the little numbers girl.' to get it. All he ever wanted was what I could give him access to. He *used* me."

Anger, searing and sudden, courses through me. The tension I've fought off through her story snaps taut up my spine. I squeeze my hands, Violet wiggling a little in discomfort. I soothe the sting by rubbing gently. She's watching me carefully, releasing my face and resting her hands on my chest. She rubs them up and down my sternum. It grounds me, leaching out the rage I rarely feel.

"I needed you to know," Violet says. "I quit my internship immediately. I informed the school I needed to be reassigned, and they were amazingly supportive. I finished my assignment working for a British soccer team. It wasn't my dream, but it was far away from hockey and gave me the space I needed to mend my broken heart. Ultimately, I knew the best way to stitch myself back together was to come home and swear off all hockey players."

There's a little knowing smile she gives me at that. It eases the ache in my chest as much as her roaming fingers do.

"I only really succeeded at one of my two goals by coming back." She leans forward, kissing me sweetly. Her mouth is hot and welcoming against mine. The smallest nip of her teeth on my bottom lip tells me to grant her more access. I open for her, a gentle stroke of her tongue coaxing mine to kiss her back thoroughly. Just as our breaths are blurring together, Violet pulls back. Her lips are plumped from our kiss, her pupils large, nearly covering the blue of her irises. She leans back a little, rubbing ever so slightly against me.

I groan at the sensation, my dick has become very aware of her proximity over the last few minutes. Violet sneaks a glance down at my lap, a pretty pink blush filling the apples of her cheeks.

"Sorry. Just ignore that. Happens a lot where you're concerned," I say. I lift her, adjusting her until she sits beside me with her legs draped across my lap. My boner will have to find a way to calm himself down because I refuse to be the asshole who takes advantage of an emotionally vulnerable woman. She gives me a little laugh, intertwining our fingers and setting them atop her legs. "Thank you for telling me. I can't imagine how painful it must have been. Your ex sounds like a real dick. It's a good thing he plays halfway around the world."

"He signed with Portland. He'll be on the ice for your next game," Violet says with a flat tone. It feels like my eyebrows have taken residence in my hairline. I angle my face to look down at her. Violet nods her confirmation.

"Is that so?" My voice comes out steely. There's nothing soft in me right now. The rage that had receded crashes over me again like a dangerous high tide in the ocean. I'm not usually a violent person on the ice. I play hard, physical, because the game requires it. But I've always tried to keep out of the penalty box since it meant less time on the ice, keeping my skills off the radar of the coaching staff. I couldn't move up the lines if I were catching a reputation as a goon. Now, for the first time in all the years I've played, I wonder what it would be like to leave someone's blood on the ice.

"You going to tell me his number, Sparks?" I have an idea, but I need confirmation. Obadiah's mood and mysterious phone call before the Columbus game comes back to me.

"Seven." Violet doesn't hesitate. If she's put off by the change in my demeanor, she doesn't show it. "He wears his lucky number. He'll be on the third line."

"Luck won't save him from me."

Chapter 16

Violet

BEA

Ready for the game tonight?

ME

I feel like I'm going to throw up, so, yes?

BEA

It won't be that bad. You won't even have to see the waste of space unless he's in the game!

ME

I told Crosby everything. It's been two days, and he still seems growly. I don't think he can keep a clear head.

BEA

He's a big boy. Let him handle himself. Now open your door, it's bloody cold out here.

I drop my phone and race to my front door, throwing it open to reveal the smiling face of my best friend.

"Surprise, bitch!" she yells before launching into a cackle that reverberates off the neighboring buildings. I missed that sound. Then I'm engulfed in her arms, the smell of Earl Grey and roses filling my nostrils as Bea squeezes me half to death.

"What are you doing here?" I cry as I pull away, patting up and down her arms like I expect her to disappear. Her curls have been straightened, sending her brunette hair down in shiny sheets along her back, and her brown eyes have slightly purple shadows under them. "Did you take the red eye?"

"Obadiah woke me up yesterday telling me a ticket was waiting for me, and under no circumstances was I allowed to miss the flight. He called my work and told them I had a family emergency and I would be gone for the next three days." She's laughing as we shuffle inside. I didn't know how much I needed Bea until I opened the door. "I forgot how pushy he can be. But he took care of the Uber to get me to his place and to bring me here."

"You're staying with Obie and Gus?" I ask. "You okay with that? Gus is harmless, just a little intense. Don't let him talk you out of your panties."

My brain catches up to the information. *Obie called her and arranged for her to be here.* It's so like my other best friend to pull something like this. From the conversation we had yesterday morning at the arena, he was just as worked up at seeing Olivier as Crosby was. Maybe even more so since he witnessed my heartbreak in real time. As kids, Obie was always my first defender in school. I guess that hasn't changed just because we grew up.

"That man is not my type. He's like a puppy, and I'm not looking to train anyone up right now," Bea assures me, sassy but teasing. She's already wandering around the ground floor, poking her head into the living room and kitchen before looping back around to me. "I'm in good hands with those boys."

I put my arms around her, hugging her close again.

"I can't believe you're here, but I'm so happy. Thank you for coming."

"Of course, Petal." She pushes my hair behind my ear lovingly before clapping her hands together. "Right. Let's get to it!"

Her excited tone and the fire flaring in her eyes have me feeling decidedly better.

The arena is loud and cold. Exactly as it should be for a Saturday night home game. The crowd is full of black jerseys and sweatshirts, only dappled in places by the sky blue of some Portland supporters. Their team is dressed in white away game jerseys, blending in with the ice except for the sky-blue accents of their logo, numbers, and names. I don't look for number seven during warm-ups, choosing to focus on the team at the other end of the ice.

The Midnight are in their signature black home jerseys; logo, numbers, and names popping out in the vibrant purple accent color. Adding a dangerous glint to their look is the silver piping that makes the stitching stand out. I scan the group to point out players for Bea.

"That's Nicky, number twenty-eight," I tell her. We watch as he goes through his rituals at his net. He stretches in ways that make me hurt just watching before sitting on the ice between the pipes and lifting his mask. I watch his lips move as he turns to each of his goalposts, kissing his glove and pressing his hand to each of the metal pipes. *Goalies.*

Off to the side, I point out a pair of players. "You might not recognize Gus in his gear; he's number eighty-seven, and Obie wears number eighty-nine." I giggle with Bea because we know Obie might not like admitting his love for Taylor Swift, but his jersey says everything. They have their helmets loose, chin straps dangling as they toy with a puck back and forth. Obie raises his head to look across the ice and then whispers in Gus' ear. I don't want to know what that means.

Closer to center ice, the trio of the starting line are running drills up their lanes, getting ready to take some practice shots on goal now that Nicky is upright again. I point out Henri in number sixty-four, the silver "C" emblazoned on his chest, Charlie wearing his number four, trying to sink a slapshot past Nicky, and finally, number ten, Crosby.

It's right then that he takes his helmet off as he skates toward the bench. His brown curls are already damp with sweat, and they flop clumsily on his forehead before he shakes them back.

"Bloody hell, Vi!" Bea whistles appreciatively. We decided to forgo the family suite for seats closer to the ice, and this is her first glance of Crosby in person. We're just above the penalty boxes, looking across at where he's leaning in close to talk with my dad. "That man looks like he'd throw you over his shoulder, fuck you twice, and thank *you* for the opportunity."

"Christ, Bea! I *work* here," I hiss. There's a man two rows down who has turned to glare over his shoulder. It's the typical reaction from a guy who thinks women only show up to the games to stare at the players without a clue as to what is going on. In his defense, my friend isn't exactly trying to deter his assumption with her commentary.

"Don't care, babe." Bea is laughing as she tosses a two-finger salute at the grumpy man; a foul gesture he certainly won't understand, so she gets away with it. "Crosby Wells is hot as hell. Is he that big everywhere?"

I slouch in my seat, the plastic giving me no assistance as I try to melt away from my best friend with the bawdy mouth. My skin feels hot all over as I think back to the other night at his house. It was a little presumptuous to show up at his place, but after being at Dad's, and one angry voicemail to Obie, all I wanted to do was see Crosby.

He was attentive, patient, and the best listener. He didn't rush me or interrupt. I can still feel the way he held me, running his hands up and down my body in comfort, never trying to push it to the next level. But when I kissed him, his immediate reciprocation sent heat flooding through my veins. I wasn't surprised our impromptu make-out session riled him up, but I was shocked at the sheer size of him underneath me. If the circumstances had been any different, I would have done some deeper investigating.

"Oh, you naughty girl," Bea's voice breaks my train of thought. She's scooted down to lean over in my ear. I cover my face with my hands, as if it will protect me from her curiosity. "C'mon then, let's have it. Don't leave out any of the dirty details."

"We haven't had sex," I say, keeping my voice pitched low and serious. I'm scanning the area around us, ever mindful of my coworkers working in the arena tonight and the clientele of the crowd starting to take their seats. Bea is giving me an indignant look, trying to figure out if she believes me. "We haven't," I insist.

A single eyebrow arch. She stares me down. One second, then two. The brow drops, but her gaze narrows.

I huff out a sigh and roll my eyes.

"But from what I can tell, the answer to your question is 'yes.'"

Bea's cackle draws the ire of the man two rows down again. I give him an apologetic smile. Bea continues to laugh, reaching for the beer we picked up before claiming our seats. She downs a healthy swallow, smacking her lips a little.

"That tastes like warm piss," she comments, grimacing and

drinking again. I laugh at her. Even shitty beer makes Bea happy when she wants one.

I look back down, watching the teams skate off the ice, preparing for the lineups and anthem. Dad is the last one off the ice for our team, looking back and forth to make sure his team is where they're supposed to be. He gives a wave to a kid banging on the glass, a move that is entirely perfect for the man he is.

In the other corner, the Portland Searchers are making their way to their tunnel. Against my will, the bright blue seven catches my eye, and I see Olivier pull his helmet off. His golden hair is longer than the last time I saw him, and beyond where he exits, some fans in sky blue wave at him. My stomach twists uncomfortably.

"Thanks for coming with me." I lean my head on Bea's shoulder. "I probably should have skipped this."

"Oh, Petal, you wouldn't have wanted to miss this for the world."

As the Zamboni finishes resurfacing the ice, and the lights dim, I know she's right. But when the opening riff of AC/DC's "Back in Black" blasts, my heart lodges in my throat.

Chapter 17

Crosby

It's eight minutes into the final period. I'm sitting on the bench for a line change, sweat rolling into my eyes, but I'm focused on Portland's right winger. Ahlman is fucking fast, I'll give him that, but he lacks a certain discipline. There's a selfishness to how he handles the puck, keeping it to take a bad shot instead of passing to someone who might sneak one past Nicky. It wouldn't be likely, our goalie is a damn wall, but it would still be the smarter play.

With a satisfying thump, Obie sends number seven into the boards when he tries to charge the crease. Down the bench, Coach is screaming at our defenseman, warning him off the uncharacteristically rough way he's playing tonight. It's the fourth or fifth time Obie's bodied Ahlman when play didn't strictly call for it, and I've been jealous of his opportunities all night long. The most I've been able to do is chirp from the bench or intentionally bump into the asshole when we've been near the line changes together. I received some confused looks, and after the last intentional nudge, Ahlman asked what the fuck was up before I just smirked in response.

"Attaboy!" I encourage Obie, ignoring how I know Coach prefers we handle things.

Ahlman looks thunderous, chirping back at Obie, who ignores him to settle back in the zone. It won't be the last time the two of them get into it tonight. I know why Obie's taking the risk, but it looks like Ahlman might just like the contact. Another hallmark of a shitty teammate: fighting everyone else instead of fighting for your team.

If I've felt nothing short of violent since seeing Violet the other night, and with the way my teammates have played since the puck dropped, I don't think I'm the only one. I slug a shot of Gatorade from the bottle, looking at Coach for the signal to shift onto the ice again. I haven't had my chance to go against the asshole who tore my girl's heart up.

My girl.

That seed of possessiveness took root after Columbus. It twisted and wrapped around me, tight as a vine, when I held Violet in my arms on my couch, brushing away her tears and kissing her sadness away. I've never felt like this before, but it settles into a space in my chest that feels right.

Violet Cameron is *mine*.

A whistle blows, and we get the signal to change. I throw my legs over the ledge and skate out to give our third line a rest. Portland can't change, so Ahlman remains on the ice. I head into position, squaring up with another Portland player as Ahlman sets up with Bones in the blue circle. I know how this series of play is supposed to go, but when the sticks clash and the puck is on the ice, I don't care. I push off my blade and head across the rink.

I let physics do their thing as I collide with Ahlman, sending us against the glass hard enough to knock his helmet loose. It skips across the ice as I back up, Ahlman's gloves dropping beside his helmet and stick. I know what's coming next because I clocked this guy as a hothead the second I saw him. He fists the front of my jersey as I drop my gloves. He draws his fist, swinging poorly for me when I lean back. I jab my own fist in an uppercut, gripping the front of his jersey in return to keep him where I want him.

I fucking hate fighting. I'm shit at it most of the time, which is why I try to avoid unnecessary scraps with other players, but tonight I'm fired up enough that I plan on making every strike count. Ahlman lands a blow against my jaw, the visor of my helmet doing a decent job of protecting my cheeks and eyes from his hits. The punch rattles my teeth, but I cock my arm back for one more hit.

He's without his helmet, giving me more targets, and I aim for his nose. I feel it crunch under my fist, satisfied when red explodes from the site.

"What the fuck, man?" Ahlman yells at me as the refs pull us apart. He's bleeding, but not nearly as badly as I hoped. "You don't even fucking know me!"

"Welcome to the NHL, you lousy piece of shit!" I call back, not caring that the official is pushing me toward the penalty box.

I trudge into the little glass box, watching the fans sitting behind it. Some are banging on the glass in near-feral levels of support, while others stare wide-eyed. Just as I turn to sit to serve my time, I catch sight of a brunette with startling blue eyes and a bright red pout.

Violet.

She's still in the crowd of chaos, now more enthusiastically cheering because I haven't taken my seat. The referee is calling a five-minute major over the PA system for fighting, and I should be hanging my head like a properly punished little boy. But I can't pull my eyes away from the woman I went to battle for. That I'll fight for again and again. She hasn't moved, and the longer we stare at each other, the more her cheeks heat.

I point at the bench before pointing directly at her. *This is for you,* I mouth.

Her lips part just before I turn my back.

Across the ice, Coach glares daggers at me, and play resumes.

Coach's office has always been a little on the impersonal side. The walls feature photos of The Midnight team and staff throughout the years. There's a particularly nice shot of the arena at night, the fluorescent purple lights splashed against the side of the building and people filing in. But there's nothing here to give away what kind of man runs the team. No framed photographs of friends or family. No mementos from his years as a player. Just a desk and his computer. A bookshelf along the back wall full of binders.

I used to think it was odd, but assumed it was because Coach was that dedicated to the game. So dedicated to the team he refused to have any possible distractions in his space. Now, I know a little better. Coach doesn't have anything personal because he doesn't want people to know about his personal life. He never wanted people asking about Violet. He's always protected her, and right now, he's pacing behind his desk, ready to yell at me for doing the same thing.

Ironic.

I'm still standing in my gear, having been called in as we marched down the tunnel from our 2-1 win. I was expecting it. After getting out of the box, Coach kept me benched for the rest of the game. Obadiah is waiting outside the door, undoubtedly next to catch shit about our gameplay tonight.

Coach paces behind his desk—his energy is all over the place. I'm used to seeing him worked up, passionate. The more intensely he feels, the more he cusses and yells. It's just his way. But a quiet

Coach is usually a scary Coach, and right now, he's not saying a word.

Another few minutes pass before he stops behind the chair, gripping it with two hands. His face is a mixture of anger and disappointment. It's almost enough to get me to feel bad for failing to be the player he expects, but I don't. I won't apologize for going after Violet's ex, and when I meet his stare, I swear I see a hint of pride flash across it.

"Sit down."

Coach swings his chair back and folds into it heavily, motioning to the large chairs in front of his desk. I look at them and back to him for confirmation.

"Sit the fuck down, Wells." His tone offers no room for argument, so I do. Being called in here immediately off the ice means I haven't even had a chance to take my skates off. It feels a little awkward to stay in them now, but I don't think Coach will appreciate it if I take them off. Instead, I stretch my legs out and hook them at the ankles, the blades making a little clink that echoes in the silence.

Coach leans forward on his elbows, clasping his hands under his chin for a moment.

"Did you know who Olivier Ahlman was before the game tonight?" It's not what I expect him to say to me. I take a deep breath, knowing there isn't any way to play this, but truthfully.

"Yes. Violet explained she had history with him. She said things didn't end well." I'm watching Coach carefully, but he gives nothing away. "He used her."

I may have only recently learned of their connection, but as I watch Coach's eyes flash with anger the same way Violet's do, it's so easy to see how they are related. He drops his hands, leaning back while he looks at me. I don't know what else to say, how much more I should offer, so I wait. This isn't just about my relationship to him as a player; it's about my relationship to him as a man who wants to be with his daughter.

"You and Violet?" It's a small question. I try to hide the smile I feel thinking about her, thinking about what that statement means —what it *could* mean—and I don't bite it back. I let it spread across my face.

"Yes."

Coach listens along to the news. He loosens the tie at his neck, unbuttoning the top collar button of his shirt underneath.

"You ever bring how you feel about her on the ice again—ever let it dictate how you play your game—I'll suspend you, understand?" I nod immediately. "This is the year you get to prove to everyone what a damn good hockey player you are. Hell, you might even finally start to believe it yourself if you're lucky. Don't fuck it up. Even for my daughter. Because she'd never forgive you."

I blink in shock. It doubles when a wicked smirk spreads across Coach's face.

"Not exactly how you were expecting this whole thing to go, huh?" He waves a lazy hand between the two of us. I huff out an uneasy laugh of agreement, my body relaxing. Coach shrugs. "What do you want me to say? 'You hurt her, I'll hurt you?' Violet's a grown woman, fully capable of making her own decisions and doing what's right for herself, whether I agree with it or not."

"She's amazing, sir." I can't help but let the truth slip.

"Don't I fucking know it." Coach agrees. His eyes turn a little soft in the corners. He stands, and I rise, too. I can tell I'm about to be dismissed. "Ice that jaw, it's already looking bad."

"Not as bad as Ahlman's face," I venture to reply. I like the darkness in Coach's face at my statement, it matches how I feel on the inside.

"Too fucking right," he answers. "But no one around here

heard me say that. *Especially* you. Can't let there be any rumors of favoritism floating about. Get out of here. No press for you tonight, I don't need the headache."

I rush from the office, giving a chin raise to Obie as I fly to get out of my gear and clean up. I pick up my phone when I reach my locker, sending a quick message to Violet asking if she's still here. I get a cheeky smirking emoji back and confirmation she's in the hallway, so I hurry to the showers, intent on seeing her as quickly as possible.

After my conversation with Coach, the post-game adrenaline reignites in my veins. It gives a remarkable high I only want to see topped by holding Violet in my arms. No, not a want. It's a *need*. I need to have Violet in my arms.

Entering the players' tunnels at the back of the arena, I look for her. About halfway down, near a small bend, I spy Violet leaning against the wall, chatting with another brunette woman. Violet looks around briefly before whispering in the other woman's ear. There's a fair amount of people in here, like there always is post-game, but most are team staff or a wayward member of the visiting team's support crew. Everyone usually is coming or going to a very specific task, and there is rarely any loitering. I'm immensely grateful our arena security is tight, and they are vigilant at keeping fans and press alike from having access.

I greet a few equipment crew members as I walk quickly along the corridor. Violet has her back to me at the moment, but her companion's eyes widen at my approach before she grabs Violet by the shoulders and turns her to face me.

"Think I'll make it to the gaffer's office before I get kicked out?" The woman's accent is decidedly English, and I definitely don't know what a 'gaffer' is. She gives me a nudge on the arm as she passes, calling back over her shoulder, "Don't do anything I wouldn't, you sexy little minx. Talking to you, Big Shoots!"

"Keep following the tunnel. Wait outside the last door on the right. Use the badge if anyone gives you trouble," Violet yells, the woman already striding along looking like she belongs, but she throws a hand up in recognition, a visitor's badge clutched in her grasp. A pretty little giggle tumbles out of Violet. I look down at her, it's something I haven't heard from her before, and I wonder if I can make it happen again.

"Let me guess: that's Bea?" I ask instead, carefully stepping closer. The crowd is thinning out, and people are used to us together when we work on social media content, but I'm still playing by Violet's rules about proximity. Even if it's killing me not to scoop her up and see if her lips taste any sweeter with that crimson color painted on them.

"The one and only," Violet replies, shuffling forward a half-step. "I would excuse her behavior on the blood thirst she acquired during the game, but it would be a lie. That's just Bea. She's off to find my dad, say hello. She's staying with Obie and Gus. Obie arranged for her to be here."

I hum a sound of acknowledgment. She's close enough now that I can lace my fingers with hers on the hand closest to the wall. It's barely any contact, but the adrenaline doubles in my blood.

"She going to be okay if we get out of here?" Propriety is telling me I shouldn't intrude on Violet's time with her best friend. I only have a vague idea of their connection, but I know it's a big deal she's here. I don't want to be proper tonight. I don't want to be patient. I don't want to be good.

The possessiveness inside me rears its head, expecting me to pay attention. It insists on being selfish and greedy, demanding I haul Violet away to keep her for myself, especially knowing Ahlman may still be in this very building. That's too close to her.

"What do you have in mind?" Violet says it quietly, and I see the sparks in her eyes. "Are the guys going to Lowry's? We could go there, get a celebratory drink to mark the occasion."

I take a risk as the tunnel quiets, shooting a quick look around, hoping we're alone in this makeshift corner. With barely a conscious conclusion that we are, I twist Violet's and my joined hands around her back, using the motion to pull her flush against me.

"I want to celebrate. But not at Lowry's, and certainly not with any of the other guys." I boldly cradle her cheek with my other hand, securing her in my hold as I run my nose along the curve of her jaw to where I whisper in her ear, "I want my 'mark' tonight to be on your skin. Here." I suck a kiss onto the tender flesh below her earlobe. "And here," I continue, letting my lips work along the column of her throat, where her pulse is picking up speed the longer I let my lips linger. "And a few more places I can't reach standing in this hallway where anyone can see us. How does that sound?"

"Yes."

Chapter 18

Violet

"Make yourself comfortable," I say as we enter the front door. I hang my coat in the entryway closet, having already tucked my shoes away. Behind me, I hear Crosby shuffling about.

The drive here had been almost perfunctory. There was a little discussion about music, a few giggles about the temperature of the SUV, and a comment about the traffic around the arena. We talked about Bea, Crosby being thoughtful and checking again that I didn't want to see her tonight. I told him we already made plans to meet for brunch tomorrow while the team met for a post-game dry-land workout. He had cringed at that, all players hated dry-land workouts, but he was looking forward to his time with the physiotherapist for a good stretch.

He kept hold of my thigh the whole time, making driving with one hand seem effortlessly sexy. His fingers traced nonsense patterns along the top of my leg before sliding along the inside and back up. If I could have pressed my thighs together to relieve the tension his teasing was building in me, I would have. But trapping his hand would have been a blessing and a curse: the relief instantaneous, but the desire for more would have grown.

Now, alone in my house, I'm determined to follow my craving. To consume this man and *be consumed* by him. There's a cage of butterflies inside me threatening to break free. I welcome the feeling. There isn't room for doubt or second thoughts when you're in free fall, and right now, I'm standing close to the edge.

Crosby shocked me during the game tonight. He went after Olivier with no other aim but to hurt the man who hurt me. It was possessive and hedonistic. A better woman would have found fault with that. She would gasp and chastise, covering her face in horror.

I am not a better woman.

When he was pulled to the penalty box, there was a hardness in his face. It wasn't his usual assessing concentration I've come to expect when he plays. Instead, he looked powerful. Dangerous. I could do little more than stare and feel my heartbeat banging inside my chest, its beat kicking up with feverish delight. Only when he spotted me in the crowd did his fierce scowl relax. The sweetness returned to the corners of his eyes, his face softening as he stared back.

He told me it was for me, and any lingering walls pitifully guarding my heart crumbled without resistance.

I turn from the closet to see Crosby standing in his slacks and the cashmere sweater he wore for walk-ins. His shoes are next to mine under a small bench against the wall, his jacket carefully draped on the seat. His hands are in his pockets, thumbs hooked over the side, and his eyes are on me. I lean back against the closet door, seeking support because those butterflies? They have officially taken flight under the weight of his heated stare, bouncing around inside me with such velocity I'm concerned my legs won't hold me much longer.

I don't need to be concerned. In two steps, Crosby is in front of me, bracketing my face with his large, warm hands. He holds me reverently as his thumb traces along my bottom lip.

"Are you okay, Sparks?" Crosby leans his forehead against mine, checking in with achingly sweet thoughtfulness. I nod once. "I just couldn't leave it alone. I couldn't leave *him* alone when I finally got on the ice with him. It probably wasn't my place, but Violet, men like him make me sick."

He pulls back, his eyes searching mine. I don't know what he expects to find. I'm grateful for him, something I have every intention of showing him in words *and* actions.

"I wasn't expecting you to do any of that tonight—go all 'caveman' on my ex. It made me feel safe," I whisper, turning his right palm, kissing it tenderly. "Protected." I turn the other way, pressing a matching kiss to his left palm. "It was kind of hot."

I can't help it. I giggle, breaking from his hold to smother my heated face against his chest. His sweater is soft under my cheek and cloaked in his spicy vanilla and citrus scent.

"That turned you on?" I feel the question through his chest. It's a low, rumbling thing, matching the throb I recognize building in my center. I silently bob my head in agreement. Crosby steps closer, pressing his hips forward, trapping me against the door. I feel the outline of his length, hard and long, near the crease of my left hip. The familiar sensation has me gasping as he grinds a little, close to my core but still too far.

"Hmm." His voice is thick as he trails his fingertips along the sides of my body, tracing the curves there, learning the map of me. They tease up the hem of my shirt, drawing on my exposed skin with such tender intention I lift my head to look at him. Crosby has a sharp smirk on his lips, curled in the corners, his eyes blinking slowly while he savors my reaction.

The heat building in me is torching the butterflies, turning them to ash, chasing away the nervous excitement. In its place, my body lights up at every brush of his touch, fueling a brighter blaze I only know one way of extinguishing.

With a determined grip, Crosby shifts me until his broad thigh slips between my own. The presence of his firm muscles pressing against my center has me bucking toward him.

"I think *this* turns you on, too," he says, leaning in. I moan, my head hitting the door with a small thunk. Crosby wastes no time attacking my exposed neck, sucking kisses along the skin leaving a trail behind while working toward my ear. "I want to learn all of the things that turn you on, Violet. What I do that makes you feel good, what you *want* me to do to make you feel good, and what you want to do to *me* that will make you feel good. I want it all. But I need your words. Does this turn you on?" He pulls me tighter against his thigh. It presses deliciously on my aching clit, and we both groan. He nips playfully at my earlobe as he waits for my answer.

"Y-y-*yes*," I stutter, ending with an unexpected hitch of my breath, when Crosby directs my hips in a little circle before pulling me against him again, never breaking contact with his leg. "Holy shit. Yes. That."

"What about this?" His hand slips further under my shirt, ghosting up my stomach to the swell of my breast. His fingertips toy with the lace scalloping at the top of the cup, tracing along the rim, never touching the skin underneath. I'm steadily rocking my hips against him, as if I can pull him closer with every pass.

"Yes."

Crosby gives a little hum, covering my breast with his large hand, a gentle squeeze drawing a moan from me. He quickly swallows the sound with a bruising kiss as my mind goes blank beyond the sensations he's pulling from me. It's an overwhelming kiss. The kind that speaks of consuming, of claiming me fully. With a stroke of his tongue against mine, there's a promise I'm hoping he'll keep.

All too soon, he's pulling back, his hand leaving its place under my shirt, the nipple inside the satin cup straining for the warmth to return. I'm squirming now, any rhythm forgotten as I search out more of his touch.

"Listen to you." His whisper is reverent as he dips his fingertips just inside the band of my leggings. I shiver at that. He removes his leg from between mine, twisting his hand to flatten his palm against my belly. The possessive action makes me feel small and delicate. But he doesn't treat me like I'm about to break, sliding into my leggings just until he reaches the elastic of my underwear.

"This?" Crosby husks out, continuing his quest before giving me another kiss and seeking my consent. His eyes find mine, widening briefly to prompt my answer. "Is this something else you want me to do to turn you on?"

"Touch me, Crosby," I say, widening my legs to make room for him to slip into my lace thong. He watches me the entire time his fingers make the journey over the top of my mound and dip into my slit. There's limited space between his large hand and the tightness of my leggings, but I like that it keeps him closer to me.

His fingers slide through the wetness there. "Fuck, baby, is this all for me?"

I only nod. My arousal has been steadily growing since we left the arena. I would feel embarrassed at the dripping mess I've made if Crosby hadn't chosen that moment to slip one finger just inside me.

"Oh." I lift up on my toes, uncertain if I'm trying to get away and adjust from the new intrusion, or if I'm angling to get him where I want him. My hand flies to his forearm, flexing as he draws his finger back, pulling out to slide up to circle my clit and back down. When he enters again, he angles it differently, moving slowly to brush against my most sensitive spots. It's been so long, and I'm so worked up for him, my orgasm is already starting to coil inside me.

"That's it," Crosby encourages as I begin to move my hips, seeking more. "You want another? Want to fuck yourself on more of my fingers?"

"Yes. Fuck, yes, I want more." I barely remember to use words, but I'm ridiculously nodding at his suggestions. I'm gasping and panting as Crosby's long and thick fingers pump in and out of me, the heel of his hand pressing against my sensitive clit.

Crosby's other hand comes up to tangle in my hair, angling my head back to offer my lips like a sacrifice. He growls as he takes the moans I make, each kiss drawing me closer and closer to the edge. His fingers are pumping faster, curling just so, and he's replaced the pressure on my clit with fast circles he's drawing with his thumb. I'm nearly there, moving with abandon, when his command falls across my lips.

"Come for me, Violet."

A strangled scream echoes in the hall as I break apart. My hearing goes fuzzy, and there are spots clouding my vision. I feel Crosby steadily bringing me down from the high by slowing the movement of his fingers inside me and gentling the swirls on my clit. He releases my hair, running his hand through it and pressing kisses along my jaw and throat while I regain my breath. A little aftershock rocks me as he tenderly brushes his lips along mine.

I'm sighing contentedly as my hearing returns, his soft words of praise causing me to smile into the kiss he gives me. A shuddered, unsteady laugh of delight threatens to break free, but I don't think I can manage it. Instead, I float in the afterglow, the buzzy high tickling my bloodstream like champagne bubbles. It's officially the only kind of drunk I want to be from now on. Drunk on Crosby Wells.

Crosby smiles, kissing me again once before pushing my hips

flush against the door and pulling his fingers free from my pants. I'm panting with desire as he raises them to his mouth, sucking each one clean. With his other hand, he palms the erection straining the fabric of his slacks. I don't recognize the whimper that escapes my lips.

"We're not done." Crosby cocks his head to the side, pupils blown wide and color high in his cheeks. "I don't know if I could ever be done with you after that. But I'm not fucking you against the door. I want you somewhere I can lay you out and enjoy it. Where I can hold you after. You have somewhere like that, Sparks?"

I love that his questions are helping to clear the lust from my head. I want Crosby like that, too. I want this slow and dirty, not fast and rough, even if my body can barely distinguish between the two right now.

"Upstairs." I point feebly at the staircase. He comes back to me, looping his arms around my waist, pulling me close. I push my hands through his hair, the curly strands soft as I scrape gently along his scalp. I like the almost purring sound he makes in the back of his throat. When I reach the nape of his neck, I leave my arms to rest around his neck. I lean forward, laying my head over his heart. The sound is soothing, a thump that is deescalating with my own. His cock presses hard, hot and needy, along the length of my thigh.

"Perfect. Time to show me more of what you like."

Then, with a smoothness I'm not expecting, Crosby squats, scooping me behind the thighs to wrap me around him. He smiles at me, the butterflies returning before he makes for the staircase.

Chapter 19

Crosby

Violet's infectious giggle bounces against my neck as I round the door she directed me to at the end of the hall. The sound hasn't stopped since I picked up speed, her tangled legs hooked behind me as she bounces perfectly just above my cock.

What happened in the entry was unlike anything I've done before. I don't usually try to take control. I don't think of myself as a dominating guy when it comes to sex. But there was a level of trust Violet gave me that felt similar. I was the one making the decisions. My lips were heating her skin. My fingers were pulling sounds from her that will have a permanent residence in my quiet moments. Now, as I take in her bedroom and guide her down from her perch on my hips, I'm looking forward to seeing what else I can do with her.

Violet steadies herself on her tiptoes in front of me, her skin glowing and her eyes shining prettily as she searches my face. I reach forward to gently cup the base of her throat, not squeezing but intentionally resting my hand there. Her pulse jumps, pupils trying to blot out the blue of her eyes. I like the little excited breath she lets loose just before I use the leverage to bring her mouth to mine.

Kissing her is as easy as breathing. It's instinctual to have her lips move against mine in a languid and lush way. The teasing taste of her tongue as it dances with mine has my hand slipping around to hold her at the back of her head. I cradle it, directing our kiss closer, harder, with more heat until her own fingers fist my sweater. A final pull of her searing mouth has me breaking off, gulping a breath, and walking her backward to the edge of her bed. The back of her knees hit the mattress, making both of us sway.

My hands lift the hem of her long-sleeved shirt slowly enough that she can stop me, but Violet reaches down, lifting it the rest of the way off. I give myself a few seconds to take in the swell of her black-satin-and-lace-covered breasts. They rise and fall with her rapid breaths. I haven't given them enough attention, something I intend to remedy another night. Right now, my cock is aching to experience the tight heat of her.

"You're beautiful," I tell her. The honesty comes easily, and I enjoy the way her blush spreads across her collarbones at my compliment. "Wish I could look at you all night like this: flushed and aching for more. Isn't that right?"

"Yes," Violet agrees. Her fingers are now running up and down my chest, stopping at the bottom of my sweater. "Can you take this off? Please? I want to see you, too."

I don't hesitate to reach behind my neck and pull the sweater off in one fluid motion. I toss it aside to join her discarded top on the floor. Violet's eyes greedily bounce around my exposed chest from the slope of my pecs to the dips of my abs. The work I put in at the gym and on the rink is reflected in my body, but I haven't paid much mind to it until she sighs and reaches a hand to follow the path of her eyes. Reflexively, I tense under her featherlight touch before leaning into her hand, seeking more.

"You've had a taste of what turns me on, now it's my turn. Does this turn you on, Crosby?" My own question is echoed back to me by the brunette giving me a wicked smirk and a challenging flutter of her eyes.

"What do you think, baby?" I put a hand on top of hers, guiding it past the waist of my pants to the bulge of my straining cock. I let go, giving her the power to do what she would like. I groan when she takes the initiative to rub me up and down a few times, ending with a squeeze that makes me count down from ten to keep from blowing my load.

"I think I want more of you." She bends at the knees, sinking onto the foot of the bed. Slowly, she unbuttons the top of my pants and then drags the zipper down. With the waist loose, Violet pushes them down my legs where I step out, kicking them idly to the side. My cock has a heartbeat. It's throbbing so hard in my boxer briefs, a small damp spot appearing where pre-cum has leaked through.

With unexpected seriousness, Violet examines the mark, swiping a thumb across it, dampening the pad, and giving the head of my cock a tease.

"Oh, fuck," I groan, fisting my hands at my sides. I squeeze hard enough for my blunt nails to leave impressions in my palms when she hooks her thumbs in the elastic of my briefs and pulls them down with ease.

My cock bounces slightly as it's released, not quite slapping against my stomach but moving with enough force. Violet gasps out a strangled sound when it draws her attention. Comically, she stares at it before lifting her eyes to me and back again. I can't help the laugh that bursts from me.

"Jesus Christ, Crosby, don't laugh! My pussy hasn't had more than my fingers for months! That... that *thing* is going to destroy me."

She's shifting back and forth on the bed, warily eyeing my cock like it's going to follow her. All pretense of our sexy foreplay from moments before is forgotten as Violet tries in vain to regain her composure. My cock continues to bob with interest despite the shift in mood. I've never considered myself well-endowed. My previous partners have never commented that I'm too much, and they never said sex was painful, but I know I'm still greater than average. And Violet's tight. I was only able to get two fingers in her earlier because of the angle and those leggings that looked practically painted on. Now, with her admission, I realize this could be a tight fit.

"We don't have to do anything more if you're uncomfortable," I say, running my hands up her sides. I mean it. If everything stops here, I'll take the pain in exchange for her comfort. I trace her jawline, hoping she hears the earnestness in my voice, even if every puff of air coming through her lips is doing little to discourage my hard-on.

Violet takes a moment, then shakes her head. "No." She looks at me and shakes her head once more. "No, I want this. I'll make it fit."

My cock swells at the thought. Any second thoughts I have evaporate as she wraps a small hand around the base of my cock and pulls me to her lips. With a final set of her shoulders, she leans forward, engulfing me inch by inch in the suctioning heat of her mouth.

She gets about halfway down my shaft, her hand pumping the remainder. The swirl of her tongue around me is intoxicating, and I'm helpless to keep my hips from thrusting forward when she draws back enough to flick the point of her tongue through my slit.

Then she's back to bobbing up and down in time to the movement of my motions.

I'm whispering words of encouragement to her as she works me. I'm not even sure exactly what I'm saying, just that I want her to keep going, and it feels unbelievably good. Violet hums as I talk, and it sends new pleasure up my spine—the vibrations are an added layer to her efforts to send me over the edge. When she releases me with one hand and guides mine to the back of her head, encouraging me to hold her in place, she almost succeeds at ending my control.

"Fuck, baby!" Instead of holding her in place, I pull her off me. Her lips are plump and pink as she continues bestowing small kisses upon me, looking up with seemingly innocent eyes. "I think you've had enough of a lesson tonight," I tell her as I step back, out of her reach, while still pulling her up by her shoulders. Once on her feet, I reach around to unhook her bra.

Her breasts fall perfectly as their lace cage slides down her arms. I trace the curve of her ribs around to her front, letting my hands rest on the underside of her tits. They're soft and just smaller than a handful when I cup them, rubbing against her rapidly hardening nipples. Violet arches into my touch while starting to shove her leggings as far down her legs as she can manage. I let go of her, kneeling to help her out of them.

Taking the initiative, she moves back to the bed, scooting back to the middle of the mattress, parting her legs just slightly, a silent invitation. Her shaved, pink pussy glistens in the low light of the room. I can't help but lick my lips as I reach for my discarded pants, digging around for the condom I slipped into the back pocket from my wallet while Violet hung up her coat.

It doesn't take long to open the package and roll the latex around my cock. It's been so hard for so long, it will take reciting the Stanley Cup winners backward in my head if I have any hope of lasting longer than a few strokes.

I climb atop Violet's pillowy mattress, working up her body by pressing heated kisses to her calves, inner thighs, the crease of her hips, a stripe up her soft belly to her peaked nipples. Her breathing sounds thready as I take care lavishing them with attention, circling them with my tongue and sucking a beat before departing with a small bite. By the time I reach her throat, Violet is writhing under me, a tumble of moans and breathy encouragement falling from her lips. She widens her legs to draw me against her hot center. I rest my weight on my forearms, looking down into her beautiful blue eyes before capturing her mouth with my own.

I pour everything I feel for her into the kiss. My respect. My desire. My hope. My growing affection that threatens to consume me at the slightest mention of her name. I'm praying it isn't my imagination that I feel the same things coming from her.

"Tell me to stop and I'll stop," I tell her, pressing one more kiss to her lips as I steady myself on one arm, reaching between us to grip my cock and guide it to her entrance. Violet groans at the first contact, and I grit my teeth as my covered head slips through the wetness gathered there.

Violet bends her knees, planting her feet apart and widening even more to let my hips drop down against her own. I don't take my eyes away from her as I press inside slowly, a tiny gasp the only noise between us.

Desert Riders, 2023

The first inch slides in, Violet's heat encompassing me, testing my resolution to give her time to adjust.

"Goddamn, Violet. You feel so good around me." I let go of guiding my cock in, content to press forward with a small thrust and the little tilt of Violet's hips. Her fingers fly to my shoulders when more than the next inch slides in. I bear the press of her nails, secretly hoping I'll have reminders of tonight to carry with me tomorrow.

Denver Snowcats, 2022

"More, Crosby." Violet's voice is strained but sure. She's nodding, pushing down into the mattress with her toes as she angles her pelvis to let me in deeper. I drop my head to kiss across her collarbone, along the pulse in her neck, and bend nearly in half to reach her breasts. Her nipples are still stiff, the dusky peaks demanding more attention, which I am more than willing to give. In this particular position, I'm able to rest back more on my knees, leveraging the angle to thrust farther.

"Yes!" Violet cries out, her legs lifting to circle my hips, guiding me the final stretch with a press of her feet on my ass. I groan and drop my head into the crook of her neck when our bodies are flush against each other. Now in to the hilt, I hold still to accommodate the new sensations for both of us.

Florida Thunder, 2021 and 2020

Missouri Jackrabbits, 2019

DC Metro, 2018

"Crosby, please—" Violet's hand is on the back of my head, pulling at the curls there to gain my attention. I leave the safety of her hair, the apples and sunshine filling my nostrils, to see her look at me pleadingly. "Move for me? Please, please move."

Violet tries to rock herself against me, but I weigh too much, the realization I'm almost crushing her prompting me to action. I give a nod to her request, rolling my neck back slightly into the scratches she's giving my scalp. With a lot of concentration, I lift my hips, pulling my cock out of the tight heat I know I'll never get over.

"Holy fuck, baby." I only make it a couple of inches before Violet tightens her legs around me, dragging me back in. "You feel so good on my cock. Look at you, you're taking all of me."

I chance a quick look between our bodies to where I disappear into her and moan at the sight.

"Touch yourself," I grit out the command. All the composure I managed to gain is quickly slipping through my fingers, and I can't remember where I left off on the list. It's a lost cause. *I'm* a lost cause. "I want to feel you come on my cock. Can you do that? Rub that perfect clit and give me what I want."

She drops the hand that had been gripping the back of my neck, wiggling her fingers to gain access to where I know she's aching. I can tell the moment she touches the overly sensitive bundle of nerves, her pussy grips me even tighter, making it nearly impossible to pull back for a full thrust. My balls are beginning to tingle, drawing closer to me, the coil drawing tighter at the base of my spine. I'm so close to coming, stars dot my vision, but I won't let go until she does.

Violet lets out a loud gasp, her breathing coming quickly, and her head arching back into the mattress. Her eyes flutter closed, matching the flutters of her pussy around me. She's close. So close.

"Oh yes!" she cries, followed by unintelligible moans as her hand works faster against my abs. With a final shout of my name, Violet is tumbling over the edge, her body shaking below me, her pussy contracting with unbelievable strength as it holds my cock in place.

"Fuck. Goddamn. Violet, I'm coming!" I give her a warning before the coil inside me snaps, my cock swelling and spilling inside the condom. I thrust once, twice, three times more, letting the aftershocks of Violet's orgasm draw out a powerful one from me.

I slow my hips, barely moving as every part of my body lights up. My cock is sensitive as I wait for my heart rate to go back to normal, drawing out slowly before it goes too soft to cause problems with the condom. I sit back on my knees as much as I can, their support feeling shakier than they do after wind sprints on the ice.

"Is that a bathroom?" I ask, gesturing to the door to the right of the bed. She nods. I rise, removing the condom and tying it off.

Inside her bathroom, I dispose of it in the trash and find a washcloth next to the sink. After running it under warm water, I return to the bed.

Violet lays in blissful repose on the bed, her eyes closed, and a lazy smile the only indication she's awake. Carefully, I climb up, stretching my frame out alongside her, kissing her shoulder before cupping her cheek, willing her to open her eyes. She does, at the same time letting out a little contented sigh, just like she did downstairs. I love that sound. I raise the cloth to her in silent question. She tenderly parts her legs to allow me to clean her up. I do so with soft swipes of the cloth before hurriedly hanging it on the sink back in the bath.

When I return, Violet has pulled the sheets back for me. I slide under the high thread count and thick duvet to rest my head on the pillow next to her. I lean over to press my lips to hers, drawing a slow, sensual kiss from her. My fingers trace nonsensical patterns on her skin.

"Please don't break my heart," Violet whispers the words between us, small and pleading. All her past hurt and the insecurities she tries to mask wrap around the request. It makes my own heart ache in return.

"Never, Sparks." I kiss the crown of her head, wrapping my arms around her and tucking her protectively against me. Her skin is warm and delicate as I run a light touch up and down her back, listening for her breathing to level out and drift to sleep.

When it does, I stay awake for hours, hearing Violet's plea on repeat, thinking through the time we've spent together over the last two months, the last few days. My final thought before sleep takes me is I'll never hurt her because I think I'm falling in love with her.

Chapter 20

Crosby

The jet's engines are a dull purr in the background, a soothing melody to relax and fall asleep to. The flight back to Connecticut from our away game in Utah at the end of November is long enough to try and catch a few hours of shut-eye, and I close my eyes, attempting to do just that. Biggest perk of flying private is being surrounded by a collection of people who feel the same way.

"They ran out of Sprite. And I like Dana—she's a great flight attendant, always takes care of me—but she's never going to convince me 7Up is a decent substitute."

A collection of people that doesn't include my best friend.

I open one eye to look at Gus as he settles into the seat next to me, mild disgust showing on his face as he slurps the can of soda.

"Why are you drinking it if you don't like it?" I ask, readjusting since I know sleep is unlikely now that Gus is next to me. I love the guy, but he can't sleep on flights. It usually isn't a problem, I like keeping him company; it's how we became friends.

At the start of the season, we pick an old television series on

Netflix and work our way through seasons on away trips, plowing through episodes and finding ourselves way too invested in what we watch. Two years ago, we became McDreamy fans, even if we both agreed that Meredith's soulmate is Christina. And last year, we stopped speaking to each other for a few days when Gus insisted that Lucas and Peyton were a better endgame than the perfection that is Peyton and Jake.

"You know I get a tummy ache if I don't have it, and it's better than that ginger ale shit," Gus rubs at his stomach. Soda can in one hand, he pulls his tablet out from under the seat. I reach over to take the drink, saving us the possibility of a spill as Gus gets the next episode of *Gossip Girl* loaded. "You know, I think Jenny might be behind the Gossip Girl blog."

"No way," I say, handing him back his soda as Netflix comes up. "She's a ladder climber, for sure, but she gets equally as burned by the 'XOXOs.' My money's on Chuck."

"That guy has everything—including Blair—what could he possibly gain?" Gus has abandoned hitting play to turn to me, shock on his face.

"I think Chuck is constantly seeking approval. He's not motivated by sex or greed, he just wants recognition. This could be a really twisted way to get it." I shrug. "I wouldn't put it past him to manipulate all of these situations so he benefits, even if it means hurting his 'friends.'"

"That's actually a good theory." Gus drinks from the can, thinking about what I said. "Damn. A guy like that in real life would piss me off. Did you think of that yourself? Lately, I can't tell if you're even paying attention to the show." He gestures to the phone on my tray table. "You already text Vi?"

"I pay attention!" I look at my best friend. His face is relaxed, but there's a bit of sadness lingering in the corner of his eyes, and guilt nudges my gut. I tuck my phone in my pocket. "Hey, I'm sorry," I offer, hands up in supplication. "I know I've been more involved with Violet, and I haven't been the best friend."

"You're always my best friend," Gus deflects, pushing out a hollow laugh behind his words as he looks away from me. I nudge his elbow, and he sobers before giving me a thin smile. "I get it. Vi is amazing. She's made doing all the social media stuff bearable. She's beautiful and kind, and I can see she means a lot to you."

"She really does." I want to tell him I've fallen hard and fast for her, but I can tell by the warmth in his words and the silent nod he gives me, Gus already knows.

"It's crazy she's Coach's daughter, though." Gus blows a breath out, a quiet whistle escaping. "I know everyone around here knows and probably suspects that you two are a thing, but do you worry about what will happen when that information officially leaves The Midnight family?"

"I'm not sure," I consider the question. I think about how careful Violet and I are at the office and practice facility; professional whenever there are eyes around but playful and passionate if we know we're alone. She's quietly steered us that way, trying to stay away from attention that doesn't pertain to her work. I've followed her direction, honestly thankful for the focus it has allowed me to keep on the ice and the distance it has created from unwelcome questions in the media. "Violet's last relationship ended when she found out he was only dating her to get close to Coach and hopefully land a try-out."

"Ahlman, right?" Gus asks, and I nod. "Wish I had known about that before we played the Portland game. I would have been happy to sit in the box for a chance to mess with him. How did that even happen?"

"Violet's existence hasn't been a *secret* her whole life," I start, working through the information Violet shared with me. "Coach didn't want to deny he had a child. I think he just preferred to keep her safe from any scavenging media trying to make a sensation out of a private decision. Things didn't work out between Coach and Violet's mom, but I don't think it was an ugly parting of ways. Just two people who wanted really different things. Protecting Violet from the media that became invested in Coach's career seemed to work for the most part.

"Violet started college when Coach came back to the team, so no reporter thought to ask about her then. He wanted her focused on school, so he never asked her to come home on breaks. He visited her for school breaks when the season allowed. She thinks it was during one of those visits to her school in London that Ahlman's agent saw them on campus together. He would have been there to discuss setting up the internship, witnessed Violet and Coach together, and went digging."

"That's so fucked up." Gus curls a lip in distaste. I agree with him. He taps a finger on the rim of the can. "You don't think people are going to think those things when you go public, right?"

"I don't see why they would," I consider.

"Just because the public is chronically online doesn't mean they like to Google any information for themselves. Just open Threads or X and you'll know what I mean." Gus shudders, and I laugh. "I just worry someone might get the wrong idea of you being on first line when they finally catch sight of Violet giving you heart eyes in a photo."

"She does not give me 'heart eyes.'" I glare. It's Gus' turn to laugh before finishing his soda in one big swallow.

"You're right. That's you."

"Damn, man," I grumble, making to pull my phone back out and ignore his good-natured teasing.

"It's not that serious." Gus bumps me with his shoulder, changing topics. "She's coming with you for Christmas Eve, right?"

"Yeah." I smile. "After that, she's agreed to be more public with our relationship—outside of working hours, of course."

"Of course."

"What about you? Who are you bringing to the party this year?" I ask. Gus' dates for team-sponsored events have always proven to be an unmatched source of entertainment in years past. How he finds someone who is so completely wrong for him is impressive. One year, he spent the evening telling me he couldn't figure out where he knew his date from. During dessert, he practically choked when the older, pretty blonde dropped the bombshell of being his eighth-grade student teacher.

"Think I might skip the date this year." He shrugs his shoulders. "Making it a guys' night with Obie and Bones."

"Cool." I smile. "That'll be good. I'm glad everyone will be there this year. I know having the first game back from the holiday sucks, but it means we get to celebrate together."

Gus squeezes my shoulder. Then, he flicks his head toward the tablet, paused and waiting.

"All right." I rub my hands together. "Let's find out who the fuck Georgina Sparks is."

Chapter 21

Violet

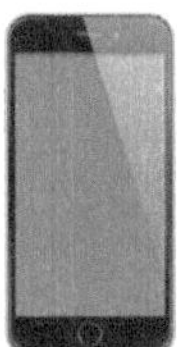

"Have you figured out what you're wearing yet?" Bea asks the dreaded question in my ear as I dig through my closet. We've been talking for so long—a good catch-up session after a whirlwind few weeks—my headphone is beginning to pinch.

After the game against Portland, Bea and I used the next two days to spend as much time together as possible while the team's schedule called for back-to-back practices and another away game. Having the opportunity to sit on the couch with my best friend and gush about my night with Crosby helped ease the nerves his unavoidable distance brought on.

But I found after she returned to England, an easy normality settled upon my life. Crosby had his job, one I was all too used to handling, and I had mine. We worked, collaborating when necessary; now with the added bonus of sneaky kisses in the empty elevator or a trailing finger along the curve of my waist, but never publicly indulging in the shift in our relationship. I double and triple-checked my contract and the handbook from HR, only finding discouraging language about romantic relationships between members of the same department. Surely that didn't apply to Crosby and me, even if he worked exclusively with me in social media.

When I finally got the nerve to seek out Ava's advice after a week, she simply smiled and told me it wasn't the first time she was aware of front office staff and members of the team being romantically interested in each other. She only cautioned me about the additional pressure of my dad's position and the increased media coverage on Crosby after the Portland game. Ava kindly recommended I talk it out with the coach, have HR make a note in my file, and get Crosby to reach out to his NHL Players Association representative.

My dad knew about us, a conversation I entered into with a particular sense of dread. But Dad merely asked me if I was happy with Crosby. When I told him I was, he let me know there would be nothing he could do to the man if things were to go poorly between us. It wasn't exactly a clear endorsement until he said of all the men on his team, Crosby is who he trusted the most.

Now, almost four weeks later, I couldn't agree with my dad more. Crosby is everything I hoped he could be and more. Tonight, we are attending the team's Christmas Eve party together, our first official public outing.

"Violet? Where did you go?" Bea calls my attention back as I continue to riffle through the offerings of my limited wardrobe.

"I'm here. Just wishing I had taken yesterday afternoon off to do a little shopping. I suddenly don't like anything I own." I flop on the floor, momentarily sulking.

"What's the dress code again?" Bea asks. I dig around for my phone, opening the email to check the details. The event is being held inside The Davis, a historic hotel downtown with an upscale restaurant, which is closed for our party.

"It unhelpfully says 'festive cocktail attire,' which could mean anything from *actual* cocktail attire to more casual festive outfits like ugly sweaters." I groan again. I think I have an old crewneck with a fuzzy depiction of The Grinch on it at the back of a drawer, but I dismiss the idea almost immediately. I switch Bea over to a video call so I can see her. "I know it's kind of stupid because we've been seen together by almost every person who will be attending, but I just want there to be this moment where I can stand with Crosby, and they think, 'yeah, that makes sense.'"

"Who doesn't want that when you manage to end up on the arm of one of the hottest men in sports right now?" Bea acknowledges, always backing me up, the familiar kindness in her eyes. She's right about that. Crosby's popularity has soared since someone took a video of his penalty box declaration. Luckily, at the angle of the recording, it wasn't clear who he was talking to, saving me from becoming a viral sensation. Despite the majority of the organization being curious, tonight will be the first time we've publicly gone out together where we didn't feel as though we controlled the situation—and its narrative. Post-game celebrations have been held at Lowry's, where Morgan's low tolerance of bullshit kept any potential non-regulars from braving the tiny dive bar, or back at one of the players' houses. I've also managed to dodge some of the more personal inquiries at work, with most of my coworkers accepting that I don't like talking about my personal life.

Crosby mentioned he would be wearing all black tonight, a standard uniform for him. He joked he would be easy to spot in the crowd when I arrived. When I gave him a hard time about basically wearing the same outfit he does for every game arrival and what the rest of the team will likely be in tonight, he smiled.

"If I wear all black, I give a background to make *you* stand out, Sparks. As much as I might regret it, I want people staring at you. I want them to know you are with me, that you belong with me, that you're mine." My heart fluttered so hard at the simple reasoning, I thought it was going to break a rib.

"What about the red dress we bought on Boxing Day last year? Do you still have that?" Bea prompts. "The cap sleeves and a sweetheart neckline? Makes your tits look great. Would that work?"

I stand up, shuffling Bea to one hand as I push to the back of the closet. The dress I had forgotten about sits on a hanger, needing a steam, but still bearing the tag from the killer day-after-Christmas sale. I bought it on a whim and haven't had an opportunity to wear it yet, but I'm glad Bea remembered it exists.

The stretchy material clings to my curves while still remaining comfortable. It's a perfectly vibrant red, readily accomplishing the "festive" directive in the email. The length hits mid-calf, keeping the balance between formal and casual. I finger the neckline Bea mentioned, remembering how it really does make my chest look amazing.

"You're an angel, Bea," I tell her, removing the dress and holding it up for her inspection. She nods, offering an enthusiastic thumbs-up.

The hotel lobby has four large Christmas trees twinkling with white lights, reflecting off the glittering silver and gold baubles hanging in the branches. From the hints of pine in the air, I'm impressed to discover they may actually be real. I gently touch the tips of a bough as I round the last one to draw close to the entrance of the restaurant. Glenn and Derek, our arena's heads of security, are posted next to the copper doors, standing sentry between the public and private space for the night. That makes me feel better as I pass a few Midnight fans lingering around the lobby couches, jerseys and phones in hand, awaiting the team's arrival.

There's a commotion behind me, and Crosby walks through the hotel doors, long, thick legs clad in tailored slacks. His black button-down has the top three buttons undone, exposing a tantalizing peek of pale skin. The final touch on his black suit is a crushed-velvet blazer with satin edging, elevating the entire look to a level of sexy I was not expecting. His hair has been delicately styled, his natural curls taking center stage. The entire effect is devastating. I duck a little behind the massive tree to watch him enter.

Halfway across the lobby, a little girl with braided pigtails and a toothy grin confidently breaks from her parents and heads straight toward him. Warmth blossoms in my chest when he immediately drops to a knee upon her approach. I'm too far away to hear the conversation, but he's looking her in the eye and nodding when she speaks to him. Her parents stand off to the side when she thrusts a black rally towel to him and a silver Sharpie. With gentle instruction, he directs her to turn around so he can use her shoulders to sign it. When he hands it back, he stands, extending a hand in greeting to her parents before reaching down a hand to the side of the girl's head when she wraps herself around him in a hug.

I admire how he's grown into handling his new level of fame. He's gracious and polite with people no matter the setting: the practice facility, the front office, at the airport, or at away games. Watching how Crosby has managed to embrace the responsibility of being a public figure while remaining kind has my heart practicing somersaults.

"Daddy says it isn't polite to stare."

I startle in my heels, teetering for a moment before turning to find the owner of the voice currently scolding me for admiring my boyfriend. With my balance regained, I see Nicky first, a sheepish look on his usually serious face. I follow the length of his arm to where he's holding hands with an adorable little girl with her other hand on her hip and a scowl on her face.

"You must be Natalia. I'm Violet," I say, squatting carefully to reach her level. "Your daddy's right, it isn't polite to stare at strangers. But I was waiting for that man, and I didn't want to interrupt him. That would be just as impolite, but I'm sure your daddy told you that, too."

"Wellsy's my friend." There's suspicion in her eyes, and I adore her protectiveness.

"He's mine, too," I assure her.

Nicky Baladin's daughter sizes me up for another moment, clearly thinking through what I've said before dropping the hand from her hip and the scowl from her face. She gives me a singular nod before turning back to her dad and asking something in Russian. His quiet *da* is the only part I understand.

"Have a good night, Vi. Merry Christmas," Nicky says, the barest smile on his face, but it feels genuine, so I smile in return. Natalia waves almost cheerfully before they start off in the direction they are heading.

I stand back to my full height, a breath passing through my lips at the exchange. I'm not sure if I passed whatever test that was, but I hope I did.

"You should hear her in the off-season when we don't beat our previous push-up count. Absolutely brutal." Crosby has laughter in his voice and a banked heat in his eyes when I look at him over my shoulder. "One time, when she was three, she sat on my shoulders because she thought I needed more of a challenge. I could barely lift my arms the next day."

"Sounds like my kind of girl," I reply, happily walking into his open embrace. I kiss him, his lips feeling smooth and welcoming against mine. His taste is becoming as familiar as home. I pull back and check that my stay-put lipstick isn't transferring; *Mistletoe Mayhem* doesn't really seem like his shade, and I'm happy when I see the advertising living up to its promise.

"You're my kind of girl." Crosby breaks into a cheesy grin before kissing me again, arms wrapping tightly behind my back, a hand wandering a little south to hold the top of my ass. "God damn, Sparks. This dress? I don't even want to go to dinner."

"Yes, you do," I tell him. I run my hands along the soft lapels of his luxurious jacket. "You've told me how much you like this party, that it's become one of your favorite holiday traditions."

He sighs as he drops his face into the crook of my neck. I skate my fingers down the buttons of his shirt until they rest on his belt. A heavy groan rumbles against my skin.

"C'mon, take me to this dinner with everyone. I'll let you have me for dessert."

I gasp when Crosby's teeth nip the sensitive skin along my pulse before he straightens, grabs my hand, and walks us to the restaurant doors.

"Evening, fellas," Crosby says to a smiling Derek and a blushing Glenn. I don't have a chance to feel embarrassed that they were well within view of us, I just giggle and offer a small wave.

Crosby pulls open the large door, ushering me into the modern steakhouse with a light touch on the small of my back. The restaurant is equally as festive as the lobby but in a more understated fashion. Large garlands of greenery and icicles hang from the exposed wooden beams across the ceiling, while centerpieces with poinsettia in red and white sit in the middle of the tables. There are enough twinkle lights thoughtfully spread throughout the space to add a gentle glow catching on the glassware and the faux icicles. It's warm and intimate, made more comfortable by the faces I recognize milling between tables and giving the room a quiet hum of conversation.

I see my dad near the large fireplace talking with Todd Montgomery, the team owner, and Ava sitting in a large leather chair just beside them. She lifts her glass of wine in greeting and winks. Crosby's arm fully wraps around my waist a second later, stealing my breath.

"These are our people, Sparks. They're our friends and family. Nothing about us being here together will surprise them, and the judgment you think they'll pass is non-existent." His words are the exact reassurance I need. He presses a chaste kiss at my temple before steering us toward our usual group of friends.

"No. Shit," Gus draws out both words, shaking his hand after touching Crosby's jacket like it stings, a silly smile lighting up his face. His shoulder-length hair has been pulled high on his head in a bun. "This jacket is fucking fire, and now I'm a little mad I let you wear it. Maybe I would have ended up with a date this gorgeous."

I chuckle as Gus steals me away from Crosby, crushing me in a tight hug. Always the radiant source of joy in this merry band of lovable blockheads, my light laughter practically turns to a cackle when he spins me a little before setting me down.

"Quick, leave this loser and be mine," he says, leaving me in near hysterics as he sets me down.

"And be responsible for breaking so many of your female fans' hearts? Never." I step back, letting my giggle fizzle before pressing a quick kiss to his cheek. From the moment he awkwardly propositioned me for Crosby's benefit, Gus has become one of my favorite people. Jovial and easygoing off the ice, he's like a giant puppy seeking attention. I adore him.

"Hands off the best friend," Obie growls from behind me. His face is all smiles, a complete contradiction to his tone. I turn to give him a kiss in greeting as well, running a finger up and down the emerald jacket he's paired with a cream sweater and black pants.

"Pretty sure we have to share them both now," Gus replies. "When our best friends become a couple, the custody gets split evenly. So, go hug Wellsy and give me back our girl."

"She's *my* girl," Crosby says from his spot next to Henri. "And it's her choice whom she spends her time with, dumbasses."

Gus and Obie open their mouths to protest or argue with each other, I'm not sure which, but I hold up a hand to stop them. With a playful wink and smile to Crosby, I cross to Charlie, who has stood stoic and silent the whole time.

"Hey, Charlie, want to get a drink with me?"

Chapter 22

Crosby

Violet walks away with Bones, her arm linked through his, hips swaying in an unconscious tease. I nearly swallowed my tongue when I spotted her talking with Nicky and Natalia behind the Christmas tree. She looks like she was nearly poured into it; the material hitting and accentuating all of her curves just so, and a color that highlights the creamy undertones of her silky skin. *God, the things I want to do to her in that dress.* Instead, I take a long inhale, willing my dick to control itself for a few hours and listen back to what Tex is saying.

"I think even if I somehow manage one, I've considered declining this year," Tex says. I struggle to find the thread of conversation he's having with Hutchinson, our left wing on the third line.

"Decline what?" I ask, finally pulling my eyes off Violet. She's just settled on a bar stool, Bones' hand hovering at her back to make sure she stays balanced.

"An All-Star invitation," Tex answers, following my eyes and looking back at me with an understanding smile. Allison is across the room with a smaller group of significant others and lifts her wine glass at him. Tex and Allison are the definition of couple goals, a compliment not easily given in our profession.

"Why would you want to decline? You've always said how much you enjoy the All-Star Weekend." I recall the stories Tex has told over the last few years when he's returned from the skills competition and friendly 3-on-3 tournament. He sounded just like we all do when talking about the privilege of being professional hockey players. The time with the fans, friends, and former teammates we rarely get to see, and the pure fun of being on the ice. I'm shocked to hear he doesn't want to go back if given the opportunity.

"I've loved it every time I've been lucky enough to go. When I first started, it felt like validation. Now it feels a little like nostalgia." Tex takes a sip of an amber liquid, thinning his lips a little at my confused face. He turns to Hutchinson, asking him to excuse us, and walks me over toward an empty table, away from the rest of the team.

"I think this is going to be my last season. Nothing official, of course, not yet. But it feels like it." Tex's hand on my shoulder doesn't weigh as heavy as the words he just spoke.

I'm not sure I can picture The Midnight without him. I don't think I can picture *hockey* without him. Henri Texier is one of the greatest role models—one of the greatest players—I've ever had the privilege of knowing. He's never stopped believing in me, even when I've had a difficult time believing in myself.

My first season in New Haven, he stayed behind every practice to "get some extra laps in," but ended up standing in goal while I worked on my wrist shot and gave me pointers on perfecting my Michigan play. I knew after a few weeks he wasn't really staying late to get in more cardio, but he never gave any other reason when the ice would clear, and I was standing at the blue line with a pile of pucks. He didn't need one, he was just being a good captain.

When I started for Bridger in the playoffs last year, I was so nervous my skates almost wore a hole in the mats of the tunnel before the game. No one would talk to me, not because they didn't care, but because I didn't want to listen. Even Gus opted for standing at the back of the tunnel in silence to keep me from going too far in my pacing. Then, Tex stepped in front of me.

"Your skate's untied." He kneeled swiftly, blocking my line of sight before I could see if he was telling the truth. After a moment he stood and cocked his head at me. "It's just a game, Crosby. Play the game, not the situation, and you'll do fine."

Every ounce of nervousness left me. It was the exact same thing my dad had told me my whole life: play the game, not the situation. Before I could say anything back, Tex had turned around to work his way down the line toward the head of the tunnel.

When I started at U of M, it was a saying my coaches and therapist had me repeat constantly. As I worked through my grief, I had to keep my feelings out of the game. I couldn't let the days I experienced overwhelming anger strip away the success I was gutting it out to achieve on the ice. With the exception of my behavior in the Portland game, I have lived by that saying. If what Tex has said comes to fruition, I'll still have a game to play.

"You're retiring?" I stutter just a little around the question. Saying the word isn't giving me more reassurance, it's like ripping open an old wound. One I didn't realize Tex had healed.

"Can't play forever." Tex releases me and sets his drink on the table. "This is good for me, Crosby. I'm not getting any younger."

"You're thirty-four. You're not dead," I push back. I try to keep the petulance from my voice, but there's this tremendous cascade of emotions threatening to fall in my next breath if I'm not careful.

"And most days I wake up feeling like I'm sixty-four." Tex's eyes are warm, the same softness in the corners I've come to expect from him over the years when we've had these private talks. "I wasn't like you. I didn't take care of my body from the start. Played injured. Played dumb. And those were just the things *on* the ice. Off the ice, I was just as stupid. I was so in love and so lost in what to do with it. Those first few seasons, I was never really able to give Allison all of me, you know?" I nod, letting myself steal a glance at Violet. Gus and Obie have joined her and Bones, all my closest friends surrounding her. Making her one of us. Another piece of my heart is stolen at the sight. "You have this more figured out than I ever did. In more ways than one."

Tex pulls me in for a firm hug. No back slapping, performative male bullshit. It's the kind of hug I got after I threw up in my helmet my second season when I thought I could get away with playing with food poisoning. It's full of the love I have for my teammate, my friend, and the man who stepped in with the fatherly guidance I was missing without ever making me see it was what he did.

When we pull apart, my throat feels a little tight, and my nose stings. Tex squeezes my shoulder and steers me toward the patio doors. He knows I need a minute.

"Why don't you catch your breath? Dinner is probably going to start soon."

"Yeah, I think that's a good idea." My voice sounds like gravel as I try to clear the emotion from it. The tip of the wave is threatening to crest, so I break for the door.

Thankfully, it's deserted outside. There's only soft lighting and the quiet instrumental Christmas music piped through the speakers that couldn't be heard in the main room. The space is winterized, large windows have been popped into place to keep the weather out. Portable heaters have been added at regular intervals to make the climate comfortable. I walk to the edge along the railing, staring out at the little garden, barren and brown at this time of year. I lean my arms against the wooden rail, cradling my head for a moment as I try to fight back the tears. It doesn't really work. I end up sniffling so much my nostrils hurt, and I'm squeezing my eyes closed so tightly there are little red starbursts behind my eyelids, but salty tracks begin to stain my cheeks anyway. I feel their little trails, my skin tightening in their wake.

A pair of arms wrap around me.

They're too light and too low to belong to anyone other than Violet. I grip her hands when they settle against my middle, grateful for the anchor she's providing. I take a couple of deep breaths before I turn around in her hold, looking down at her as I weave my own hold around her. She's unbearably beautiful. Her blue eyes are concerned as she silently observes me. She kept her hair down tonight in voluminous curls, the ends brushing my hands at the small of her back. She doesn't protest when I bend down to take a kiss of reassurance, her lips soft and pliable under my own. Her small hand climbs up my torso to where her fingers can just touch my cheek tenderly.

"Do you want to tell me?" she asks when I pull back, noting she doesn't immediately check her face despite me leaving behind the evidence of my tears. I swipe at it, careful not to smudge any of the makeup I know she applied for tonight. I love that she doesn't push, and that alone makes any hesitation to confess what I'm feeling disappear.

"Tex is thinking of retiring at the end of the season."

Violet doesn't speak, just angles my head to the crook of her neck, using her smaller frame to hug me tight. I breathe her in, marveling that this amazing woman took a chance on me. That she's here. If I play my cards right, she might be here for a very long time.

"Does it surprise you that he's considering it?" I lift my head, breaking our embrace at her question.

"No. It makes sense." I lean back against the rail, pulling her with me until she's resting against me, rubbing her bare arms. I enjoy the feeling of her against me for a moment, letting the silence settle comfortably around us. I toy with the ends of her hair as she leans into me, getting as comfortable as she can. "It made me think about my dad."

She gives me a slow nod. I see the questions burning in her eyes, the silver flecks jumping with curiosity. I can't give a good reason why I've put off talking about him all this time. We're not exactly where I'd like to have this conversation now, but Violet deserves to hear why I've turned into a little bit of a mess. Preparing for the conversation, I take my jacket off and drape it around her shoulders. Despite the somber feeling in the air, she flashes a warm smile of thanks. I kiss her forehead and help her thread her arms through the velvet blazer.

"When I was a senior in high school, my dad and I had a stupid argument. He was pushing me to defer my draft placement. He thought I could use a little more development and time to grow up. I told him he was trying to keep me closer because he was afraid of being alone. It had been only the two of us for as long as I could remember; mom left before I could walk. I went even further, accusing him of wanting me to defer because he didn't believe I was good enough. I was such a self-righteous asshole." Violet straightens, moving to rest on the railing next to me, angling so she can listen. "I left the house without trying to make it right because the state championship was that night. We were playing our biggest rival for the title, and it was going to be my first time playing in a real arena."

I twist to mirror her position. The usual phantom guilt creeps into my gut, my previously still emotional waters have ripples, churned up by an innocent announcement.

"I didn't say goodbye when I left. Just picked up my gear bag, grabbed my keys, and hit the road. I ignored the calls from him as I drove and shut my phone off as soon as I hit the locker room. I was so angry." Violet reaches out her hand, lacing her fingers through mine in support, instinctually knowing I need it. "After the game, my coach was waiting in the parking lot with a pair of State Troopers. They notified me that Dad had been in an accident. Someone ran a red light. The impact pushed my dad's car off the road, pinning it against a tree. He died on the scene."

"Crosby—" Her voice is a reflection of her shocked face. Her hand squeezes mine, but I don't move to hold her.

"I was eighteen." I shrug off the feelings the memory brings up. Scared. Devastated. Alone. They're mostly phantoms now, creeping from the shadows but not threatening the way they were then. "I buried my dad, finished high school, and deferred my draft by a year. You know how I came up through the league after that, how I ended up on The Midnight. And Tex—well, Tex, he...."

"He became more than your captain," Violet finishes for me, a sad smile of understanding on her lips. "Oh, Crosby. I'm so sorry. Thank you for telling me."

I can't bring myself to say more, I just pull her close again. She soothes me with gentle kisses and strokes of her hands up and down my back. She pulls back to keep them consoling instead of heated but still heals the ache in me with her lips.

"Do you want to leave?" she finally asks. As soon as the question leaves her lips, it's like my hearing returns, cluing in to the sounds from the dining room: plates and cutlery, glasses clinking together, the constant hum of excited conversation. My team is just beyond the doors. I can see them through the windows: my friends. The men and women I have embraced as my family.

I look at Violet, the newest person to own my heart.

"No," I tell her confidently. I smile, turning us to rejoin the group. "Let's go enjoy being with our family."

"I like that idea." Violet blushes a light pink. I kiss her until the color in her cheeks reflects her dress, laughing when she swats at my chest.

Chapter 23

Violet

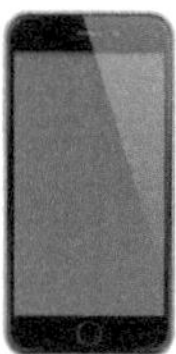

"So you work in the social media department?" Allison asks from across our table.

Dinner has come and gone, a delicious and decadent meal that has left me full and floaty on the flavors. Our group is all around one table, Crosby to my left and Charlie on my right, the easiest decision to keep Gus and Obie from fighting over me. Again. We're winding the night down over large slices of pie, spiced cider, and holiday mead. Everyone has a high flush in their cheeks or slightly glassy eyes as the conversation continues about life and the schedule post-holiday.

"That's right. I started at the beginning of the season. It's been an interesting side of the game to learn. I'm surprised how much I enjoy it," I answer. I don't know many of the players' supporting partners, and talking to Allison tonight has been really nice. She co-owns an apparel company that works to create sports merchandise designed by women for women, a corner of the market that has shown room for growth over the last decade. With her experience as a player's wife all these years, I was blown away by the mockups she showed me on her phone. Everything looks comfortable, on-trend, and clearly for sports fans but with a subtlety the league tends to miss when trying to market to female fans.

"I bet they're lucky to have you!"

"I'm not sure about that. I can run the numbers on the data the platforms bring in, but I'm not sure I'm the most creative member on staff." I laugh. Crosby is smiling at me, his hand snaking under the table to squeeze my thigh. "You can ask any of these guys, I've had them doing some ridiculous things in the name of my job."

"I kind of like the singing bits," Gus says. "I didn't think I had a good voice."

"You don't," Charlie and Obie quip at the same time.

"Fuck the both of you. The comments say otherwise." Gus looks affronted. Allison laughs and wraps her arm around Henri. He unconsciously leans over to press a kiss to the side of her head. They really are adorable.

"Don't believe everything you read online," Crosby wisely says next to me, taking a sip of water.

"If online comments were true, you'd have slept with half of Connecticut this season," Obie shares, looking at Gus.

"No shit?" Gus shrugs. "Guess Wellsy's right: the internet is full of lies."

Conversation breaks up among the group again, but I'm losing the threads as Crosby's hand traces little patterns, causing sparks of arousal to pulse in my blood.

It took him the majority of the appetizer to come back from the pull of his revelations to me. Even as he gave nods and smiles to everyone who spoke to him, traces of sadness and dark memories played in the corners of his eyes. It was a devastating piece of himself to share with me, but the trust he gave with it was a precious thing.

His history hasn't been a major part of his player narrative in the media. I can see why he's worked to keep it quiet, and I have a feeling that my dad has also done his behind-the-scenes magic to blacklist as many questions about those painful events as possible. It's something Cal Andrews does: he protects those he cares about. I settle against Crosby's arm realizing that even before we were together, my dad cared enough about Crosby to try and shield him.

I look across the room to where he's sitting with Ava, Todd, Ethan, and some other members of his coaching staff. He's sitting quietly as Ava leans across to say something to him. He gives a small nod and looks up at me. Dad smiles at me, and I think maybe, despite how I tried to fight it, he helped me figure out exactly where I belong.

"You okay?" Crosby kisses my forehead, keeping the question between us.

"Yes. Perfect," I reply. I look up at his beautiful eyes. The shadows of earlier have cleared, and there is an almost palpable amount of joy in his gaze now. I suck in a sharp breath. I'm trying valiantly to believe the love I see is for the collective group of people around him. I'm trying to convince myself that no matter how badly I want it to be only for me, there's no way we're there yet.

"You, um, you didn't eat your dessert." I break my eyes away from his, flicking my gaze to the plate with a full slice of pumpkin pie in front of him. Crosby manages a quick glance before a slow, heated smile spreads across his lips, and his hand flattens on my leg.

"It's not the dessert I want." He leans in, feeding the words into the gap between my parted lips. The sparks of arousal are threatening to morph into an inferno. If we were anywhere else, I'd let the intensity of the heat consume me.

"Oh?" I breathe back. Crosby shakes his head, somehow moving even closer. His lips brush mine, his body turned so much in his seat, I feel surrounded by him. When he wraps himself around me like this, I feel every piece of myself being consumed by him.

"This is a hotel. I'm sure they have rooms." Charlie's deep voice travels in from my other side. It's the exact dose of metaphorical cold water I need. As the bubble of Crosby-induced haze clears, I see the entire table watching us. Gus leans forward on his elbow, tucking his chin into his hand with an exaggerated, dreamy look. Obie just shakes his head with a teasing smile on his face. Allison and Henri are whispering and smiling, a fondness in their matching expressions. I take in Charlie's face, the usual stony pout replaced with a lighter, kinder smile. An embarrassed little giggle spills from my lips.

Crosby smacks a kiss to my cheek to break the moment, good-natured laughs circle the table. The hand on my lap disappears, but I don't have time to miss the absence of its reassuring warmth. It returns with a cold, distinctly rectangular shape pressed between palm and leg. A key card. I look up at Crosby's mischievous face.

"They do have rooms. Want to get out of here?"

"This fucking dress," Crosby growls the words against my neck from behind me as soon as the heavy hotel room door closes. His arms circle me, hands roaming the material of the garment he finds so abhorrent. His fingers inch the skirt higher up my thighs as he walks us to the plush king-size bed.

As we reach the white comforter, skin meets skin when Crosby finally pulls high enough. His touch sears into me even when he keeps it light and teasing. I lean back into his chest, reaching up to hold him behind the neck, directing his mouth back to the exposed skin under my ear and at my shoulder. I sigh happily when he complies, kissing the sensitive area with languid, heated pulls of his lips against my pulse.

His hands traverse along the tops of my thighs, fingertips dancing against my flesh before ghosting back down. With each pass, he inches higher until he brushes at the satin covering my core, drawing a gasp from me. Crosby's answering chuckle makes my fingers tighten their hold on the ends of his hair, pulling him off my neck and back to my lips.

I kiss him hard, a passionate dance of tongues and teeth that he matches stroke for stroke. I love how responsive he is when I press my ass back against his hard length. It earns me a little nip on my bottom lip as he breaks away. I suck it back between my teeth, and he turns me around, reaching for the hem of my dress and dragging it up and off me.

"Look how beautiful you are." Crosby's voice is dark, thick with arousal, matching the predatory gleam in his eyes as he takes in the sight of me. I'm clad only in my matching red satin underwear and black stilettos, but I may as well be naked for the appreciative look crossing Crosby's face.

I don't feel a trace of embarrassment when Crosby delicately directs me to turn around for his inspection. My body feels alive and beautiful as his fingertips connect briefly along my hips before brushing along my shoulders. The hum of satisfaction he gives as I finish my turn emboldens me to reach for the lapels of his blazer. He only lets me pull him a step closer—a firm, bruising kiss delivered to my hot lips before he pulls back again.

"I want my dessert, baby." His hands reach around my back, unhooking the clasp of my bra. With decisive action, he pulls it off, letting it drop to the floor. "Can I have it, Violet? I'm a hungry man."

Crosby's thumbs trace along the elastic of my panties. I take in the look he gives me: pupils blown so wide they almost blot out the beautiful two-toned color of his eyes and flushed cheeks under evening stubble. I lick my lips at the possibility of what it will feel like against the tender flesh of my inner thighs.

I hook my own thumbs into the waist of my underwear and pull it down my legs before he can. Crouched after stepping free of them, I sit back on the mattress, scooting until I'm properly supported. Boldly, I widen my legs, setting the pins of my heels on the comforter to balance, leaning back on my elbows in invitation.

"I'd never want to keep you from a meal."

He takes a moment to remove his blazer before climbing between my parted legs still fully clothed. *Holy shit, that's hot.* The *need* in his face is almost enough to undo me as his eyes reverently glide up my thighs to my pussy. I'm wet and aching for more attention than from just his eyes. One hand follows the same path, skimming along my skin, leaving gooseflesh in its wake, before he hooks it underneath my thigh, his strong grip ensuring I can't close my legs to keep him from his goal.

The press of his lips against my inner thigh sends a jolt through my body. His stubble rasps against my skin in a way that is not wholly unwelcome. It leaves a slight sting as he moves toward my center. I fist the comforter in my hands as he climbs closer and closer to where I want him most.

I throw my head back at the first swipe of Crosby's tongue, my back bowing off the mattress. He responds with several other passes up and down my slit as he situates my legs over his shoulders, his hands both wrapping from underneath to spread me wider.

With me fully exposed, I begin to fade from consciousness, succumbing to the heated ministrations as he works toward my clit. He gently laps the exposed bundle of nerves with the flat of his tongue. When he seals his mouth over it and sucks, I can't help the cry that escapes me.

"Crosby!"

I look down to see his gaze locked on mine, one hand abandoning its post to spread out across my middle to hold me down. It is only then I realize I'm thrusting against his face. I bring my own hands to my breasts, squeezing their fullness and toying with my peaked nipples. Crosby groans at the sight, the sound vibrating through me and pulling a mirrored sound from my own mouth.

"That's it, baby, touch yourself." Crosby kisses my inner thigh gently, a finger from his other hand coming up to touch my wet heat. I gasp at the sensation. A wicked smirk appears on his face as he does it again, angling to tease my opening before moving up and circling my highly sensitive clit. "So wet. So responsive." Crosby drops, sucking at my clit for a moment before looking back up at me. "Give me everything, Violet. I'll spend all night here until I get my fill."

At that, his mouth returns, alternating a steady pattern of flicks with the tip of his tongue and broad strokes with the flat. Coupled with the rhythm he sets with his finger, thrusting almost lazily just inside my entrance, I feel myself barreling toward the edge of a devastatingly powerful orgasm. Especially when he slides a second finger in. Then, a third.

"Fuck," I gasp, my fingers flying to tangle in his curls. They're soft and strong under my grasp. I twist a little when Crosby's fingers slide deeper, hooking slightly to stroke at that soft, sensitive tissue just right. "Oh my God... Crosby, I'm coming!"

My vision goes white, and I can't hear anything for a moment. There's just the blissful suspension of release. It should be a vulnerable state, but even through the haze, I feel the softness of Crosby's lips as he kisses my legs tenderly and the soothing strokes of his hands against my skin. Blindly, I reach out to be met immediately by his own fingers twining with mine.

Crosby guides me through the aftershocks with gentle care and affection. I feel him slip my shoes off as he slides my legs off his shoulders. I open my eyes to him gazing at me with a warmth I've never seen before. My heart flutters in my chest as I let myself bathe in a momentary thought that I'm seeing a reflection of my own feelings. Feelings I've tried in vain to keep from naming, but for a breath, I acknowledge I'm falling irrevocably in love with him.

"You okay?" Crosby crawls up to me, pushing sweaty strands of hair off my face. I give a hum in response, reaching up to thumb at his collar.

"I'm perfect," I answer, curling toward him, propping myself up enough to undo the buttons of his shirt. His eyes flick down to where my fingers move. "Did you get what you wanted?"

"Hmmm," he considers. I push his unbuttoned shirt off his shoulders, appreciating the way his torso flexes and moves, his muscles enhancing the beauty I find in him. "I've always been a greedy boy, so I think I'll be going back for seconds."

"Not until I get mine."

Chapter 24

Crosby

"Let's fucking go! Keep it simple, Bones!" Coach yells from the bench as I charge up my lane, trying to help my wingman get the coverage he needs. "This is our fucking game!" I swiped the puck from Bridger late in the third, passing quickly to Bones who has the most space in the neutral zone. With their defenders pushing too close to our blue line, he's making Miami eat their mistakes as he speeds in the opposite direction toward their net. "Low to high! Low to high! That's it! Fuck yeah! Fuck yeah!"

Charlie lives up to his nickname, surgically putting the puck in the smallest space between the goalie's glove and the post. The buzzer is almost deafening as we swarm him in the corner of the rink.

"That's how you fucking play, baby!" Tex screams, hitting our teammate on his helmet with his glove in celebration. We've gone up by a goal with less than three minutes to play. We all skate over to the bench for a line change. It's time to take a few breaths and suck down some water before we go out one last time when Miami pulls their goalie.

It's two weeks into January, our season well and truly underway. We've sat comfortably near the top of our division for the last month, and every game counts to keep us there. Tonight isn't a divisional matchup, but it is the first time this season we've faced Miami, bringing a different kind of importance. It's been a hell of a media shitstorm leading up to the game with a lot of chatter about facing our former star, which earned more than a few eye rolls from everyone on the team.

Violet was originally tasked with crafting some voiceover video that would have had me acting tough and confrontational, an idea she explained came from Ethan but everyone else hated. I told her I would do it if she needed it, but I was quickly shut down.

"No way are you going to do something like this for me," she says, "I'm not sure it's the best way to convey the narrative of a rivalry—feels really aggressive for social media. Let's just do a scene from 'The Office' with Gus. You can play Jim, he can be Dwight. Gives the same 'rivals vibe' without the shitty take. It'll be fine. Everyone in the department makes changes on the fly, it's okay— Ethan's told us we can."

Miami charges back toward our end, but their passes are getting sloppy. Their right winger manages to hold onto the puck just inside the blue line, and he slaps a shot at the net. Nicky drops into a butterfly, the puck deflecting off his pads, and Miami can't secure any kind of rebound. My team clears it back up toward center ice, and Coach is yelling at us to change.

I jump over the wall as fast as I can, taking in the formation shifts in the players wearing Miami's white and electric teal jerseys. Tex scoops the puck securely against the blade of his stick, deftly maneuvering it away from a Miami defender. He swipes it and spins, sending it in my direction, but his aim and my speed are out of sync. The puck ends up behind me, traveling back toward our zone where Gus has swept it up.

With that, there's enough breathing room for Miami to pull their goalie, adding a sixth attacker to the ice. No whistles mean we're stuck on the ice, and I can just barely see we're near the ninety-second mark.

I twist again, trying to regain some control of my lane, especially now that I have to contend with another skater. Bones is coming up next to me, arcing wide to draw his Miami counterpart with him. I turn, skating backward for a moment to see where the pass will go. Gus slips it to Obie who dekes against a Miami player and shoots it up the ice between his legs back to Tex.

Skating hard from the middle toward Tex's lane, I catch his pass as I cross in front of him. I lift my head to see the empty net, but my teammates are too deep in coverage to pass to. I could take the shot.

I crouch to slap the puck in.

A blurred streak of white and teal in the corner of my eye hurtles itself at me too fast. I can't see who's coming, and there's not enough time to brace for the hit.

There's a blinding pain as I'm smashed against the boards. My head hits first, my helmet making a sickening sound in my ears. The rest of me is crushed, and I crumple to the ice, unable to keep my feet under myself. Blackness seeps in at the edges of my vision. I can't blink it away, even as my eyes pop open, and the air whooshes from my lungs when I hit the ice. The moment of panic as my body struggles to reinflate them is the last thing I remember before the blackness takes over, and I lose sight of everything to the fuzziness.

I hear my name. It swims through a muffled sound, like my ears know what to do, but my brain can't figure out how to make it clear. I try to shake my head, but the tiniest movement makes it feel like I strapped a cement block to it. I can't move without sharp, piercing pain in my skull.

My name is called again. A little clearer, and this time, I think I recognize the voice. It's then I realize everything is black. My eyes must be closed, but I don't remember closing them. I lift my eyelids, something that is oddly difficult. *Why do they feel like they're bench pressing one hundred pounds?* I focus on the feeling, willing my eyes to open. It takes a few tries and some blurry blinks, but I manage to get them to obey my commands.

It is blindingly bright. Suddenly, all my senses seem to come back online at once: I smell the familiar frigid coldness of ice that has a distinctly chemical after scent. The cold is seeping through my jersey and pads, making my skin tingle as it mixes with sweat. I want to shiver to shake it off, but moving that many body parts seems like too big of a challenge after opening my eyes took so long.

I hear my name being called by Coach. My coach. That's right. I was playing a hockey game. The arena is oddly quiet except for concerned murmurs around me and Coach Andrews talking to me. He's hovering just above my head, meaning he isn't speaking loudly, but my head registers it as a shout. I want to get up. Everything about the way I've played this sport for nearly two decades insists on it. But my head is throbbing in a way that is familiar and horrifying at the same time, so I just kind of roll off my side a little, looking up to the source of my name.

"Crosby!" There's relief in his voice. I blink stupidly in response, not sure what else to do. I've never taken a hit like that before. My brain oddly supplies what's happened to me at that exact moment, and all the pain comes with it. "Holy shit. Can you move?"

I offer a groan and try to get my hands under me to sit up. A couple of members of the training staff immediately reach under me and get me to a seated position where I can lean back against the side of the rink. A cacophony of noise almost sends me back to the ground.

Cheers. The crowd is cheering.

"Get me the fuck out of here." I look directly at Coach. He nods at me and starts giving directions. Pain explodes behind my eyes again, and I don't need to ask for anything else before I'm awkwardly lifted to my skates and helpfully shoved toward the bench. I'm surprised I'm moving under my own power as I pass through the back door and into the tunnel, but aside from my head and a little twinge in my right ribs, it seems my body handled the assault well.

I stumble a little as we get into the training room off the locker room. Someone turns the lights off, releasing a little tension in my shoulders. It's much easier to see when there's just light spilling in from the hallway, the pain less intense without the harsh fluorescents above me. The door closing helps shut out the sounds of my team coming back to change. The game must be over.

With some help, I get up on a padded table, the staff taking my gloves and helmet off. I just sit and let them work. Doing too much else hurts. There are questions and exams, imaging with the x-ray machine and more removal of my gear, the pile growing at my feet. *Someone removed my skates, that was nice of them.*

Our team doctor—only known to us as "Doc"—gives me a diagnosis of a concussion and at least two bruised ribs among the other various aches. I think I nod in reply, but my head still feels like a lead ball, so I'm not sure I was effective.

"You're off the ice for at least a week, Crosby," Doc tells me. "Stay home tomorrow, but I want to see you here first thing the day after that. Report every day so we can reevaluate and start you back on some dry land exercises in a couple of days. For the next forty-eight hours, I don't want you doing anything crazy, you hear me? Rest. Minimal screens and lots of sleep."

"You got it, Doc." I grimace as I slide off the table onto my feet. *Fuck, this is going to suck.* I try to bend to pick up my discarded pads.

"Let the equipment guys get them this time," Doc continues as he steps to the door. "You have someone who can come stay with you?"

"Do I need someone to?" I answer, looking at my gear one last time before following him to the open door.

He nods. "It's usually helpful. You're going to feel like shit. Plus, if you lose consciousness again or begin vomiting, you'll need more imaging."

I try to laugh at that and end up groaning. Doc gives me an apologetic smile, walking with me to the locker room. As I reach the threshold and we break apart, I realize it's quiet inside. More time than I realize must have passed during my exam, leaving the place almost empty.

At my locker, I see my helmet on the shelf, my gear bag gone, and a towel for the showers draped across the bench. I pull my phone from the combination safe we have in the back of our units and lower to the wooden bench slowly. It takes a moment for my eyes to focus on the screen without wincing and even longer to get through the messages as I try to follow Doc's orders. THE RUBBER PUCKIES have been busy.

NICKY

Locker room should be empty. Made
sure the rest of the boys cleared out fast.
We've got your gear bag.

TEX

I think everyone was happy to give you the space. And maybe try and catch Bridger in the hall before he made it to the bus.

BONES

What a fucking asshole.

GUS

I'm in the hall. Give a shout if you need something. Then, we'll make sure to get you home when you're ready.

TEX

Allison will be happy to follow us in your car.

BONES

Meals are being delivered for the next three days.

OBIE

I called Violet. She's meeting us at the house.

Emotion clogs my throat. I don't have it in me to type a response, staring at the screen even this long is starting to make my head hurt again, so I send a thumbs up to let them know I read everything. I switch back to the unread messages, quickly picking out Violet's.

SPARKS

I'll be waiting at your place. You can't be alone right now. And I'll be staying until you tell me to go home.

I barely manage to keep myself from responding with *I never want you to go home*. It's a truth I've felt since Christmas, but it isn't the kind of thing to first say over text. I try to take a deep breath, but it hurts enough to draw a grunt from me. I settle on a heart reaction to her message.

The early morning light is gray in my room. It seeps in through the edges of the curtains, painting everything with a light wash that will grow brighter soon enough. But for now, it doesn't permeate the space strongly enough to chase away the lingering night in the stretches of shadows. The push and pull between the dawn and the dark is one of my favorite times of the day, when neither wakefulness nor sleep rule. There's a wistfulness that feels like the remnants of a dream, but unlike when I'm unconscious, I control what happens.

As I roll gingerly to my uninjured side in bed, it feels like I'm still inside a dream when I take in the sight of Violet next to me. She doesn't seem real, the light in the room giving her an ethereal glow.

Her brunette waves spill across the pillow behind her, dripping down to thinly veil the bold print of my last name across her back. The old practice jersey in signature black she pilfered for bed contrasts where it brushes against the skin of her creamy thighs. She's kicked off the covers, curling her legs up against her body and away from me. I carefully lift myself against my pillows to lean enough to catch her face. It isn't in the peaceful state I've become accustomed to waking up next to. There's a slight pinch between her eyebrows as though, even in sleep, she's deep in thought, and her lips are parted around quiet breaths.

When I arrived home, Violet was waiting. She hugged me with care before guiding me into my bathroom and helping me soak in my large tub. There was nothing sexual in the way she stripped my clothes before shedding her own and sliding in behind me. She quietly and diligently worked her small fingers into my aching muscles to ease my body into a temporary state of comfort before helping me climb into bed.

Every time I woke through the night, she was there with the next dose of ibuprofen or acetaminophen and murmured words of reassurance. Violet never complained, waving off my attempts to tell her I was fine, and pointedly dismissed my comment to get some sleep of her own.

I slouch back down in the mountain of downy comfort, content to watch her sleep for a bit, thinking of last night. I've been injured before; in my line of work it's a guaranteed hazard of the job. I've played with a fractured foot, a dislocated pinky, and a few concussions that didn't knock me out. It was never a big deal, and I certainly never asked to have someone look after me.

But not having to ask is different. Having a person fill the need without prompting heals me more than any pill could begin to.

Violet was here.

Is here.

An adorable snort sounds before Violet jerks a little and rolls over to look at me. She's alert, eyes wide with concern, hands reaching out to touch me before she pulls them back to herself and sits up.

"Are you all right?" A loose strand of hair floats down along the side of her face. She's a perfect mess sitting before me, and it makes my heart swell. "Does something hurt, love?"

Now, she does reach for me tenderly, as her quiet endearment shatters me wide open inside. With her warm hand on my cheek, I ignore the pain that rips up my side when I wrap an arm around her and drag her against me.

"Crosby!"

It's a toothless protest. Violet's completely pliant in my hold, all soft curves and gentle breaths. Her blue eyes look up at me, beautiful and sweet, as she waits for what I'll do next.

"I love you." I eagerly watch her eyes widen briefly before they soften at the edges, turning glassy. Her mouth parts, her pink, pillowy lips forming a perfectly round shape before she closes them, and a smile spreads. It turns upward, her cheeks plumping in the apples and blushing beautifully. "I do. I love you. I think I was half in love with you the first time I saw you." I press my forehead against hers, sweeping the hair off her face before holding her between my hands. "The other half fell into place when you told me you didn't date hockey players."

A breathy laugh bubbles up from her before it turns fuller, mixing with my own. Not letting go, I pull back enough to see her face. The blush has mottled a little on her fair skin while twin tears cascade over the full curve of her cheeks. I catch them easily with the pads of my thumbs, cocking my head to assess if she is sad or happy.

"That did me in. I was an absolute goner," I continue. More laughter and a blinding smile from her. "I didn't know why you were against hockey players, and I wasn't sure I really cared. I just knew if you gave me a chance, I would do anything to show you that playing hockey wasn't even half of who I am or what I could offer you. What I will *continue* to offer you, if you'll let me." She smiles again before I press my lips to hers, sealing in my words. Kissing her is different with the depth of my feelings between us.

"I love you, Violet. For all that you are. For the joy you bring. For the kindness you show. For the confident way you won't settle for less because you've learned your worth. For how deeply you care. For how hard you try. For the courage you had to start over again. For taking a chance on me—I think I love you the most for that." I look at her, soft and beautiful in my arms, the morning light turning a gauzy gold around us, and I'm not surprised to feel I want this scene every morning for as long as she'll have me.

"I love you, too."

Her voice is quiet but confident. I ignore the pain in my body and the dull throb in the back of my head to keep her as close as I can hold her. Violet presses her forehead to my sternum, a deep sigh escaping her to fan across my chest. We sit together for what could be hours, breathing each other in until sleep returns.

Chapter 25

Violet

Two days after Crosby's injury, my hand is clasped in his, swinging a little as we walk into The Midnight's practice facility and offices. I stayed with him yesterday, even if it probably wasn't entirely necessary. I know how tough these guys are, but I'm certainly not regretting my choice. I just want to be there for him.

It was a day of floaty feelings, gentle touches, and soft, whispered words of love between naps and meals on the couch. Reading a book with Crosby's head in my lap while he slept felt precious after his early morning confession. I ran my fingers through his hair, trying to memorize the moment. I wasn't sure if it was the concussion talking at first; maybe he was still half asleep. But the more he opened up to me, the more my heart split to welcome the words he was saying.

From the very beginning, there was something effortless about falling for Crosby. Even when I was scared to admit it, terrified I was repeating past mistakes, Crosby has been safe. He's loyal.

Protective. Gentle and understanding in all the ways I've needed. It took little thought to tell him I loved him in return.

This morning, I floated through getting ready at his house, the high of new love permeating every part of me. As desperately as my body craved to show him the depth of how I felt, sex had to take a backseat to healing. Instead, we showered together, exploring each other with unbridled attention, intention weaving through every touch, kissing as often as we breathed. Lost in the steam and the perfect elation of holding nothing back, my body buzzed with the same feelings of a powerful orgasm.

I helped Crosby pick out a thermal long-sleeve and his trusty black joggers, giggling through his protests when I tied his shoes. I found a pair of black skinny jeans in a drawer Crosby had cleared out for me, matching them to one of his well-worn team hoodies, his last name emblazoned just above the curve of my ass. It earned a pained growl from him that had nothing to do with bruised ribs.

"You're really going to walk around the facility with my last name on your back, and I'm just supposed to be relaxed about it?" he grumped, grabbing my hips tightly before walking me against the wall of his bedroom. I couldn't give an answer before his lips crashed into mine possessively, a bruising and heated kiss I can still taste as we enter the lobby.

"Violet!"

We both turn at the sound of my name, Ethan walking quickly toward us while he tucks his phone into his pocket.

"Hey, you two," he greets as he stops before us, turning his attention to Crosby. "Are you feeling alright, man?"

Crosby's shrug is noncommittal. He's here to be evaluated by Doc and line up what his return to play process will look like, it doesn't surprise me he's not forthcoming with any information to the head of the social media department. Ethan doesn't seem bothered, as though his question was more perfunctory than personal.

"Well, hopefully, it's all fast healing." Ethan nods to himself. "You heading upstairs, Vi?"

"Yeah," I answer, turning to Crosby to give him a hug goodbye on his good side. He presses a soft kiss to my forehead.

"I'm going to catch a ride out with one of the guys when morning skate is over," Crosby informs me. I force down my concern, but Crosby hasn't had any worrying symptoms over the last thirty-six hours. I only took one day off, and there's only a couple hours until morning skate is over. I've messaged Gus, and he's promised to hang out with Crosby this afternoon while I work.

With a slight chin raise in farewell to Ethan, Crosby disappears down the hall leading to the locker rooms and physical therapy offices. Alone with my boss, I give a tight smile as we walk to the elevators.

I take in Ethan's furrowed brow and the way his hands are shoved deeply into the pockets of his black chinos. His hair is sticking up a little, as though he's run his hand through it, a vastly different appearance than his usually put-together look. He glances back at me before illuminating the call button on the wall. Silence hangs between us, but there's tension in Ethan's shoulders.

Waiting for the elevator, I consider my boss. He's been a good department head to work for. He runs a fair department, distributing responsibilities in an equal manner, supporting professional development, and generally leaving our personal lives outside the office. I've learned how to succeed in a field I wasn't comfortable working in, and some of that has been through the environment he's created for his employees. The trial and error we've been given space to experiment.

But I haven't missed how there have been subtle shifts over the last few months. Little moments where, despite my personal creative growth and the metric data to back up my performance, Ethan has been frustrated with my work. With me. He hasn't been forthcoming enough to address it, only my intuition seems to indicate a problem. With Ethan's demeanor darkening by the second, that gut feeling tries to tell me that today might finally be the day he says something.

The elevator chimes, brushed chrome doors opening. We walk in together, Ethan pushing the button for our floor. He's staring straight ahead, jaw tight.

"You didn't post the video we discussed before the Portland game," Ethan grinds out before the doors have finished closing, turning pointedly to face me. The look on his face is unlike any I've seen from him before.

"Yeah, it seemed a little aggressive. The players weren't interested in playing into that narrative with Bridger, so I asked them to film something else." I blink back at him, unsure of his reaction to my decision.

"That wasn't your choice to make. I gave you an assignment." Ethan lifts his chin at me. During our weekly Monday meetings with our team, I've seen his irritation when his ideas get outvoted. I've seen his disappointment when the staff doesn't secure a desired player interview. I've even been in the room when our staff is on the receiving end of a stern dressing down when videos don't perform. But I've never observed this indelicate way he's withholding his anger. An anger that is pointedly aimed at me.

"You've let us change things up before, and I was following the players' discretion. They didn't want to make it. I thought the sketch still highlighted the rivalry." An apology is sitting on the tip of my tongue, but confusion keeps it from slipping loose. I fight the urge to cross my arms despite how defensive I feel, knowing it will likely come across wrong.

"Don't tell me your boyfriend wouldn't have done exactly what you asked of him if you just told him to." Ethan steps toward me. I move automatically until I feel the support bar on the side of the elevator at my back. His hand lifts at his side sharply before he seems to control it, lowering it slowly as his fingers curl into a fist. "It was the perfect opportunity for the team to go viral—a foregone conclusion, given the way the game ended last night. Maybe that bump on loverboy's head would have been worth something at least."

I have nowhere to move. Ethan's face, twisted with anger, is mere inches from mine, the invasion of space nearly suffocating. I search his face, past it, around the small space, for what—I'm not sure. But there are clear alarm bells ringing in my head, the overall feeling of *wrongness* growing stronger. Just as the edges of panic claw their way into me, Ethan steps back, and the faint ding of the doors announces our arrival.

"Careful, Vi. *I'm* in charge of you, and no boyfriend or powerful daddy will change that. From now on, what I say goes."

It's a parting shot lobbed at me as the doors open, Ethan sliding between them like oil. I grip the bar at my waist, pulse racing. No one enters the elevator as I take a few shuddering breaths, willing the fear from my system. The doors close again, the lift making a return trip to the lobby. I lean my head back, closing my eyes, counting down from ten. When I reach zero, I open them, the adrenaline waning. I hear the dull ding signaling that the doors have opened.

"Hi, Violet. How's Crosby—" Ava's voice cuts off as she steps into the elevator. I stand a little taller, trying to look unbothered, but she sees through me instantly. With a gentle hand on my arm, she says, "Let's go to my office, shall we?"

Ava's office smells like jasmine, the rich, sweet floral scent tying together with a deeper, earthier undertone. I can't figure it out, but it's familiar. I'm contemplating it from where I'm perched on the gray sofa. The same one I sat on my first day.

"Violet?" Ava calls as she stands in the doorway of her office. She's dressed in black slacks and a brilliant emerald tee. On anyone else, it might look a little casual, but Ava's natural grace and impeccable tailoring make the outfit look refined and powerful. I feel neither of those things as my eyes focus and my brain kicks me back to the present.

"Did you say something?" I ask. With a soft smile, Ava sits gracefully next to me, concern etched at the corners of her eyes.

"I asked how Crosby is doing?"

"Oh, he's sore, and his head hurts off and on. He's down with Doc right now. But if you know anything about hockey players, they'd rather die than admit any weakness." I laugh a little thinking of the way Crosby tried to hide the painful grimace on his face this morning as he tried to tie his shoes before I took over. It's a good distraction, and I latch onto it.

"Physically or otherwise. But it's good for them to have someone there when they finally do," Ava acknowledges with her own knowing smile, patience infusing her words. I'm sure in her time here, she's dealt with her fair share of the man-children on skates. It feels nice to have her understand. A beat passes before she clasps her hands over her knees and looks at me. "What happened this morning, Violet?"

I consider my exchange in the elevator with Ethan. Suddenly, I'm unsure if I should say anything. He was out of line and definitely unprofessional, but maybe there was a reason for it. I made a judgment call, and as my boss, he has every right to question it. He could be facing pressure from the sales department because a missed chance to go viral online can really impact the team financially. A quick search online this morning shows the hit Bridger laid on Crosby was headline news; the former teammates-turned-rivals narrative can be extremely lucrative. *Was I wrong?*

"Hey," Ava gently prompts from beside me. Her palm covers my hands which are beginning to twist in the hem of Crosby's hoodie. I lift my eyes to look at the silent question on her face. She presses her lips together and gives my hands a squeeze. "Start at the beginning. We'll figure it out."

I start with the pre-game content assignment, taking her through my decisions and ending at the confrontation I had with Ethan in the elevator.

"I think I might be overreacting now that I've said all of it out loud." I give an uneasy laugh, tapping my fingers against my lips. "That, or I'm too sensitive from the lack of sleep and worry."

I don't think I believe myself even as I speak. I can still taste the bitter, unexpected, and potent fear of being in an enclosed space with Ethan—a man who already has power over my life, teasing close to the edge of something potentially violent when he lifted his arm for the briefest second. But there's a part of me that wishes I did believe my words. The part that drops my eyes to my lap at Ava's silence that knows how much easier everything would be if I didn't speak up and complain.

"We're not going to do that." Ava's voice is firm. I look up quickly at the demanding tone. She's not angry, but there is fire in her eyes and a determined set to her jaw. "We're not going to fall on the proverbial sword of someone else's bad behavior because we've been taught it only happened because we think *we* caused it."

Ava rises from the couch, irritation clear in her measured strides as she paces. I remain still as I watch her work through her thoughts as she rounds her desk to lean on the back of her chair. Whatever clarity she seeks seems to hit her at once when she sends her chair spinning and returns to the couch next to me.

"Thank you." Ava leans against the back, propping her head on her fist and nodding absently to herself. I sit a little straighter, twisting to face her. "I mean it, Violet. Thank you for telling me."

"I appreciate you listening," I say, waiting for whatever guidance she has to impart. Ava smiles, but it doesn't quite reach her eyes and falls faster than is reassuring.

"Do you want to report this to Human Resources?" Ava asks. I sigh dejectedly. I've been thinking about that since the moment Ava walked me into her office. There were no witnesses. It would be my word against Ethan's. My boss. A tenured employee with status.

"I don't think so." Tears sting at the back of my eyes. I don't like the idea of leaving this unreported, but even with Ava's support during my recounting, I don't think I have it in me to escalate it. I made a mistake in changing the assignment. I can protect myself by doing what I'm supposed to. I clear my throat and press the back of my hands to my cheeks, blotting out the shame.

Chapter 26

Crosby

"I don't like it," Bones says, voice rumbling and thunderous, just like his expression.

"You never like it, but we have to film," Tex counters, stretching his legs out to cross at the ankles on the ottoman in my living room.

"Of course I don't. It makes me fucking uncomfortable. I'm here to play hockey." Bones leans forward on his elbows from his spot in the club chair. "But I'm not talking about the videos. I'm talking about how Vi was treated."

There are general rumblings of agreement from the rest of The Rubber Puckies as I look around the room.

After finishing with Doc, I waited for the guys to finish morning skate. I wish I had been able to pull up the next episode of *Gossip Girl* to pass the time, but I wasn't allowed that much screen time yet per Doc's orders. Using my phone for communication was okay, but it would be another day before I could try to watch anything longer than a few minutes. The rest of Doc's plan already has me a little agitated, but he reminded me that I have only been dealing with my injuries for a couple of days. Thinking positively and acting conservatively would only help my recovery in the long run. Doc emphasized that I'm not allowed any strenuous physical activity for another twenty-four hours, and then I can slowly work on dry land until I'm no longer suffering headaches. The ribs will continue to ache for a few weeks, but not much can be done about them. The concussion is the main concern Doc and the team want to address, and I'm not going to complain about taking care of my head. Even if being off the ice for at least a week is going to suck.

Gus stuck around for a bit after bringing me home, promising to return with reinforcements and dinner in a little while. I'm thankful for my hockey family.

When Violet showed up after work, filling me in on everything that happened with Ethan, I wanted to make her drive me back to the offices so I could get him alone. Show him what it means to be afraid. Violet just shook her head.

"Please don't, Crosby." Tears in her eyes as she lowers herself to the couch.

"Then at least report him, Sparks. Please?" I want to pull her into my arms, but I have been doing that too much since the injury. My ribs protest almost every move I make now. I settle for holding her small hand between mine, rubbing my thumb along her soft skin.

"No." She shakes her head. "It would just make things worse. I like this job—so much more than I ever thought I would. I don't want to lose it. I made a mistake, and while it doesn't excuse the way Ethan handled it, I can make sure I don't make another."

I didn't agree with her, but she looked so defeated, I didn't want to push. She wasn't ready for that. Instead, I convinced her to take a long bath, letting her know the guys were coming over, but she shouldn't feel a need to socialize if she wasn't up to it. As soon as she disappeared and the food was settled, I filled the guys in.

"I think I can make it look like an accident," Obie states, eyes drifting off to some imagined scenario. "The next time he comes down to the rink... pucks go astray all the time."

"No good. He knows you're her best friend," Gus says. He's stretched out on the floor, feet on the arm of Obie's chair. "It has to come from someone he wouldn't suspect."

"We can't physically hurt him. Coach—and Violet—would have our asses," I say. I'm propped up on a pillow on my smaller loveseat under the windows. I can't really extend my legs, but I'm trying to limit my movements in general, so it works. "And I'm not sure who I'm more afraid of in this case."

My comments draw soft laughter from the group before we lapse into silence, each of us thinking about how we can help. Suddenly, Nicky stands from where he was sitting with Tex. He paces a couple of times, all eyes following his movements.

"Natalia's nanny quit yesterday." He looks at all of us. Despite the subject change, we offer up words of sympathy. That has to be the third nanny since training camp who has come and gone from the Baladin household.

"Sorry to hear that, man," I say. Nicky nods. "Any particular reason this time?"

Nicky shakes his head. "Don't know anything for sure. She just said that Natalia stopped speaking to her. Then, she stopped doing what she was told."

"Kids," Gus lobbies unhelpfully from his spot on the floor. "Guess it's back to the agency for a new nanny." Obie gives him a *what the fuck was that* look, but Gus just shrugs. Obie swipes his feet off the chair. I give Obie a subtle chin raise in gratitude for dealing with Gus' behavior. The guy means well, but his timing can be shit.

Nicky grunts in acknowledgment but turns to face me.

"The nanny quit. Not because Natalia threw a temper tantrum but because she silently and strongly protested." A smile spreads across his face. At least, I think it's a smile. Nicky rarely looks anything but focused or mildly pissed off. It takes a second to move past the odd facial expression and process what he's said.

The entire room reaches the same conclusion at the same time.

"Kids," Tex echoes.

"No shit," Gus says, beginning to laugh so hard he has to sit up. "Nicky, your daughter is such a fucking mastermind."

Nicky shuffles back to his spot on the couch. Bones grabs everyone's attention when he starts planning aloud.

"We can't start right away. It will be too suspicious. We stick to business as usual until Wellsy gets back." He taps his fingers on his knees. "But then, we take action. Slowly at first, then we quietly stop doing what Ethan asks of us. We do what Violet says. We can't make the target any bigger on her back."

"We have to tell Violet. I don't want this to negatively impact her," I caution, agreeing that any tampering with her job requirements could end badly for her.

"Tell Violet what?"

Her voice floats in from the entryway. Every head turns to her, and a little flush paints her cheeks. She's in gray sweats and a black tee, messy bun piled on top of her head with the hair near her face sticking against her skin. Her head is tilted slightly in question, but her eyes don't show any signs of suspicion. I love how comfortably my girl fits in with my friends.

"Our diabolical plan to deal with that asshole you have to call a boss," Obie says, opening his arms to her. I should be jealous, but I'm aching more than I'd care to admit tonight, and I can't hold her the way I want to. Even if the desire still flares red hot through me.

She gives me a little smile of understanding before climbing onto the small space of Obie's chair and leaning against him.

"To be fair, it was actually Nicky's idea," Tex tells her.

"Natalia's, if we're giving credit where credit is due," Bones corrects.

"Leave it to the pint-sized puck baby to have a natural ability in passive resistance strategy." Gus leans his head on Violet's knee. She looks down at him for a moment before threading her fingers through his hair, pulling it from the elastic it's secured in. His eyes close, looking exactly like the puppy dog we all know him to be.

"I knew I liked her," Violet says, smiling warmly at Nicky. The twist to his lips says he appreciates it. "Well, let's hear it."

The boys inform her of the mostly complete plan, with Violet only interjecting to add important pieces of advice about fulfilling our contracted agreements for working with team media. She quietly requests that no one mention to her dad what happened. I sense it's because she doesn't want him to step in; it would only make matters worse. There's begrudging agreement around the room. I'm barely keeping my eyes open by the time Violet discusses her own decision to do exactly as she's asked during working hours with us, the dull ache of my head threatening to pull me into sleep.

"We're going to head out." Gus' hand is on my shoulder. I blink up at him, aware that it wasn't just a thought. I fell asleep while my teammates and girlfriend brainstormed.

"Yeah, sure," I say, standing slowly, tamping down the urge to stretch like usual. Violet's suddenly under my arm, wrapping herself around me with care to guide me to the front door, trailing behind the group.

"See you both in the morning?" Tex calls from the driveway, opening his car door.

"You bet. Still have to report. Have a stretching session scheduled and hydrotherapy," I answer.

"Yes. Unfortunately," Violet grumbles from beside me.

"I hate ice baths," Bones comments as he walks past. He steals Violet out from under me, squeezing her tight. "Don't let Ethan get you alone again, you hear?" He pulls back, a serious look on his face. "I don't like that he tried to intimidate you. Never be alone with him. You want everything he says to you to have a witness."

"Okay, Charlie." I don't miss the way Violet's breath hitches a little at his concern, but it makes me happy to see my friends look after her the way I do. She leans in for another hug with him, and our eyes lock over her shoulder. I give him a smile of gratitude, and he just nods once.

"You still coming to the Kansas City game in a couple of days?" Obie's next up while Bones jogs to hop into Tex's car.

"I'll find out if I'm cleared for travel tomorrow," I say, but Obie laughs.

"I was asking Letty."

"I'm scheduled to, so I guess." Violet shrugs her shoulders. "How weird would it be if I went and Crosby stayed here?"

I don't fight the way my lips downturn at the idea. I don't like it, but at least Ethan won't be on the trip. Plus, she's surrounded by my teammates and her dad when we're on the road. There's nothing to worry about except how much I would miss her.

"Lighten up, Wellsy." Gus slaps my injured side. At my sharp intake of breath, he steps back. "No. Shit. Sorry." He reaches forward and rubs out the sting, jostling me a little in the process, which doesn't help matters. Behind him, Violet and Obie smother their laughter with their hands, apologetic eyes wide at me. "I just meant if you aren't cleared, we'll take care of the little flower."

"Don't call me that," Violet groans, eyes lifting as if asking for patience, even though she smiles when Gus stalks toward her.

"But it's true! You're just so little compared to me, and your name is '*Violet*.'" He scoops her up under her knees bridal style and holds her in place. She gives him an unimpressed look before twisting to reach for Obie.

"Why is everyone picking me up tonight? I am a perfectly average-sized woman and fully capable of standing on my own." She lets out a long-suffering sigh. "Get me out of here, and get him home." She wiggles, leaning farther to reach for Obie who helps her out of Gus' hold with ease, setting her on her feet. He throws his arm around Gus, putting him in a headlock, and walks them down the drive to where his car is parked, calling back a farewell.

As the engine fades down the street, I turn to Violet in the quiet of the evening. She's staying with me again tonight, just like she promised, and the thought cuts through the January chill when we walk through my door hand in hand.

Violet

"I know you're missing and worried about Crosby, but I'm not going to complain about having some one-on-one time with my best friend." Obie bumps my shoulder as we sit at the hotel bar in Kansas City, numbing our post-game depression with the Old Fashioneds sitting on the counter before us.

Crosby wasn't cleared by Doc, who expressed concerns about flying with his continued headaches. It was hard to leave him behind so I could complete my work assignment, but I'm glad he wasn't here to watch the 3-0 loss The Midnight endured. When the team made it back to the hotel, Dad gave me a quick hug as he grumbled about new drills for practice once they got back to Connecticut and asked me to run my own stats report on tonight's performance.

"We eat lunch together at least once a week!" I look at Obie, assessing if I've let my closeness with him lapse in favor of my relationship with Crosby. Obie gives a tight smile, and I wrap my arm around him in silent apology before resting my chin on his shoulder. "I'm sorry."

Obie tilts his head, looking sideways at me kindly before he puts his own arm around me. A little press of a kiss on my forehead tells me I'm forgiven.

"Not all of us get to be dick drunk, so I suppose I can let it go and be happy for you," Obie whispers in the small space between us. My shoulders shake with laughter.

"It's more than dick drunk, Obie. I love him. Crosby isn't like anyone I know. He makes me feel so safe and so seen. I've never felt like this, and it should scare me a little, but it doesn't."

"I'm so glad you gave him a chance." He pulls us apart, a genuine smile on his face. "I've just missed you."

"I've missed you, too." I love the warm, comfortable feeling of being with my oldest friend as we pick up our glasses toasting to each other. I slowly sip down the smoky, bitter alcohol, swallowing thickly around the less-than-pleasant taste, and make a mental note not to let Obie pick my drink next time. Surreptitiously, I push the tumbler a little farther away before brightly looking back at Obie. "Give me an update. How's life?"

Obie considers my question, running his fingers through his black hair. It dried at funny little angles after his shower at the arena, it reminds me of when we were kids. His green eyes catch the light reflecting off the bottles behind the bar, giving him a mischievous look, even though the words he says are serious.

"I'm really glad I came back here to play. Having Cal at my back is something I didn't know I needed. And the team—these guys feel like home." I love the way he reflects on the last six months, positive memories overriding years of professional but distant interactions with his team in Los Angeles.

"I love that. I'm so happy for you." I grip his hand with mine, his larger fingers squeezing in return. Next to my glass, my phone lights up with a text notification.

"That Crosby?" Obie gestures with his chin. I glance to confirm, my smile growing.

"He can wait." I flip my phone over. "I promised him I'd call once I was getting into bed, but I'm sure he'll be asleep."

Obie smirks. "God bless technology, right?"

I shove at him, joining in with my own laugh, even if some heat rises in my cheeks.

"He's injured. I just wanted to tell him good night!"

"Letty. The man's hands work just fine. He won't want to just say good night," Obie deadpans. "Besides, a side effect of concussions can be increased libido. You want to take care of him, right?"

"Oh my God." I smother my face in my hands as Obie continues laughing loudly next to me.

"What's so funny?" I look up to see Gus standing in the open spot on Obie's other side. His hair is down, brushing at the top of his shoulders, and he's swapped his suit for jeans and a long sleeve. He has his hands buried in his pockets as he rocks back on his heels. "Hi, little flower."

"I was explaining to Letty one of the less reported side effects of a concussion." Obie waggles his eyebrows. Gus' face scrunches as he considers what Obie isn't saying out loud, then his own eyes widen, and he gives a few enthusiastic nods.

"Oh, yeah. The sex thing. It's wild; you can become completely disinterested in it for a while, or you suddenly want nothing but." He climbs on the empty barstool, leaning comfortably on the counter toward me. "Best threesome of my life came in the wake of my last one. Probably not worth the headaches again, though."

Obie's shoulders shake with laughter as he regards his teammate. Gus just shrugs but gives me a playful wink. Sometimes, I think Gus plays up the carefree playboy image fans have cultivated for him online, when really he's pretty low-key and sweet.

"I think that's all for me tonight," I announce as I hop off my barstool. I lean in and kiss Obie's cheek before leaning forward to blow an air kiss at Gus. He catches it and presses a palm to his own cheek, batting his eyelashes.

"You didn't finish your drink," he says, pointing down at the nearly full tumbler.

"All yours, big guy." I slide it down the bar. Obie gives me a flat look, trying to hide his offense at my rejection of his preferred drink. I lift a shoulder. "You two behave yourselves."

"Only if you do," Obie answers.

"I'm going to my room." I pop a hip, securing my hand on it, feigning an attitude I don't really have.

"To FaceTime your boyfriend goodnight." Obie lifts his wrist, consulting his watch. "When it's nearly 1:00 a.m. for him."

"I promised. I'll be surprised if he's even up." I know it's a lie as soon as I say it.

"Oh, he's up." Gus chuckles into the glass he raises to his lips. Obie smirks again. I spin on my heel, throwing a hand in the air and an exasperated goodnight over my shoulder.

ME

I'm heading up to my room. Are you still awake?

I send the text after hitting the button for my floor. The answer comes before the elevator doors close.

MORE THAN A HOCKEY PLAYER

Yes

ME

I thought you'd be asleep. You're supposed to be resting. Just because you have your screen privileges back doesn't mean you should stay awake all night rewatching Lord of the Rings for the twentieth time.

MORE THAN A HOCKEY PLAYER

It's a comfort movie. It's soothing.

ME

Oh, yeah. The screams of the Nazgûl are such an amazing lullaby.

MORE THAN A HOCKEY PLAYER

You say all the sexy things, baby.

ME

But seriously, you're not tired?

MORE THAN A HOCKEY PLAYER

Honestly, if anything, I feel really awake. Kind of restless. Been this way for a day or so.

The elevator chimes. I walk down the hall, pulling my keycard from the front pouch of my purse. As soon as the door closes, I secure the deadbolt and flip the swing bar before throwing my purse on the desk next to my laptop. My conversation with Obie and Gus replays through my head as I brush my teeth and wash off my makeup.

ME

Still want me to call?

MORE THAN A HOCKEY PLAYER

Of course I do. I'm not too proud to admit I've been a mopey son of a bitch today without being able to touch you.

I laugh as I pull on the oversized Midnight shirt I swiped from Crosby's closet and open my laptop, settling it on the bed next to me. I initiate the FaceTime call, not surprised when Crosby connects barely a second after the chime starts.

"Hey, you," he says. His camera is sitting on the nightstand, but he's moved down from the headboard to be more directly in front of it, propped up on his elbows, leaning off his uninjured side. The curls of his hair are a little more haphazard, as though they dried after a shower while he was napping. The weary dark circles that had been under his multicolored eyes have waned, and I love how there's a little crinkle at the corner of them as he smiles at me.

"Hi," I answer. With my laptop near the foot of the bed, I lean back against the pillows comfortably. I like how his eyes move, clearly tracing the expanse of my bare legs, and the heat behind them makes it feel like a caress.

"No wonder I couldn't find my favorite shirt to sleep in tonight. You look good in it, Sparks."

"This old thing?" I toy with the hem, letting it ride up over my hip. I trace my fingers along the seam of my panties, barely flashing the pale blue lace.

Crosby groans, his gaze intensifying, as he flips fully over to his side. It gives me a beautiful view of his trimmed and defined torso, left bare by my thievery. His favorite black joggers rest low along his hips, untied and gaping away from his skin where the faint cut of his Adonis belt directs my eyes lower to the bulge of where his cock rests.

I let out a breathy sigh. *I guess I've missed touching him today, too.*

"See something you like?" His voice, pitched low and gravelly, pulls me from my wayward thoughts, refocusing my attention on his face. There's a teasing smirk on his lips, but his eyes are full of mirth.

"Not anything I can't be patient for," I tell him, rolling to my side to mirror him, dragging the computer up the bed.

"I have headaches and a bruised side. You want me, you can still have me, baby." Crosby skims his hand down his abs over his sweats to grip himself and rub his cock. His pupils expand, the black blotting out his hazel and green, desire eclipsing the usual warmth. I follow his hand as it lifts, fingertips dipping just below the waistband, moving back and forth. My nipples tighten below the fabric of the soft shirt, every movement creating sweet friction as I weigh the choice before me.

"Are you sure you feel okay?" My own hands are rubbing up and down my thighs, skating closer and closer to the trim on the bottom of my panties.

"I'm about to feel a hell of a lot better." He laughs, the sound jagged as he reaches inside his sweats to stroke himself. "Now show me, Violet. I want to see how wet this is making you."

With a little quick thinking, the laptop is set on a pillow near the foot of the bed, lifting Crosby's view higher and in between my legs. I sit straighter against the headboard before spreading my legs apart to show the damp spot that has formed in the center of my panties.

"So pretty," Crosby purrs through the screen. He adjusts the camera, setting it so that I have a broader view of him from his face to his thighs. He lays back against his own pillows, hooking his thumbs into the waistband of his sweats and pulling down, kicking them off at the ankles. "Are you going to pull the lace to the side so I can watch that pussy glisten while I stroke my cock?"

"Jesus, Crosby." I'm frozen in place while his words burn under my skin. Crosby's a vocal lover but never like this, and something about it fills me with the confidence to do what he asks. I drift a hand down to my heated center, applying slight pressure as I glide past my clit, and let a finger pull the fabric over to one side, exposing myself to him.

"That's good, baby," he says, his hand working up and down his hard shaft in long, firm passes. His other arm hooks up behind his head, elongating his body to show off every ridge and valley of his hard work. I moan, dipping a finger into my wetness before dragging it up to circle around my clit. The light touch already has me building quickly to release. "Yes, just like that." His wrist twists a little on the downstroke, drawing a pleasured grunt from his parted lips. "Wish those were my fingers right now. Or my tongue. Miss how you taste."

Matching his movements, I push two fingers inside, breath catching at the slight stretch. To ease it, I use my other hand to tweak my hard nipples, distracting me as I begin to thrust in and out. I throw my head back as the familiar tendrils of my release begin to coil deep in my center.

"No, no, no, let me see your face," Crosby's command comes out rough, strained, as he leans closer to the camera. "Want to watch."

My rhythm increases, and I keep my eyes on Crosby's. His hand is a blur near the side of the screen, and his breathing becomes harder. Seeing him close to the edge brings mine within reach.

"Crosby," I gasp, abandoning my breasts to rub circles around my clit. "I'm close."

"Fuck, baby." Another moan. Longer. Louder. "Going to make me come seeing you like this."

His words are my undoing. A final few thrusts of my drenched fingers and the sharp pressure to my sensitive clit has my pulse pounding in my ears, just as Crosby's body goes rigid with a stran- gled noise parting his lips. My own gasp dwindles into a loud groan at the sight of his cum shooting up over his hand to paint his lower abdomen. The sound of my name repeats in a reverent chant as he works himself through it.

Slowly, I draw my fingers out, chest heaving from the aftershocks. I strip my ruined panties off, wiping my fingers on them before tossing them aside. My legs shake as I twist around and settle on my side, moving the laptop closer to my face. Crosby reaches beyond his camera for a few tissues to clean up and find his sweats. Tucking my hand under my head, I curl toward him, noticing the wince cross his face as he pulls the joggers back into place.

"Are you okay?"

"I'm good." He brings his camera close to his face so I can see him. His pupils have receded, and the hazel and green halves of his eyes sparkle with love. "Was that all right? You're okay, too?"

"Yeah." I smile, bliss floating through my veins. "I've never done something like that before."

"Me neither, but I'm putting it into rotation the next time I'm away without you." The chuckle that rumbles from his chest is a warm, comforting sound. I release an airy laugh in return.

"I'd be okay with that. Maybe I'll finally buy some toys. Pretend one of them is you." I lift my eyebrows at him, and he looks up to the ceiling.

"Fuck, you're going to make me want to go again."

"Then it will be a solo mission. I'm spent." I wiggle down into the comforter. "But if you really have that kind of drive, I think you settled a debate I was having with Obie and Gus earlier."

"Oh?" he asks, a yawn breaking across his face, a sleepy smile falling into place in its wake. "What was it about?"

"They said sometimes concussions result in higher libidos." I lift the corner of my mouth in a prompting smirk.

"Can't say this had anything to do with a hit to the head,

Sparks. This had everything to do with how much I love you and how much it's killing me to be here and have you there."

The bliss I've been resting in skyrockets to euphoria at his words. Being with Crosby is more than I ever believed I was allowed to want. My cheeks heat with a blush I'm surprised he still brings out of me.

"I love you, too. I can't wait to come home."

"I'll be waiting for you this time," he tells me, clicking off his bedside lamp and setting the camera down again. His face is painted in a bluish glow, and he sighs happily as he gets comfortable against the pillows. I roll over to shut off my own lamp and just gaze into the face of the man I love.

I wake to a laptop with a dead battery and a text on my phone.

MORE THAN A HOCKEY PLAYER

You sound like the Nazgûl when you snore. It was the perfect way to fall asleep. 🤍

Chapter 28

Crosby

"This is your first All-Stars appearance, and you're coming off an injury. How are you feeling being here?"

I take a second to consider the question Tara Upton—reporter for *Center Ice*—is asking. She flashes a bright smile in the glow of the lights of this makeshift studio, set up in the ballroom of The Majestic where press is taking place for the weekend. She's my first interview of the day, and I know I'm going to get this question a lot, but I can't answer it until we address something else.

"I'm going to answer you, but I would feel absolutely awful if I didn't let you know there is a little lipstick on your teeth. Do you want to take care of it, and then we can start over?" I look around the space, past the cameras to where the crew stands. "Anyone have a tissue back there and a mirror?"

Tara flushes furiously as a makeup artist walks quickly to her with the necessary things to address the problem. Once they both feel her sparkling white teeth are unblemished, Tara reaches across the space to tap my hand with a genuine smile on her face.

"Thank you," she says before settling back into the uncomfortable upright stools they have us perched on. "I don't think anyone has ever done something like that for me. It was honestly so refreshing. I would much rather have a second of embarrassment than the rest of my career be a barrage of TikToks dedicated to a lipstick smile."

"Sure," I reply.

Tara's good at her job. She's personable and professional, asking the same questions as her male contemporaries but with an added kindness. But I've seen how some players in the league still easily dismiss her because she's a woman in sports and takes a couple of extra minutes to fix her hair before the cameras roll. It's not her problem that society cares more about how she looks than what she asks, while I'm afforded the privilege of looking like I rolled out of bed, barely stringing five words together. I can still make the highlight reel because I'm a man who hits a frozen rubber disk with a stick for a living.

"Ready to go again?" she asks, looking around at the crew.

"We've been filming the whole time," the segment producer calls back. "That's going to be brilliant."

"Oh." Tara smiles again. "Better make this count, then."

She seems to like that what could have been a blunder is going to turn into gold. I clear my throat in an attempt to move things along since I have three more interviews before I can get to the arena. Today is media day, full of interviews, photos, and a brief practice in the arena. Tomorrow is the skills competition, which I'm not participating in but will attend, and Sunday starts the three-on-three tournament. Sandwiched in there are a couple more media commitments and time with Violet and the members of my team who came out to support me. Tonight, we're all going to dinner in celebration of the halfway point of the season.

With a quick breath, Tara gives me a dip of her chin and

launches into her question with repetitive ease. "This is your first All-Stars appearance, and you're coming off an injury. How are you feeling being here?"

"Having the opportunity to come represent The Midnight feels great. I certainly wasn't expecting it." I think of Tex's smile when Coach announced I would be going to Vegas for the weekend. Before I could question it or feel guilty, Tex threw an arm around me, telling me he was proud of me and he'd be cheering me on. "I'm excited to participate and show the fans they made the right choice. I've had an excellent predecessor in Henri Texier for the last few years, and he's been really supportive. I'm glad we're here together."

"And how was the recovery? You missed a week of games and scratched for another week. We've only seen you on the ice for one game, which resulted in a loss. Seems like there was a delay to get you back to play."

"I'm grateful for our team's medical staff. They take head injuries seriously, and as much as I was willing to lace up my skates and play the next day, I think it's really important to take the advice of medical professionals. They wanted to ensure I wouldn't be doing anything that would cause further injury or result in lasting damage." I pause. I've gone over and over this answer in my head and with Coach and Ava for the last week. "As far as the delay in my return, I wanted to make sure I was at my best again. Our team has worked hard this season to experience the success we have in this first half. That shouldn't be put in jeopardy because one person is eager."

I let out a light laugh, hoping to soften my answer and detract a little attention. Tara nods good-naturedly.

I hated sitting on the bench, watching the guys play their guts out, and losing when I finally did make it back on the ice was brutal. But Doc didn't like that my headaches hadn't fully gone away after I'd practiced. It was frustrating that it was out of my control, but I had never suffered a concussion so severe. I had to trust that I wasn't being held back without reason. The extra time helped. My headaches have cleared, and even my ribs have healed to the point that taking a hit doesn't feel like I'm dying.

I felt strong and focused on Tuesday night when we played Baltimore. I'm glad to have the last few weeks behind me. Except for how it brought Violet and me even closer together.

More of her clothes have moved into my closet and dresser.

Her toothbrush sits next to mine on the counter.

There's a gaudy coffee mug in the kitchen full of British iconography, and I make sure it has an Americano in it every morning when we're home together.

I know she's spent the nights we've had away games back at her place, but she's always at mine when I get back.

The only way it could be better is if it were permanent.

"Well, I think there will be quite a few eyes on you this weekend to see just how back to form you are and where you can take The Midnight in the next half of the season."

"It won't just be me who takes us even further after this break," I counter. It makes me cringe every time the media's narrative insists I don't have a full team of capable, talented people behind me.

"Of course," Tara replies with a smile on her face. "Before I let you go, I couldn't miss the opportunity to ask about your new relationship. Any conflicts of interest there?"

The neutral smile I've held the entire interview slips from my face for a moment when I press my lips together. Instead of the professional upturn of my lips, they pulse quickly in a painful smile. I squeeze my hands together.

For nearly two months, Violet and I have been open about our relationship. We haven't hidden anything, but we don't tend to go to public places that could draw unnecessary attention. This is the first time anyone in the media has directly asked about it.

I think of Coach's office. The impersonal gray walls and empty desk.

I think of how far he went to protect her from the media when she was little.

I think of Violet's reluctance to reveal their connection at first.

I take a deep breath before I answer, buying time to craft my response carefully.

"I've worked to keep the focus of the media on my time on the ice, what I contribute to my team, and even where I fall short as a player. I can address questions about those topics comfortably. But my personal life isn't a topic I'm willing to contribute to in a public forum. I might not choose to hide who I'm involved with, but aside from expressing my happiness at being with a woman of her character, I won't say more."

"So, being involved with your Coach's daughter hasn't resulted in preferential treatment?"

"I think you already have your viral moment, Tara." I give her a tight smile and see the moment she realizes the interview is over.

"Best of luck with the tournament, Crosby. It's great to have you back on the ice."

"Ethan has not stopped blowing up my phone since that video of you with Tara Upton dropped an hour ago. I told him that tonight is for the players, no outside media allowed at a private function. We're just having dinner," Violet calls from the bedroom of our hotel suite. I'm in the sitting area, dodging my own messages from the head of our social media department, begging me to call him. I swipe to clear another as a knock comes from the door.

"Sounds like we've got company. Are you decent?" I stand from the couch, pulling the sleeves of my button down through the suit jacket, adjusting the cufflinks a little.

"You tell me."

I lift my head as Violet leans against the doorframe. She's all long lines with the strappy heels at her feet and the arm extended up the side in a sassy pose. She has on a fitted two-piece outfit in a purple vibrant enough to honor her name. The crop top flashes a hint of skin above the high waist of a slim, fitted skirt. She's covered modestly, but the tight fit shows off her curves and has me detouring from my path to the door.

In a few strides, I crowd her up against the doorframe, leaning close to run my nose up the length of her neck, breathing in the intoxicating summer scent she wears. One hand grips her hip, my thumb reaching up to brush the teasing flash of skin there, while the other leans next to her head, caging her in. When she sucks in a breath, her breasts brush against my chest before her exhale comes out uneven.

"You're gorgeous." I press a kiss below her ear, tasting the soft and tender flesh. "But the thoughts this outfit gives me are definitely of the *indecent* variety."

I pull back to look down into her eyes, the silver flecks reflecting the light in a dazzling display. Her chin lifts up, angling as I bring my lips to hers.

"Wellsy! Open the damn door, I need to pee!"

I drop my head to Violet's shoulder that's shaking with laughter to match my own. I look back up to see her eyes pinched in the corners as she smiles wide.

"Gus," we say in unison.

I press a chaste kiss to her crimson lips, careful not to smudge her lipstick, and turn for the door. I open it to reveal my best friend hopping back and forth before he gives my shoulder a slap and beelines for the bathroom. Tex and Allison follow him inside the suite with Obie and Bones bringing up the rear.

"I thought we had him trained to go before he leaves the house," Violet says to the group as she gives Allison a hug. Everyone laughs, settling into various spots around the sitting room. I take a moment to feel the warmth bloom in my chest that they all came out to support me this weekend.

The bathroom door opens, and a relieved-looking Gus exits.

"I didn't account for standing around for ten minutes at your door." He levels me with a narrowed gaze, eyes scanning up and down, looking for evidence of what caused the delay. I flick my eyes to Violet in explanation.

"Your room is two floors down. Why didn't you just go before you got on the elevator?" Bones asks. Violet has made her way over to him to say hello, and he's immediately tucked her into his side. Before this season, Bones barely spoke unless spoken to; he was quiet and reserved. He still is with anyone he doesn't know or like, but something about Violet has brought him out of his shell. He's exceedingly protective of her, and she's taken on a big sister role with him.

"Wanted to see if this bathroom was any better than mine. It's the fanciest room I think Wellsy's ever sprung for." Gus shrugs, like evaluating hotel bathrooms is entirely normal behavior.

"And?" Obie prompts.

"It's not," Gus replies, walking around and looking curiously through the door to the bedroom. He turns back to the group, hooking a thumb over his shoulder. "But that is. Damn."

"What time is the reservation? We should probably order the Ubers." Allison saves us from the rest of Gus' room inspection, and I shoot her a grateful smile. She's already pulled her phone out, arranging for transportation to the restaurant. Tex presses a kiss to the top of her head before leading everyone back to the door with practiced efficiency.

I pick up Violet's clutch from the end table as she walks out the door engrossed in a discussion with Bones. I pass it to her as we fill the elevator. She slips her other hand in mine, leaning sweetly against my arm as the chime announces the lobby.

Our walk through the lobby is interrupted a few times by various people stopping to ask for pictures or autographs. Allison and Violet eventually break off together to walk faster and claim our ride shares, while the rest of the guys and I stop for a kid with his family near the entrance.

Giving one last high five to the young fan, I stand to catch up with everyone else. Violet is at the curb, laughing at something Allison says. Her brown hair is pulled into a high ponytail, the curled ends swaying down past her shoulders as her head tips back. I pause a moment to take in the sight of her: beautiful, carefree, and happy.

Gus slings an arm around my shoulders, leaning in to keep his words between us.

"She's something else, Crosby. I'm really happy for you."

"Thanks, man." I reach my own arm around to squeeze his shoulder. "If I'm lucky, she'll want to stick around for a long, long time."

Chapter 29

Violet

"Wait, wait, wait. *That's* why your parent-teacher conferences always involved Principal Marshall?" Obie looks truly gobsmacked next to me, while our friends continue to laugh around the table.

"I think once your third grade teacher hits on your Dad, it kind of becomes necessary." I look at him as I take another sip of sweet red wine.

"I didn't know Miss Thomas had it in her." Obie shakes his head. "Wow."

The laughter dies down as dessert is served. It's been an evening of good food and good conversation centered around the accomplishments of the team, celebratory and joyful. Nearly everyone is here; the most notable absences—that of Nicky and my dad—make sense. This is the only break in the season my dad gets until it's over, and he's always used it to practically barricade himself at home. He likes to tackle all the little home projects he swears he can't hire out. Nicky chose to stay home with Natalia, deeming Las Vegas a city he doesn't want her exposed to until he's too old to remember what it's like.

Crosby has kept a hand on my thigh nearly all night unless his arm has been draped over the back of my chair like it is now. His fingers play in the ends of my hair before sliding down to ghost across the skin exposed between my top and skirt. This outfit made him look at me with a feral energy, as if he was one second away from taking me against the doorframe. I don't think I would have complained. Even now, it's difficult not to press back into his hand and sink into the idea of something else sinking into me.

Henri clears his throat, standing for a moment. Our table is in a secluded corner of the high-end Italian restaurant, affording our group a tremendous amount of privacy. The captain waits a moment before he fixes his eyes on Crosby, lifting his tumbler of amber liquid in the air.

"To Wellsy," he begins. I turn to see Crosby's face still, focused on his captain. "We're so proud of how hard you've worked—not only this season but for years—to have this kind of attention. It would have been easy to stop challenging yourself and become comfortable, especially after last season. Instead, you've pushed forward to become one of the best players in the game right now." Crosby's lips twist, a quiet acknowledgment of the words before he dips his head to look at the tiramisu in front of him. Henri initiates the lifting of our glasses in a toast. We all follow, drinking and cheering. Henri remains standing, and our attention is once again on him to continue.

"But it isn't just what you've brought to the ice that makes you worth celebrating. You're a good teammate... but you're a hell of a good man. I'm glad to know the guys will always have someone to look up to."

Crosby's head snaps up, and I whip my head back to Henri. He laces his fingers with Allison, who gives him a little nod, and turns to offer a watery smile to the group. He looks around the table at each of his teammates.

"I won't announce it publicly for a while, but I am going to retire this year whenever our season is over."

There are little gasps from the guys, and Crosby pinches his lips together before gripping my hand. He's working to hold back the emotion the announcement brings, so I soothe a thumb over the back of our clasped hands, hoping he understands it's okay.

"I've been thinking about it, but we got some news that made the decision for me." Henri smiles broadly before looking at Allison again. "We're going to be parents. Allison is pregnant!"

The table erupts in surprised cheers. Bones reaches the couple first, shaking Henri's hand and gingerly offering a hug to Allison. Then Obie is there, hugging them both, barely releasing them before Gus takes over.

"This is the only way I want to become an uncle!" he boasts as everyone laughs. I can barely hear the lecture Obie starts in about how Gus won't get to control his sister's life.

Crosby and I round the table last, where I give a quick hug to Henri as Crosby brushes a kiss on Allison's cheek. We switch places, and I shuffle Allison and myself a little further away as the boys hug each other tightly. The tears Crosby held back leak out of the corners of his eyes, the reason entirely different now, and I'm so thankful this news will rewrite how he remembers this evening.

I hold Allison's hands, looking at her face for a moment.

"There's so much excitement in here right now, but how are you feeling about it?" I ask. She blinks back at me for a moment in surprise. "It's a huge change, and if no one else has said, it's okay to feel more than one thing. Even if everyone around you is thrilled, I'd rather take my cue from you."

"Oh, Vi." Allison pulls me in for a quick hug. "I promise I'm ecstatic, but that is the most thoughtful response I've had so far. It really is overwhelming."

"If you're happy, I'm happy for you!" I tell her, hugging her tightly once more.

It takes more than ten minutes for everyone to settle back in their seats, the energy of the group buzzing with excitement and questions for the soon-to-be parents. There's a shuffling of seats, Gus sneaking in next to me while Obie grumbles.

"I've been meaning to ask," Allison says as things die down. "How has the quiet resistance movement been going? Henri told me about the boss and how he treated Vi."

"It's been fucking amazing," Gus answers. "Vi keeps doing everything she's supposed to, but every time we get a new request from the douchebag, we've all slowly been declining."

"And he hasn't been suspicious or giving you shit for it?" Allison asks, looking at me. I shrug.

"Ethan's definitely beginning to get frustrated. Monday Morning Meet-ups for the department have become tense, and I think he'd like to blame me. But I've continued to do exactly what he asks, down to the very punctuation in the captions on the accounts. The numbers on those posts can't reflect my ability, only on his ideas, and he's getting pissed. Having the team slowly turn down his requests is just making it harder for him. He's kind of stuck because the players are following their contracts, and I'm doing my job, but he's feeling the pressure." Crosby's hand is back on my thigh, a squeeze of encouragement.

"Brilliant little disrupter." Gus beams at me.

"I'm trying *not* to disrupt things, Gus. I want to keep my job." I sigh. "I just want to be able to do it without fear."

"What an asshole." Allison blows a breath between her lips. "Are you sure you shouldn't report him for what happened?"

Crosby collects me around the waist, pulling me closer to him protectively as though Ethan were standing in the room with us. "No, I don't think it would help. My dad got me the interview—maybe even helped secure the job, I don't know—and Ethan's clearly been struggling with that favoritism. I can't open an inquiry like this without it feeding into that idea. I think his anger is doing enough right now. It's clouding his judgment in making decisions for the department."

"Giving him enough rope and all that?" Allison nods. I bob my head in agreement. I've had to put faith in the idea that if Ethan is as stubborn as I think he is, he'll find a way to fail on his own—without taking me with him.

The skills competition might be my favorite part of All-Star Weekend. During his appearances, Dad only did the skills competition once, but he said it was the most fun he's ever had.

As I sit in the section of the arena designated for players and their guests, I see why he loved it so much. The crowd is supportive and slightly unhinged as they cheer on every player, team designation not factoring in as much as usual. Everyone wants to see the best of the best, even if it might come from their biggest rival.

Crosby is yelling next to me, cheering on his counterpart from Kansas City. His face is lit up with joy, eyes flicking back and forth at what's happening on the ice, but he keeps an arm tightly wrapped around my waist as we stand with everyone else losing their minds at the talent of the veteran center. I can't help but lean a little into Crosby's side, safe and content in his presence. As the group on the ice readies for the next segment, he looks down at me.

The Midnight hat he wears shadows his eyes a little in the arena lighting, but his smile is impossible to hide.

"Hey there," he says, squeezing my side. He tips his head down toward me and then pauses. He reaches up with his other hand, quickly turning the hat backward before finishing his journey to my lips, where he presses the sweetest kiss on them. When he straightens, he leaves the hat backward, and butterflies dance in my stomach.

An official announcement comes over the loudspeaker, informing the crowd of the change of standings for the competitors between events. The KC center has pulled into first, eliciting a deafening roar from the majority of the fans.

"Fuck yeah, Matty!" Crosby shouts, pumping his free hand in the air. I clap, happy to see Matt Dempsey is still proving why he has the Conn Smythe *and* Hart trophies for top player in his tenure. "I want to be like him when I grow up," Crosby jokes in my ear.

"I don't think that's unrealistic if you keep playing the way you have been," I tell him, wrapping both of my arms around him. "Your stats have done nothing but improve this season. You've always been good, but something changed this year. Whatever's gotten under your skin has been good for you."

His lips sink against the top of my head. Once. Twice.

"What if I said it was you?" His breath is hot against the side of my neck as he dips to whisper in my ear. Suddenly, despite being in an arena of 20,000 people, no one else exists except for him. I twist a little to catch a glimpse of the sincerity in his eyes. "I mean it, Sparks. What if it's you?"

"I'd say that's a difficult correlation to statistically track."

"Maybe we'll need a few more seasons' worth of data."

The butterflies skitter through my body, heat fanning the beating of their wings, and the only way I can contain their impending escape is to bury myself into Crosby's chest. The spicy sandalwood and crisp citrus scent he always wears fills my senses, and I try to float away on the feeling.

"I think I'd like that," I tell him when I break my face away, tipping my head almost all the way back to look up at him. Without the brim of the hat blocking them, I see how his eyes brighten with joy. The green parts appear like chipped jewels, while the hazel glows like warm embers against them. I reign in my composure, a mock-serious expression as I purse my lips. "It would be for mathematical accuracy, of course."

"Of course." He kisses me again before holding me tightly against him, turning us to watch the ice once more.

"Violet Cameron?" the accented voice calls clearly from the aisle next to me. A tall and slight man with white blonde hair and crystal blue eyes stands two steps down in a three-piece suit.

Anders Lasch.

My stomach drops at the sight of my former boss—and Olivier's agent—closing the distance between us with a flat but professional smile on his face. He slips his phone into his pocket as he draws level with the end of the row we're seated in. He lifts his arms slightly in a welcoming hug.

"Anders," I acknowledge without stepping into his embrace. He doesn't show any signs of offense. Merely drops one arm as he reaches a hand across me toward Crosby, who has stiffened behind me.

"Anders Lasch," he offers by way of introduction. Crosby politely shakes his hand.

"Crosby Wells." I see the way they both squeeze firmly, Anders pulling back first. I want to smirk but quickly rearrange my features to be impassive.

"Violet worked for me in London." He looks down at me, a flash of white teeth before ignoring me to speak to Crosby. "Did some excellent things in 'client relations.' I see her methods have improved, too."

Crosby's arm tightens around me, his fingers curling into a fist against my hip, not missing the insulation dripping through Anders' congenial statement. Before anyone can say anything else, Olivier climbs the stairs behind Anders. His features morph from indifferent to wolfish as he looks at me, then darken when he looks over my shoulder to Crosby.

"Wells." Olivier lifts his chin.

"Ahlman." Crosby's voice is as tight as his grip on me. "Didn't realize you'd been invited this weekend."

"Last-minute alternate." Olivier's smile looks painful as he tries to make it believable. Anders leans back to speak in his ear, checking his phone. Olivier nods and continues up the stairs, calling over his shoulder, "See you on the ice."

"And at the reception tonight, yes?" Anders does a better job of sounding friendly. It makes my skin crawl. "It will be good to catch up."

Chapter 30

Crosby

"I'll support whatever decision you make," I say.

Violet is sitting on the end of our bed in the fluffy hotel robe, hair artfully pinned to her head in swirls and curls. Her makeup is almost completely finished, but she emerged from the bathroom ten minutes ago to sit down and watch me put my suit on. She hasn't said much since we made it back from the skills competition. I kneel in front of her, running my hands up her thighs, dipping my chin to look up into her eyes. They're flat and closed off when she locks them on mine.

"You have to go." She cradles my cheek, an absent brush of her thumb against the skin there before it drops. "Even before you were trending on every platform, it's expected that the invited attendees would go to the reception."

"But if it makes you uncomfortable to be there, I'm sure we can call our friends, and they would come up here to keep you company until I've shaken the hands and kissed the asses I need to. Tex has managed to bow out." I lift the corner of my mouth in a half grin. I get one back before a shove on the shoulder.

"Because Allison isn't feeling well. You're the only other Midnight player here, you really have to go. Do you think we'll have to see them?" Violet asks, voice smaller than usual.

"I'd love to tell you we won't, but I don't know," I tell her honestly. "If it's like any other event the NHL throws, it's likely we'll see them. I'm just hoping the celebratory atmosphere and media presence will keep everyone on their best behavior."

"Even you?"

"I can try." I cradle her face in my hand. She looks so small in my hold as the faded hurt of her past tries to color her present joy. "But I think my track record speaks for itself. I don't like how he hurt you."

With a breath, Violet draws her shoulders back and stands. I watch her slowly walk back to the bathroom.

"He's not going to hurt me again. Let me finish putting on my armor."

As soon as the door clicks shut, I'm pulling up THE RUBBER PUCKIES chat.

ME

Olivier fucking Ahlman is here. And he's brought his agent, Violet's old boss, with him. The guy is the walking definition of sleaze. I can't even repeat the things he was insinuating about her.

NICKY

Now I wish I was in Vegas. And I hate Vegas. But I hate that little prick even more.

GUS

Who died in Portland for him to get a spot? There's no other way he made it in.

ME

I guess he was an alternate. Violet's really upset, and we have to go to the reception tonight. I think she's plotting how to spill a drink on his head and get away with it.

BONES

I'm plotting a lot more than that.

TEX

Easy, now. Murder isn't on the list of things I'll bail you out of jail for.

BONES

I blame Gus. He brought up death.

GUS

This was not my fault.

ME

NOT HELPING. I want us to get through the evening without death, jail, or mental breakdowns.

GUS

Sounds like a boring night.

OBIE

Wellsy, I know your girl. She wouldn't go tonight if she didn't think she could handle it. Having you there is all she needs.

NICKY

It's a busy event. Unlikely you'll have to see either of them again.

ME

That's what I'm hoping for. If not... well, Tex, is assault on the list of bail-friendly offenses?

TEX

When it is in defense of the woman you
love? It's at the top.

GUS

We'll be on standby, buddy.

"Ready." Violet's voice is sure. She stands in the doorway of the bathroom in a black cocktail dress, the skirt flaring out at her hips slightly before hitting her calves. The bodice is fitted and cut low between her breasts, with thin straps supporting it. When she walks toward me, she offers a little spin, showing the backless design, her smooth skin bared from shoulders to just above the curve of her ass.

"You look amazing." I blink in awe. With her hair still up and wine-colored lipstick on her lips, she's elegant and fierce. She's to be admired but never touched in a crowd, and it somehow is the perfect outfit for tonight. As I wrap my hands around the curve of her hips, anchoring her in place to watch for signs of uncertainty, I vow no one will make her feel less than the flawless woman she is tonight. "We'll leave as soon as we can, I promise."

"It will be fine, Crosby." She links her hands behind my neck, fingers dancing through my hair. Her touch sends a pleasant shiver down my spine, the desire for her making my fingers twitch where they hold her closer to me. "This is about you, and there are far more friends than enemies in that room."

"Sometimes, I'm still not sure what I did right to deserve you," I tell her, pressing a kiss to her lips. I'm mindful of her makeup but want her to feel reassured as I gently coax her mouth to part. I swipe my tongue gently against hers, teasing. As her soft moan tries to escape, I pull her more firmly against me. We're flush, chest to chest and hips to hips, deepening the kiss when I grip the back of her head and angle it where I want her.

Violet's fingers have stopped toying with my hair. She scratches the blunt tips of her nails against my scalp as she weaves them through the curls to pull at the strands. It's my turn to groan at the sensation. I bend my knees slightly to tilt my hips and grind up against her, my cock swelling from her touch and taste.

My phone vibrating inside my jacket breaks us apart.

"Fuck." I laugh as I fight to regain control of myself. Violet's pupils are wide, but I can finally see the silver flecks in her eyes again, and she smiles at me as she touches her lips, slightly swollen from our kiss. I run a thumb under the bottom one, checking that the line of her lipstick is still intact, impressed when the deep-red color doesn't transfer.

"Saved by the phone." I sigh, pulling my phone out as Violet steps back. She brushes at my curls that have migrated out of place from her touches. I clear the alert from my phone, a reminder to leave on time, and lace my fingers through Violet's. "C'mon, let's get this over with."

The ballroom in The Majestic is a beautifully expansive and functional space with crystal chandeliers and baroque-patterned carpets. It's been outfitted for the occasion with bold splashes of black, silver, and white, the NHL All-Stars logo projected on the walls and worked into the centerpieces on the tables around the room. There's a small dais set up at one end for the welcoming toasts and acknowledgments, and a high-profile DJ is situated at the back, ready to transform the affair from formal to party with the turn of a song.

As we enter the double doors, I immediately direct us to the right, edging along the wall to avoid the group of gathered media personnel catching arrivals for more relaxed soundbites to add to their stories. Tara Upton's interview has likely stirred up more interest in Violet and me appearing together, and tonight isn't the right night to embrace our newfound popularity.

I have a duty to make an appearance, but after today, I want to get Violet and me settled around people we're comfortable with first. Her hand is snug in mine, gripping tightly as she steps closer to my side. I know she wanted to stay back at the hotel, the effects of our earlier run-in with her past lingering as she scans the crowd beside me. I lean over to kiss her temple, the smallest gesture of gratitude and pride that she didn't let those feelings keep her from being here.

"There's our table." I gesture to one near the middle of the room but still on the outside of the cluster. It's not too far from one of the many bars in the ballroom, and I'm a little relieved to see it's close to an exit. I don't plan on us being here any longer than strictly necessary. Violet puts on a smile as we approach the group assembled around it. I recognize the defenseman from Detroit, Ben Lawson, and Meghan McDonald, the leading scorer in the Professional Women's Hockey League. With them are their guests and a few other members of the NHL offices.

"Excuse me," a voice interrupts after we've offered introductions and taken our seats. I twist over my shoulder to see a woman with black hair and a lanyard with extensive credentials hanging around her neck. "I was wondering if I could borrow Mr. Wells for a moment. It's about the tournament tomorrow."

I know I can't actually say no. The woman clearly works for the network carrying the broadcast tomorrow, but I don't like the idea of leaving Violet. Despite my constant searching, I haven't found Olivier or Anders. The last thing I want is them approaching her when she doesn't have someone from our circle of friends with her. I look at her beside me, the same uncertainty is in her eyes, but she gives me a nod.

"I promise it won't take long," the woman says at my hesitation.

"Go ahead." Violet lifts her chin in gentle dismissal. "I'm going to stay right here. Meghan and I are going to argue with Ben about how long it will be before the PWHL players get invited to participate in this whole thing."

She looks around the table with a mischievous smile, like she's conspiring with old friends instead of strangers, but grips my hand tightly when I reach for it. I bring it to my lips, kissing the back and smoothing my thumb along the inside of her wrist.

"I'll be right back."

I follow the woman to a small, curtained-off area in the back corner of the ballroom. I can't see Violet clearly, but I'm still looking around the area of our table when the woman introduces me to a member of the production staff whose name I immediately forget. The guy starts talking, but I'm only half listening, catching words like "locker room" and "wires" when I see a flash of blonde hair weaving through the crowd. It is only professional courtesy that anchors me to the spot long enough to absently agree to the question asked of me.

"Great," the production member says. His face floats in front of me, smiling, but blocking my view of Olivier Ahlman drawing closer to where I left Violet. "We'll set things up with your coordinator before the tournament starts tomorrow. Thanks, Crosby."

"Uh, sure. Great." I thrust my hand out to shake, my body already in motion to cross the room. I still can't see Violet, but I know Ahlman is on his way toward her. I shouldn't have left her.

I offer tight smiles and head nods when I hear people say my name as I persistently push through the tables and bodies in the crowd. I keep my eyes on Ahlman as he stops, my stomach dropping when I note it's right next to Violet. I can't hear what is being said. I can only focus on Violet's body language. Her shoulders are square, chin raised defiantly as she barely turns her head to him.

I'm almost to them when a body steps in front of me.

"Crosby." Anders smiles in greeting. "So glad to run into you again."

"I can't really talk right now." I make to side-step him, a move he counters. My patience is wearing thin, his presence feeling too coincidental.

"There aren't any obligations tonight." Anders slips his hands in his pockets. "I'm sure you have a moment to spare."

Beyond him, Ahlman has bent to Violet's ear. Whatever he says has her rearing back from him, twisting to look at him. I see the anger in her delicate features, but there's a hint of fear in her wide eyes.

"I don't. Excuse me." I turn, putting my shoulder into the motion of passing him, a small check to emphasize my point.

Not far from Violet, my hands flexing at my sides. The same protective and irrational anger I felt when I met Ahlman on the ice all those months ago comes rushing back, fueling my adrenaline and need to reach her. I'm two steps away when his hand curls around her upper arm and jerks.

Chapter 31

Violet

"So, you think it's important for women to wear cages on their face masks but support it's an individual choice for the men?" I ask Meghan next to me.

"I think it ultimately comes down to two things: control and product." She shakes back the blonde hair that curls just past her shoulders before she leans her elbows on the table. "Because fewer women play the sport or have had fewer opportunities to build their skills, as a whole, the league has a lot less control in handling the puck. It goes rogue more often than anyone wants to admit, and that's how you get your teeth knocked out."

I think of Gus and his gaped smile. I'm as used to seeing him with his implant retainer in place as I am without it, but I've never asked how he lost his tooth.

"And the product?" I prompt her. A thin smile presses her full lips together before she shrugs.

"You're looking at it. For better or worse, the popularity of women's sports is still tied up with the societal image of what a woman should physically be. How she looks plays a big part in that. Sure, there are a lot of women in sports who are unapologetically themselves, and they challenge that concept with an ease I'm still learning to grasp. But it doesn't mean they're ignorant of how their teammates and contemporaries across other disciplines are treated when they present themselves in full glam outside of a game."

"That's absolute shit," I say, shaking my head.

"It's the truth," Meghan replies, reaching for the flute that holds her champagne. "It's going to be a long time before there's going to be the type of fairness we want to see. But compared to twenty years ago, there's already been change, and it gives me hope we might accomplish what we want before I have to hang up my skates."

"You're amazing," I tell her, sipping from my water glass, eyes scanning the room. It hasn't been long since Crosby left with the ESPN assistant, but keeping engaged in conversation has helped ease some of my anxiety. Now, with the natural lull, I find myself searching for him, unease tickling up my spine.

"Violet, how do you like working in The Midnight offices?" Ben Lawson asks from across the table. He's a veteran in the league, a defenseman with a solid record and looks that have had fans torn for years in online forums. His unruly blonde hair and dark green eyes contrast with his pockmarked and slightly ruddy complexion. But his megawatt smile seems to put everyone at ease, which tips most fans into the swoon-worthy side of the argument. He's been around long enough I remember watching tape with Dad in high school when Ben first joined Detroit out of college.

"It's an interesting job. I like being able to interact with so many different elements of management and still be close to the game." I twist once more in my chair, hoping to see curly dark hair and two-toned eyes making their way back to me. But I can't.

"Is that how you met Crosby?" Meghan asks, curiosity in her voice.

"Kind of?" I take a breath and try to focus on being present at the table. "My best friend plays on the team, and I met everyone through him. Then, we were assigned to work together on some content, and well, he just never really went away." The laugh I give sounds a little hollow.

"He's had an impressive season. It's good to see him on the first line," Ben says. "I've only had a few opportunities to play against him until this year, but he's got a killer trick shot."

"I was happy to see him get moved up the lines as well." I can't help but smile. "He's definitely earned it."

"I bet he has."

I freeze. I could recognize that voice anywhere, and right now, it's coming from right next to me. There's sarcasm dripping from Olivier's words, but I know if I turned to look at him, he would be offering up a dazzling smile to cover it.

I don't look.

"I'm sure it's difficult for you to recognize achievements made through merit alone." I angle my lifted chin just enough for my words to carry in his direction while staying focused on the ugly black and white centerpiece before me. I don't want to make a scene, but I desperately wish I could leave.

Where I used to think if I was around Olivier again it would cause me nothing but heartache and sadness, now fury flares through me. I see so clearly how he used me, manipulated me, and had help doing it. Even if there are moments I chastise myself for allowing it to happen, I feel greater amounts of betrayal and anger.

There's breath against my neck, hot and scented with the sharpness of alcohol, before he whispers his venomous words in my ear. The tiniest thread of fear weaves through my veins at his proximity.

"Does your boy know how you spread your legs for me? How devoted you were to me? That you would have gotten me his spot if I had just asked?"

I rear back in disgust when he growls angrily, turning in my chair and all sense of propriety flying out the window. The breath I suck in after the shock is painful in my lungs, as though I've inhaled this man's vile and evil essence. Before I can reply, Olivier's hand curls aggressively around my arm, fingers tight and pinching, a swift jerk lifting me painfully from my chair.

"Take your fucking hand off her."

Crosby's voice is dark. A dangerous threat issued from behind me. I'm immediately relieved with him near, even as my arm stings under Olivier's grip.

Slowly, deliberately, Olivier removes his hand one finger at a time. He takes a step back as Crosby wraps an arm around my shoulders, guiding me to stand against him. I go all too willingly, even as I watch Olivier square up against him.

The other members of our table are watching raptly at the silent, but intentional, exchange. Crosby's body is strung tight like a bow, the tension practically vibrating off him, as I wrap an arm around him, wishing I could wrap all of myself instead. The adrenaline and anger are starting to fade even as the fear lingers bitterly. Common sense returns as the standoff between the two men continues, and more faces turn to where the energy in the room is decidedly more murdery.

"Wells, maybe you should take your girl out of here for a minute," Ben suggests. I catch Anders stepping up behind Olivier, a hand coming over his shoulder. "And I think this guy's business is done for the night, right, bud?" His eyes flick to Olivier as he stands up from the table himself.

"I was just on my way to find him. Olivier's drinks were made a little too strong tonight," Anders offers as a small crowd has formed. "I already lodged a complaint, but everyone please look out for yourselves tonight," he placates the bystanders who have only arrived to hear the well-practiced agent smooth over the situation. "Come on, Olivier, there's still a tournament to play tomorrow."

Crosby turns me from the table at the same time Anders begins to direct Olivier in the opposite direction.

With nearly surgical swiftness, Crosby steers us out of the ballroom and back up the elevators to our room. My mind has been swirling from the first step, a mix of emotions until there's the distinctive click of the hotel door, and I'm surrounded completely by Crosby. His breathing is audible, his scent lingers around me, and his touch refocuses my vision and thoughts.

Crosby guides me with gentleness toward the bed, helping me sink backward to sit on it, crouching before me.

"Did he hurt you?" Crosby's voice is strained, his hands hovering next to me, wanting to touch but never reaching. His eyes coast up and down my exposed flesh, homing in on the upper part of my arm. I lift the opposite hand to indicate it. "May I?"

The request is immediately softer than his first question, and at my nod, he tenderly lifts and cradles my arm between his hands. He frowns as he examines the area that is still red and slightly raised with irritation.

"It's going to leave a bruise," I tell him. His frown deepens, matching my own displeasure at the idea of a mark of Olivier's handprint imprinting on my skin.

"I'm sorry I wasn't there." He drops his hands, his head following in shame. I lift his chin to look at me. His brows are pinched together in the middle. He's trying to keep his anger in check, trying to remain calm for me. I run my fingers along his jaw until I cradle his cheeks between them. "I was almost there, but Anders stopped me. I don't know why, but it felt intentional. It makes me feel like I let him hurt you."

"No, you didn't." I lean Crosby's forehead against mine. "Olivier hurt me. More times than tonight—although never like this—and despite what I believed until I left London, it was only ever *his* fault."

I kiss him sweetly, softly coaxing him from the emotional upheaval of the last hour, willing him to return to me. Slowly, his lips become pliant and hungry under mine. I encourage him with small nips at his bottom lip and opening to stroke my tongue against his, fighting a smile when I finally draw a groan from him. It's a deep, reverberating noise, the dark tone full of longing instead of anger. The sound banishes the rest of the fear from my system.

Crosby breaks from me, our heavy breaths mixing between us. His hands lift to my hair, gently searching for the pins I used to keep it up. Methodically, he pulls each one, setting them on the side table before diving his fingertips back into the waves, massaging at my scalp. I lean into every touch, closing my eyes and letting the tension leach from my body.

"I don't like that he touched you."

There's a pained edge to his words. I open my eyes to look at the seriousness in his face. It's mixed with the love he has, but there's more. Fear. Crosby was afraid, and my heart swells.

"Then do something about it," I tell him, slipping my hands under his suit jacket, pushing it from his shoulders. "Erase it. Touch me where he can't."

The jacket hits the carpet as my words sink in. Crosby's eyes flare with heat, the hazel turning a liquid amber and the green deepening just before his pupils begin to widen.

Piece by piece, our clothing falls to the floor or is thrown haphazardly on the nearby chair until I sit in only my thong before him. While still on his knees before me, I feel like an altar he is praying to, every touch a deeper devotion. I've never been worshipped before, but as Crosby kisses his way up my inner thigh, I think I might be open to the idea.

I sink my fingers into his thick hair, contentedly settling back onto the plush mattress. It doesn't last when he traces a path over my hips to hook into the elastic and lace, sucking a kiss so hard into my skin just above his fingers, I arch at the intensity.

"Violet, I want to take these off." Crosby sounds uncertain. I look down at him as he toys with the waistband. He's deep in thought, not looking back at me.

"Okay."

"I want to switch places and have you ride me."

I nod along eagerly with his plan, too easily forgetting he can't see my agreement as he focuses on his task, fingers trailing teasing paths up and down the curves of my hips and back to the apex of my thighs.

"Yes," I offer instead, head still bobbing up and down.

A frustrated groan bleeds into my skin when he leans forward to press a kiss to my sensitive clit through the thin material.

"I want you so bad, I don't want to get a condom from the bathroom." His finger follows the intricate lace to the gusset, damp with my arousal. He slides it up and down, close to where I want him, stopped by the only barrier we have. I consider how much of an interruption it would be for him to get the protection. I begin rocking my hips against the motion. The friction of the lace and the pressure of Crosby's finger feel delicious, but I need more, and I know I don't want to wait.

"Do you have any reason why we would need one?" I ask hesitantly. Crosby immediately stops, both hands reaching to grip my hips, eyes lifting to mine.

"Are you saying you want me to go bare?"

"I'm saying I was tested before I started seeing you, and all my results were negative. I have never missed my pill." I link my fingers with his against my hips. "I'm okay with this."

He presses a lingering kiss to the inside of my knee, resting there for a moment.

"I was tested at the beginning of the season for my physical. All of my results were negative, as well, and there hasn't been anyone but you since." His hands squeeze mine once before he curls them back around the fabric, sliding my panties down my legs with agonizing slowness.

I don't need time to process what we've agreed to. Just because I've never gone without a condom doesn't mean I don't understand what's going to happen. Sex like this is going to change everything. And as I drop my hips back down to the bed, I know I've never wanted to do this before because I was waiting for Crosby.

"You're so wet, baby." His voice drops as the fabric hits the floor, and his hands reach back up to widen my knees before creeping up to tease at the folds of my pussy. I should feel exposed with the way he's putting me on display, but instead, I arch my back and cup my breasts, enjoying the attention. "Is this all for me? You going to let me put my cock in here? Fucking fill you up?"

"Yes."

A gentle tap on my leg pulls me from where I'm plucking my hardened nipples, imagining the feeling of his hard cock touching me in ways no one else ever has before. Crosby is standing, his cock jutting out in front of him and a bead of pre-cum on the tip catching the light.

"Up for me. I want to watch you take every inch of this." He squeezes his cock, pumping deliberately, swiping the tip with his thumb. He offers it to me. "Want a taste?"

I don't hesitate before wrapping my lips around his offering, swirling my tongue to ensure I have every bit of the salty essence. Then, I stand, switching places with him, growing hungrier for him when he moves back against the headboard. He spreads his legs, relaxed and beautifully large, a man of hard lines and flexed muscles. But it's the restrained look of need on his face that has me straddling him and pressing a kiss to his lips.

"We're not done until you're dripping with me," Crosby growls against my mouth, helping me lift with one hand, using the other to grip the base of his cock, lining himself up at my entrance.

Chapter 32

Crosby

Sinking into Violet makes me see stars.

I've never gone without a condom before. The risk wasn't one I was willing to take as a bumbling teenager or as a rising star in a professional sport.

But as Violet's tight, slick heat swallows inch after inch of my cock until she is fully seated on my lap, I can't think of a single reason why we haven't been doing this all along.

Her arms are loosely around my neck. Her fingers trace the veins before settling in the ends of my hair, fingernails gently scraping the skin as she swirls them around. Her head is thrown back, lips parted in ecstasy as her body works to accommodate me. I hold her hips in place, enjoying the way her pussy flutters slightly around my cock, and how in this position, her breasts are directly in front of me.

Their soft roundness is topped with tight and firm rosy nipples. Perfectly pebbled in arousal, reaching forward with an unspoken request for attention. I provide it by leaning forward and sucking one into my mouth, swirling my tongue around the peak, and switching to its not-to-be-forgotten twin. She moves her hands to my chest, pushing to gain leverage as a moan comes out on a stuttered breath.

"Attagirl," I encourage, popping off her breast and lifting her hips. "You took all of me. I'm filling you up, aren't I?"

"Crosby, fuck," she says, looking down at where we're joined before sliding back along my length. I guide her on the downstroke, tilting her hips to rub her clit against me. It makes her pussy tighten a little. A few more and Violet finds a rhythm she likes—a slow lift with her knees until the tip of my cock almost slips from her, followed by a fast drop and rock. Her tits bounce with every movement, and her nails dig into my skin. I love the little half-moon indents she momentarily leaves behind, wishing she would press harder so I could see them in the morning.

Soon enough, Violet begins to lose her pace, her breathing growing more erratic, and she abandons holding on to me in favor of running her hands up and down the sinful curves of her body. My fingers dance up her porcelain skin to cup her breasts and skate back down the smoothness of her stomach to sink lower to tease the base of my cock.

"Please—" she gasps out.

"What do you need?" I ask, one hand curling harder around her to keep her steady, the other traveling to hold her chin between my fingers and thumb. "Eyes on me, Sparks. Tell me what you need. You need to come?"

"Yes!" Violet's eyes lock on mine, the flecks of silver hazy with sinful delight, but the blue clear and sharp. She leans forward, crashing her lips to mine, taking for a moment exactly what she wants without words. A fierce and needy kiss, all teeth and tongue, as her hips begin to roll and rock instead of rise. Just as swiftly as she fuses our lips together, she breaks away, keeping her forehead on mine. "I can't—I need you to fuck me. Hard and deep. Please, Crosby. Please."

Her begging shudders around the trembling breaths she draws in, stealing them from me in the small space between our bodies. I give them freely, content to let this woman have anything she wants. Anything she needs.

"I'll fuck you, baby." I wrap both arms around her waist, lifting and depositing Violet underneath me on the mattress. I balance on my knees, widening them to keep her legs parted. I slip out of her for a moment as I fall forward to cage her in. She whimpers, wide eyes looking up at me. "It's okay," I tell her, thrusting back in, slow and deep. I rock my hips forward, grinding hard enough for her to gasp. "I'm going to make sure you come. Just the way you like it. Then, I'm going to fill this pretty pussy up until you're dripping with me."

Violet moans, hitching a leg over my hip. The adjustment draws me impossibly further into her, testing my resolve to get her there before I lose it. I drop my head on the next thrust, kissing her sternum and back up the column of her throat. She tilts her head back, giving me more access.

"Do you want that? Want to show me you're mine?" I whisper against her skin, using one hand to keep me steady, the other sneaking between our sweat-slicked bodies to rub my thumb against her sensitive clit.

"Yours." It's a sigh of agreement. A heated confession with love and desperation. I can tell Violet is close by the way she struggles to focus on me, the pulses of her pussy as she begins to tip over the edge. "I'm yours. Make me come!"

I increase the pressure on her clit, swirling around once, twice, then pinch it between my fingers. I feel the exact moment she shatters around my cock, and I swallow the scream that threatens to tear from her with a devastating kiss.

It's never been like this for me. I've never fucked with an urge to claim. But as Violet scratches down my back, clawing at the curve of my ass to keep me thrusting into her, that's exactly what it feels like I'm doing.

When I follow her over the edge a few thrusts later, it's to the declaration of her love. She holds me to her as the aftershocks work through both of us, calmed by tender kisses and gentle touches.

We lie together for a thousand heartbeats before I slip from her, sitting back on my knees. Violet begins to close her legs, but I reach a tentative touch to her calf, a silent request she grants by sitting up on her elbows.

"Can I—" I swallow, pushing the request out in a rush, "Can I see? Please?"

A shy and secret smile spreads across her wine-stained lips. She nods, planting her feet flat on the bed and widening her legs. I watch with fascination as a small pearled bead of my cum begins to drip from her. Instinctively, I trace a finger through it before pushing it back in. Violet's back arches, a sharp inhale parting her lips, eyes flashing with heat.

"Don't want to waste any of it, right?" I smirk. "Want to keep everything exactly where it's supposed to be."

"Holy fuck, Crosby." Violet squirms, hips wiggling and laughter lacing through her words. But her nipples stand at atten-tion, and a beautiful blush spreads across her chest, climbing to paint the apples of her cheeks. She's just as affected by this as I am. I move to her side, cuddling her close for a few minutes before I move us to the bathroom to clean up in the shower.

"Crosby!"

I turn at the sound of my name, seeing the last person I

expected. Ethan stands just inside the locker room in a dark-gray pressed suit and black tie. He has one hand in his pocket, the other holding his phone, eyes flicking between it and me.

I cross the carpet in my breezes, superstition making me careful to skirt the logo, and stop in front of him with my arms crossed.

"What are you doing here?" I ask, working hard to keep my voice neutral. I'm in the middle of suiting up for the tournament, trying in vain to ignore that my team of three drew a scrimmage against Ahlman. I just want this weekend to be over.

"You're wearing a microphone for us today. Mitch said you agreed last night, so I'm here to facilitate." Ethan finally puts his phone in his jacket pocket. "You did say yes, right? I'm not here for nothing?"

I search my memory from the last twenty-four hours and remember the brunette at the reception. I met someone last night at her introduction—Mitch, apparently—and agreed to something. I wasn't paying any attention, so I guess this is what I get. I don't really care. I've had a hot mic once this season, nothing much came from it, just a few soundbites of me chirping and cheering.

"You seriously flew to Vegas to watch someone put a mic on me, Savoy?" I cock my head to the side, weighing the truth of his appearance and hoping to piss him off a little.

"I've been here the whole weekend. I just came to the tunnels to make sure this was done correctly." Ethan turns and waves a hand back at me. "C'mon, they're waiting on you."

We head down the hall to a media room where the same woman from the night before is waiting. She doesn't do more than nod a greeting and set to work. With the microphone and pack secured, she dismisses me with a soft "good luck." Ethan stands off to the side with his phone back in his hand, furiously typing and swiping.

Ethan gives me a curt "thank you" in the hall before wandering in the opposite direction of the locker rooms. I shake my head as I walk back to the locker room and get into my pre-game headspace. Even for an exhibition, if I don't get my head on right, I can't be my best on the ice. While there isn't a real win on the line, there is the enjoyment of the fans to consider. They voted me here, and making sure I give them a good show feels important for my first All-Star appearance.

Back inside the locker room, I finish getting my gear on and taping a few sticks. Another production member comes in, letting us know it's time to go, and the familiar buzz of competition stirs under my skin.

I sit on the Vegas home bench, cheering and laughing with my fellow players throughout the first few rounds of the tournament. The league is evenly split, forming the bases of the teams, with the extra fan-voted players filling out the ranks. We have eight goalies to share, and they rotate in and out for the rounds of play. I have my teammates for the match—Ben Lawson and Elias Torvik from Milwaukee—on either side as we yell at Tex to shoot.

The crowd is going wild for the fun and fast matchup on the ice. The guys are having a blast as they take the game at 75 percent seriousness, leaving the opportunities for trick shots and good-natured roughing as the final seconds tick away. My group plays next, so I take a moment to double-check the laces on my skates, shake out my wrists to get loose, and pick a stick. The other two I don't play with will likely find their way to a fan before the end of the night. I smile at the reminder that I'm lucky enough to call this my job.

Finally, we take to the ice, five minutes for warm-ups. Ben, Elias and I go through some basic drills, the routine making it easy to find a way to play together. Elias plays right wing and Ben defense, so we balance out pretty well. We have the Vancouver goalie on our side, and we'll be shooting at New York's tender. I'm excited about that. It reminds me of our season opener, which makes me think of Violet.

Unconsciously, my eyes lift to the seats behind the penalty boxes. A few rows up, Violet is smiling in a black sweater, the bright purple accent color of our team's home jersey spelling out "Rise" in big letters across the front. She's jumping up and down as she waves. I shove one hand under my arm to pull it free from my glove so I can wave back. The rest of our friends are around her, and while I can't make out what they're shouting at me, I know it's encouraging.

Just before I turn to focus on the officials at center ice, I blow her a kiss. Gus' hand shoots out in front of her face, catching it before he presses the "kiss" to his own cheek. Violet pushes his shoulder while Obie rolls his eyes. Even Bones smiles at the child-like joke before he pops a quick kiss to Violet's head to make up for it. She beams at him and turns to send me one of her own in return.

"Has she moved on to being shared now? Guess it makes sense she'd take care of her daddy's whole team. Do you like getting in on it, too? You do seem awfully close to a few of your teammates."

My friends' faces darken in the crowd, and the smile slips from Violet's face. I don't have to turn to my left. I know who's standing there. A rough exhale rushes out my nose.

"Motherfucker," I practically chew the word through my rising anger.

"If it weren't for Violet, I never would have realized finding the right puck bunny is just as important to my career as daily skate. Of course, I didn't get it right the first time, like you probably did," Ahlman continues, as though he's talking about the weather and not how he tried to use Violet to secure his NHL career. Anger, pure and wild, courses through me. I bite down—never more grateful for a mouthguard—as my jaw tenses enough to almost crack a molar. "Kind of a shame, though. Violet sure is a good fuck."

I know I can't get away with hitting Ahlman during the All-Stars. So far, the most violent thing to happen has been an accidental tripping that resulted in a Los Angeles player sliding into the back of the net, hitting his face on the pole on the way in. Both players involved gave back-slapping hugs to clear the air after and play resumed. But I really, really want to beat the shit out of this guy.

Instead, I turn to him, locking my spine to revel in the three inches I have over him. I cut my eyes down, enjoying the way he adjusts on his skates like he can draw level to me.

"I'm going to need you to shut the fuck up and back the fuck away from me. Now."

"Or what?" he taunts, a fist coming up to push at one of my shoulders—hard. It barely registers. All I know is he made the first move. I still can't hit the guy, but I can—and *do*—grab the back of his neck to shove him away.

It lasts less than a second. There is no opportunity for anyone to jump in to keep a fight from escalating. We're already separated, pushing off the ice to get to our spots for play.

Instead, Ahlman gets in the last insult.

"Trying to pull my hair, Wells? I liked it better when your girlfriend did it."

The buzzer announces there won't be the opportunity for more. This might be an exhibition for fun, a celebration of the game and the fans who watch it, but it just got personal for me. I can't use my fists to settle the score, but I can still fucking win, and I plan on doing just that.

"That guy's an asshole," Lawson acknowledges as we skate into position. "I can't wait for the season to start back up so I can fuck with him." He shakes his head and leans toward the ice, eyes focused on our opposition.

I crouch into a face-off stance, my muscle memory keeping me present even when my mind is playing out a million different accidental murder scenarios. None of them are helpful. When the puck drops, I slap it to Torvik and shut everything else in my brain down. I just have to get through this and get back to Violet.

Our match is rather tame as we go up and down the rink. They score. We score. Everyone plays exactly like they should but unlike the previous matchups, an undercurrent of tension thrums throughout the game. With the mechanical way everyone plays, there's limited excitement, and even the crowd is subdued.

I look up to check the clock.

One minute remains.

I move up my lane, maneuvering the puck with a little extra flare I wouldn't normally play with. When no player is charging you, it's easier to show off a little more. It's a one-on-one match as I get closer to the crease. I like that Lawson and Torvik have their players handled. Giving me the chance to square up on Ahlman.

With blazing eyes, tense arms, and a painful scowl, he looks like he's playing game seven of the Stanley Cup. I smirk a little, causing his eyes to narrow at me as he lunges. I dodge, circling the net around the back side with him giving chase.

I suddenly hear Tex's voice bellow clearly across the ice to me, "Michigan!"

My body works automatically to comply. All the post-practice shooting sessions of that trick shot flooding back to me at once.

With the puck tucked closely against the blade of my stick, I flip my backhand and lift, balancing the puck there. New York's goalie is still twisted the other way, even though I'm sure he knows what's coming. As I round the corner of the net, I flick my wrist into the top corner, sending the puck into the back of the net.

The arena erupts with cheers, my trick shot injecting a little life back into the atmosphere. Lawson and Torvik skate forward to tap me on the head. I reach a gloved hand out to the tender, bumping fists with him, thankful he let the play go ahead, even if it meant a loss for his team.

The officials blow the whistle, the announcer calls the final score 2-1, and I glare at Olivier Ahlman until he leaves the ice.

Chapter 33

Violet

Watching Crosby and Olivier on the ice together again is almost unbearable. I can sense that Crosby is keeping his emotions in check, but only just. Olivier is restrained only by his own sense of self-preservation. If I learned anything from the fallout of our relationship, it's that Olivier can follow the rules if it means they give him something. Playing nice through the 3-on-3 game is necessary for him at the moment.

If it weren't for the presence of The Midnight boys and Allison, I'd likely be throwing up or fleeing the arena. Instead, they stand tall by me, cheering Crosby on and encouraging me to do the same. At one point, Gus worms his way behind me to lift my arms in the air and wave them around until I can't keep in the giggles from the absurdity.

Allison holds my hand as the clock expires, her support quiet and unwavering.

There's an undercurrent of dread pulling at me, even when I cheer for Crosby's trick shot to win the game.

When it's over, the guys surround us, bodily moving us through the electrified crowd to the checkpoint for credentialed personnel. We huddle together, waiting for Crosby and Henri to wrap up in the locker room and head back to the hotel. Our weekend in Vegas is almost over, and I can't wait to be home again.

No one says anything, but there's an awareness that something isn't quite right in the game. Watching Olivier and Crosby exchange words before pushing and shoving doesn't sit well with any of us. My nerves are in overdrive as we try to be patient. Something is off. I can't explain it, I just *feel* it.

I need to see Crosby. I want to hold him. I want to know what the fuck Olivier had to say.

"Hey guys." Henri's voice carries as he approaches. His hair is damp, and he has his gear bag over his shoulder. He pulls Allison in for a kiss before looking around at the rest of us. "Crosby's in with the audio crew. He had a mic today."

"No shit," Gus says with veiled amusement. "That's either going to be the best sound bite all year or the worst. Fuck." He shakes his head, walking over to the wall to lean against it.

I don't feel good that whatever was said between my ex and my boyfriend might get past the censors for a national broadcast, considering the last time they clashed, Olivier ended up with a bloody nose, and Crosby was benched the rest of the game.

My feelings must show because Obie is draping his arms over my shoulders from behind, securing me against his chest like armor. I reach up to curl my hands around his forearms, grateful my best friend knows what I need without asking.

"It's all right. I'm sure it was just a little shit talk," Obie says, low enough for my ears only. "Olivier wanted to get in his head, fuck with his confidence."

I'm about to agree when Ethan steps out from the tunnel, head bent low as he talks with Anders. Unease, anger, and confusion sink like lead balloons in the pit of my stomach. Before I realize what I'm doing, I'm wiggling out of Obie's arms, heading toward them just as they smile and shake hands. Seeing these two men together has dread racing up and down my spine. Something about it isn't right.

"Do you two know each other?" My voice isn't as confident as I'd like to be. The pair lift their attention to me. Anders is smiling and relaxed as always. Ethan's eyes narrow as he tries to paint on a thin-lipped smile. It's the same one he always wears in my presence now; the friendly man I met my first day is long gone.

"Why, Violet, I should have guessed you'd be down here." Anders flashes his white teeth. It reminds me of a shark about to bite. "Ethan and I were just catching up. One of the strangest parts of the league is how many people you can speak to without ever meeting in person. It's lucky we both had players involved this weekend to afford us a chance to meet face-to-face. We've even had a chance to swap stories about what a dedicated employee you are."

There's heat at my back. I don't even care which one of the team has stepped up, but the tension bleeds from me when a familiar sandalwood and citrus smell enters my nostrils, and a large hand I know so well rests on my hip.

"Guess it really is a small world after all." Crosby's voice rumbles through his chest behind me. I lean further back, trying to wrap him around me. "Everything all right?"

"Of course," Ethan answers. "Anders and I were just walking out together, wrapping things up." At this, Anders gives a little nod and disappears along the curved hall. Ethan surveys all of us, and I'm suddenly aware the rest of the group has fanned out around me. "Glad you're all here. Our drivers are waiting to take all of you back to the hotel and then directly to the airport."

"What about you?" Henri asks, relaxed, the picture of a confident captain processing all the information before making a play.

"I have a few more meetings, I'm afraid. Try and keep things from spiraling too much further out of control." Ethan's voice trails off, vague and ominous. Then, as if he were a general addressing his troops, Ethan gives one final glare and walks away.

"What's going on?" I turn in Crosby's arms, his curly hair damp and his eyes following Ethan's exit before they crease.

"Not here, Sparks." He looks around. Everyone pulling in, closing ranks, concern showing in their tight expressions. "Let's just get on the plane."

"Weather looks pretty clear for the duration of our flight. A few spotty storms over Tennessee, but we're hoping they'll move on by the time we get there. Flight attendants, prepare for take-off."

The pilot's intercom turns off, and I stretch my legs out in front of me, eyes unfocused but looking out the small window of the private plane. The lights from The Strip in the distance fade and blur as we speed down the runway and lift into the darkness.

"All right," I breathe out, turning from the window to the man beside me. His shoulders are hunched from exhaustion or the size of the seat, I can't tell, but his eyes look far away. The colors are dull and lifeless, reflected by the circles beginning to form under them. Crosby's joy from the weekend has officially been sucked away by the hasty way we left Las Vegas, the little glowing dot growing smaller and smaller behind us. "Let's hear it."

Bodies shuffle around the cabin as everyone gathers to hear Crosby recount what happened on the ice with Olivier. The blatant sexual accusations and the toxic admissions. Silence descends after, thick and heavy, while we all process it.

Crosby threads his fingers through mine, his thumb rubbing along the inside of my wrist. It reminds me so much of the first time we touched that—despite the way my stomach shifts riotously with hints of shame and anger—I take comfort in it.

"What do you think is going to happen?" I ask, leaning heavily against his arm.

"I don't think Ahlman knew I was wearing a mic. This was an internal directive to build content. It was approved by the network, but it was arranged by our team, so hopefully, it won't make it to air." He lifts a hand to run it through his curls, tugging a little at the ends. He tips his head back, a weary exhale blowing past his lips.

"You're probably right. It's not like the audio makes Ahlman look too good, and with the way Ethan and Anders were getting along, I'd say they'll try to bury it," Henri says. Allison's legs are thrown over his lap as they sit across the aisle on the couch.

"Let's hope you're right. No one needs their sex life splashed all over the media," Gus counters behind me. I tip my head up to look at him. He smiles, but it's pinched, an unnatural expression for my usually happy friend. "Trust me, I speak from experience."

"I'll never understand why who someone sleeps with is anyone's business. Ever." Obie stands from his seat, pacing the aisle in three short strides. I can tell by the set of his shoulders he's working his way into full-blown protective mode. "The insinuation that Crosby used his relationship with Violet to get to the first line is absolutely stupid. He made the line before they even met."

"That's right," Allison echoes. "Crosby and Violet's relationship doesn't have anything to do with that."

The conversation continues, but I block it out.

I pull my legs up to my chest, wrapping my arms around them, desperate to keep myself small enough to disappear.

"No, no, no, Sparks," Crosby's voice is quiet, and his arms

strong as he lifts and maneuvers me to sit across his lap. He tucks me against him, safe and secure, pressing a kiss to my forehead. "Don't hide. Talk to me."

"I can't help thinking none of this would have happened if I had just stayed away from you."

"Nothing *has* happened. We don't know what will happen with the audio. We don't know what the team is going to do with it. Right now, the only people who are making a big deal out of this are on this plane." He hooks a finger under my chin, lifting my eyes to his. "I'm never going to regret taking my shot with you. I'm never going to regret falling in love with you, Violet."

My heart swells with love. Crosby is so *certain*, and it gives me the fortitude to push back at the thoughts that want to circle all the worst possibilities that could come out of today's altercation. He's right: nothing has happened.

As I look at Crosby, my face now cradled into his warm and calloused palm, I know I can handle any outcome because I won't be alone. I'll have him. I turn to press a kiss into his skin. He guides me back to the spot under his chin, my head resting against his chest. His heartbeat is slow and steady under my ear. I exhale the last of my fear and fall asleep.

Crosby

March in Connecticut is unpredictable. There are days the sun shines bright and warm, spring teasing with every small green leaf you see on a tree. But two days later, a late snowstorm covers the ground in white, and icicles start forming on the same tree. As Coach yells from the bench during the third period of the game, the shifts in the weather feel like an appropriate analogy for the way our team has played.

The puck sails past me, and I groan, cutting deep on my skates to turn and chase after it.

"Get your head in the fucking game, Wells!" Coach's voice booms as I pass him. He has every right to be pissed at me. I'm playing like shit tonight. We're only up by one against the worst team in the league, and everyone is feeling the pressure of it. We've slipped into second place in our division since the All-Star game, and I carry every ounce of the blame on my shoulders.

I try to offer a nod, but the winger from Houston has scooped the puck and is charging up the lane at me. I keep my head on a swivel and skate backward, the change in momentum making my calves burn. I give it one, two glides before I swipe the puck back from him, sending a pass to Tex, who's open on the other side of center ice.

The crowd roars against us, the Houston fans desperate to see their team steal a win from us in their home arena. I'm determined not to let that happen, but I also can't wait for this game to end. We've been on the road for nearly a week, and I can't help but let my mind wander to the plane ride waiting for us tonight.

Tex shoots, a slap shot that echoes even with the noise, and the buzzer of the goal nearly assures us the win when I check the clock to see only three minutes remain. I skate toward my captain to give him a pat on the back, then make the switch with the other line at the players' bench.

I get to rest for the duration of the game, cheering on Hutchinson and his line as they continue to put pressure on Houston, especially when they pull their goalie and add an extra player to the ice. Coach paces back and forth behind us, calling what he sees and cussing at the good and bad. When the final horn sounds, his hand drops to my shoulder. Normally, it would feel encouraging or warm, instead, I feel the severity of it. A sentence I have put off serving.

"You're sitting next to me tonight, Crosby."

I nod before being released to head for the locker room with the rest of the team. It's hard to indulge in the joy my teammates feel at our win—another step to solidifying a playoff run—when my head has been anywhere but on the game for the last three weeks.

We made it back from Vegas without landing to a barrage of headlines and videos. Other than a short segment highlighting the clear animosity between Olivier Ahlman and me, there didn't seem to be anything to report. The audio was never shared, Ethan's meetings effectively killing any bigger story.

It was eerie and unsettling until the next morning when I was called in to see Todd Montgomery. The entire experience was a little like being in the principal's office as a kid, only this time my literal future was at stake, as the man who signed my paychecks glared at me from behind his oak desk.

I was told a decision had been made to keep the recording from the tournament out of the media.

"This is the kind of shitstorm I hate, Crosby." Montgomery leans forward. "I have always ensured—and will continue to ensure—that people who want to headline gossip columns over record books leave The Midnight behind. There's no place for that in a franchise so close to getting its first Stanley Cup in nearly forty years. So, don't become one of those people, and there will always be a spot here for you."

It wasn't much longer after that I was unceremoniously dismissed, asked to never speak of the weekend again. My post-game press conferences were canceled until further notice to avoid questions, and I was to go nowhere near the social media department while in the building. Ethan would coordinate all my obligations, and my previous demands to work exclusively with Violet were void.

So much has gone on like normal: practices, games, meetings, nights spent next to Violet. But there has been a dark cloud hovering over each day. The feeling that there's unfinished business. We keep waiting to be pulled back into the storm we can't understand how we escaped. As much as there's been relief, there have been questions.

What happened to the audio? If there isn't any concern over it, why has so much changed?

"Good recovery out there." Tex's voice brings me back to the locker room. He's bent over the bench, tying the laces of his oxfords. He's readying to do a few interviews before we board the bus for the airport. He puts his hand on my shoulder, giving it a squeeze before heading to the door.

I shove the rest of my gear in my bag, reaching to the back of the shelf to open the safe for my phone.

SPARKS

Good game.

SPARKS

Even if you did miss the pass at the end that a pee-wee could have handled. 😉

ME

Would it be acceptable if I said I was thinking of you?

SPARKS

Absolutely not. You're now one point from first place in the Eastern Conference. I also would have never forgiven you if you lost to Houston. They're terrible.

ME

I'm looking forward to getting home to you. This road trip wasn't the same without you with us.

The typing bubble pops up at the bottom of the screen and disappears twice before Violet gives my message a heart in acknowledgment. I lift my bag over my shoulder, typing as I follow Gus out of the locker room and down the hall.

ME

See you soon. I love you.

"By the time we step off this plane, the audio from your microphone in Vegas is going to be the lead story on every sports website and maybe even some that don't normally give a fuck about hockey."

Coach has been a silent seat partner for almost an hour. The plane has been at cruising altitude for a while, the cabin filled with the hum of the engines and the snores of our assistant coach in the back row. Cal Andrews sits next to me, glasses perched on his nose as he reads on his phone, fingers flying across the screen from time to time, but never looking at me or speaking.

"I'm sorry, what?"

Coach puts his phone in his lap, the glasses pushed up on top of his shaggy black hair. He gives me a look that is equal parts tired, concerned, and annoyed.

"A snippet of your exchange from the All-Star game is minutes away from being available to the media. Portland's offices and our own personnel are trying to track down where the leak originated, but it won't matter. The world is about to learn you are currently dating Olivier Ahlman's ex." He leans on the leather armrest between us. "Violet's dating history, your current relationship, and what all of it means are about to be discussed in detail."

My stomach feels like it has plummeted 35,000 feet to the earth below. My brain is in a horrific state of free fall. Numbness bleeds through me, fusing me to the seat, and hollowing me from the inside out.

"Does she know?" I ask. I turned my phone on Airplane Mode out of respect for Coach.

"Yes," he replies. "I have Ava handling things with her, and I called in some backup."

"Good," I say, rolling the information over in my brain. I find my head bobbing up and down, unable to do anything else. I know what kind of stories will be run about Violet. None of them will paint her in a flattering light. The comment sections will be full of trolls calling her horrendous names: puck bunny, slut, whore. Every part of her life will be up for discussion and—worse—dissection. Every choice she has ever made involving her dating life and hockey will be examined.

It won't matter that our relationship isn't connected to my position on the team. But Violet's job with the team, her success, will be called into question. There will be rumblings that I'm given preferential treatment. What was a fairly innocent question by Tara Upton a month ago will be replayed over and over. My non-answer will likely be twisted to fit whatever narrative someone wants to spin.

This is everything her father spent his life trying to prevent. It's everything Violet tried to avoid.

"Crosby." My eyes refocus at the sound of my name. Coach has a firm grip on my shoulder. "It will be okay. I have a plan."

"Coach, I think you can go to jail for trying to hire a hitman. Especially since we don't know who leaked it."

"You absolutely can go to jail if you get caught." Coach drops his hand, a wry smile on his face. "But no, there's no murder for hire in my idea. And I'm not searching for the leak. I'll leave that up to Ava."

"Little disappointed." I try to laugh, but it comes out pained.

Coach looks around. Half of our team is sleeping, the others are looking a little more alert than I would expect. Some have their phones in their hands, and I realize I'm not even going to make it back to New Haven before the story gets out. When I look back at Coach, I can't help the sting of tears filling my eyes.

"I'm sorry, Coach. I tried. I wanted to protect her, too." My words come out in a rush, emotion choking me up. "I thought we did all of it right."

"Hey." He leans close, eyes crinkling in the corners with kindness. "This isn't on you. Of all my guys, I'm glad she chose you, Crosby. It's because you did everything right that I think there's a way through this."

I nod again. Once. Sharp. The familiarity of following instructions guides me out of the self-doubt that threatened to overwhelm me. With a decisive sniff of my nose, I listen closely as Coach outlines what he thinks will help.

"You and Violet both declared your relationships to HR and the Player's Association when you started dating. There are no violations of conduct by being together. But I think there is a strong case to be made against Ahlman for sexual harassment under the NHL Code of Conduct."

I can't help but frown. It's rare for players to bring complaints to the NHLPA. For all the good the official code does, there are deeper ones among players. Unwritten and unspoken rules you absorb as a player. The least of these is keep your mouth shut and do your job. Things that happen in the locker room, or between players, stay exactly there.

My gut reaction is to balk at the suggestion. Opening an investigation is going to keep this story going for longer than I want. There's potential for a lot of negative professional fallout.

But it's also an unexpected and intelligent move. It could result in Ahlman being questioned, maybe even suspended. It will take the heat off Violet, and that is the most important reason to agree to it.

"Will Montgomery get behind it? He's made it clear he doesn't want me to bring more drama to the team."

"I'll worry about Todd," Coach says. "If he doesn't put the full force of the organization behind killing this story and finding the person who leaked it, I'll walk."

"Are you serious?"

"As a hitman with a clear shot."

Chapter 35

Violet

Video plays of Crosby and Olivier on the ice next to each other. The audio comes through clearly.

"Has she moved on to being shared now? Guess it makes sense she'd take care of her daddy's whole team. Do you like getting in on it, too? You do seem awfully close to a few of your teammates."

A quick edit jumps to the moment Olivier shoves Crosby and the vice-like grip Crosby puts him in in return.

"Trying to pull my hair, Wells? I liked it better when your girlfriend did it."

I want to look away from the television as the story cuts back to the familiar faces of the anchors for *Center Ice* on the NHL channel. But I can't do it. Not when my face appears in a small split screen icon in the upper right corner, set between Crosby and Olivier's roster photos. The horrible headline, *Pucking Around*, sits under the headshots.

"Our coverage of the audio from last month's All-Star tourna- ment explaining the altercation between New Haven Midnight

*center Crosby Wells and Portland Searchers center Olivier Ahlman
is still developing, but as you just heard, this drama is taking place
on and off the ice,"* Dave Poston, the show's host begins.

Despite my dad's warning the story was going to go live
tonight, I'm unprepared for how desperately I want to sink into the
couch. I wish Crosby were with me. Or Obie. Or Bea. Or anyone I
know I could trust to hold my hand and tell me everything will be
okay, even if it feels like the ground is crumbling beneath me.

*"When we reached out to both teams, we were told a comment
would be forthcoming after internal reviews with team personnel
and the players. In the meantime, I want to bring in some of our
own experts to talk about what this story means and what we do
know."* The camera changes angles to a wide shot of Dave, Tara
Upton, and former player Gabriel Belanger. *"I want to start with
you, Gabriel."*

Blond with kind blue eyes and blinding white veneers, I
remember Gabriel from my dad's retirement party. I spent most of
the night trying to keep Obie calm in a room full of his heroes and
sneaking sips of champagne. But Gabriel's three-year-old son was a
holy terror, wrecking havoc as his dad tried to talk with people
until I corralled him on my lap, determined to teach him rock,
paper, scissors. I was thanked profusely when Gabriel was finally
able to say hello without being interrupted for the next twenty
minutes.

"This is completely unacceptable." Gabriel's face is twisted in
disgust, his pen tapping against the desk in emphasis. I feel the
smallest flutter of appreciation for him. *"Locker room talk belongs
in the locker room. It should never make it to the ice, should never
be talked about in a game-play setting. If two players have both
been with the same woman, they can talk about it behind closed
doors like regular men. On the ice, the only thing that should come
between them is the puck."*

The flutter abruptly dies.

As Gabriel continues to wax poetic about the importance of player code, a.k.a. the beyond antiquated and pathetic sports equivalent of "bro code," I check my phone. Given the circumstances, it's pretty quiet. My Instagram profile was already set to private, my contact information for The Midnight was never publicly accessible on the team's website, and most people who would need to be calling me are unreachable, asleep, or have already checked in.

"I have to interject here." Tara's voice is sharp, her hand slicing the air. The camera zooms in on her. *"I refuse to accept that discussing a woman in such a degrading manner is ever acceptable. In a locker room or out of it."*

"I'm not suggesting it is." The camera cuts wide to show Gabriel looking equal parts angry and offended.

"But you are not advocating against *it, either."* Tara does little more than smirk at him, her annoyance clear. *"I can appreciate your history with the sport, Gabe, respect the relationships you built as a player and as a broadcaster. But you're selling an old song here. One I'm quite tired of dancing to. Women deserve better."*

I sit a little taller.

"I think we're focusing on the wrong part of this," Dave interjects. *"This audio implies Violet Cameron, daughter of Midnight head coach Callum Andrews, might have a history of helping players through her relationships with them."*

"That's a fair point, Dave," Gabe eagerly jumps on the change of topic. I feel sick to my stomach as they begin theorizing timelines they clearly can't comprehend. *"We know from the audio that she was once romantically involved with Olivier Ahlman and is currently in a relationship with Crosby Wells. Is she responsible for the relative success both of these players have had this season?*

Ahlman was practically unknown to anyone outside of Europe, and Wells was promoted to first line."

"*You're actually suggesting these guys didn't get where they are on their own?*" Tara asks. I appreciate her lending some common sense to the discussion.

"*Not exactly,*" Gabe returns. He folds his hands together on the desk in front of him. "*But there are hundreds of players out there just waiting for their shot in the NHL or to get more ice time. Wells and Ahlman are both excellent players in their respective positions, but it feels a little too coincidental to ignore the connection both of these guys have to a woman with connections to the league and the huge changes to their playing careers this season.*"

"*Crosby himself refused to give you answers during your interview before the very game this exchange took place in, Tara,*" Dave adds.

The camera cuts back to Tara for a response, but I've reached the limit of what I can tolerate tonight. I switch off the television and consider the texts my dad sent.

DAD

The media is going to talk about you, kid. As much as I want to hope it won't, the sex part of this story is going to sell. There will be a lot of theorizing you helped get these guys where they are. They're going to imply you make sure they are treated favorably, given opportunities they wouldn't have otherwise. It won't take long before people start poking holes in that logic, but it won't mean the damage isn't done. I want you to keep your head down, focus on your job. We're going to do all we can to get this to blow over fast.

ME

Okay. I'm so sorry, Dad.

DAD

This isn't your fault. I don't want you to think any of this is because of you. We'll get through this. I love you.

My cubicle feels small today. Even as I face the glass wall to look out over the empty ice, a vast, expansive space, I feel like the walls are closing in on me, and I can't escape them.

I barely slept last night, only managing to drift off in the early morning hours when Crosby's arms finally wrapped around me after he quietly arrived home. Truthfully, I've only had a handful of good nights' sleep in the last month. They've always been on nights I can't hide my exhaustion anymore. Every day has been a trial of worry and relief, no matter how irrational it is. Worry the unreleased audio will leak. Worry I will be fired from my position if it does. Having my workload reduced hasn't been a good indication of the "what-ifs" outcome.

Relief only comes when I make it to the next morning without a seismic shift to my entire world. But it's fleeting because the cycle starts all over again.

Crosby has been a huge support, but I see the strain on him as well. He's become quieter, more withdrawn. Instead of stopping to talk with every employee he sees, he politely says hello and sets about his tasks in the building. When we spend nights together, we split time between our houses, making dinner and watching sports documentaries in bed.

We avoid talking about the worst-case scenario, but now, as I sit here, I wish we had. I wish I had been better prepared, even if I didn't know what I was preparing for.

I've spent the morning trying to work, follow my dad's advice, and trust he and Crosby are making headway in their meeting in the conference room with the NHLPA representative. But it's been difficult to manage with the looks my coworkers have sent my way in the halls or their attempts at a casual drop-in, asking if I want to take a coffee break.

I don't.

I don't want to awkwardly stand around with a terrible cup of coffee, pretending they're not mentally asking a million questions. Or that by standing with me in the break room they're not pitying me. My phone buzzes against the surface of my desk. I scoop it up, hoping it's a good notification instead of one I've been dodging since last night. Even with precautions in place, people on social media are persistent.

BEA

Catching up on all of your messages. Do I need to get on a plane? I can be there in 10 hours.

ME

Is it really needy of me if I say yes?

BEA

Not at all. In fact, I'm already on one.

ME

Are you serious? Bea, you have a job—a life—you do not actually need to come here!

BEA

Too bad. Can't change it now. When I get there, I'll do whatever I can to help you get this sorted.

ME

I don't deserve you.

BEA

No one really does. <kissy emoji>

Buoyed by the support, I send the information of Bea's impending arrival to Crosby. Taking a deep breath, I refocus on my computer and the latest report on metrics from Instagram. No surprise the account has seen an uptick in traffic over the last twenty-four hours, but I'm working on the monthly numbers. There has been a steady downturn of interaction since All-Star Weekend, with comments skewing negative. I've just started examining the common threads when a sharp knock on the top of my partition has me jumping.

"Violet, I need to see you in my office. Now." It's Ethan, delivering a brusque summons before continuing down the hall to where his office door stands ajar. I grip the edge of my desk, unease slithering up and down my spine.

It's taken a lot of professional creativity, but I've managed to avoid being alone with Ethan since that morning in the elevator. I've sent emails or texts to avoid in person conversations, and I've only had to face him when we have our weekly department meetings. This has seemed to be acceptable to him, as well, because, until right now, he has not sought me out. It's an unwelcome development on an already difficult day. I hesitate for a breath before I square my shoulders as I walk toward the open office.

"Have a seat," Ethan says the moment my toes cross the threshold from behind his desk.

"I'd rather not." I'm proud my voice doesn't waver. I stay just inside the door, across the office from him. I meet Ethan's gaze, watching as a flicker of annoyance passes in the next breath. "What did you need to see me for?"

Ethan pushes up from his chair, rounding the desk with his hands in his pockets, an apologetic look on his face that doesn't quite reach his eyes. Behind his glasses, they are practically alight. He doesn't walk toward me; just leans back against the surface of his desk before letting out a long sigh.

"After reviewing your recent performance, and with careful consideration to what is best for the team, it's been determined that your skills are no longer needed. The Midnight organization thanks you for the work you've done, but your termination will be in effect at the conclusion of business today. Make sure to send all of your current projects to me. Human Resources will be expecting you this afternoon to sign your offboarding and review anything else necessary. Security will collect your credentials in the lobby." Then, as if he hasn't just gutted me, Ethan nods once, the barest hint of a smile playing at the corners of his mouth, and returns to his chair. "Close the door on the way out. I expect those projects within the hour."

I walk back to my desk, numbness making the motion automatic. Sinking into my chair, I let Ethan's words sink in. *The Midnight organization thanks you for the work you've done, but your termination will be in effect at the conclusion of business today.*

He fired me.

Chapter 36

Crosby

"I don't want to come across as dismissive, but I want to make sure all of us walk out of here with realistic expectations of what will happen next." Anthony, my NHLPA representative, is slowly packing up his papers and tablet into a sleek black shoulder bag. "I can't predict how the NHLPA will process this complaint. Additionally, it will be filed anonymously, but Merrick Daniels, as the team owner in Portland, will have access to what the complaint details since it involves one of his players. It's also likely the media will be able to draw their own conclusions should any disciplinary actions follow."

"Understood." I stand from the plush conference room chair, reaching across the large table to shake hands. Anthony has been here for the last couple of hours, explaining my rights as a member of the association, the steps of the filing process, and the various possible outcomes. Next to me, Coach stands, extending his hand as well. He's been a silent supporter, sitting next to me, never offering more than a nod or shake of his head, but as Anthony sees himself through the glass door, he turns to me.

"This can't be easy, but I can't thank you enough for doing it." There's a tightness in his voice, a quick twist of the corner of his mouth, the only indicators that a heavy emotion sits behind his words. When he puts his hand on my shoulder, he gives it a firm squeeze.

"Ahlman's a world-class dipshit on his own, Coach. But I'd do more than fill out a complaint about it if it kept Violet from being dragged through the mud. She doesn't deserve it."

Coach steps back, making for the exit as I pull my phone from my pocket, switching it off silent. I see a string of notifications I ignored during the meeting, including a slew of texts from Violet.

> **SPARKS**
>
> Bea is on a plane! On the way here! I told her she didn't need to, but it's not as though anyone can tell that woman anything. I'm not going to lie, it will be really nice to have her here.
>
> **SPARKS**
>
> I'm also going to really owe her a visit after this.

The final message has me reading it twice, shock making it near impossible to comprehend. The timestamp is nearly twenty minutes ago.

> **SPARKS**
>
> I just got fired.

"Holy shit," I let out, looking up at Coach. "Violet said she's been fired."

With chilling ease, Coach shifts from the calm, stalwart man I've known for the last few years into a tempest. A man who has quietly stood by as his daughter endured, defended herself, and proven her strength is replaced with a father who will tolerate no further injury to the one he loves.

"Call her. Ask her to come here," Coach instructs, pulling out his own phone. I hit Violet's contact, and she picks up on the first ring.

"Crosby, I don't know—I've done everything he's asked." Her voice sounds so small, so far away, even though she's in the same building.

"We'll figure it out," I assure her, looking up to see Coach talking quietly into his phone across from me. All the concerns from the meeting I just had fall away, my focus narrowing to what's happening with Violet. "I'm with your dad. We're still in the conference room. Can you meet us here?"

"Uh, yeah. Okay. Yeah, I think—I'll be right there." The line disconnects.

Several things happen in the next few minutes. Ava enters, face grim, when she acknowledges me with a terse nod. She makes quick work heading to Coach.

"Is he coming?" she asks. Coach nods, but before I can wonder who he's referring to, the door opens again.

Violet steps inside, eyes flicking between me and her dad, momentarily considering where she should go first. It doesn't escape my attention when Coach gives her the slightest indication with his chin in my direction. The significance of that small gesture isn't lost, even as Violet rounds the table, eyes watery and face turning blotchy as she tries to keep her emotions in check. I open my arms, enveloping her tightly when she walks into them without hesitation.

"I'm sorry, Sparks," I breathe the words into her hair, hands coming up to soothe her back. I give her my full attention, letting her hold onto me as long as she needs. When she takes a small step back, there are silent tears falling down her cheeks. I don't know if they're made of sadness, anger, or defeat. I wipe them all away just the same, my thumbs erasing their salty tracks while keeping her face cradled between my hands. A throat clearing calls our attention back to the others in the room. Coach and Ava have been joined by Todd.

"Hello, Violet. I'm sorry we're seeing each other like this." Todd's voice is coarse, the gravelly sound harsh, but he tries to temper it with a tight smile.

"Hello, Mr. Montgomery," Violet answers, stepping away from me to leave a professional amount of distance between us, even as she threads her fingers through mine. I squeeze them in reassurance.

"Todd. Please," he clarifies, gesturing to the seats around the table. We all sink into the chairs.

"Todd," Violet says.

"There's a lot that has gone over the last twenty-four hours," Todd begins. "First, Crosby, Cal has informed me of your right to pursue a complaint against Olivier Ahlman through the NHLPA. I am sorry it came to this. Part of my directive in keeping that audio from being released was the disgraceful and disgusting tone of the exchange. Out of my respect for Cal, I didn't want there to be a discussion about Violet."

I'm glad I'm sitting down. As far as owners go, Todd Montgomery hasn't given too much indication he's aware of or involved with his team. He's in his late fifties, with graying hair and a poor color-match dye job. His face was likely handsome in his prime but now is oddly stuck from too much Botox and has an intentional dusting of five o'clock shadow along his jaw. He wears a black suit and white sneakers, the uniform of a man trying hard to appear cool and approachable in the sports world. He has zero athletic background, having made his money in the tech industry, and most of his decisions involving the team reflect that. Alex

Bridger's disastrous tenure sticks out as a prime example. But now, there's a humbleness in the way Todd is talking, the way his face shows as much remorse as it is able to.

Next to me, Violet sucks in a sharp breath. I remember she's likely met Todd many times in her life, even though she has never flaunted the familiarity through the course of her work here. Her dad played for this man his entire career, took up the coaching mantle, and has built a formidable team during that time. I can see now, however well compartmentalized Violet has kept her life and work, the respect her family has earned will shape things now.

"Unfortunately, that choice has been taken out of my hands." Todd spreads his own fingers wide, palms up, as though in supplication. "The official team statement has been 'no comment.' But I want to inform you that, internally, we are taking this very seriously."

Todd looks at Ava, a prompt for her to continue where he left off.

"I understand you had a meeting with Ethan this morning, Violet," Ava hedges, easing the conversation in a new direction.

"Yes," Violet replies, all attention shifting to her. "A little while ago, he informed me I would no longer be employed by The Midnight organization after today." She folds her hands in her lap, keeping her shoulders back and head high. "I've emailed him all of my open projects, and I'm due to fill out my offboarding paperwork in Human Resources after lunch."

"Did he provide a reason for the termination?"

"He said after a recent review of my performance, and with consideration to what is best for the team, my skills were no longer needed." Violet's voice is tight, professional, but I sense her anger is rising. The immediate shock has worn off, the sadness dissipating, leaving behind justifiable ire.

"Do you feel as though that assessment is accurate? Did he

have an evaluation available for you to review his claims?" Ava asks. Todd has leaned back in his chair, quietly observing. A quick peek at Coach shows he is paying close attention, gaze volleying back and forth.

"It has been my observation that the metric data from our—from The Midnight—accounts trend down on the content I have been assigned to complete in recent weeks, supporting his assessment," Violet answers. "Ethan did not provide a formal evaluation for my review."

"But the data has only shown a downward trend recently? It was higher before?"

"Yes, it was once higher. The current video with the best performance is one I created." Violet lets a little smile creep across her lips at that. An echo of one ghosts at the corners of my mouth as well, pride swelling in my chest for her.

"What changed?" Ava probes gently. Violet tries to hide the way her body stiffens at the realization of where Ava's questioning is going. Her fingers twist painfully in her lap, and I don't resist the urge to cover them with mine. She squeezes at them. I hold her tighter, offering the support I can. She licks her lips before she speaks, and I turn my attention to Coach, carefully taking in the way his expression changes as Violet recounts the day in the elevator with Ethan.

"After that, I stopped posting and contributing any content that wasn't explicitly given to me by him. Until today, he hasn't sought me out for any individual conversations, and avoiding him has been easier than I expected," Violet finishes.

"Vi, why didn't you say anything? Why not report him?" Coach asks gently, but I see the rage behind his eyes. The intensity isn't directed *at* her, just banked into an inferno of righteous indignation *for* her.

"He told me the day I was hired he was unhappy with me

being here." Violet's face twists as she keeps her tumultuous feelings at bay. "I just thought it was because he didn't get to make the decision of hiring me, that's what he said. But he slowly became more awful. First, when everyone found out I'm your daughter. Then, when Crosby and I started dating. Coupled with how I started getting to know the team and the way my work was performing? If I had reported him—or told you about it—I think the response would have only validated his belief I've been shown favoritism here." She hangs her head, quietly adding, "Maybe I have, but I never wanted it. I tried to prove I could do this on my own."

Coach is in front of her a moment later with a tissue he's acquired from somewhere. He offers it to her and holds her cheek for a moment in a parental display of affection so tender my heart hurts. He bends down, pressing a kiss to her forehead before returning to his seat. I watch, fascinated, as his professional demeanor falls back into place, but his eyes now softened at the corners, continue to flick back to his daughter and then to me. I give him a nod, hoping I convey I've done everything I can to protect her.

"Ava, were you aware of this?" Todd asks. He leans forward on his elbows, eyebrows pinched unnaturally because his forehead can't furrow properly, but his rough voice indicates further how uncomfortable he is at this revelation.

"I saw Violet directly after. I've been monitoring Ethan Savoy ever since," Ava replies.

"And what have you found?"

Tension builds thickly in the room. Todd seems to know the conclusion before any of us do, but when Ava speaks, it's as though all the puzzle pieces click together.

"Confirmation came through this morning that Ethan is responsible for the leaked audio."

Violet

By the time Bea bursts through my front door, I'm nearly exhausted, but the sight of her curly hair, understanding smile, and full-body hug have me perking up. And if her proximity didn't have me finding a new level of comfort and relief, her infectiously bright attitude does.

"I'm never going back to flying commercial. That was bloody fantastic. Remind me to thank Cal."

Crosby comes down the stairs, swooping her into a hug as Gus and Obie wander in from the living room. I pull her bags out of the way, stacking them on the entryway bench, unsurprised to hear it was my dad who brought Bea to me when I would need her.

"Why does Wellsy get the first hug?" Gus grumbles when Bea and Crosby break apart. Obie rolls his eyes at his teammate. Everyone shuffles around to make room in the space, which is feeling entirely too small with the presence of three professional athletes. Bea just opens her arms. "I don't need a pity hug," Gus grouses, but a bright smile breaks across his face as he steps toward her. "But I could never deny Bea anything. We all know she might fly across the Atlantic for you, little flower, but she'd stay for *me*."

"In your dreams." Bea sighs as Gus practically folds himself in half to be cuddled, her shorter stature trying to accommodate him. He nuzzles against her shoulder for a moment. Everyone laughs and begins moving back to the living room, where we all arrange ourselves into the available space. My townhouse isn't as spacious as Crosby's, but we manage to make it work. Bea and Gus are on the long sofa, Obie in a wingback chair to their left, and Crosby and I snuggled into the oversized armchair across from him. Bea takes a measured look around at all of us before drawing her legs underneath her. "Catch me up."

Before I can start, Gus jumps in, "Violet was fired. But our team owner and Ethan's boss know it was Ethan who leaked the audio from Vegas." He props his head up on a fist, arm resting on the back of the couch, completely relaxed as though he's swapping neighborhood gossip, not the events of the last few hours. Bea gives him her full attention, and I try not to feel offended, but Crosby's light laughter next to me has me giggling along. "Coupled with the day he assaulted–"

"He did not assault me," I gently correct. "Tell it right, or you won't get to tell it at all."

Gus rolls his eyes but complies, starting again.

"Fine. Coupled with the day he cornered Violet in an unprofessional and physically intimidating manner in the elevator, it was enough for Ethan's job to be terminated."

"And what about you, Vi? What about your job?" Bea looks at me. Crosby's hand finds mine, and I lean into him.

"It's still mine. Ava—she oversees the department and was Ethan's direct supervisor—says there wasn't evidence in his firing of me." I sigh. Three little pulses of Crosby's hand remind me he loves me. "But this has been a lot. My dad suggested I take a few days and consider what I want to do, and I'm taking the advice."

"Smart girl." Bea offers an understanding and soft smile before giving her attention to Gus once more. "Okay, but why did he do it? Not firing Violet—it sounds like maybe he's wanted that for a while. Why did he release the audio?"

Gus shrugs his shoulders, lost as to the reason a successful, respected man decided to make it his mission to tear me down. Slowly. Professionally, at first, before finding a way to attack me on a deeply personal level.

"Greed," Obie says. His face is hard, the usual sparkle of his green eyes dull and jaw locked tight. It's a face he reserves for games against difficult opponents. It's also the look he wears when he defends his family. When he feels everyone's attention on him, he takes a deep breath. "That guy has been trying to figure out how to make everything he does bigger or better for who knows how long? We've all heard how the team talks about him: Ethan is the least-liked member of his own department. Getting to tell him 'no' the last few weeks has been freeing." He leans forward on his spread knees, elbows resting lightly as he continues, "Then Violet came along, helped into her position because of her familial connections. No offense, Letty." He shoots me a quick apologetic twist of his lips. I hold my hands up in resignation. It's the truth. "But she's not just some nepo-baby working for Daddy's team. She's smart. A quick learner. She understands the game *and* the players. She became good at what she did. The guys all loved her from the beginning."

"No shit. Some more than others," Gus jokes. Crosby lobs the throw pillow from our chair at him, hitting his best friend square in the face. "Hey!"

Bea reaches across just as Gus cocks back his arm to throw the fluffy square back at us, Crosby's arm already extended in front of me as a shield.

"Children, the adults are speaking." Her accent makes the admonishment even more severe, but she smiles when she gracefully flourishes a hand at Obie to pick up the conversation.

"I could have it wrong, but all he did was talk about getting the accounts to go viral. I think he just thought this would be one more opportunity to get people talking about The Midnight, and he could build from there. He didn't care it had fuck all to do with hockey, and it only served as a bonus that it would hurt Violet in the process," Obie finishes. The room lapses into silence. I let Obie's logic work through my mind.

I don't think we'll ever fully understand why Ethan did what he did. I'll never personally know why he disliked me the way he did, but there's a lot Obie said that seems to fill some of the gaps. Ethan was obsessed with success. I don't think I had been there long enough to understand that, maybe, he was counting the department's success as only his own. That he was willing to do whatever he could to achieve his goals.

"What a wanker," Bea finally says just before she stands up and stretches. "All right, you lot—clear out. I'm knackered, and you have a game tomorrow."

Gus and Obie begin to object, but Crosby extricates himself from my side, gesturing to the guys it's time to leave. There's lighter conversation as everyone finds shoes and coats before slipping out the front door.

Crosby presses a lingering kiss to my lips, a silent reassurance, before turning to Bea and offering her a peck on the cheek. "I know I'm leaving her in good hands," he tells her, referring to me.

I wrap my arms around Bea's middle just as she reaches for me. "Thanks for being here."

"Are you sure you want to go to the game tonight?" Bea asks. I finish swiping on a coat of mascara to focus on her in the mirror. She stands behind me, looking at two Midnight home jerseys, one in each hand. We were both too tired last night to stay awake any longer. Any conversations about my job, The Midnight, or how I'm feeling were set aside in favor of sleep. Today, we avoided a little more, staying cocooned in blankets on the couch, fueled by takeout and the latest Netflix series with Kristen Bell and Adam Brody, escaping reality.

"It will be weird." I spin and lean against the sink in the bathroom. "But I want Crosby to know I still support him. They're down to their last few weeks of regular season games. Every single one of them matters. This stuff with the audio took a toll on him this past month. We both kept waiting for the other shoe to fall, and now that it has... it doesn't change the fact he has a job to do. I think he'll be more focused tonight. All the other chatter is white noise for him. He wants the work he does on the ice with the guys to matter more."

"You're a good person, Petal." Bea smiles before looking back and forth again at her potential wardrobe possibilities.

"Who are you trying to pick between?" I giggle as the decision drags on.

"Gus and Nicky."

"Nicky? Really?" I can't keep the surprise from my voice.

"Gus gave this to me last time and begged me to wear it the next time I was at a game. However, that boy does not need the attention, so I made sure to have another option. Figured that big, sexy Russian wasn't a bad idea." With that, Bea tosses the number eighty-seven jersey onto the bed behind her. She slips the number twenty-eight over her head, curls bouncing as she settles it over the black long-sleeved shirt she has on. With a little flourish, she twirls to show off the look.

"Gus is going to be so salty later." I laugh. I turn back to the mirror, my favorite tube of red lipstick in hand. "Dad gave us the suite tonight, so I invited Allison to sit with us. Is that okay? I know you've only met once, but she and Henri are trying to keep the pregnancy secret for as long as they can."

"It's more than okay." Bea slips into her sneakers, the purple of the side swoop perfectly matching the piping on the jersey. "It's nice to get a glimpse into your life. You seem happy here, Vi. Ex-boyfriends and toxic bosses notwithstanding."

I apply my lipstick, mindful to keep the lines precise, even as I watch Bea in the mirror. She picks up her phone and settles on the edge of my bed. I watch her lips turn down, the entire countenance of her face shifting, and her shoulders rounding a little. I grab a tissue to blot off the excess and head back to the bedroom for my sweatshirt. It's one of my dad's old ones, worn and comfortable. With the soft fabric dwarfing me, I push the sleeves back, sitting next to my friend.

"When all this dies down and the season is over, how about I fly over for a week?" I place a hand on her forearm. The offer doesn't feel like enough. Twice, in the time since I left London, Bea has shown up for me. Dropped whatever was going on in her life, flown across an ocean, and stayed by my side when I needed her. Suddenly, I feel like an awful friend. I hang my head and blink back tears. I won't make her feel responsible for my shortcomings. I clear my throat and look back up at her. "I'm sorry I've been such an awful friend."

"Friendship doesn't work like that," Bea gently admonishes. "It doesn't keep score. There is no quid pro quo. Right now, you need, and I have the ability to give. It won't always be this way, and I have faith that when my time comes to need you, you'll be there."

"Of course I will." The vow comes easily. Truthfully.

"Then, let's leave it at that for now, hmm?" She brushes a tear that escaped off my cheek, then pats gently under her own misty eyes. "I'm ready to drink piss-poor beer and yell at grown men acting like cavemen."

We dissolve into giggles, getting the rest of our things ready and heading downstairs to the Uber.

Chapter 38

Crosby

I wind my way down the hall toward the locker room, doing my best to look focused and unbothered for our team photographer and other media staff. I'm surprised to see Amelia, one of Violet's coworkers, camera in hand and a look of concentration on her face. She's sitting on the floor, her camera angled up, and she's set a row of lights along the wall behind me to create an interesting backdrop for walk-in shots. It's a more elaborate setup than I'm used to. Her camera clicks away as she twists and turns in a crouch.

"Did you get what you need?" I ask, nearing the bend where I'll disappear from view. I turn back over my shoulder, checking she's satisfied with the photos. She clicks through, and I see a smile bloom as she continues. She practically bounces on her toes.

"Yeah," she calls back. "Thanks, Crosby."

"You got it. This is new, yeah?" I turn fully to give her my attention while gesturing at everything.

"Oh, yeah. I've been wanting to try this for weeks," she looks at her camera screen, cheeks pinking slightly as she pushes some buttons to make adjustments. She turns it for me to look at the picture. With the exposure, lighting, and angle, I definitely look more intimidating than I am. She's great at her job. I give her a thumbs-up.

"Wow," I say, genuinely impressed. "I can't believe you haven't done it this way before."

"I'm finally allowed to." Amelia bites her lip like she let something slip. She takes a step closer, another secret spilling from her. "Ethan never let me."

I'm not sure what to say, so I just nod at her, even though I'm rocked a little by her admission. Maybe Violet wasn't the only one dealing with problems. Instead of trying to unravel it in the middle of walk-ins, I squeeze her bicep and pivot the conversation.

"Are you going to be rink side tonight, too?"

"Yeah! I'm so happy I'm leading on this tonight. The closer we get to the end of the season, the more exciting the games get. Even with everything this week, I have a good feeling about tonight!"

"Me, too!" I reply as she steps back, kneeling in her preferred spot, readying for another shot as one of my teammates approaches. With my head turning over the information Amelia gave, I blindly get to the locker room and begin changing into my gear.

Halfway through, Gus nudges my shoulder.

"Did Midnight Mary show up in your room last night or something?"

"What?" I blink at him. He pops his retainer out, storing it away in his locker before giving me a gap-toothed look.

"Either you saw a ghost, or you're about ready to puke. What's wrong?" He sits on the stool next to me.

"Just something Amelia mentioned on the way in," I lower my

voice and lean closer to him. "You know that cool setup she had tonight?"

"Hell yeah. She showed me the pictures. I looked badass." He gives a little flex of his arm.

"Anyway, she said she's been wanting to do it for weeks, but Ethan wouldn't let her." I let the implications hang between us. Gus nods in understanding.

"That sucks," he says, securing his shoulder pads. "I wonder how many others would say the same thing. I wonder how long it was going on for."

"I don't think we'll ever truly know, but it makes me happy he's finally gone. Even if it means dealing with all this shit."

"It's over now, right? Let's celebrate by fucking some shit up out there tonight!"

"Save it for the game." I laugh, pushing aside the uncertainty of the NHLPA complaint. But for the first time in weeks, the fog that's been permeating my brain has lifted. I pull on my pads and smile. "Tonight's going to be a good fucking game."

Tex hears me and calls back from a few stalls down, "Fuck, yeah!" The energy in the room intensifies. Everyone around me begins to talk animatedly, and I sigh in relief. An excitement hums under my skin as I finish suiting up and settle in for pre-game announcements. Coach comes in, his usual solemn expression firmly lodged in place. He stands at the head of the room, careful to keep his toes off the edge of the logo in the carpet.

The room quiets, the team sitting down, waiting patiently for him to speak. He looks around at all of us, his eyes holding mine a fraction of a second longer than the rest before he looks down and taps his leg with his thumb.

"It's been a fucking time of things, hasn't it?" he starts, easy and soft. The guys all lean in a little from their stools. "Team's sitting high in the standings because of the tremendous amount of hard fucking work and deep fucking commitment over the season. Unfortunately, every single one of you has had to deal with things that don't belong in this fucking game, instead. Some of you are being asked stupid fucking questions that take the focus off what we do."

I drop my head, my guilt rising. I don't feel blamed, but there is an unshakable sense of responsibility I carry for how the last few days unfolded. It twinges that I haven't stopped to consider that everyone in here still has to face public scrutiny when they do press for the game or see notifications on their phone from social media.

"It'd be understandable to let it distract us. To let it bury us," his voice begins to build, momentum shifting as he amps up. I swallow down my emotions and focus in, letting my coach guide me back to where I need to be. "Maybe it has," he begins a slow loop around the logo, hands in his pockets. "Maybe with every fucking microphone, every fucking comment... every fucking disgusting opinion shared, we've had another shovel of dirt thrown on us."

There's a shift as Coach deepens his analogy. I look around at my friends to see if they feel it, too. My leg begins to bounce as the energy builds.

"Shovel after fucking shovel until we're buried six-feet under." As he passes me, his hand lands softly on my shoulder pad. It's brief, but the feeling of his support will linger the entire game. "It's just too bad they forget who they are trying to bury."

"Yes, they fucking did!" Tex unleashes. Coach smiles darkly. It's unusual for our captain to interrupt, but I can tell they are on the exact same wavelength, and I love being swept up in it.

"Midnight?" Coach asks of us, looking around again, the

familiar prompt causing all of us to stand before answering in unison.

"Rise!"

It's our most decisive win since before All-Star Weekend. Nicky shuts out Boston, and we scored six. All traces of distraction vanished when our blades hit the ice, and every period had us growing stronger, more confident—and ultimately—more dominant. Boston sits above us in the standings, but we have the advantage by winning our matchup. It could mean a lot when the playoff picture comes into sharper focus in the next week.

The locker room is loud. The atmosphere feels more like we've advanced to the Stanley Cup than won a regular season game. But the change in morale is incalculable. I'm finally starting to feel like myself again, and while there is still a lot to face to move on, it will be easier if I can hold on to this feeling.

"You fucking killed it tonight!" Tex grips the back of my neck, shaking me in celebration. "One goal, two assists, no penalties. Damn, Wellsy."

"What about you?" I slap at his back. "A hat trick? When was the last time that happened?"

"Hell, if I know."

"Violet would," I tell him. He laughs because it's true. "She's probably upstairs with Allison talking about it right now."

I strip out of my gear to head to the showers. I'm actually happy I no longer have press requirements because I want to kiss the shit out of Violet. I want to wrap her up in the high I'm feeling. I want to share with her the certainty I have that things are going to get better.

I've just finished buttoning the last button on my shirt, rubbing the towel one final time through my hair, when Coach calls for me across the room. He gestures for me to follow him.

We slip through the hallways quickly and quietly, only offering small nods to anyone we pass until we reach a service elevator I've never been in. Coach pushes a floor button, and the silence continues. When I look over at him to prompt a comment, he just shakes his head, a clear request to wait.

When the doors open, we're at the end of a long hall. Coach seems to know exactly where he's going, so I follow along next to him. We end up exiting through a set of double doors on the level of the arena where the private suites are located. He immediately ducks into the closest one.

Inside, I see Violet, Bea, and Allison. Allison and Bea say a quick goodbye before they squeeze my arm as they pass me to leave. The door stays open, Todd slipping inside with Anthony, my NHLPA representative, behind him.

Coach shakes hands with Todd, nods respectfully at Anthony, and hugs Violet briefly. I've come far enough into the comfortable-looking suite not to be stuck to the walls, but I still wait for any clue about what's going on. Violet crosses to me, wrapping her arms around my waist before popping up on her toes to kiss my cheek.

"Great game," she whispers in my ear before dropping back down. She threads her fingers through mine and guides me to one of the supple black leather chairs that litter the upper sitting area of the suite. Everyone slips into a space before Todd speaks.

"Hell of a game, Crosby. Coach," he turns his head to acknowledge both of us. He leans forward on his knees, letting his clasped hands hang between them. "Anthony has an update about your complaint, and I figured you'd want to know the outcome immediately."

I blink in surprise. I wasn't expecting the Player's Association to come back so quickly. I don't know if the fast response is good or bad. I steal a quick glance at Coach, but his face doesn't give anything away.

"I'm sorry to tell you that the NHLPA has dismissed your complaint," Anthony says. A mixture of anger and frustration flushes through my veins, but there is also a strange mix of relief. Without the league investigating, I hope it will mean the story can fade into obscurity. So what if Ahlman doesn't have to face the repercussions for his words? I'm sure he'll face retribution at the hands of myself and my teammates for the rest of his career. We may be forced to forget, but I know I'll never forgive. "The Player's Association will not investigate the claim because the player is no longer employed by the National Hockey League."

"What?" I say sharply. Violet sucks in a breath.

"When Portland was notified we submitted the complaint, we also included the recording," Anthony continues. "It appears Merrick Williams, their owner, was very interested in the exchange. Turns out his daughter, Lucy, is responsible for bringing Olivier Ahlman to her father's attention. Convinced him to give Ahlman a try-out. When Ahlman made the team, he broke up with Lucy. Given his boasting on the recording, I guess Merrick was only too happy to find a way to end Ahlman's contract when the complaint was filed."

"Oh my God," Violet whispers. Her shoulders have deflated like a balloon, the realization of what could have been her life—and what is the unfortunate turn of events for Lucy Williams—sucking the energy from her. I give Anthony a nod of thanks, letting him dissolve into specifics with Todd while I lean over to check in with her.

"Are you all right?"

"Surprisingly, yeah, I am." Her voice is strong, even if I can see her still processing. Coach joins us, kneeling down in front of her, assessing her. I see their silent discussion before he stands, leaning down to press a kiss to her forehead and return to the executives across the suite. "Crosby?"

"Yeah, Sparks?"

"Let's get out of here." She stands, reaching a hand back to me. I don't let the offer linger, rising from my chair to tuck her against me, making a hasty exit at the approving nods of the others.

Epilogue: Crosby

Four Months Later

"We're not going to be playing any games where we have to smell diapers, are we?" Gus asks warily as we walk up the sidewalk.

"What?" I ask, confused, stopping in my tracks.

"I googled some of the things that happen at baby showers. There's a game where you smell things smeared on diapers and have to guess what it was. You know, like figuring out poop." Gus looks absolutely horrified, and I'm inclined to agree with him. I'm happy we're here to support Allison and Tex, but I might draw the line at guessing possible poop stains.

"Violet didn't mention anything like that, so I think we're okay. She said they want to just keep things casual, a BBQ to celebrate with their friends," I reassure him. Violet, Bea, and a few of Allison's other friends have spent months planning this shower, a welcome project after the chaos of the end of the season.

After the drama and distraction of Ethan's firing, Violet went back to work, where the department was restructured at Ava's insistence. Under the new organization, Violet was given the role of Head of Analytics. She was all-too-happy to give back the creative content to coworkers who wanted to design, film, and upload things to the team's social media platforms. Now, Violet puts her energy into reviewing the metrics associated with the content, organizing focus groups that interact with our public relations staff, and fact-checking the statistics associated with player profiles online. She's happy and thriving at work, especially with the addition of Bea in the Public Relations department. An unexpected change that also found Bea making a move into Violet's old place when she moved into mine.

"Well, I'm letting you know now, Cap, I'm out of here the second someone waves a diaper in my face," Gus replies as we start back up the sidewalk.

"Don't call me that in there," I request, stomach churning nervously over the new honorific. Tex announced his retirement when we lost in game seven of the conference round of playoffs. That was a hard night, emotionally. Losing when we were even closer to the Stanley Cup than the year before and losing our captain left more than a few of the guys in tears.

"But you're captain now. Going to have to get used to it sometime," Gus just shrugs at me as I shake my head.

I wasn't expecting the phone call from Coach last week when he let me know I would be serving as The Midnight's new captain. I was deeply moved, honored to carry the "C" on my chest to advocate for my teammates on the ice and lead them off. I'm also painfully aware Henri Texier leaves big skates behind to fill.

"I don't think today will be that day," I tell Gus as I push open the side gate of the house. The baby shower is being held in Tex and Allison's expansive and beautiful backyard of the place they bought last year. I hear music playing from hidden speakers and the chatter of the other guests as we round the house.

The yard comes into view, delicate decorations of pastel green and neutral taupe make the space feel inviting and festive. I smile at the amount of work Violet has put into making today perfect for our friends. I scan the space, looking for a flash of brown hair, red lips, and bright blue eyes, only to come up wanting.

"She's gone inside," Obie greets us, handing over a couple of newly opened beers, answering my unspoken question. "Something about shoes, I think? I don't know. She's been running around here all morning."

"Thanks for coming to help. I offered, but she told me she wanted 'best friend time,'" I say.

"We got some of that, too!" Gus chirps, slinging his arm around my shoulder. Obie laughs.

"We are not lacking time together," I shove him off me, laughing with the others. I bring the cold bottle to my lips, taking down a sip of the pale-amber liquid. I look around at the other attendees, nodding to the guys on the team and smiling when I see Violet emerge through a part in the crowd, a pair of sandals in her hand. She walks directly to Allison, kneeling to switch out the heavily pregnant woman's shoes for the pair she can slip on easily. Tex is holding Allison's arm to keep her steady, but I see him thank Violet before pushing the discarded footwear off to the side of the patio. Violet gives a squeeze to Tex's forearm and turns toward me.

Almost as if she felt me watching her, the smile that illuminates her face is bright and warm, just like the sun today. I cock my head at her as she makes her way through the guests to me.

"There's my little flower!" Gus crows, stepping in front of me. I drop my head back in exasperation at being denied the first hug from her, but my shoulders shake with laughter when I see how happy it makes Gus to scoop Violet into a tight hug. He presses a sweet kiss to the top of her head before turning her loose.

"I know he says we have to share custody of you two," Obie says, sharp green eyes bright with laughter as he takes in the exchange before turning to me, "but I'm never going to do that with you."

"Fine with me," I acknowledge, clinking the necks of our bottles together.

"I think you're still jealous that she loves me more than you," Gus tells Obie, smiling devilishly.

"Not true," Violet quickly assures Obie before she finally steps into my side, arms wrapping around my middle, head resting against my chest. I look down to see her beautiful face turned up to stare at me. "And I love *you* the most."

I dip down to kiss her perfectly pouty lips, the usual ruby color replaced with a soft pink today. I feel her hand run up the length of my spine, fingers toying at the base of my neck in a quick tease before she pulls back. My heart races from just that brief kiss, and I love that she can still make me come undone so easily.

"Everything go okay this morning? It looks beautiful," I tell her, gesturing to the yard full of smiling guests. Allison and Tex are laughing with Coach.

"Yes, it was great. Allison insisted on hiring out almost all of it, so I just had to point to where things should be set up. Bea and I honestly felt a little guilty," Violet says. I know she did more than that, but if she wants to be modest about the last few late nights I found her and Bea in our downstairs study preparing, that's fine.

Movement in the corner of my eye draws my attention. Bea holds Natalia's hand as she guides her over to a giant calendar where we can guess when Baby Texier will make their appearance in the world. Nicky follows behind, a bemused expression on his face as he talks to Bones, and I lift an eyebrow at Violet. She shrugs but winks at me.

"I put my gift inside. Is that all right?" a sweet voice asks from behind us.

"Maeve!" Violet squeals, shooting from my side and into the arms of Gus' little sister. "I'm so glad you made it!"

"We were supposed to bring a gift?" Gus asks, confusion and concern twisting his face. "Tex said they had already bought more than they needed for the baby."

"They did. You didn't have to bring anything, but it's thoughtful. I'm sure they'll appreciate it," Violet diffuses as she smiles at the girl with the same amber eyes as her older brother. Gus thinks it all through, then he snaps his fingers.

"I've got it!" He nods enthusiastically, clearly proud of whatever solution he has come up with. "I'll volunteer to babysit!"

"God save that kid," Maeve jokes. Gus leaps at her, trying to swipe her into a headlock or something, the siblings falling into a natural rhythm together. They tear off around the side of the yard, drawing shouts from a few members of the team.

Violet quietly grumbles beside me, her eyes narrowed on where the pair are kicking up a ruckus, but the rest of the guests have already returned to their previous activities and conversations.

"Maeve got into Yale. She's going to be around a lot more," Obie says. "But I'll go get them to break it up and remind them they're not in the basement in Minnesota anymore."

"Thank you." Violet follows him a few steps. I wrap my arms around her from behind, feeling her relax back into my chest. I play with the little bow at the waist of her pretty green dress, its delicate skirt swishing against my knees. I press a kiss to her cheek, inhaling the apples and sunshine smell that blends perfectly into today.

Her hands come up to hold mine, lacing between my fingers.

"Where's your ring, Sparks?" I say low in her ear, noting that she's missing the new accessory I gave her this morning before she slipped out of bed. Her thumb rubs at the empty skin of her left ring finger.

"I left it in my purse inside," she answers. "I didn't want anything to distract from Allison and Tex's perfect day."

I nod.

I hadn't planned on asking her. Not for another month. But the way she looked curled up in the sheets, the soft light filling the room, I didn't want to waste one more second before asking her to be mine.

"That's fair." I turn her around to hold her more firmly in my arms. Her blue eyes are happy and warm as she looks at me. I dip my head, giving her a soft kiss. She hums a little in pleasure before breaking apart.

"Remember when you told me you didn't date hockey players?" I tease when her arms wind around my neck. Her eyes narrow just the slightest as I repeat what she told me the night we met.

"I don't," she sasses, lifting up on her tiptoes to whisper in my ear. "I marry them."

Acknowledgments

First, a huge thank you to the readers that have taken a chance on a brand new author and read this book. Having your support and trust as a storyteller is the biggest motivation to see my books go to print and continue writing.

Thank you to my family: Your understanding, patience, and love made this entire dream possible. I could not have done this without you behind me, beside me, and with me. I love you.

To my beta team: Erin, Aliyah, and Aimee. You took on the task of reading an unpolished manuscript with enthusiasm, kindness, constructive criticism, and humor. Entrusting you as the first set of readers was forever the right decision. Your comments, suggestions, and messages helped guide Violet and Crosby's story to be better than it started. Thank you.

To the ModSquad and HSBC: never has there been a better collection of pocket pals. It was through your love of hockey, romance books, and the multiple combinations of both that the idea to even attempt this book was born.

To Kim, Lemmy, Michelle, and Juni: brilliant, creative bad asses who tirelessly support this community with their visual interpretations of our words. Through your abilities you connect readers and authors, and I count myself lucky to have had you on my team.

To the author friends and professionals I've met along the way: thank you for your encouragement and counsel. From those that have done this before (Dani, Chelsea, and Grayce) to the ones figuring it out alongside me (the Diamond Dolls), having you as resources and touchstones made me feel less alone. Special recognition to Katie, who was endlessly kind while holding my hand through some of the more technical things, and the moments I had big feelings.

Lastly, to my editors: thank you for all the lessons learned.

Hockey Handbook

Lines (first, second, third, fourth): A set combination of three forwards that play together in shifts.

Forward: Offensive position. Players may take this position at right wing, center, or left wing to cover the offensive zone during their given shift.

Defenseman: Defensive position. Usually plays closer to the goalie for additional support, but can play across the ice. Defensemen play in pairs for shifts during the game.

Salary Cap: The set amount of money every team has to pay players every season.

AHL: The American Hockey League is a professional league that serves as the primary developmental league for the NHL. Players can be called up to their team's NHL counterpart or sent back throughout the season.

Draft: The annual selection of new players for the NHL. Athletes may enter the draft as young as eighteen years old.

Deke: A deceptive movement that induces an opponent to move out of position.

Goon: A player who has little purpose on the ice other than to get in fights or deliver big, sometimes illegal, hits.

Chirping: Trash talk during games between opponents.

Michigan: A lacrosse-style trick shot.

Conn Smythe Trophy: Awarded annually to the most valuable player of their team during the Stanley Cup Playoffs.

Hart Trophy: Annual award for the most valuable player of their team, voted by the Professional Hockey Writers' Association.